Acknowledgments

To my family and friends—Thank you for supporting me and believing in my dream.

To Jovana Shirley, Kate Marope, Carol Tietsworth, and Zara Dash—Appreciate your help!

To Jeff—Your support, guidance, and love are immeasurable.

To Connor and Brennan—Having you in my life brings me more happiness than you'll ever know.

To my mom, sister, and brother—I'm not only blessed with a wonderful, supportive family, but you are also the best friends I'll ever have.

To Amy—Thank you for all your help and love. You are simply the best.

Finally, to my father—Thank you for teaching me to love books, and although you will never be able to read this, I dedicate this book to you. I miss you.

Last Goodbye

LAUREL OSTIGUY

Third Edition

Visit me at:

www.laurelostiguy.com

www.facebook.com/AuthorLaurelOstiguy

http://twitter.com/authorlaurelo

Email: authorlaurelo@gmail.com

Cover Designer: RBA Designs | Romantic Book Affairs

Cover Model: Kerry Logan, www.KerryLogan.actor

Photo Credit: Lucian Maestro

Editor and Interior Designer: Jovana Shirley, Unforeseen Editing, www.unforeseenediting.com

This book is a work of fiction. Names, characters, places, and incidents either are products of the author's imagination or are used fictitiously. Any resemblance to actual persons, living or dead, events, or locales is entirely coincidental.

ISBN-13: 978-0692693124

OTHER BOOKS BY LAUREL OSTIGUY

Prologue

MARCH 1, 1995
ABIGAIL

"I was thinking maybe we could just spend a few minutes together," James said, almost sounding desperate.

I wrinkled my face, and as I did, he turned toward me and whispered softly, "Come on, Abigail. I'm not that bad."

I quickly snapped out of it.

"James, I didn't..." I trailed off, knowing I didn't really need to finish my sentence.

He continued to drive down the long road.

He was handsome. Everyone in school thought so, too. He had gray eyes and shaggy blond hair. He always wore a zip-up jacket and a baseball hat that made his hair stick out on the sides and the back. He was planning to go away to college in the fall, like most of our graduating class. He could carry on intense conversations with me. I liked that about him.

Unbeknownst to me, he had been trying to ask me out since sophomore year but never did until the prom of our junior year. When he'd finally gotten the courage to ask me, it'd made a lot of the girls in our class jealous, something I could never understand. They all presumed I was too brainy for James—whatever that meant. I wasn't your typical bleached-hair and frosted-pink-lipped girl liked by the majority of the boys our age.

James pulled the car by the back fields at Glens Falls High School. My heart began to pound. He sat up straighter in his seat, which made him appear sure of himself. I was not used to him being so confident. He parked the car and opened his door. Before he could come around, I pushed hard against the car door with my shoulder. It popped open, and I got out.

As he walked toward the football field, I followed him in silence. He slid through the gate and then held it open for me. I eased my body through the chain-link fence, just as he had.

"Feeling nostalgic?" I asked him, half-laughing. "You're more of a soccer guy, aren't you?"

"That's funny, Abigail, considering you're the one going to Onondaga State, the *ultimate* football school." He wrapped his arm around me.

It was an unusually cool evening in March, and this forced me to pull my hands into my sleeves.

"You know me so well. Avid sports fan that I am, it's not like I'm going for their top-ranked biology program," I quipped with my usual sarcasm.

He smiled down at me. He led me over to the bleachers and climbed up a few tiers and sat down. I followed his lead and took a seat next to him on the cold metal bench.

"What are we doing here? Looking at the full moon?" I asked. It was sort of an inside joke.

He slid closer to me. "It's nice but no. Like I said, I just wanted to spend some time alone with you." He locked eyes with me.

He always remarked that my navy eyes showed my intellect and innocent view of the world. I could tell he was searching my face—for what though, I was not sure. He turned away, gazing out toward the field lit by the spectacular moonlight above. He seemed to be deep in thought. I, too, gazed at the beautiful moon that hovered above us. I could hear his breath begin to deepen. I shuddered with the cold.

"Can I ask you something?" he probed with a husky voice.

Finally. Let's get to why we are sitting out here and not at the diner with our friends.

"Sure," I said cautiously.

He was acting so strangely.

"Why…" He hesitated. "Why don't you like me the way I like you?"

I nearly choked, but I tried to control myself by clearing my throat. I couldn't believe he'd asked me that, that he'd actually noticed enough to ask me that. There was silence as I wondered how to respond to his question while sitting in the middle of the bleachers on this unusually frigid night in March.

"Why would you ask me that?"

"You know exactly why I'm asking you that." He sounded a bit irritated.

I started to get a weird feeling. Something in my gut told me to touch him, so I did. I moved my hand onto his leg. He stiffened a bit, knowing how little we had touched. I knew he had not expected it but that he wanted it badly.

I thought about all the girls at school who were always after him—the cheerleaders, the jocks, even the artsy girl who he'd said used to stare at him during class—but our friends kept telling me that all he ever talked about was me. When he'd finally asked me to the prom, I guessed I'd answered so halfheartedly that it completely threw him off his game. He'd become timid and shy around me, nothing like he usually was. I preferred the confident James who seemed to rule the hallways of our high school. We had been dating for almost a year, and as far as I knew, he'd remained faithful to me in spite of all the distractions from the girls in our class.

"Aren't you going to answer my question?"

"Yes. I mean, I do like you. Of course I do. You know that. What have I done?" I asked, putting it back on him.

I felt confused, a bit sad even, because he'd noticed and waited until now to say something. Maybe I did give off an unwelcoming vibe, but I wasn't trying to. Honestly, I just wasn't ready. I wasn't ready to give my purity away just yet.

"Are you playing hard to get then?" he asked matter-of-factly.

No, not hard to get. I'm only seventeen. It's never crossed my mind to play any sort of game.

I started to remove my hand from his leg, but he grabbed it before I could.

"Don't pull away from me. *Please*."

He moved his leg to one side of the bench, so he was now directly facing me. I swallowed hard.

"I'm not," I barely whispered.

I felt so overcome all of a sudden. It was like I was getting weaker, and he was getting stronger.

"Look at me then." He inched closer to me. "You know how I feel about you. Don't you feel the same?"

I observed his handsome face, but I was still unsure of what I was feeling. "I just told you how I felt."

He had this unbelievably sly and somewhat sneaky smirk on his face. It was the kind of expression a person might have when gaining a slight victory over his opponent.

"Then, come here." His voice was unfamiliar to me. It was deep, confident, and alluring. I had to admit, I kind of liked it.

He put one hand on my back and the other around my waist, pulling me toward him. My heart was beating fast now.

He repeated, "Come here."

He took his hand off my back and drew my face up toward him. He softly kissed me—at first. He held me tighter around the waist. I resisted, but he pressed his lips to mine with a passion I had never felt from him before. He moved his other hand up the side of my body until he was

3

gently caressing my breast. He kept going up until he reached the back of my neck. He tugged on my long sun-kissed hair. My instinct was to move my head back, and as I did, he began kissing my neck. I could feel his intensity, and I, too, became overcome with the same feelings.

I abruptly stood up in front of him.

The glimmer in his eyes said, *I told you so.*

I didn't care. I wanted him the way he wanted me. I pushed him back on the bleachers and leaned over him. He grabbed my face and drew it toward his. My body was now on top of his as we kissed again. I could tell he was excited as he moaned and kissed me harder.

"You want me."

I started to move away from him, but he grabbed me.

"James, can we go somewhere warmer?" My cold body clearly shivered from more than excitement.

I moved back as he stood up. He gave me the sexiest smile I had ever seen from him. I did like James, and in that moment, I was asking myself why I had so often forced my feelings for James out of my mind.

"Of course." He sighed as he motioned toward the end of the bleachers.

I glanced at my watch. It was seven forty-five. Rebecca and the rest of our friends would be wondering where we were, but for once, I didn't care about anyone else.

I walked first and hopped off. He followed suit. Much to my delight, he put his hand on my shoulder and turned me toward him. He started to lean down, and with one swift motion, he picked me up. I laughed, and he planted a kiss on my cheek. He carried me to the gate and put me down. He went through first and then held open the gate until I slid through.

We walked back toward his navy 1990 Toyota Corolla. He went over to my side of the car because that door always got stuck in the cold, so it required a bit of extra muscle to get it open. I stood behind him, as I always did, while he pulled on the handle.

"Let's see how long it takes you to open the door. It's seven forty-eight. Go!" I laughed.

With his back to me, I heard him chuckle as he started to pull on the handle.

Suddenly, a wave of anxiety washed over me. I blinked feverishly, yet all I saw were white spots in the pitch-black sky. *What is happening?* I couldn't speak. My heart rate increased rapidly. Then, almost as soon as it had, it seemed to slow to a crawl. I could feel each beat, one at a time, pounding deep within my chest.

Thump, thump, thump.

James still had his back to me as he yanked on the door handle. My knees weakened, and I tried to speak as my body became weightless. I stumbled backward and hit the earth.

I heard James finally pop the door open. I stretched out my arm toward him, desperate for help. No sooner did I reach out than my arm started to shake violently, my body writhing on the ground.

Then, he screamed, "Abigail!"

MARCH 1, 1995
JONATHAN

I am dying. This much I am sure of. No matter how many times the doctors flutter around my bed, attempting to stick another needle in my vein, I know nothing more can be done. I can't blame them for trying. It's their job. They care. I genuinely believe they care about me. But the facts are the facts. My life got cut way too damn short.

If you asked me if I thought life was worth living, I would say, yes, absolutely, without a doubt. I know what is happening to me, and it still doesn't change my mind. It's going to happen to all of us at some point. I guess, in some ways, I'm lucky. I get to choose when, and I'm choosing to be here with you, Tank, my best friend. I know my family couldn't be here today, but I knew you would be.

I close my eyes, and I can feel you squeeze my hand. You have the strength of a man even though I know you're really too young to deal with this. In fact, I know a lot of people, me included, think I'm too young. Abby's too young to be a part of this, too, but somehow, we have been chosen. I'm not exactly sure why, but I would do it all over again, even knowing what I know now because I met you, my family, and ultimately, Abby. I believe in Abby and what we had, as strange as that might sound.

I would have told the world about us, but instead I told you, Tank, and now, you'll have to find her. I want to believe that wherever I'm going next, she'll be there...eventually. I now believe there are angels on earth. We pass by them every day. They are the ones who make our heads turn, the ones who make us believe there is something better out there, the people who make us feel that, despite it all, this life is worth living.

I can feel my body relax. It feels like it is sinking into the bed. I feel comfortable. My mind is still active. I can see her sitting on the bleachers. I can see how beautiful she is under the glow of the moonlight. I know this moment will affect her. I know she will feel this, and I can only hope, someday, she will find the peace I am feeling now.

The room is quiet. There are no more sounds from machines. This is how I want it. My eyes remain closed. I am smiling. I can see a gray illumination, and in the middle, I see the light of her beautiful navy eyes. I feel so peaceful.

I know you're still next to me, Tank. I know this. I'm not able to feel sad because you are sad. My body won't let me. It wants me to feel okay about all this. I have no regrets, and I'm so very glad you can be here with me. I know you will take the box and keep it safe, and I know you'll be able to move on. This will wound you, it will scar her, yet somehow, I believe we will all be better in the end. I have faith in this because I know that you will find her, just as I once found her.

I can feel my mind and body begin to slow.

Please know, she will be happy, and one day, you, too, will be happy again.

That is my promise to you, my friend.

I squeeze your hand back, and I take one more breath.

MARCH 6, 1995
TANK

Tank—that was what my friends and family had called me since I first took to the football field when I was eight years old. I'd grown out of the name Thomas.

My mom had told me that when she was pregnant, she could have sworn she was having twins with the way her belly had stretched and expanded. Not surprisingly, when I was born, I'd weighed a whopping eleven pounds and four ounces. The doctor had said it was a hospital record.

Today, I stood about six feet four inches and weighed around two hundred eighty-five pounds. At the age of eighteen, I wished that were the only thing that made me stand out, but I had shocking blond hair, almost white, that touched my shoulders. I also had wide-set silver eyes, and I'd been told they were very striking. People would say they could see me coming from a mile away.

I was always recognized for my size and appearance, but I was actually a pretty soft guy off the field, and I took my family and friends super seriously because they'd supported me as I spent every waking moment working to earn a Division I college football scholarship.

And I did.

I was supposed to be leaving in the late summer on a full ride to my top-choice school, Onondaga State University. But it was so difficult to envision leaving for school without him. How could I leave Jonathan's family, my family, heck, even this town when we needed one another now more than ever before? I had a good reason to feel the way I did—at least, that was what I kept telling myself every time I wanted to cry.

But again, my size defined me. Everyone just assumed I was some kind of cold, heartless rock. But I was not. I was just a confused, sad, and broken-down eighteen-year-old kid. And all I really wanted to do right now was bawl my eyes out. Yes, I wanted to cry like a child because of how much I was badly missing my best friend.

In fact, Jonathan Higgins was the greatest friend I could have ever asked for. I guessed that was why I was the only one Mrs. Higgins could have asked to pick up the hundred or so balloons from the store after his funeral. She'd asked me as a favor, yet it pained me to pick them up. Who in their right mind would want to pick up balloons for their deceased best friend's memorial? Not me, but I was doing it anyway. After all, when I'd become his best friend twelve years ago, there was no way for me to know that I'd be here today.

Everyone from the football team, the school, and pretty much anyone in Fairmont, New York, who had ever come into contact with Jonathan was waiting for me to arrive. My truck moved sluggishly down the paved road, passing the high school and heading toward the football field, with balloons billowing out of the back. I had this overwhelming sense of gloom wash over me as I saw the crowd gathered up ahead. For the first time in a week, it really dawned on me that I would *never* see Jonathan again.

I parked in one of the last spots in the lot and killed the engine. I took a deep breath before opening the door. I put on my black suit coat and buttoned it tight. It was sunny today but cold.

Fitting really, I thought to myself as I grabbed the hundred or so strings attached to the balloons.

I hesitated, and then I turned and walked through the parking lot and toward the gate to the football field where Jonathan and I had entered side by side a thousand times before. This was the first time I had been on the field since he passed. The football field was our home. This was where we'd excelled, and this was where we had belonged. There was a lump in my throat as I walked across the field to the crowd standing on the fifty-yard line.

The gathered mourners parted as I approached. I walked over to Jonathan's parents and stood next to them. Mrs. Higgins reached up her hand and patted me on the arm.

Principal St. Gibbons had asked the Higgins if he and our head coach could say a few words in an attempt to comfort us. Unfortunately, it was quite obvious to those who had been close to Jonathan that words would not be able to fill the void we were left with after he passed. He had been the guy who made you laugh, he had been the one who helped others, he had been the reason I loved football. I owed much of my success on and off the field to him. He'd kept me focused and grounded. He was, in a word, awesome.

After the moment of silence, all eyes turned toward me. I opened my fist and released the blue and white balloons into the air. Our school colors that had once been a symbol of pride were now a symbol of misery for me. Mrs. Higgins gazed up at the sky only briefly before returning her eyes to the torn grass below her feet. I immediately put my arm around her shoulders as she quietly cried.

I squinted at the sun but kept my eyes on one balloon in particular, wishing that it would somehow be a beacon for Jonathan so that he'd know I was desperately missing him. It went up, up, up until it finally blended into the cobalt sky. It was gone, just like him, forever.

Mr. Higgins stood just outside the circle, clutching Jonathan's brother's hand. I could almost read Mr. Higgins's mind as he glanced at Will.

Jonathan and Will looked so much alike. Will was just a slightly younger version of his brother, right down to the dynamic smile. As he gazed up at his dad, Will tried to muster up a grin, but his eyes filled with tears. He dropped his father's hand to wipe the tears away with the sleeve of his dress coat.

I hated being a witness to this.

I hated all of this.

The crowd gradually dispersed, walking toward their cars. Now next to Mrs. Higgins, Mr. Higgins took her hand and ambled slowly toward their SUV, glancing back only once toward Will and me. In their car now, they watched us stand in complete silence. I could tell Will was too afraid to make eye contact with me.

I attempted to bring closure to the day by saying, "Hey, I'll see you around, okay?"

Will understood that I meant it. After all, we were practically family.

I headed for my truck.

Will spoke up, "You weren't just Jonathan's best friend, you know? You were like a brother…to us both."

I stopped and turned slightly. "I know." I stayed still, searching for the right thing to say. "I miss him, and I'm…I'm so sorry, Will. But you will always have me, no matter what."

I hurried to my truck, afraid I might cry. I waved to the Higgins as I fumbled in my pocket for my keys. I had no idea where to go, but I just had to get away. I climbed in and turned the key in the ignition. My trusty dark green Ford F-150 roared to life. As I adjusted the volume on the stereo and accelerated to the main entrance to the high school, I thought of my friend and the last time we had been together.

His words had been playing repeatedly in my mind, causing me excruciatingly painful, sleepless nights. I just couldn't stop thinking of the days leading up to today. There was more to digest than I'd let on to anyone, and I was suffering for it. After all, I had been the last one to see Jonathan alive, and no one knew what I knew.

MARCH 25, 1995
NATHAN

I came running in through the door. I could feel my heartbeat in my throat. My eyes widened like saucers when I saw my father sitting at the breakfast bar, nearly in tears.

"Dad, what is it?" I choked out.

"You're in, son. You made it. God, Mom would be so proud of you!" My dad jumped up and squeezed me tight.

He'd said so few words, but I knew exactly what he was referring to.

I'd made it. I'd been given a full scholarship to play football at my top-choice school, Onondaga State University.

My dad released the embrace. My knees got weak, so I sat down on the stool in the kitchen. I tried to smile back, but I was too scared to let this be real.

It can't be real, right?

Then, it all began to connect. I unintentionally let out a deep breath. I reflected back on this past year of grueling training and recruiting visits, of academic and physical tests, of my father crunching numbers and talking about loans and scholarships, and of the nights my father had spent leaning over a calculator while on the phone with his brother, Dave, discussing assets and credits. With my dad being a single parent, I imagined it was hard enough, but losing my mom, his wife, so suddenly had made it even harder. It might have given me all the motivation I'd ever needed to make sure my dad wouldn't have to pay a cent for college.

I took a moment to let it all sink in. A moment was all I needed to realize that if I continued to work as hard as I had my whole life, I would, come August, be the starting quarterback for the Onondaga State University Hawks. I had reached my goal. I would call it a dream, but a dream was something you imagined or wished for. A goal was something you set for yourself and worked hard to accomplish. This had been my goal since the first day I touched a football.

"I'm so proud of you, Nathan. You've earned this. Now, keep it up." He was grinning from ear to ear.

"I will, Dad. I promise." It was as though my words were coming at the same pace as my mind was absorbing the information.

"Coach mentioned he would send over some paperwork. He's going to FedEx it to my office. I'll get it in the morning. He wants to talk to us tomorrow night before you sign and make sure you don't have any more questions about your scholarship, okay?"

"Okay."

Just then, the phone rang. My dad reached over and grabbed the receiver.

"Where's the fire?" I heard Uncle Dave bark.

My dad quickly told my uncle the news about Onondaga State. I could hear the elation and pure joy in my father's voice. It was something I hadn't heard often. I knew I had made my father proud.

I stood up, forced a smile, and went down the hall to my bedroom. I closed the door, and I walked across my room. I grabbed the small Nerf football off my nightstand and collapsed on my bed. I needed some time alone to absorb this.

With news such as this, one might think that I would be running down the street, knocking on my neighbors' doors, telling all the friends I'd known my whole life that I, Nathan Ryan—the skinny kid from Halifax, Pennsylvania, who never wanted to come in from playing football—had done it. All my hard work had finally paid off.

Quickly, I faced this reality that was unfolding before me because it was happening. It was really happening.

I closed my eyes, took a deep breath, and then opened them. I stared at the ceiling. I had no idea how long I'd been lying there, motionless, until I finally heard my father's footsteps coming down the hall.

My father knocked on the door. "Nathan, you okay?"

"Yeah, Dad." My voice cracked. "I'm better than okay."

One

Nathan Ryan took a deep breath before he pulled open the heavy metal door to the locker room. He felt his nerves rise when all the players turned toward him as he headed over to his locker. He unhooked the latch and saw his practice jersey hanging inside. The incredible feelings of excitement wrapped tightly with fear came over him as he reached in to grabbed it.

Am I really ready for this? He tried to shake his nerves by letting out a long sigh.

He dropped his gym bag to the floor and sat on the bench, holding the jersey with the number twelve on the back. He took another deep breath. *Thank God they gave me my favorite number. I'm too superstitious not to wear the number I've worn since I was seven.*

It was the first day of preseason camp, and he had to summon all his will not to get too emotional about it.

It is just like any other day. Dad told me not to freak out. I can handle this. I'm ready for this.

He wanted to believe his own thoughts, but deep down, he knew this was no ordinary day in his life. In fact, this day could change his life for years to come.

"Nathan!" an unfamiliar voice yelled.

"Yeah? I mean, yes, Coach?" he stammered a bit.

"Coach wants to see you now," Assistant Coach Stanfield pointed toward Coach Bromley's office.

Coach Stanfield was about six foot two inches and had the build of a twenty-five-year-old, only he was forty-six. He'd played pro football for the Chicago Bears for two years before a knee injury left him without a contract. Even worse, he'd then become a liability that no team was willing to risk big money for. It had taken him no time at all to realize he was just another player without a place to play. So, as the old saying went, those who couldn't play, coached. He had been the assistant coach at Onondaga State for four years. He had quite a record to speak of, last year being no exception. Part of what made him and his team so successful was his unwillingness to settle for less than the best.

Nathan quickly got up, tossed his jersey back into his locker, and followed the assistant coach toward the office.

"Have a seat." Coach Bromley peered over his glasses, sizing up Nathan from head to toe.

Nathan nervously ran his hand through his dark hair. Nathan was a little over six foot three inches. He had his parents to thank for his height. On a good day, he weighed two hundred fifteen pounds, tops. There was barely an ounce of fat on him. In fact, his body was more similar to that of a swimmer than a Division I quarterback.

"You do all your drills this summer, like we talked about?" he asked, full well knowing the answer.

"Yes, sir, I did."

"Good, good. You ready to start it off today, son." It wasn't a question but rather a firm remark.

"Yes, sir, I am." Nathan tried his hardest to sound confident.

"Okay then. Coach Stanfield will take you and the offense out onto the field. You'll get to know your linemen and coordinators really well over these next four weeks. Work hard, son." He picked up the newspaper that was on his desk and started thumbing through it.

Nathan took this as his cue to leave, so he stood up and walked out.

The first day of practice was hard—*really* hard. The temperature reached ninety-two degrees inside of Menton Stadium—which was named after Class of '41 Hall of Fame running back Josh Menton—and the atmosphere felt like one hundred percent humidity. Nathan was feeling as though he was merely running on adrenaline and nerves. The team worked for a solid three hours. It was a grueling practice, but he'd known he would be pushed to the limits. This was the big time now, and he had to step up to the challenge.

Two other quarterbacks were vying for the starting spot, but after seeing what they could do, Nathan knew the spot was his to lose, and he had no intention of doing that. He had worked so hard to get here, going to summer camps and winter training camps and playing football day in and day out for the past ten-plus years. He was not about to let that go to waste now. But he would be lying if he said he couldn't wait for the final whistle to blow.

As Nathan and his teammates walked back toward the locker room, they were silent from exhaustion. He peeled off his equipment, dropping his soaked clothes into the wash bin.

Then, he went and stood in the shower. The cool water felt great on his skin and tired muscles. The sounds of the other players bantering, the spray of the water as it hissed out of the old showerheads, and the yelling of players' names asked to go see the coach filled the air around him, yet he was somehow zoned out. He went over the plays from practice as the soap ran down his skin and disappeared into the drain.

He knew his dad was anticipating hearing from him, and he was just as anxious to talk to his father. This was the longest they'd gone without speaking to one another. Since Nathan's mother had died, they had not only leaned on each other as family, but as friends, too. This time apart was proving to be more difficult than Nathan had anticipated. At least he had school and football to concentrate on. In some ways though, that made him feel guilty for moving on and leaving his father alone.

Nathan stepped out of the shower, tightly wrapped a towel around his waist, and walked to his locker. He pulled out his white T-shirt with the words *Onondaga State Hawks* on the front and *Football* on the back. He dressed quickly. He needed to get to the cafeteria before it closed.

The campus, which was located in the heart of Syracuse, New York, essentially had different hours during the preseason month than the academic year. In fact, everything was still in summer mode around here. The campus only allowed athletes and dorm monitors early access to move in. Most of the academic offices were open but for just a few hours each day.

For the next month, Nathan would really only see the field, the gym, his dorm room in Boyd Hall, and the cafeteria. It was a shame because the campus was beautiful. The old, pristine buildings had ivy vines growing up the sides, brick walkways were encased by perfectly manicured shrubs, and the tree-lined streets had colonial lampposts adorning each doorway to the academic and dormitory buildings. These were some of the many reasons he'd fallen in love with this school to begin with.

He tossed his towel in the bin as the equipment intern did one last round.

"Thanks, man," he said to the intern.

"Oh, sure, Nathan. Anytime." He pushed the wet towels further into the bin, making room for more.

He knows my name already. "I'm sorry. I didn't catch your name."

"Max. It's my second year with the team." He extended his hand to Nathan.

Nathan gladly took it. "Well, thanks, Max. Appreciate all you do for the team."

Although it was only the first day, Nathan knew that being an equipment intern was anything but glamorous. Who would want to pick up after a bunch of dirty football players? He closed his locker, took his bag off the bench, and put it on his shoulder.

"You got it! Good luck this year. The students are really excited to have you as our quarterback. It's going to be a great year. I just know it!" He had a goofy grin on his face.

"Well, I gotta run if I'm going to make it before the cafeteria closes."

Max glanced at his watch. "Yeah, you'd better hurry."

"See ya, Max," Nathan called out.

He rushed down the hall toward the metal doors at the side entrance of the field house. He jogged slightly across campus toward the cafeteria, passing all the beautiful buildings. A different kind of excitement entered his body.

I'm really in college, he thought as he jogged past the English and science buildings. *This is it—my home for the next four years.*

The cafeteria had been renovated a few years back and was much more modern than many of the other buildings. It didn't have as much charm as the older buildings, but it was state of the art. As Nathan approached the cafeteria, the electronic doors slid open. He could smell the food as he walked in, and his mouth began to water.

"We're closing in ten minutes," the lady behind the register remarked as she swiped his card.

"Understood."

Decisions, decisions. His eyes danced over the massive bread and pastry section that stood before him.

Instead, he went through the hot-food line. He left with a plate of pasta with meat sauce, a piece of plain chicken, and two helpings of broccoli. He spotted the salad bar, and his mouth began to water. He couldn't resist. He filled a bowl with lettuce, cucumbers, carrots, and mushrooms, and then he covered them in ranch dressing. He turned around to the empty room.

Boy, I have my pick of tables.

Only a handful of people were left in the cafeteria.

He was just late enough that all his teammates had already come and gone. He put his tray down on an empty table and dragged his chair in close. Then, he began eating as though it had been years since he had a decent meal. In record time, he devoured his dinner, barely breathing between bites.

He was the last one in the cafeteria.

The lady politely came over and took his tray for him. She smiled and asked, "Football?"

"Yes."

"Good luck this year."

"Thank you."

He pushed open the metal exit door to the cafeteria and strolled back across campus to his dorm. It was a rare opportunity to see the main part of campus with such little activity. The few times he had visited the school, the walkways had been packed with booths, clubs trying to get people to join, and students everywhere, hanging out and enjoying campus life.

This is nice. He approached his dorm. *Might as well enjoy it while it lasts.*

He twisted his key in the front door of Boyd Hall. He pulled on the heavy glass door and walked through. He took the stairs to the fifth floor despite the ache in his legs.

Once inside his room, he took inventory of the hard Formica floors and the concrete walls. His room was anything but attractive—not that he'd expected something other than this, but it was dreary and bare. He hung his posters on the wall near his bed and placed a few pictures of his mom and dad on his desk. The small window in between the beds was just high enough that he couldn't see out of it, but it would let in a bit of sunlight. Thankfully, the windows in front of the desks were large and made Nathan not feel as closed in.

He unpacked his clothes and then took out all his bathroom stuff and dumped it into the shower caddy he'd gotten as a graduation present. Finally, he emptied another box of school supplies and put them in one of the desks.

Feeling his unpacking ambitions fading, he found the old phone his dad had given him from the garage and plugged that into the wall. He had no idea what kind of stuff his roommate was going to have, and since he would be solo for the next few weeks, he had brought everything.

Nathan's roommate was a biology major. His name was Webber Littman.

Webber. What kind of a name is Webber? Nathan had thought when he read the letter.

Nathan was sure he'd gotten his answer after speaking with Webber on the phone. He'd seemed a bit odd, much like his name. He had called Nathan after receiving the room assignment letter. Their conversation had been painfully awkward. Once Nathan's status as a football player had come to light, Webber's tone had changed drastically. In fact, he had not sounded thrilled to be sharing a room with an athlete.

So, Nathan planned to enjoy these days alone in their room while he could.

He plopped down on his bed and kicked off his sneakers. He picked up the receiver on the phone and dialed his father.

"How is it going?" his dad asked with sheer enthusiasm.

"Good so far, Dad. Tough first practice, but it was decent."

"Glad to hear. Your teammates and coaches?"

"Yeah, all good, Dad. Coaches are really determined. I know I'll learn a lot from them. Don't know anyone yet, but that'll take some time."

"Of course," his dad said reassuringly. "You doing okay?"

"Yeah, just tired; that's all. Didn't sleep great—you know, first night and all."

There was silence. It was as though his father wanted to say, *Me, too. I didn't sleep well either.* But he didn't. His dad would never intentionally make Nathan feel bad for leaving home.

Guessing this, Nathan quickly added, "I'm going to try to go catch *SportsCenter* in the rec room. I'll call you tomorrow, okay?"

"You got it. Let me know if you need or forgot anything."

"Will do." Nathan paused, knowing that he should acknowledge that this was hard for them. "Dad?"

"Yeah?"

"The house is too quiet, isn't it?" he asked.

"Yes, Nathan, it is, but there is a good reason for the quietness. Now, don't worry about me, okay?"

Nathan could hear the strain in his father's voice.

"Thanks, Dad. I love you." He added with heaviness in his heart, "Call me anytime, and I promise I will call more, too."

"Of course." There was a brief silence on the line, and then he said with a crack in his voice, "I love you, too, and I'm so proud of you."

Nathan smiled and waited to hear the click, and then he hung up. He tried not to think about his father being alone in the house for the first time in eighteen years. If nothing else, he hoped that his being at Onondaga State would give his dad something positive to focus on.

Nathan slipped on his Adidas flip-flops, took his student ID, and headed down the hall toward the stairs.

He walked into the recreation room. It had a pool table directly to the left of the door, and two soccer players were arguing over the rules of nine-ball. On the far end of the large room were three large vending machines. To the right were couches and chairs lined up in rows facing a TV mounted on the wall. There was only one guy sitting on the furthest couch from the TV. His baseball hat was tipped over his eyes, so it was hard to tell whether he was sleeping or not.

"Hey, man," Nathan said. "Mind if I switch it to *SportsCenter*?"

The guy kicked his feet off the seat in front of him. "Yeah, sorry. Sure. Whatever." Clearly not caring, he slowly stood up and began to exit.

"Well, I didn't mean that you had to leave," Nathan mumbled.

As the guy walked out, Nathan noticed how large he was. He couldn't be a soccer player. He was way too big, and his shoulders were too broad. He glanced back at Nathan, never saying another word.

The next day, Nathan awoke to the blaring sound of his alarm clock. He wanted to be the first one at the field house, so he would have time to get in and relax a bit. Then, he'd have the trainers warm up his shoulder, like Coach Bromley had suggested the day before.

He stood in front of the mirror in the dorm room, rubbing his eyes, as he tried to wake up. Once he could focus, he laughed a bit to himself, as his dark brown hair was sticking straight up. He always cut it short to start the season even though he wasn't a fan of having his hair short, but it was easier to manage in the summer. The golden-colored skin on his face showed signs of three-day-old stubble, and he rubbed that to wake up his face.

He gave himself one last scrutinizing glance before dressing in his Adidas gym shorts, T-shirt, and hat. He grabbed his keys and a protein bar and closed the door behind him.

His mind was focused on football as he jogged over to the field house. When he entered, it was exactly as he had imagined it would be at this hour—dead quiet. Opening his locker, he put his keys on the top shelf, sat down on the bench, and opened his breakfast bar. He took a bite and then another. He was almost finished when he heard Coach Bromley's door open.

"I know you being here is hard on you and your family. But we all have to move forward, even in the face of something as tragic as your loss. We understand why you couldn't be here on the first day. It'll just take a bit of time, son." His voice was unusually soft. "You'll be okay. Just continue to work hard, and it will get easier."

From where he was sitting, Nathan couldn't see whom Coach was talking to. All he could see was this enormous guy walking with Coach toward the back door. He had never heard Coach Bromley speak so delicately to anyone. He was a straight shooter. In fact, he seemed to have little tolerance for softness. But this was something different.

Nathan closed the door on his locker and went to the training room. He stripped down to his shorts and climbed into the hot tub. He rested his head on the edge and closed his eyes. He only had a little time before the trainers would want to start warming up his shoulder.

Once out of the hot tub, Nathan was rested and warmed up, ready to go. But more importantly for him, his mind was clear, something he required to perform at his best.

He dressed in his practice pads, laced his cleats up tight, and wrapped white tape around his ankles for extra support. Near the back door to the field, he took his helmet off the shelf and went out into the steaming hot summer sun. He felt his energy rise within him as he jogged over to the players gathered on the fifty-yard line. He stood next to one of the assistant coaches, letting his helmet hang from his hand.

Coach Bromley gave them a quick rundown of his plan for practice that morning and then called out the players' names as he motioned toward where they should stand on the field. As the players started to split up into their groups, Assistant Coach Stanfield waved over to the sideline.

"We got a newbie," Coach Stanfield remarked. "This here is Thomas McPherson. We'll be trying him at tight end." He gave Tank a shove on the back, as if to say, *Now, get in line with the rest of them.*

McPherson stood among his teammates and didn't say a word.

For the next several hours, they went over play after play.

Nathan had big targets to hit. These guys were twice the size of those on his high school team, and they were faster, too. Route after route, whistle after whistle, he worked with the running backs, the wide receivers, and the tight ends. He was confident and was really getting a feel for his teammates this time. He seemed to connect with McPherson often and accurately. His confidence grew as the morning session came near to finishing.

Nathan drew his arm back, and like a bolt of lightning, he threw up a Hail Mary in the direction of McPherson. McPherson reached out but barely got a piece of the ball as he went sliding on the ground. The ball went wobbling into the end zone.

Visibly pissed off as he popped up, empty-handed, he yelled in the direction of Nathan, "Come on, Two!"

Confused, Nathan thought, *Who is he yelling at? My number is twelve, not two.*

Tank, on the other hand, knew exactly why he'd called the guy Two. As he stood, without the ball in the end zone, he deliberately brushed the dirt and grass that covered the front of him and glared in the direction of Nathan.

Jonathan would never have overthrown that, he thought as he jogged back toward the field house.

"It would have been nice to end practice with a touchdown," he mumbled to himself.

Nathan was beginning to form a routine. For him, it was part of his superstitious behavior that some would find charming but others, like his friends who were not athletes, only found weird. But he had to stick to a routine in many ways, so he could focus on football and school. He kept a schedule for himself, and it had been working well for him thus far.

So, once he showered after practice, he made it to the cafeteria right before it closed. He ate alone, and he began his nightly walk from the cafeteria back to Boyd Hall. The quiet summer breeze and the fading sun behind the English building were enough to make him smile slightly to himself.

He entered his room, kicked off his sneakers, and went right over to his bed.

He picked up the phone and dialed home. "Hey, Dad. How are you?"

"Wonderful. All good here. How was practice today?"

"Tiring. Had a new guy join. He's a pretty solid tight end. I think we are looking competitive overall."

"Awesome." He slightly laughed, and then he said, "Getting your routine down?"

"Yes." Nathan chuckled. "You know me; I like to keep a schedule."

"Oh, don't I know!"

"Funny. Am I that bad?"

"Nah. Well, let's just see what your roommate thinks. Who knows? They say college really changes people. I know it changed your mother and me—and for the better."

"Hey, wait a second. For the better?"

"I'm kidding. Of course it's a good thing, Nathan. You're focused and disciplined, and no doubt, it will only propel you forward. Now, quit chatting with me and get some rest or go hang with your teammates or something."

Nathan's brow furrowed as he thought about how many meals and such he'd already eaten alone and how he hadn't really had any time to get to know anyone on the team. *Maybe I am too focused. Maybe I should get out of my routine and live a little more.*

"Oh, yeah, sure. I'm going to go down to the rec room right now and maybe play some pool or something."

"Good. I'll call you soon. Love you."

"You, too, Dad."

Nathan headed down to the rec room to watch some TV. When he entered, a bunch of guys with Onondaga soccer T-shirts on and a couple of cross-country guys with similar apparel were sitting on the couches, staring at the TV. They all resembled how Nathan felt—tired and sore. He sat down on a chair toward the back and put his feet on the edge of the empty couch in front of him. His body ached as he became one with the chair.

His eyes were growing heavy as he stared aimlessly at the TV. He was paying little, if any, attention to what was on the screen. He was about to close his eyes when he noticed the same big guy from the day before walk into the room. He walked past Nathan and toward the vending machine. He swiped his card and pressed the button for a Gatorade. After retrieving the bottle, he opened the cap and took a big gulp before walking to the couch in front of Nathan. He sat down, and as the guy draped his arm across the back of the couch, Nathan reluctantly put his feet on the ground.

He turned slightly toward Nathan. "What? Ya can't hit a big target like me?" he asked in a deep voice.

Nathan chuckled. He knew exactly who this guy was now. "McPherson, right?" he asked.

"Tank." He had this air about him that Nathan couldn't quite place.

This guy has some nerve, questioning my ability, when he was the one who joined late. And what is with his attitude?

Tank wouldn't turn around, which frustrated Nathan.

"Whatever. Okay then, Tank"—he yawned—"you'll know it when I hit you." Too tired to engage anymore, he got up and patted Tank on the shoulder before making his way through the door.

"Let's see it tomorrow, Two!" he yelled after him, but Nathan was already gone.

Two

SEPTEMBER 17, 1995

Abigail Price was settling nicely into her dorm room in Willis Hall.

Her roommate was Laura Chase, a relatively quiet math major from Stockbridge, Massachusetts, who had mentioned she wanted to be a teacher. Laura was an attractive girl with an athletic build despite the childhood she'd spent avoiding any and all athletics. She had a great smile, an adorable brown bob hairstyle, and striking hazel eyes. She was just a bit shorter than Abigail at about five feet four inches. She had been kind and polite thus far, and it appeared to Abigail that it came natural to her. Abigail could tell she had been raised well, just by how she spoke. She had probably been voted Friendliest Senior in her high school yearbook.

They'd just met for the first time while moving into the dorm.

However, they had spoken numerous times over the summer, getting to know one another as best they could through stories about their friends and their home life and how excited they both were to go to college. They'd coordinated the necessities, like who would bring the VCR, TV, phone, and mini fridge. They'd bought whatever else they wanted to share, like snacks and drinks, but the rest was just their own clothes, toiletries, and school supplies.

They helped one another move in boxes and garbage bags filled with clothes while their parents chatted nervously, not wanting to leave their daughters to fend for themselves at such a big university. After the cars were unloaded, the two of them stood quietly, smiling at one another, while anxiously waiting for their parents to leave.

"You sure you have everything you need, honey?" Abigail's mom, Natalie, asked.

"Yes, I think so. I'll be fine, promise. I love you, Dad." Abigail hugged her father, Edward, tightly around the neck.

"I'll call you if we need anything," Laura whispered to her mother.

Finally, after tearful stares and hugs that had more of a squeeze to them than one might like, the parents left, and the two of them were left alone in the silence of the cement dorm room they would call home for the next nine months.

"Well," Laura said, "it really is nice to finally meet you!" She moved closer and gave her new roommate a hug. "You're even prettier than in the pictures you sent me over the summer," she admired. "You always this tan, or is it just during the summer?"

"Oh, geez. Thank you. I appreciate that. I guess I do tan easily—for a blonde." She bashfully lowered her large navy eyes.

"Oh, I've embarrassed you. So sorry, but you must be used to people gushing over you."

"Oh, boy. Well, yes, I guess I am," she stumbled through her words. "I'm just so excited to finally be here." Her cheeks burned with heat.

"Me, too. Couldn't sleep last night because I was thinking about today! It's finally here!"

"I know. Seemed so far away a few months ago, yet here we are. So, want to unpack all this stuff?" Abigail motioned around the room. "Then, we can go check out the rest of the dorm."

"Sounds perfect!"

They took a few hours to unpack their boxes and bags. One of the many reasons Abigail had liked OSU so much during her initial tour of the campus was because the dorm rooms were actually two rooms. When you walked into the door, the first room had the desks and chairs, and the second room had the beds, dressers, and closets. The wall perfectly separated the sleeping area from the study area.

Abigail hung her posters of The Cranberries and Bruce Springsteen near her bed. Before she'd left for school, she had also picked up a poster of the cast of *Friends* since she'd discovered over the summer that it was both of their favorite show on television.

Laura hung her Nirvana and Beck posters above her bed. "Mind if I put some of my family pictures on our dresser?" she asked.

"Of course not."

Abigail put a picture of herself and her best friend, Rebecca, from their high school graduation on the nightstand next to her bed. She also had a picture of her family that had been taken at her graduation party, and of course, she had a picture of her dog, Skyler.

She missed her dog terribly. As she'd grown up as an only child, her dog had become like a sister. Skyler had slept in her bed since she was a puppy, so aside from a few vacations here and there, this was the first extended amount of time that her dog would be without Abigail. She hated thinking about how lonely and confused Skyler must feel, not having Abigail around. She knew her mom and dad would take good care of Skyler despite the fact that they would not let her sleep with them.

After Abigail and Laura unpacked and recycled their cardboard boxes in the facility center on their floor, they went down to the main floor and were in awe of all the students still coming into the dormitory with their parents.

Hundreds of wide-eyed teenagers shuffled in and out of the lobby and elevators, carrying bags and boxes filled with their most important possessions. Parents nervously followed. Their expressions landed somewhere in between pride that their children would soon be college-educated and sheer panic at the thought of leaving their teenage kids, only to have them instantly become adults.

"Do you think our parents looked that nervous?" Abigail asked as a family walked by.

"Yes, one hundred percent." Laura pointed at another mother as she took a deep inhale. "But not as bad as her. Poor woman appears like she is going to faint."

"Geez, now, I feel kind of bad. I was just waiting for my parents to leave. They must have been…I don't know…feeling a lot, I suppose."

"Of course. Hey, call them later and tell them that we're doing fine."

"Yeah, I will. I'll do that." Abigail gave her a slight smile.

Laura glanced at her watch. "Let's go in the rec room and watch *Friends*."

Abigail noticed two kids collide as they tried to make their way to the elevator, neither seeing one another over the boxes piled in their arms. Clothes, CDs, and toiletries crashed to the floor in a combined pile, and their parents rushed in to quickly pick up the mess.

"Oh, boy. We have to get out of here. This is madness!" Abigail exclaimed.

The first two weeks of classes had gone by quickly, and Abigail and Laura were starting to get into their own routines.

Abigail found her level-one Biology class to be too easy. She had taken all Advanced Biology classes in high school, so from day one, she had been able to easily follow along. She was also really enjoying her Microbiology and Chemistry classes as well.

Unfortunately, in her first few weeks at school, she had done little socializing, unlike many of the other girls on her floor. The girls were nice enough, but some of them seemed to be mostly focused on parties and boys. Abigail hadn't really even had a chance to meet them all yet. They'd had a few small floor meetings with their dorm monitors to talk about the rules of the dorm and such, but other than that, it was like they were all just ships passing in the night. It did, however, make her feel good that some of their floor mates had at least tried to get her and Laura to go out even though it was clear they were content with staying in and studying.

Abigail was determined to get off on the right foot with school. There would be plenty of time for parties this year. In the back of her mind, she worried, too, about having another seizure. Although she had not had one since last March, she would think about it often and couldn't help but get anxious from the mere thought of it.

It had come on so suddenly that night with James that she constantly felt like she was just lying in wait. When was the next one going to come? Would she be in class and all of a sudden just start convulsing? Or worse, would she be at some random party where no one knew her? She feared more than anything that she would just bear a resemblance to some drunken freshman passed out on the floor. All the partygoers would be passing her by, too afraid to call for help with the fear of getting caught for underage drinking. These were just some of the dark and twisted thoughts she would have, and they were enough to keep her glued to her dorm room at night.

Her parents had pleaded with her to take it easy at school, and they'd all but begged her to tell her roommate just in case something happened. Reluctantly, she had told Laura after their first week at school. Deep down, Abigail had known it was the right thing to do. Laura had taken it well, asking few questions, and they'd left it at that. They hadn't spoken a word about it since. Abigail would often wonder if her seizure was the reason Laura would stay in with her night after night.

It wasn't until the third Saturday of the first semester that Abigail was finally starting to get stir-crazy. She had seen the cafeteria, the student union, the library, and the rec room in her dorm, but that was about it. She needed a change of pace. The days were starting to blend, and she was beginning to get that feeling of time slipping away with not much to show for it. Besides, if winter in Upstate New York was going to hit as hard as it had every year before, she'd better enjoy these fall days more while she still could.

She finally took out her journal for the first time at school.

I'm bored. I have done nothing really but go to the cafeteria and library. Am I really the world's most boring freshman? Poor Laura always hangs with me, too. She must think she got a real dud for a roommate. But, seriously, she is awesome. I really like her. She is so easy to live with and is polite and kind. I think it will be a great year if I can ever get my nose out of a book and start socializing a bit more. It's just that school is so important, and while it's not hard yet, it will be. I really have to keep the momentum going if I'm going to get into the veterinarian program. Anyway, I do like school so far, but I'm just getting a little bored. I need some excitement!

She closed her journal and put it back in her desk, hiding it under a bunch of papers and photos. It just always made her feel better to write her thoughts down. Her journal was her therapy.

It seemed like perfect timing when the entire floor decided they were going down to Menton Stadium to watch the football game. Abigail quickly agreed to go, much to the surprise of the other girls on her floor. The Hawks were hosting the Georgia Tech Yellow Jackets, and it was slated to be an exciting game. This, of course, was according to the school newspaper, *The Weekly Blue*.

"I'll go if you go," Abigail said to Laura.

"Sure. Why not?" Laura gave her a halfhearted smile.

On numerous occasions, Laura had expressed her disinterest in sports. She had grown up playing the stand-up bass, and that had turned into the bass guitar. She had a deep interest in music. She appreciated good music and loved to talk about it, more than any other girl Abigail had known growing up. That was the reason that Laura and Abigail had connected so fast. Abigail also had a love for music. She had spent hours in her room, making mix tapes, in high school and had even sent Laura one over the summer once she knew of their common interest.

The entire sixth floor gathered in the lobby before heading down to the field. Group after group of freshmen and sophomores strolled out the dormitory door, dressed in the school colors.

Abigail walked out the front door of Willis Hall with her floor mates. The warmth of the autumn sun was a welcome feeling on her skin. It was a perfect day with crisp air, the bright sun, and a slight breeze. She pulled her hair back into a ponytail and put on her black sunglasses. She was wearing a navy T-shirt with the word *Hawks* across the front—every freshman had gotten it in their welcome package—along with tight blue jeans and gray Adidas sneakers.

The stadium was crowded with students, alumni, and parents. She could barely make her way through the crowd to the student bleachers. When Abigail and her floor mates finally got to the metal stands, they were packed with scarcely any room for them, but they slid down, one after the other, until they finally took their seats.

The game was already in the second quarter, and Onondaga State was on top with the score at ten to three.

Abigail found herself watching the people more than the actual game. She couldn't believe how many spectators filled the stands. It was loud and full of energy. Laura seemed like she was having fun, and so was Abigail, much to her surprise. She had to admit that since she'd started school, this was really the most she'd seen of campus life. She was disappointed in herself that she had not spent more time doing activities like this. As the marching band played their fight song, it made her feel more alive than she had these past few weeks while just going back and forth between classes, the cafeteria, and her dorm.

After the game, Abigail and the girls walked back toward campus and to the cafeteria for an early dinner. Many of her floor mates wanted to eat early, so they would have plenty of time to get ready for whichever frat party they decided to go to later that night.

She walked through the line and got her usual turkey sandwich on wheat, a garden salad, and a hot chocolate. The cafeteria was pretty crowded for four thirty on a Saturday. The girls all sat at a long table in the back. They ate and discussed who would hook up after the party. Almost all of them joked they hoped they would.

By the time they tossed their trays on the belt and returned to the dorm, it was almost six thirty.

"You sure you don't want to go out with us tonight?" one of their quieter floor mates, Maddie, asked Abigail and Laura.

Laura glanced at Abigail, trying to gauge her thoughts.

Abigail didn't need a babysitter, so she spoke up before Laura had a chance, "You should go, Laura. Maybe I'll meet up with you guys later. I know where it is." She tried to hide the fact that she was lying. She had no intention of going out tonight.

Laura then turned to Maddie. "Yeah, I'll go. What time are you going out?" she asked.

"Nine, and Bree says not to be late."

"Bree?" Laura asked with a quizzical expression.

Casey, one of the other girls in their wing, eyed Maddie and then the two of them. "Oh, I take it, you haven't met Bree?"

"No, I guess not," Laura said.

Abigail stood quietly, watching the scene unfold.

"Well, just be in my room before nine," Casey said rather than requested.

Laura added in a hushed voice, "I'll come down when I'm ready."

Abigail actually enjoyed watching and helping Laura get ready. She appreciated the fact that Laura had not once asked her if she would come. Laura knew if Abigail wanted to go, then she would go.

Abigail pulled out a few shirts from her closet and showed them to Laura. They were the same size, so sharing clothes was easy. She held up a bright aqua polo shirt, and Laura's eyes lit up.

"What a pretty color!"

"It would look great on you." Abigail took it off the hanger and handed it to Laura.

Laura slipped it over her head. The color made her hazel eyes even more amazing. She took a step back and showed Abigail her outfit. "Good?" She smoothed down her dark brown bob.

"Great!" Abigail fumbled on her dresser, searching for her perfume. "Try this." She handed the bottle to her roommate.

Laura pulled off the cap and smelled it. "Thanks!" She sprayed it on her wrists and neck.

Abigail eyed the clock hanging on the wall. It was eight thirty-five.

"Do you want to go down to Maddie's room with me? Or are you not coming because you want time alone to talk to James?" Laura asked.

James? What the hell made her ask me about James?

"How the—I mean, how did you know?" Abigail's cheeks flushed.

"I know I'm not a genius, but give me some credit, will you? Every time you pull open your nightstand drawer, I can see the picture of him—or I assume it's the same guy who is always calling here and leaving messages on the machine. You never talk about him, so I'm guessing he's your high school love? No?"

Love? Not sure I would call him my love, but we do have a connection, one that I can't possibly explain.

"So, you going to spill the beans to your roommate or what?"

"Sorry. I'm not trying to hide anything. I'm just not sure where we stand. We go to school hours away from one another, and I guess we never really talked about what was going to happen next." She let out a long sigh. Then, with a slightly awkward laugh, she said, "I avoid complicated relationships. My name is Abigail Price, and I'm an avoider. I'm currently seeking help for it."

Laura started laughing, too. "Ah, yes, the old if-you-sidestep-it-it-no-longer-exists trick. Well, I'm no expert, but that could come back and bite you in the ass one day!"

"Thanks for the advice," Abigail quipped as she rolled her eyes. "Shouldn't you be leaving now anyway?"

"Trying to get rid of me?" Laura laughed and checked her reflection one last time in the mirror.

"Have fun meeting this Bree girl. And have a great time!" She walked over to her bed where she kicked off her sneakers and sat down.

Laura waved her hand and quietly closed the door as Abigail lay back on her bed.

With Laura's conversation now fresh on her mind, Abigail grabbed her journal from her drawer and began feverishly writing down her thoughts. This was both therapeutic and a good way to pass the time. She wrote until well after nine, filling several pages with her thoughts on school, James, and how much she missed home.

Being an only child was in some ways a blessing. When she wanted to be alone, she could. It was easy for her to be by herself. Many of her friends always had someone around whether they wanted them to be or not. It had, however, created a sense of quietness in Abigail that never quite went away. Sometimes, when she was not talking, it could be mistaken for her being shy, uninterested, or disconnected, but really, it was just a product of her environment. It was neither right nor wrong.

After about forty-five minutes, when she knew all the girls were gone, Abigail stripped down, leaving a pile of clothes at her feet, and pulled on her terry cloth robe. She grabbed her shower caddy and walked down toward the bathroom. She turned on the hot water and let it warm up a bit before stepping in. She took her time in the shower. She was glad to have some alone time for once. After she turned off the water, she dried herself with her towel before putting on her robe.

When she returned to her room, she pulled her men's button-down shirt on. It was large enough that it almost went to her knees. She twisted her wet hair on top of her head and secured it with a pen from her desk.

The clock on the wall read half past ten. She sat down at her desk and gazed out across the campus, wondering if Laura was having a good time.

Is the party fun? Should I have gone?

She quickly shook those thoughts away as she opened her Biology textbook. Her professor had told her that she could test out of 101 and move right into his 201 class, if she so desired. Of course she did. It would make life so much easier, not to sit through an entire semester of information she already had down pat. In fact, nothing would make her happier.

Three

Maybe this is a mistake. Abigail sat down in the only open seat left in Biology 201. She sighed as she pulled her notebook out of her bag and placed it on the desk.

"Welcome, Abigail," Professor Rhodes announced.

Abigail noticed that he gave her a wink. She blushed at his gesture, as seemingly innocent as it was.

He then turned his attention toward her neighbor. "Webber, would you mind pairing up with Abigail since you do not already have a lab partner?"

Abigail turned toward Webber, and he bashfully nodded in her direction.

For a moment, she regretted leaving her last class to join this one, but she knew it was ultimately the right decision for her studies.

Abigail found the class somewhat easy to pick up in terms of where they were, but she had no idea what she'd already missed, and this was what she'd feared the most. She felt anxious as Professor Rhodes referred to the upcoming exam. She would absolutely need to get someone's notes and soon.

When class ended, Professor Rhodes called for Abigail to come to the front of the room. She grabbed her notebook and bag and approached him.

"Welcome again, Abigail. I hear you tested out of one-oh-one. Any particular reason you were placed in that class?"

"I already knew the material in the other class. I took all AP classes in high school."

"Excellent. I'm sure you'll do just fine, Miss Price."

"Thanks, Professor Rhodes. I'll try my best to get caught up before the exam. I'll have to borrow someone's notes during the next class."

"If not, come see me. I have office hours on Thursdays from four to six." He smiled at her.

"Great. Thank you again. Sorry, I have to run if I'm going to make it to my next class."

"Of course. See you on Friday."

Abigail headed down the stairs. She noticed her new lab partner standing by the double doors. He seemed to be nervously shuffling back and forth as she approached.

"Abigail?"

"Yes. Hello." She smiled warmly, trying to put him at ease.

"I'm Webber." He stuck out his hand in what appeared to be an attempt to shake hers, but at the last minute, he just waved at her.

He was average height and definitely on the thin side. He wore wire-rimmed glasses and had spiked, dark hair. It appeared as though he'd tried to put some kind of gel or something in his hair to keep it from getting out of control.

"Nice to meet you. I guess we'll be lab partners. Hope you don't mind me coming in late."

"Uh, no—I mean, it's fine." He snorted.

"Well, I've gotta run to my next class. Tuesdays are my busy days." She went to turn and walk out the door, but then she hesitated. "Hey, any chance you'd let me borrow your notes? I'm feeling like I really need to get up to speed."

His grip tightened around his notebook, and he seemed panicked at the thought of giving up his notes. The last thing she wanted to do was upset her new lab partner.

"If it's easier, we could meet sometime?"

Tension released from his shoulders.

"Sure, uh…I'm extension seven-eight-two-five." He gave her his campus phone number.

She quickly jotted it on the front of her notebook. "Okay, Webber, I'll call you."

As she left, she let out a huge sigh of relief. Starting college was one thing, but coming into a class four weeks in and not knowing what to expect was another. But now that the first Biology 201 class was behind her, it made her feel so much more at ease.

Abigail didn't have her Biology 201 class again until Friday. It was Wednesday, and she couldn't wait until then to study.

She met Laura and some of their floor mates in the cafeteria at their usual time—five thirty. After another turkey sandwich for dinner, she walked back to her room with Laura. Abigail put her bag and ID on her desk and picked up her notebook. She dialed Webber's extension.

He picked up on the first ring. "Hello?"

"Is Webber there, please?" she asked politely.

"This is he."

"Webber, it's Abigail, your lab partner."

"Hello, Abigail."

"I was hoping we might be able to study soon. Before Friday?" she asked, hoping he would be okay with the short notice.

"Sure. When do you have in mind?"

"I could meet you at the library in twenty minutes?"

There was a pause.

"Sounds good. I'll see you then."

She heard the phone click, so she hung up, too.

Abigail arrived at the library before Webber did. She stood inside the doors and waited for him to show up.

The library was virtually empty, so after a few minutes, she decided to go in and grab a table. She was sure he wouldn't have a problem finding her. She walked in the direction of the back row of tables and placed her bag on top of the wood table. She opened it up and took out her pen, notebook, and Biology textbook.

She glanced at her watch again. It was seven thirty. She flipped open to the first chapter and began skimming the pages. Before she knew it, another fifteen minutes had gone by.

Maybe I missed him. Or is he waiting somewhere else for me?

She was about to get up and walk around when she saw him hurrying through the front door. He barely acknowledged the woman at the desk when he showed his ID. He barreled straight toward Abigail with a concerned expression.

"I am so sorry I'm late," he whispered.

"Oh, no problem."

"My roommate lost his key again, and I had to wait to let him in," he added, sounding exasperated.

"Okay. I understand, honestly. I was just catching up on my reading anyway." She skimmed her textbook while he got settled.

He seemed somewhat agitated. Although she hardly knew him, she sensed this.

"All right." He opened his notebook. "Where would you like to begin?"

"Well, I read the first chapter and think I'm pretty good with that. Any particular things Professor Rhodes talked about?"

"Not really." Webber slid his notebook closer to her.

She skimmed his notes under the title *Chapter One*. She noticed his notes were concise and well written. She was impressed.

"Okay, looks about right. On to chapter two?" she asked.

"Yes. So, in chapter two, he gave us this quiz."

Abigail glanced at the quiz. Webber had gotten a grade of ninety-seven.

"Okay, great. Would you mind reading me the questions, and I'll see what I know?" She opened her notebook to a blank page.

"Sure." He held up the paper, so she could no longer see it. "Question one…"

In a hushed voice, he proceeded to read all fifteen questions to her. She jotted down each answer on her notebook. When she was done, he took the paper from her and went over each answer.

"Wow." He shook his head. He moved her notebook back toward her and gave her a crooked smile. "One hundred percent."

She tried hard not to smile too wide.

"Lucky, I suppose." She turned her book open to chapter three. "Do you know what chapters the midterm will be based upon?" She started to scan chapter three.

"Yes, chapters one to five. There will be a bonus essay. He hinted that it might be on a topic of our choice—with a few wrenches thrown in."

"Great. Do you have time to catch me up on chapters three, four, and five?"

"Yeah, sure. I'm free." His awkwardness was wildly apparent.

They sat in the library for the next two and a half hours before calling it quits. It was a bit after ten thirty when they left. She was satisfied that she was now caught up before Friday's class.

Abigail started heading down the stairs in front of the library. She stopped when she reached the sidewalk.

After spending the past few hours with Webber, Abigail knew he was smart. She could tell by the way he talked that he'd read a lot of books. She wondered if he enjoyed other things besides biology. When he spoke to her, he always seemed to hesitate, giving her the feeling that maybe he hadn't conversed a lot with girls in high school.

She tried to put him at ease, but she wasn't so great at this either. "Where do you live?" Abigail asked as he started down the stairs.

"Across campus. You?"

"Me, too. Willis Hall."

"I'm in Boyd Hall," he said.

They crossed the street together and silently walked along the lit path through campus for a few minutes. Frankly, Abigail liked the quiet. The air was a bit cool but felt nice on her face as they moved in between the buildings. She noticed that Webber kept walking in her dorm's direction even though he could have taken another path straight to Boyd.

"Didn't you say you're in Boyd?" she asked.

"My mom would kill me if I let you walk home alone in the dark."

Abigail couldn't help but laugh. Thankfully, he started to laugh, too.

"Well, I wouldn't want my lab partner to die before my second class."

He chuckled again, pushing his glasses up his face.

They got close to Willis Hall before Abigail turned to him. "Thanks, Webber. I think I can take it from here. I'll see you on Friday."

"Okay. See you." He turned and headed toward Boyd.

She observed him for a moment. She was struck by the feeling that she'd made a new friend with a common interest in science, and it made her feel good.

She gazed up toward the sky and sighed to herself. "So, this is college. I think I'm going to like it." Then, she turned and went inside.

She took the elevator to the sixth floor and walked down the hallway to her room. She opened her dorm room door. Abigail could see the light on Laura's desk. Laura turned to face her as she walked in.

"How did studying go?" Laura asked.

Laura was sweet. Abigail really liked her, and they were getting closer more and more every day. Their differences were what made them good roommates, but much like Abigail, Laura was courteous, neat, and quiet. Their lives were blending well together. They were never tripping over one another or getting in each other's way. It was perfect.

"Good." Abigail plopped her book bag on her desk chair. She saw a note on top of her desk, and she picked it up.

"Yeah, James called again. Want to talk about it?" Laura asked, already knowing the answer.

"No, but thanks." Abigail stared at the note. She had a lot to think about, and that was partly because of the note.

James called at 9:56 p.m. If he doesn't hear back from you by Friday, he will be driving here to see you.

Abigail walked to the other side of the room, holding the paper, and she sat down on her bed. She stared at the note for a few moments before she put it down next to her. She started to undress. The best thing about her dorm room was the wall in between the desk area by the door and the other side of wall that had the beds, dressers, and closets. This gave them some privacy, and it also allowed them to study late without letting the light from the desk lamp bother the other one while sleeping.

As Abigail crawled into bed and switched off the light, she heard Laura say, "Remember, I'm going home to my parents' house this weekend."

Ugh. Now, what am I going to do?

Would James actually drive four hours just to pop in on me? Would he take the chance that I might not even be here? She wrestled with these thoughts back and forth in her mind as she tried to drift off to sleep.

After an hour of lying there, eyes wide open, she realized that if she didn't turn off her brain, she would undoubtedly be awake to see the sunrise, and she could not afford to be tired in the morning. She had a full day of classes.

She finally stopped thinking about James. She had done this so many times before tonight, but for some reason, this time was much harder.

Four

Nathan could barely sit up in bed. His alarm was beeping at what seemed to be a louder decibel than normal. He reached over and hit the snooze button. He pulled back the covers and swung his legs over the side of his bed before allowing his feet to touch the floor. He hurt. His whole body hurt. He rested his head in his hands, anticipating what it would feel like when he finally stood up.

The alarm went off again. He couldn't believe it had taken him seven minutes to move. The pain that had radiated down his leg all night long was now in a full throb, pulsating each beat like it was chanting, *You're in pain, you're in pain*, over and over. He was in agony partly due to the fact that he had refused to take any of the medication he had been offered. He reached over and turned off the alarm. He had forty minutes to shower, eat, and get to class. He could not miss classes—team rules.

Nathan stood in the shower and let the hot water move down his body. He knew by the sheer ache in his left hip and the massive dark purple bruise, that his injury might in fact end his season.

In yesterday's practice, he'd taken a hit so jarring that he'd actually left practice on a stretcher and been taken directly to the medical center on campus. His pride had been significantly more wounded at the time he was escorted off the field than the actual discomfort in his leg. Thankfully, the X-ray had determined that it was only a deep contusion and not a fracture, so he had been sent back to his room to rest. Due to the commotion surrounding his injury, he'd accidentally left his keys in his locker and had to get in touch with Webber to let him into the room last night. After letting him in, Webber had immediately left the room, and Nathan had gone to bed. Nathan was a little disappointed that his own roommate had rushed out of the room even though it was obvious the condition he was in. But then again, he had been so busy with football that he hadn't really had a chance to get to know Webber and to try to change his mind that not all jocks were idiots.

Nathan took his time while getting dressed, pulling on the loosest pair of sweatpants and sweatshirt he could find. He put on his baseball cap, grabbed his bag, and left a note on the dry erase board that Webber had put up for just these sorts of things.

> *Spidey: I'll get my keys from my locker. Sorry about that. See you later.*

Nathan called Webber Spidey as in Spider-Man because he was always playing this Spider-Man game on the Nintendo. It was a long stretch, but Nathan gave all his friends nicknames. He thought it was a subtle way to let Webber know that he did want to be friends, even with their obvious differences. He hadn't asked Webber how he felt, and since he had not rejected it, Nathan continued to call him that.

Nathan locked the door from the inside, closed it behind him, and headed toward the cafeteria. He had about twenty minutes to grab something to eat, and he was starving.

He smiled at the woman as she swiped his ID to let him into the cafeteria. She always made some kind of remark about football, and this time was no exception.

"You ready for Saturday?"

"Yes, ma'am," he said politely.

"You hurt?" she asked, eyeing his leg.

"Just a little banged up. I'll be okay."

He noticed two girls behind him in line as they started to giggle.

The woman noticed, too, and spoke first, "You girls know Nathan, your star quarterback?" She winked at him.

He blushed as he moved out of the line and grabbed a tray. He glanced back at the girls as they handed the woman their IDs. The smaller girl with the long, curly brown hair gave him an incredible smile. He turned away and got in the hot-food line. He glanced back again and noticed the girls were close behind.

"What can I get you?" the server asked. His hand was ready with a spoonful of eggs.

"I'll take eggs"—Nathan motioned to the spoon—"ham, potatoes, and sausage."

The server gave Nathan an extra scoop of scrambled eggs. He reached over and handed Nathan the plate piled with food.

"Thank you."

"Hungry?" the girl with the curly hair asked. "I'm Jessica, by the way, and this is Kelly." She pulled down on one of her long brown tendrils and then let it spring back to life.

He turned, as her voice had startled him. Her friend just stood there, staring at him. Jessica smiled again.

"Oh, hi. Yeah, I guess I'm hungry." He went over to the drink counter and took two empty glasses. He filled them with milk.

Again, Jessica and Kelly appeared next to him.

Jessica reached across him for an empty glass. "Excuse me." Her voice sounded different, almost sweeter than before.

"No problem." He took a step back.

She filled up her glass with milk. In a hushed voice, she said to him, "Milk does a body good."

She turned and walked away. Her friend followed closely behind her.

It was no surprise to anyone with eyes that Nathan would grab someone's attention. He had strong, distinct features—a hard jawline but a perfectly proportioned nose and pouty lips. He always had flushed cheeks, like he'd just gone for a run, and his hair was naturally wavy and a darker brown, which made his steel-gray eyes stand out even more. With his glasses, the girls at his high school had often giggled at him, telling him he resembled a young Clark Kent. His handsomeness and bashful looks would drive girls crazy, and no matter where he went, he always drew girls to him. This might sound great to some people, but all it did was make him recoil and avoid the girls in his class. He was too shy to be chased.

Nathan sat down at a table with a few other football players. They hardly spoke to one another as they shoveled in their food.

Nathan suddenly realized he had only ten minutes to get to class. He could not be late. As he stood, he popped two more potato wedges into his mouth and grumbled, "Good-bye," to his teammates.

"Don't be late, Two!" Tank yelled after him.

"Whatever," Nathan growled with his mouthful of food. *That guy is really starting to irk me! Is he trying to piss me off?*

As he put his tray on the conveyer belt, he could hear Tank laughing. Nathan walked past some tables near the door, and he heard a girl yell after him.

"See ya after the game, Nathan!" Jessica called out.

His skin heated as he hurried out the door.

What a strange breakfast.

He jogged across campus. By the time he got to his classroom, his left side was throbbing. The pain was radiating down his hip and into his leg and calf. He began to cramp up. He cursed himself.

"You idiot. Had to run all the way to class," he mumbled under his breath with just under thirty seconds to spare until class started.

He took his usual seat in the front of the room, per Coach's request. Coach did not want any of his players to sit in the back of the classroom. He had made that clear to the entire team before school even began, and if he found out a player had sat in the back, it would be extra laps for the whole team. He'd alleged he had spies in each of the buildings. Nathan was not so convinced about that, but he would never put it past Coach to pop into a classroom, unannounced. He was a hard-ass on and off the field.

It was difficult for Nathan to concentrate due to how much pain he was in. He kept shifting in his seat in an attempt to get comfortable. When the professor started writing on the board, Nathan rummaged through his bag for some ibuprofen. He popped them in his mouth and swallowed hard. They gradually moved down his throat.

He had to make it through the next four hours of classes before he could head down to the field to see the trainers. Today was one of his longer days, and he needed to excel in school in order to keep his scholarship and remain playing on the team.

School had always been important to him, but his life downright depended on him being an exceptional student. It was a lot of pressure. His dad, his friends, and his teammates from back home and now Onondaga State were all counting on him, and just thinking about it would keep him awake at night. College was difficult enough. In a lot of ways, it was a full-time job. Only now, he had two full-time jobs—student and scholarship athlete. He had to find a balance and make this work.

He limped to his Economics class. Moaning, he sat down in his seat and dropped his bag on the floor next to him. He began to worry.

Will I be ready to play on Saturday? A bead of sweat formed on his brow. *What if I have to give up my spot? What if Coach makes me sit this one out? Worse yet, what if the trainers won't clear me to play?*

Panic set over him, and all he could think about was the game.

One more hour, and he could make his way down to the field. One more hour, and he would know the answer to his worst nightmare—whether or not he would be playing.

When class ended, Nathan was dreading the ten-minute jaunt to the field. He went across campus and to the main road. He tried hard not to limp, but it was becoming impossible.

A truck pulled up alongside him, and he heard the squeaking of the window as it moved down into the door.

"Get in," the voice said.

Nathan turned and saw Tank sitting in the driver's seat. Nathan grimaced but opened the door anyway, and he leisurely slid his way into the seat.

"Jesus, you look pathetic." Tank laughed as he pressed on the gas.

"Yeah, you see what it feels like when a guy who weighs three hundred pounds hits you on the side," he mumbled under his breath. He was in too much pain to argue.

"How's your arm?" Tank asked, ignoring Nathan's comment.

"Fine."

"Good," Tank said with another laugh. "That's all I care about."

"Dude, what is your problem?" Nathan quipped. It was unnatural for him not to get along with people, let alone a teammate.

"Hey, if you're going to play football, then *play football*. No one said this was an easy sport."

Nathan's jaw dropped, and he was about to respond when Tank turned up the radio.

"Love this song!"

Aerosmith blared from the speakers.

When they got to Menton Stadium, Tank pulled into the first row and parked his truck. He hopped out and started walking to the double doors of the field house. Nathan paused, trying to get the energy to open the door and move his legs.

Tank turned, and without hesitation, he yelled, "Come on, Grandma! You need an invitation?"

Nathan grumbled words he knew he shouldn't say as he climbed out and closed the door.

He walked into the training room. Everyone turned toward him, particularly the head trainer, Rob. He knew by their expressions that they were anxious to find out about the X-rays and whether or not he would be playing. The Hawks had one of their toughest opponents on Saturday—the Clemson Tigers—and to top it off, they would be playing at home. Playing at home in front of their own fans was something every player strived for. Flyers and posters were all around campus, promoting the game, and many had a picture of Nathan posed mid-throw.

The week before he had gotten injured, Nathan and the team captain, Marcus, along with a few of the senior players had been asked to do a photo shoot, so the school could have some promotional pictures for print. He actually liked the shot of himself, and he'd get a bit of a rush each time he saw the poster on campus. He knew the school, the fans, and his teammates would be so disappointed if he wasn't able to play.

Rob rushed over to Nathan and escorted him to the back trainer's table. "How are you doing?" he asked.

"I'm okay."

"Let's take a gander."

Nathan put down his bag and took off his sweatshirt and sweatpants. He knew it was bad when Rob gave him a pained expression.

Rob walked around Nathan, inspecting his hip and leg. After a few minutes, he added quietly, "I'll be right back. Stay here."

Nathan stood motionless. He didn't notice Tank walking by the open doorway.

Tank observed Nathan standing in the training room. He had never seen a bruise like the one Nathan had. Tank thought for sure that Nathan would not be playing this Saturday. He didn't think Nathan was tough enough to handle the pain.

Jonathan would have played. No doubt about it.

After a few more minutes, Rob came back from the trainer's medical supply closet that was always under lock and key, no exceptions. "Nathan, I did review all the medical records the hospital sent over from the other day, and I consulted with Dr. Brown in Orthopedics. He recommended I give you an injection of lidocaine. Not going to lie; this is going to hurt a bit," he said as he pulled out a needle and a jar of liquid.

"Wait, what is Lidocaine?"

"Lidocaine is used to numb an area of your body to help reduce pain. I understand it's hard for you guys to have anyone inject anything into your bodies. Christ, they are your temples after all. I get it. Trust me. But you have my word; this is legal and approved by the NCAA to treat these types of contusions," he said with sincerity that quickly put Nathan at ease.

"Okay. I let my doctor at home know everything, too. He's a brilliant sports doctor, so I always consult with him and my dad."

"Smart kid. Coach knows, too, and everything that happens in here is recorded and reviewed. I can give you a copy of this"—he held up a sheet with today's information on it— "for you to send home."

He opened the kit and took out a needle and a small jar of liquid. He put the needle in the bottle and drew the liquid into the syringe. "Turn on your side. Ready?"

He quickly put the needle into Nathan's lower back just above his buttock. Nathan winced and then felt a warm rush under his skin.

Rob put his hand on Nathan's shoulder. "It will help with the pain. Now, let's get you into an ice bath, okay?"

"Sure. Uh…am I practicing today?" Nathan's tone was sad.

"Not today. Let's just get you through the next few hours. Coach said you could throw later, if you could stand on your leg, okay?"

This is not good news.

A terrible feeling of dread started to brew inside of Nathan. He had to suppress it and move forward. He couldn't change what had happened. He just had to get better and fast.

It was Thursday afternoon, and if he didn't practice tomorrow, he most likely would not play on Saturday.

Five

SEPTEMBER 25, 1995

Early Friday afternoon, after grabbing a quick bite, Abigail walked back from the cafeteria to her dorm room. She was hoping to catch Laura before she headed home for the weekend. This would be their first weekend apart since moving in together, and Abigail had mixed feelings about having the room to herself. Not having the comfort that Laura brought to her made her feel uneasy. She knew Laura was the only one who knew about her seizure. It was as though Laura was her safety net, and that net was leaving for a whole weekend. Besides that, she would miss her social buddy, too.

She had not heard from James since the message he'd left the other night, so she had all but written him off at this point. She planned to call him before her afternoon class today. She owed him at least that. It wasn't as though they had not spoken at all, but they had both been busy, and they had done their best to keep in touch. After all they had been through, she hoped that he, more than anyone, knew her intentions were always in the right place.

When Abigail approached her door, she could hear Laura talking to someone. She pushed it open and announced herself, "Hey, Laura, I'm back." She walked in and noticed someone standing in their room, picking mindlessly at their nail polish.

"Abigail, this is Bree Van Tousen." Laura continued to pack her sheets and laundry in her bag.

Bree beamed at Abigail. Their eyes locked for a moment, and Abigail was suddenly struck by how beautiful this girl was. She was like a vision, standing there with her long brown hair cascading down one side, and she had these big, gorgeous brown eyes that showed she was a bit of trouble.

The room smelled like lavender and sandalwood, and Abigail assumed it must be Bree's perfume since the scent was so unfamiliar.

For some reason, just her presence made Abigail blush. "Nice to meet you, Bree."

"It's actually Aubrey, but you can call me Bree. Nice to meet you, too."

"Are you on our floor?" Abigail asked.

"Yes, just a few doors down. I've been in and out this past month, finishing up some modeling obligations I had from over the summer." She flipped her mane of hair to the other side and twirled it around her hand.

So, that explains why I have not met her.

"Oh, great," Abigail said.

"Yes, Bree and I are in Calculus class together," Laura added.

"It's so boring," Bree quipped.

Laura nodded slightly.

"Well, I should get going." Laura zipped up her backpack. "Abigail, I took a few of the items I borrowed from you to wash at home as well. I'll see you on Sunday." She gave Abigail and Bree a quick hug each.

"Sounds good. Enjoy your weekend!"

"I'll walk you down. I'm going to grab a water," Bree said. "It was nice meeting you." She eyed Abigail up and down.

Abigail's body shuddered at her stare. There was just something about her coolness that made Abigail feel so uneasy.

"I left my parents' number on a notepad in case you need me for anything, okay?" Laura added.

"Of course. Please tell your parents that I said hello."

Once they were gone, Abigail picked up the phone and dialed James's number.

It rang a few times before someone answered, "Hello?"

"Uh, hi. Is James there, please?" She was half-hoping he was, half-hoping he was not.

"Nope," his roommate, Michael, said. "He's gone for the weekend."

"Oh, okay. Do you know where he went?" she asked.

"Uh, no. Sorry. He just said he was going to see his girlfriend or something. Who is this?" He probably realized he might have told her too much.

She was frozen. *This can't be happening.* She had assumed that he had just been playing with her to get her to call him back. *Is he on his way to campus right now? Or did he just tell his roommate to say that to freak me out?*

She could barely whisper her own name, "Michael, it's Abigail. I'll call back. Thanks." With that, she hung up the phone.

She glanced at the clock. It was almost two. She had Biology class at two. She had little time to digest this.

She went over to her dresser to grab her water bottle when she caught a glimpse of herself in the mirror.

Ugh.

Her blonde locks were messy. Her ponytail was barely holding in her unkempt hair. She appeared tired and boring in the sense that she had done little, if anything, to spruce herself up. She pulled the rubber band out and ran a brush through her hair. Thankfully, it seemed to bounce back to life.

She studied her clothes. She decided that she didn't like what she had on, so she slipped out of her khaki pants and hiking boots and reached for her favorite jeans. They fit her body so perfectly that she'd bought three pairs of them in different shades of denim. She carefully pulled her T-shirt over her head and removed the plain white bra she had on. She opened her drawer and picked out a black lace bra. As she put it on, she started to get a nervous feeling in her gut. She wasn't positive that James was coming here to see her, but something had told her to go through the trouble just in case. She wanted to at least look nice for him.

She reached for a tight navy V-neck sweater and put it on before smoothing down her hair again. She rummaged through her makeup bag and grabbed her mascara, bronzer, eye shadow, and eyeliner.

Before she'd left for college, her mom had taken her to the makeup counter at Macy's, and a beautiful cosmetician named Amy had applied her makeup for her. Abigail had squirmed almost the whole time while she was in the seat, but she had gone along with it to make sure her mom knew she appreciated the gift. Her mom had spent over two hundred dollars on makeup for her that day.

As Abigail leaned into the mirror, she tried to remember what Amy had instructed her to do. She closed her eyes and tried to envision the beautiful woman with a fistful of brushes, explaining the art of applying makeup. She opened her eyes, took a deep breath, picked up her eyeliner, and began by lining her upper lids with the charcoal pencil. She then swept on a little bit of peach eye shadow. It did make her blue eyes stand out, just like Amy had said it would. She applied two coats of mascara and just a touch of bronzer on her already-golden skin. She dabbed on a little bit of cherry balm on her pouty lips. It had just a hint of color, and that was good enough for Abigail.

She stood back and examined her work. She was pleased with what she had done in such a short time. Then, she noticed the clock on the wall.

She panicked and grabbed the water bottle, her bag, and her keys. Then, she ran out the door and down the hallway. She hit the button to the elevator a few times. When it didn't come fast enough, she went straight for the stairwell. She hurried down the stairs and ran out the front door of her building. She glanced at her watch. Class would be starting in five minutes. She had at least a seven-minute walk to class. She walked at a brisk pace across campus, weaving in and out of other students. At this point, she was going to be late, but she had to try to get there as close to the beginning of class as possible.

She entered the science building and headed up the stairs. She took note of the silence. There was no one around, and class had started. She reached for the door handle when it suddenly flew open.

Professor Rhodes must have heard Abigail running up the stairs, and his eyes lit up when he saw her. She hurried inside.

"Nice to see you, Abigail."

"So sorry I'm late." She gave him a halfhearted smile as she hurried to her seat.

Abigail hurried across the room and down the aisle, and then she took her seat next to Webber. She took out her notebook. Professor Rhodes began to talk about how the laws of thermodynamics related to the biochemical processes that provided energy to living systems. She started jotting down every word he said. When she finally glanced up, she noticed Webber watching her.

She slightly turned her head toward him and whispered, "Hello."

"Hello." He snapped back around and started writing in his notebook.

Class flew by, and before Abigail knew it, Professor Rhodes was giving them a few questions to answer for homework. "I also want to remind you all that Tuesday's class will not be meeting in this classroom but rather in the lab, which is located in the basement of the building. If no one has anything else, then class is dismissed. Have a safe and wonderful weekend."

Webber and Abigail walked out of the classroom together.

"You, um…you look different today. I mean, really nice."

Abigail blushed. "Wow, thank you, Webber. That was kind of you to say."

He pushed his glasses back up onto his nose. "If you want to study before Tuesday," he said bashfully, "just let me know."

"Okay, thanks. I will."

They walked down the stairs and out the front door. The campus was packed with students leaving their last session of classes.

There was silence for a few moments before Webber asked, "Got any plans for the weekend?"

"No, not really. My roommate is gone, so I actually have the room to myself. I'm excited for some alone time."

"Yeah, I hear you. My roommate is never really…"

Abigail stopped without warning and stared straight ahead.

"Abigail?"

She snapped out of it after a second. "Oh, sorry. Webber, I have to go. I'll call you to study, promise. Is Sunday good maybe? Or, well, you can call me, okay? I'll see you later. Sorry to run off like this." She started walking toward the student union.

Abigail felt badly about leaving Webber just standing there. She could feel his eyes on her as she marched straight toward James. He stood there, looking around with an anxious expression on his face. He seemed lost in the middle of the crowd of students. When he caught Abigail's eyes, a smirk grew on his face.

Abigail's skin turned red hot. *James looks handsome.*

His shaggy blond hair had gotten longer. He had put on some weight, and it suited him well. He no longer was the skinny kid she remembered. He was more muscular. College had treated him just fine so far.

She approached him and stopped. A smile crept across her face. She couldn't help it. "James," she said softly, "what are you doing here?"

"Didn't you get my message?"

"Yes, of course I did, and I called you back…"

He stepped closer to her and gave her a big hug. Then he stepped back. "It's good to see you."

They couldn't stop staring at one another. Students walked by them, around them, and between them, but neither seemed to care. It had been weeks since they last saw each other, and they had only spoken briefly on the phone. James had called once a week to check in, and out of all those calls, they had spoken three times. They could never seem to catch each other. Their timing was always off. They had both been busy with school, and they seemed to be on opposite schedules, but James knew how important school was to Abigail. It always had been. So, he would never make her feel bad for not calling.

"Want to get something to eat?" he asked enthusiastically. "I'm starving!"

"Sure," she responded, not having a chance to tell him that it was good to see him, too. "How about we go downtown and grab something?"

"Got any good Chinese food places around here? Ours are terrible!" he exclaimed. "I'm dying for some good Chinese food."

"I know just the place."

They started to walk down the street toward the main road. They hopped on a student shuttle that took them downtown. They chatted back and forth about school, classes, and the new friends they'd each met at school. James mentioned he was considering pledging a fraternity, and Abigail spoke mostly about her biology classes. The conversation was light, and Abigail was just fine with that. They eventually got off the shuttle and walked for about another five minutes before seeing the sign for Panda Palace. The restaurant was all but deserted. Maybe three other tables were filled with students out of the forty or so available tables in the room.

A young girl who Abigail recognized from campus took them to a table near the back. They sat down and opened their menus.

After a few moments, he put his menu down. "You look really pretty, Abigail."

She glanced up at him. "Thank you. You look good, too."

"Thanks. So, you know what you want to order?"

She let out a small sigh. "Yes," she responded, putting down her menu. "I'm going to have the number seven with wonton soup. You?"

He laughed. "The number seven with wonton soup."

They sat across from each other in silence until the waitress came over to take their orders.

James ordered for both of them. Once she walked away, he took a deep breath. "So, now that we got the small talk out of the way and school is going well and all"—he paused— "we should talk."

"I know." But she just sat there, playing with the straw in her soda.

"Okay," he said after a few minutes of watching her squirm. "But you're not going to do it. Is that right?"

"I'm sorry. I just wasn't expecting to do this today, ya know?" She tried to muster up a smile.

"I've missed you, Abigail."

"James, I am sorry that I've been so flaky. My head just isn't right or something, but I don't expect you to have—I mean, I don't want you to have to chase me or whatever. Am I making any sense?" She moved back in her seat.

The waitress came over and put a cup of wonton soup in front of each of them.

"Who said I had to? Abigail, you don't exactly make this relationship very easy on me, but I'm here, aren't I?"

Although his words seemed a bit harsh, he was right. Ever since day one, she'd never made anything easy for him.

"You're right." She pushed her soup away from her.

"Oh, come on, Abigail. Don't do that." He moved her soup back toward her and handed her a spoon.

"No, you're right. We should talk about what happened. I owe you that much. I know I do. Like a jerk, I tried to avoid all this over the summer. With you away at soccer camp for most of August, it was kind of easy for me not to deal with it."

"Okay. Well, do you feel like you need to *deal* with me now?"

"You know, I'm capable of talking, but those kinds of comments are not going to help." Abigail was agitated for the first time since James had arrived. "You're not the only one who has gone through a hard time. I was a part of it, too."

He smirked at her.

"What?" Her shoulders tensed.

"Nothing. But you realize that you are *dealing* with us, with me."

"See? You're still doing it." She put her spoon down and seriously contemplated leaving.

"I'm sorry, really. I'll keep my smart-ass comments to myself. I promise."

"I'm just saying, things got hard for me and you after what happened in March with the seizure and all that. I was just so confused afterward, and my memory was affected and…" She wondered if she should tell him about the sensation she had been unable to shake, even after several months. It was not a feeling she could articulate. It was more like a heaviness in her heart that never seemed to go away.

Considering him now, she knew if she tried to tell him about how she had been feeling all these months that he'd think it was about him or their relationship, but it wasn't. It was about her. It was about that day on the field last March and all those terrible days after, days that had stayed with her and haunted her. When she'd finally woken up from the coma, she'd felt alone and changed. That event had changed her, and she had no idea why.

Why do I always feel so sad and so alone, even with my family and friends around me?

Even worse, she no longer actually wanted to be with James, like somehow that event had led her to realize he was not the one for her. She had another destiny, only there was no one else in her sights. So, it just seemed like a foolish thought, but one she could never shake.

Jesus, this is about him, but it's nothing he's done. That's what is so hard to pinpoint. I'm so afraid to tell him, for fear he'll never get it and he'll just end up hating me.

So, instead of telling him all that, she simply replied, "I just want to say I'm sorry, too. That's all."

He regarded her with a sincere and longing gaze. "I know. It was just a tough time."

"You know how much I appreciate what you did for me. That's never changed."

There was a break.

"I have to get this off my chest," he said.

"Okay, of course."

He took a deep breath in and then slowly let it out. "That night on the bleachers, when I finally asked you why you didn't seem to feel the same way about me that I obviously did about you—and still do—maybe that wasn't fair to ask you. Maybe I was just being insecure, but it just sucked because for the first time, we were actually moving ahead before the seizure. I became resentful about what happened but also so terribly frightened. Just thinking about all the what-ifs…heck, it still keeps me awake at night."

He continued, "Abigail, without even thinking, I just scooped you up and put you in my backseat. I drove like a madman directly to the hospital. You were lying so still on the backseat that I didn't know if you were dead or alive. When I pulled in front of the emergency entrance, I barely even put the car in park before I ran into the emergency room with your lifeless body draped in my arms. I yelled for help. This nurse and an ER doctor came running toward me with a gurney. They took you from my arms and whisked you away."

Abigail's eyes were wide.

"I wasn't allowed to see you for hours. In fact, at that time, I didn't know if you were going to make it or not. I had no idea what had happened. I paced in the waiting area, feeling scared and alone, and I feared the worst."

"Oh, James, I'm so terribly sorry." Tears stung her eyes. She knew most of this story from the days following the incident, but it was evident by his tone that it bore repeating.

"It's not your fault, but damn, it feels good to tell you all this."

Abigail nodded and waited for him to continue.

"As soon as my mother walked through the doors, I just started to cry. I was devastated at the mere thought of losing you, and I started to question what had gone wrong. In fact, there were too many questions." Again, he paused. "When your parents arrived, they were understandably cold toward me. I realized later that they were just scared, too. I blamed myself for bringing you out to the field, and I racked my brain, trying to think of what could have caused your seizure."

He drew in a deep breath. "You were in that damn coma for almost a week. It felt like forever to me, to our friends, and more importantly, to your parents. Everyone came and went during that week. Friends from school brought you flowers and balloons, filling your room. It was an embarrassment of riches, which you deserved ten times in excess. Almost every day after school, I sat in the waiting area—pacing back and forth, catching up on homework, and eating three-day-old sandwiches from the vending machine—but I never cared, not once. I only cared about you. The nurses were only allowed to tell me so much since I had no legal rights, but I begged them for any updates. They would nod at my questions and give short sentences in response to my endless queries. Your parents, despite their appreciation for me bringing you into the hospital, only allowed me to see you once, but I understood they were just doing what they thought was best for you.

"When you finally woke up, you had little memory of what had happened, and you seemed distant. The doctors were baffled as to why a healthy young girl had had a seizure and gone into a coma. In fact, at one point, they questioned me about why I had taken you to the field that night. They even asked if I had given you anything that would have caused you to go into a coma."

"You mean, drugs?" Her voice quivered. "Of course not. You would never do that to me."

"Oh God, no, but they did the toxicology report anyway, and I was glad they had. But, once those rumors got out, people started talking about it, and—oh hell, I don't even care about that anymore. People can be real jerks."

"I know, like all those stupid rumors that you had started dating that junior, Marcy Reed. I have to admit, James, that even though it was a rumor, I pulled away. I needed a reason to focus more on me—on getting better and finishing school. I used it as an excuse, and I'm really sorry."

"But you didn't even ask me if it was true." He sounded hurt. "You just pulled away from me. That wasn't fair, Abigail."

Before she could say anything, he cut in, "It wasn't true. None of it was. Marcy came after me, pretending to care about you. She told me she was worried about you. I knew she hardly knew you. One day, she came by my house after school and tried to kiss me. That was it. John was stopping by on his way to work and saw her at my house, and he told a bunch of people. My own best friend, spreading rumors about me. Then, the tales began."

Her eyes got wide.

"People were searching for any reason to make me out to be the bad guy, but I wasn't."

If she didn't know him better, she wouldn't have noticed the mist beginning to form in his eyes. He was telling her the truth. He had always told her the truth. He was being one hundred percent honest with her. It had been killing him all this time, and she had done nothing to ease his pain. She was ashamed of herself.

"Wow. I guess I never asked you directly because, James, I knew you wouldn't do that to me."

The waitress brought the chicken lo mien and put a plate in front of each of them on the table.

James sat back and took a deep breath. "It feels good to hear you say that. I've waited months to tell you all this. It has been weighing so heavily on my mind. I never liked Marcy. In fact, I hadn't even noticed her. All I cared about was you. All I thought about was you, Abigail."

"Thank you for caring so much about me. Truly, James."

"You're welcome."

"I mean it. I know I can be a real pain in the ass. Well, anyway, it is nice to have you here."

"I'm glad I came. Now, remember when I said I was starving? Well, mind if I eat?"

She laughed. "Of course not."

They ate in silence for a bit. They both needed a break from talking.

Abigail noticed that it was getting darker outside. She had no idea what time it was, but she knew she was getting tired. She had her jam-packed class schedule to thank for that.

James put his fork down, crumpled his napkin on his plate, and pushed his plate to the edge of the table. The waitress came by and removed his plate.

Abigail picked at her dinner. "I'm sorry you never had the chance to tell me all of that."

"If it counts that I'm saying it now, then that will make me happy."

He'd come all the way here from Albany University, a four-hour drive from her, just to talk to her about what had happened over seven months ago.

She'd thought a lot about that night, too. She had worried and scared just about every person she cared for. On the road to recovery, she'd pushed some people away, but she couldn't help that now. She had gone through some dark and depressing days. Those days, everyone had treated her like she was made of glass, constantly hovering and asking how she was feeling. She'd felt like a fragile china doll that constantly needed to be monitored, and it'd depressed her.

She'd sensed a lack of freedom, the freedom she'd once had to come and go as she pleased. And the worst part of it all was that she couldn't explain it to anyone, not even Rebecca. She'd tried, but nothing had made sense. She'd hated getting those sympathetic looks from her family and friends, like she was crazy or something. So, she'd just pushed people away, or at a minimum, she'd acted as hard and unfeeling as she could, as if all were fine in her little world. But on the inside, she was a completely different person. It was like her soul had been changed and not necessarily for the better.

"It counts." There was so much more she wanted to say to James, but she honestly didn't have it in her. "And all I can say again is that I'm sorry. And thank you. I didn't mean to hurt anyone. I didn't know what was happening with me, and I guess I shut down."

"I understand. I do." He waited before saying, "God, it really is good to see you."

"Thanks. You, too." She grabbed the straw out of her drink and began playing with it.

James took the check from the waitress and paid the bill. "You ready to go?" he asked.

"Yes. Thanks for dinner." She grabbed her book bag and stood up.

They walked toward the door of the restaurant, and James held it open for her. The air was crisp but welcome. She hugged herself as they headed toward the shuttle stop. James took off his fleece and offered it to her. She accepted it, and the warmth of the jacket made her shoulders relax. She needed that. She needed this. He seemed more stress-free and confident than he had before, and that made her happy.

The shuttle bus dropped them back at the student union. From there, it was only a short walk to her dorm room. Her heart began to beat harder in her chest. She was incredibly nervous about being alone with him.

"Where is your car?" she asked him.

"I parked it in the visitor lot over there." He pointed to the lot across from the student union.

Without saying a word, they both began to walk toward his car. Abigail tried not to be obvious when she checked her watch. It was a little past six. If he left now, he would be back at school around ten. As they approached the visitor lot, a wave of emotions swept over Abigail, and she started to wonder if the same thing would happen that had happened seven months ago. She feared the worst.

James stopped before they got close to his car. He turned to her. "Feels weird, right?"

Without him saying another word, she knew exactly what he was talking about. "Very weird. I feel nervous."

"Don't be, Abigail. You are fine." He put his hands on her shoulders and looked her squarely in the eyes. "You're fine. Nothing is going to happen to you tonight. I promise."

He had a way of making her feel better. She believed him. She knew that as long as he was around, she would be fine.

"I don't want you to go, James."

He laughed. "Who said I was leaving? Wait here." He walked over to his car.

He opened the door to the backseat, and from what Abigail could see, he took something out and shut the door. As he walked back toward her, he held up a bag.

"I was just getting my bag."

She laughed.

They walked in silence toward Willis Hall. With his body close to hers, she suddenly felt a shiver of excitement come over her. She had never really been alone with James before. When they had been living at home, they had spent a few hours here and there alone, sneaking off to his basement for make-out sessions, but nothing like this, with no adult supervision whatsoever.

Once on the sixth floor, she unlocked the door to her room, and with a clumsy push, the door opened. She quickly turned on the light near her desk. She unzipped his fleece jacket and placed it on her desk chair.

James kept his bag on his shoulder until he walked into the bedroom side of the room. He noticed her photos as he dropped his bag next to her bed.

"Can I get you a drink?" she asked.

"Sure. What do you have?" he asked.

"Water or Gatorade," she said, opening the mini fridge.

"Water is fine."

She turned to hand him a bottle of water. Their hands connected briefly, and she felt this longing to be touched. She wanted so badly for him to hold her.

"Nice room," he remarked.

"Thanks. It'll do, right? Is your room this small?" she asked.

"Yeah, pretty close." He leaned over her dresser to get a closer glimpse at the photo of her and her family at graduation. "So"—he straightened up— "Laura is gone for the weekend."

"Wait, how did you know that?"

"We talk," he said, half-joking. "She fills me in on how you are doing. She told me she was going home." He winked at her.

"That little sneak," she squealed. "I can't believe the two of you."

"Well, don't give her all the credit. I told her I was coming to see you first." The seductive tone in his voice caught her off guard. He put the water bottle on Abigail's dresser with authority and started to approach her.

Her heart began to pound. He eyed her with mischief. She had seen that look before and knew he wanted to kiss her. As he got closer, she glanced at the floor, too afraid her knees might get weak if she locked eyes with him. He put one arm around her waist and pulled her close. He leaned down, their faces close now. His breath was warm on her face. She was breathing hard. She was nervous and excited and wanted so badly to kiss him.

He tipped his head, his lips only centimeters from hers. They were so full and inviting. He gently ran his fingertips across her jawline until his fingers rested behind her neck. He pulled her in toward him, and with his lips on hers, he kissed her. They were soft and warm against hers. She closed her eyes as her body began to melt into his.

Oh, James. How could I have been so selfish and foolish that I almost let you slip away?

She grasped his hair as she kissed him back, tangling her fingers in his soft and shaggy mane. She heard him moan, so she kissed him harder.

It was a long time before she opened her eyes and took a step back. He smiled at her then pulled her in again. He kissed her, and as he did, she reached up under his shirt and began to pull it up over his body. He followed her lead and took it completely off. Standing in front of her, his body was firm and muscular. He tossed his shirt on the bed. He was definitely bigger than she remembered.

He could only wait for a moment before he drew her back close and kissed her over and over. Their mouths were becoming one as their tongues intertwined. His skin was incredibly soft as she moved her arms around his sides, tracing the beautiful lines of his muscles. She rested her hands around his back. He kissed her harder and harder, his mouth all over her lips and neck.

Their breathing was heavier and stronger now. She knew then that she would not be able to stop. She *didn't* want this to stop.

This was long overdue. There was so much history between the two of them. They had not kissed in months, and she realized just how much she had missed him.

James started to move his hands up her waist, dragging her shirt up and over her head. Her hair fell over her shoulders, and then he rested his hands on the sides of her face.

"What?"

"I-I don't know, Abigail," he said with a breathy tone. "I just want you. I've always wanted you." He pushed her hair back over her shoulder and gazed deep into her eyes. "You look amazing."

"As do you."

He ran his hand down her neck before resting it between her breasts. She closed her eyes for a moment, allowing the sensations to take over. She began to moan softly as his hand ran over her breast, teasing her slightly. The tingling sensation that ran all over her body was so intoxicating that it made her want more, more of all of this.

"James," she purred.

He pressed his body against hers. "Yes?"

"I want you, too," she whispered.

"Good," he answered.

She could tell he was no longer in the mood to take this slow when he began to kiss her. His mouth was all over her before he made his way to the top of her breasts while his fingertips danced over her skin. Her moaning got louder. He eased the strap of her bra off her shoulder and lightly cupped her breast. He pulled the other strap down as well, and she sensed the coolness in the air as it touched her exposed chest.

She walked backward, still holding on to him, and they both landed on her bed. He pushed her hair out of her face and wrapped his entire body around hers. She could feel every inch of him now, and she was elated.

And then, without warning, the old Abigail came back, almost as soon as she had been set free. They were no longer two high school kids sneaking around. This was real, and Abigail had a decision to make, one that would stay with her forever.

Am I really ready for this?

Six

SEPTEMBER 26, 1995

Nathan woke up early on Saturday morning. Webber was still sound asleep, mainly because he'd slept with earplugs in and a sleep mask on. He'd snored slightly throughout the night. Nathan didn't make a big deal about it.

With only a towel wrapped around his waist, he went down the hall to the showers. He let the water run as he leaned toward the mirror and rubbed his eyes.

The bruise on his hip was turning a bit darker now with a little bit of yellow around the edges. It was awful and hurt like hell. He had practiced yesterday, but it had been a no-contact day, and they'd just run light drills. Coach had explained that his decision as to who played on Saturday wouldn't be announced until closer to the start of the game, so Nathan wanted to get down to the field house early to make sure he had ample time to warm up.

When he entered his room, he could still hear Webber snoring. He dressed quickly, grabbed his keys, and closed the door but not before leaving Spidey a note.

See you after the game. Wish me luck.

With Nathan spending so much time in their room lately and Webber only having a few friends of his own, the two of them had started to get a little closer. Nathan didn't talk much about football off the field, and that might have surprised Webber. They talked mostly about music, video games, and school. In fact, after almost a month's worth of football games, it was actually Webber's idea for him to come down and check out this Saturday's game, much to Nathan's disbelief.

When Nathan arrived at the field house, he was the only player there. Rob was sitting in his office with a desk lamp on, a cup of hot coffee, and the morning newspaper spread out in front of him. Nathan unwrapped the paper from the bagel and cream cheese he'd bought at the student union and waited for Rob to speak.

"How are you doing?" Rob asked.

"Not bad actually."

"Good." He continued to read the newspaper. "Finish that, and we'll get going."

Nathan popped a piece of the bagel in his mouth and went into the training room.

So much work went into getting ready for games. Nathan knew this and shockingly didn't mind the extra preparation as long as he could play. He had spent half of his life in a training room with heating pads, ice baths, deep-tissue massages, and getting taped up every day, to name a few of the physical things he did to get prepared. Then, he'd get into the mental part of preparation, and that was a whole other animal. A player's mind could be their best asset or their worst enemy. Thankfully, Nathan had spent just as much time on preparing his mind for tough situations, particularly not panicking under pressure. It was probably why he was such a good quarterback.

Nathan got up on the trainer's table, and Rob hooked the electrical stimulation machine, or e-stim, to both his arms and to his left hip. Then, he covered Nathan's body with heating pads. Nathan tried to relax and let his mind go. He had to trust that Rob would do his best to get him physically ready, but it was up to Nathan to prepare mentally.

"Hey, try and unwind, kid. I'll leave this on for about twenty minutes, okay?"

"Sounds good."

"Yell if you need me. I'll be in my office."

Nathan closed his eyes as Rob switched off the light and closed the door. The e-stim made his muscles tense and tingle, essentially treating the pain while reeducating his muscles to hopefully perform how they had pre-injury. This treatment had worked well for him in the past, but he *truly* needed it to work today.

Twenty minutes later, Rob entered the room. "Let's get you up and warming up on the bike, okay?"

"Sure thing."

Nathan walked out to the weight room and got on the stationary bike. He turned ESPN on one of the TVs in front of the row of bikes and began pedaling. His body was already nice and warm from the heating pads, and his muscles were relatively loose. He pedaled slowly at first and then finally worked his way to a pace where he was sweating. It felt good to be moving like this again. Even though he had practiced yesterday, it had still been considered an easy day for everyone.

Nathan rode the bike for forty-five minutes during which other players started trickling into the weight and locker rooms. Some ran on the treadmill, others lifted weights, and some just hung out in front of their lockers, eating PowerBars and sipping on Gatorade.

Nathan stayed focused. He was determined to play and to have the best game of his life. If he could get through this, he could get through anything.

After an hour, Rob came over to the bike and told Nathan to take a shower, to get his undergarments on, and to meet him in the back room. So, he did just that.

He opened the door to the back room to find Rob and Coach Bromley talking.

Oh no, this cannot be good.

"Hey, Coach."

"Hello, son. Rob tells me you're doing well. How do you feel?"

"Great, Coach." He hesitated briefly. "I feel ready to play."

"You feel ready, or you *are* ready?"

"I *am* ready, Coach," he said without foot-dragging. "I am."

Nathan eyed Rob, as if to say, *Back me up!*

Rob gave Coach a firm nod.

Coach walked toward Nathan. He put his hand on his shoulder, stood in close to Nathan, and stared into his eyes. "Okay then." He tapped Nathan and walked out of the room, closing the door behind him.

Nathan cheered inside.

Rob moved to the left of the table, and Nathan saw his trainer's kit behind him. Rob turned and reached into the bag for a needle and a clear jar of liquid.

"Another dose of lidocaine. I think this should be it as long as you don't reinjure yourself, okay?"

"Yes, I'm feeling a lot better than a few days ago. I think the shot definitely helped."

"Good. So, I am recording this one as well and will let Coach know." He wrote Nathan's information down in his logbook.

Nathan walked over to him and lowered the left side of his padded bike shorts. Rob didn't ask him if he was ready this time. He just stuck the needle in. Nathan winced.

"Coach wants you to warm up your arm for ten minutes, rest for ten, and then throw for another ten minutes. Jason will warm up with you. Got it?"

"Got it." Nathan pulled the left side of his pants back up.

Jason was the backup quarterback, and for all intents and purposes, he was a pretty nice guy. He wasn't as good as Nathan. He'd played for a good high school program, and his team had made him seem better than he was. Still, he was here, in his sophomore year, and was pretty content with being the backup. Nathan didn't fully trust any player who would say that they were willing to settle for second, but then again, maybe he just liked all the perks that came with being a college athlete. But regardless, having someone waiting next in line for his job gave Nathan that driving force he sometimes needed to keep going, particularly on days like today.

Nathan walked into the gym to find a bunch of the guys stretching and jogging around the track. Jason was at the farthest end of the gym, talking to the offensive coordinator, Jackson. Nathan approached, and as he did, he put his hands up, and Jason tossed him the ball.

"How are you feeling, buddy?" Jason asked.

"Not bad." Nathan tossed back the ball.

"Good. Glad to hear it. I know that was a tough hit you took, and the guys were worried," Jackson added.

"So was I." Nathan gave him a slight grin.

Jason threw the ball back.

After their warm-up session, Nathan walked in the locker room and sat in front of his locker. He needed a few minutes to relax before he got dressed. He did this before every game. It was superstitious, and it was a necessity. He sat with his head in his hands and closed his eyes. He envisioned the ball, the game, the first snap, his first hit, his first throw, and a touchdown. It went like this for a few minutes until he felt a hand on his shoulder. He jerked up.

Who would dare interrupt me?

"You sitting this one out, Two?" Tank snickered.

Nathan stood up and got right in Tank's face. "Nah," he said sarcastically as he pushed past Tank, walking over to the table and grabbing his shoulder pads.

"It's okay, Two. Everyone gets a boo-boo."

Nathan was getting so sick of Tank. He had a bad attitude toward him, and he always made rude comments. But mostly, he hated that it always seemed like Tank was working against him and not with him. He tried not to think about Tank, but they were constantly around one another. Nathan didn't want to go to the coaches and complain about him. That would be breaking a code among his teammates. You didn't whine about other players—ever. But this was getting crazy. He had never had such issues with another player before. Right now though, he needed to shake off Tank's comments and just focus on the game.

Last Goodbye

The team gathered in the tunnel. The old metal doors that led out onto the field let in just enough sunlight that the hallway was illuminated. The referees were getting their final instructions, and the coaches were gathered near the back of the team, trading their play cards and final thoughts before the doors were pulled open. Nathan could hear the crowd cheering and the loud thump of the drums from the marching band as they did their final lap around the field. Then, he heard the boo and hiss of the spectators when the other team was announced as they took their place on the field.

It's showtime, Nathan thought as he heard the roar of his teammates.

They began to circle around him, like a pack of wild dogs, praying to be released.

Nathan began jumping up and down along with the rest of his team.

"Are we ready, Hawks?" he yelled.

A loud round of, "Ooh-rah!" came right back at him.

"Are we ready, Hawks!?" Nathan yelled louder.

"Ooh-rah!" they all screamed.

Then, as the team manager threw open the metal doors, Nathan, followed by his teammates, ran like a thousand bolts of lightning through the tunnel and out onto the field while the band burst into the Hawk's fight song. It was nothing short of spectacular, and it got Nathan's blood pumping each and every time.

This is why I play college football.

The crowd roared and started yelling his name as he came into the fans' sight.

This is why I play!

Seven

SEPTEMBER 26, 1995

Abigail woke in the morning to James caressing her arm up and down. She opened her eyes. He was adoringly gazing at her. She wondered how long he had been watching her.

"Hey." She stretched her arms over her head, and as she did, the blanket pulled down, exposing her breasts. The cool air touched her skin. She lowered her arms. She pulled the blanket back up to her chin.

He smiled as he watched her.

"Don't look." The blood rushed to her cheeks. She had never been nude in front of anyone before. She was incredibly shy and uneasy with her own nakedness.

He leaned over and kissed her on the lips. "I can't help it. You are so beautiful, just as I imagined you would be in the morning." He kissed her again. His hand rested on her hip, and he pulled her toward him.

She didn't resist. Instead, she put her arms around his neck and faced him. She kissed *him* this time. As she did, the memories of last night came flooding back. She thought about them rolling around on her small twin bed, their bodies intertwined, and the feeling of his hands as they ran all over her. Her heart began to pound. She kissed him harder. He squeezed her body against his, and suddenly, he stopped, pulling them apart.

"What is it?" she asked.

"I have to leave today." His voice was somber.

"You do?"

"Yeah, I borrowed Michael's car, and he has a family party he has to get home for, so by the time I drive back…well, I'll be cutting it close as it is."

"Oh, okay. I understand." For the first time, she honestly felt like she was emotionally in a good place, that she was in control of her feelings, but she was shifting toward her lonely place again. She did not like how it was making her feel.

"Besides"—a smirk started to creep onto his face—"my girlfriend must be wondering where I am." He started to laugh.

She reached over and pinched him hard on the arm. He grimaced and jerked his arm away but not before he grabbed her and pulled her on top of him.

"Your girlfriend, huh? Must be nice." She squirmed to get away from him.

He pulled her in again and gave her a deep kiss. He gradually released her. "I hope you do think it's nice."

I do, James. I really do, but the sadness is tiptoeing back in, and I don't know why.

"Can you at least stay for coffee and a bagel?"

"Yes, of course."

She pulled the top sheet around her body and stood up. She slipped into her jeans and a tank top before turning around. As she did, she saw he was standing there, naked, in the middle of her room. She blushed as he pulled his pants from the chair and slipped them on.

My God, he really is beautiful. Why can't I just be with him, like a normal person? Why do I have to overthink everything?

"He's not going to wait for me forever," she mumbled under her breath as she pulled on a sweater.

"You say something?" He took a clean T-shirt out of his bag and slipped it over his arms and chest.

It fit snuggly, and she noted how handsome he was in the morning, messy hair and all.

"No, sorry. We can be fast. I know a good place downtown to grab a bite."

"Sounds good."

When Abigail and James were finished eating, they walked back up the hill to the visitor parking lot. James stopped before they got near his car.

"I'll call you, okay?" He gazed into her beautiful blue eyes.

"Okay."

She got up on her tippy-toes as he put his arms around her waist. They kissed, and he gave her a big squeeze.

"You'll actually call me back, right?" he asked.

"Of course I will."

Before he got in the car, he grabbed her hand and kissed it. He winked sweetly at her as he let go, and then he closed his car door and started the engine. It roared loudly. Abigail waved as he began to pull away. Her heart sank as she swiftly realized how much she was going to miss him. She hadn't felt like that since she left for school. A connection to her past, her home, was driving away, and it made her blue. Then, before she knew it, he was gone.

She stood in the same spot for a moment as she contemplated her next move. *What will I do for the rest of the weekend with no Laura and no James?*

She decided to head back to her dormitory. After climbing the stairs, she walked down the hallway to her room. Many of her floor mates were still asleep. She opened the door to her room and glanced at the clock. It was only nine thirty. She grabbed her bathroom stuff and walked back down the quiet hallway to the shower.

She turned on the water and undressed. As she stepped into the hot water, her shoulders began to relax. She let the water run over her face, and the makeup from last night ran down her cheeks. As she rubbed soap on her body, she felt different. She knew it was probably all in her head, but she was somehow surer of herself, like she was finally making her own decisions as an adult. She hadn't been able to do that much since last March.

She thought of James being here and then gone, and her emotions started to move quickly and erratically, like a roller coaster.

Don't go to your dark place, Abigail. Stay happy!

She remembered what her mom had told her. *"Sometimes, Abigail, if you want to change your mood, just smile. Such a small change can make you feel happy."*

So, for the rest of the morning, Abigail had this perpetual grin on her face, willing herself to stay in a good place.

She even took more care when she got ready. It was a perfect day, and honestly, she felt beautiful. She put on dark blue jeans and a tight navy V-neck T-shirt. Over it, she put on a green gingham button-down shirt from J.Crew. She rolled up the sleeves and put on her watch along with her favorite silver ring. She took time to blow out her hair, making the waves almost cascade down her back. She applied makeup and lip gloss. Then, she sat at her desk and read over some class notes.

She heard some of the girls talking in the hallway and opened her door to see who it was. Bree and Melissa sat on the floor outside Bree's room and sipped coffee while they chatted about the night before.

"Hey, Abigail!" Melissa said, almost surprised to see her. She patted the floor next to her.

Abigail walked over and slid down against the wall. Bree viewed her as she sat down.

"You look pretty." Melissa's eyes sparkled.

Melissa was quickly becoming Abigail's favorite friend at school. Although they didn't hang out often, she was comfortable around Melissa, and that didn't come easy for Abigail. It was the way Melissa regarded her with such kindness that made her instantly want to be friends with her.

"Yes, you do. Going somewhere?" Bree asked, her voice sounding cool.

Bree, on the other hand, made Abigail uncomfortable and unsure of herself. She was secretly known as the queen of the floor. She made most of the rules and could get her floor mates to do anything that she wanted. Above all, she was gorgeous.

"Thanks." Abigail's face turned red. "Just had some time this morning; that's all."

"So," Bree continued, "do you want to go to the game with us? We're heading down in about forty-five minutes or so."

Abigail had almost forgotten it was Saturday, and there was a football game at noon. She thought about just sitting in her room and studying, but then again, it might be nice to get out and enjoy the afternoon.

"Sure," she said.

Bree started to stand up and walk to her door. "I've got to get ready," she said, opening her door.

"Oh, I thought you already did?" Melissa asked, checking out her put-together outfit and her flawless makeup and hair.

Bree scoffed as she flipped her hair to the side and walked into her room. They could hear her in there, rummaging through drawers, and then the blow dryer went on.

"This could take a while." Melissa rolled her eyes.

Abigail started to stand up. "You can hang out in my room, if you want. Laura is gone for the weekend."

Melissa stood up and started following her. "I know."

Abigail turned to her as she walked into the room.

Melissa was average height with an athletic build. She had brown hair and caramel-colored eyes. The thought of calling her eyes brown seemed to do them an injustice. They were striking, and by the way she carried herself, it was obvious she had yet to realize how pretty she was.

"So, who is he? The guy I saw you getting coffee with this morning? I would have stopped, but the queen needed her latte." She laughed. "Not that I'm trying to pry, and I promise, I won't say a word to Bree."

Startled, Abigail began fumbling with the keys on her desk. "Yes, please don't tell Bree."

Bree was famous for meddling in other people's business. She wasn't always the most popular girl on their floor despite her illicit reign over them.

Abigail couldn't help but smile as she briefly told Melissa about James, their somewhat untraditional courtship in high school, and how he'd just shown up on campus yesterday afternoon. She tried to tell as few details as possible because she didn't want to sound off any bells. She wasn't prepared to announce that last night was the first time she had been naked in front of her high school boyfriend—or anyone else, for that matter.

Melissa was kind and asked just a few questions about James. "You guys looked cute together."

"Thank you." Abigail went over to her dresser to get her ID and lip gloss. She applied a new coat and smoothed down her hair. "This look okay?" she asked.

"You always look great."

"Oh, well, thank you."

Melissa laughed, which caused Abigail to cock her head to the side.

"Something I said?"

"We all think you're prettier than Bree. It's this little floor-mate thing we all talk about behind your back," she said matter-of-factly.

"Really?" Abigail laughed as her cheeks pinked. "I didn't know it had been debated."

"Well, not exactly. But Bree thinks it's a competition. She's been eyeing you since the first time she met you. I think it's just how she is. Actually, did you know she was in some sort of Miss Teen pageant?" she asked.

"I had no idea. She's very pretty."

"Well, she thinks you are, too. Just don't ever tell her I told you so." Just as Melissa was talking, she heard Bree yell for them. "Ah, the queen is calling."

Melissa flicked her hand toward the door and laughed again, as she started to exit. Abigail followed.

When they walked into the hallway, they were taken aback at how done up Bree was. She had put curls in her hair, applied more makeup than was needed, and changed into black jeans, a tight white T-shirt, and open-toed sandals. She had a light sweater draped over one arm. She obviously was beautiful, but now that Melissa had mentioned Bree's participation in a teen beauty contest, Abigail thought Bree's overdone style was probably what she was used to.

"I know what you guys are thinking. I look too good for this place, don't I?" Bree winked. "Now, let's go break some hearts!"

Ugh, Abigail thought. *What have I gotten myself into?*

Eight

SEPTEMBER 26, 1995

Abigail, Melissa, and Bree walked outside their dorm and into the cool, beautiful fall afternoon. Crowds of students began to gather on the sidewalk as they all started to walk down to Menton Stadium. The sun was shining, and there was a slight breeze. The day was perfect. These were the times that you pictured college to be like, and Abigail was glad she had decided to get out and enjoy a little more of the social aspect of school.

They crossed Main Street, and Abigail noted that the trees dividing the main road had just begun to change colors. As she viewed them, she barely noticed that Bree had been chatting almost the entire way to the field.

"I recently received a call from a casting agent in New York. My mother was so mad because she wanted me to focus on school and not modeling. I keep trying to tell her that I can do both."

Abigail grimaced. "I don't have much advice to give in this department. But maybe now is a good time to focus on school, being so early on in the semester."

Bree squinted her eyes at Abigail. "What is your major again?" she asked.

"Biology."

"Makes sense. See, as a marketing major, the only way to market yourself is to get out there and make yourself available. And that is what I plan to do—be available. Besides, she'll never know if I go or don't."

"Oh crap," Melissa interjected. "The score is already ten to zero. We missed the first touchdown." She pointed out the scoreboard as they approached the gate.

They showed their IDs to the gate attendant at the stadium entrance and then walked over to the bleachers. From what Abigail could tell, the crowd was certainly into the game. It was rowdy and loud. She could feel the energy as the fans screamed and cheered for the Hawks.

Abigail did more daydreaming during the first half of the game than actually watching the game.

Bree chatted in her ear about which players were the cutest in their uniforms. "Check out number seventy-three. Yummy." A huge grin spread across her face.

Melissa, on the other hand, talked specifically about the game. "This is a great game. My dad is a high school football coach back home in Texas, so I grew up around football, football, and more football. I can even tell you some of the plays. Daddy used to make me watch game films with him—you know, to pick out play patterns and new routes. Instead of watching the girlie shows I wanted to, I'd watch a bunch of high school boys run around." She glanced up at the sky before saying, "Actually, now that I say that out loud, maybe it wasn't so bad after all."

"Sounds good to me," Abigail added.

"Sounds *great* to me!" Bree added slyly.

As the game went on, it became more and more apparent that something special was happening.

Melissa tried to explain, "So, for a freshman quarterback to throw five touchdowns and complete this many passes, we are experiencing what many fans would call an unbelievable game. Really, I can't wait to tell my dad about this." She peered over the crowd in front of her to get a better view.

People everywhere were screaming and jumping up and down. More screaming ensued when the announcement was made that freshman quarterback Nathan Ryan was now leading the league in pass completions.

The crowd started chanting, "Twelve, Twelve, Twelve, Twelve!"

The crowd roared as the last seconds of the game ticked off the clock, and Abigail observed the quarterback take a knee. He shot up and raised his arms in the air. He was quickly scooped up by three of the linemen on his team, and they paraded him down the field. Even the coaches ran onto the field to celebrate.

Abigail found herself cheering along with the rest of the crowd. She could feel the enthusiasm radiating through the stands. The fans started to hurry off the bleachers and onto the field. A wild scene unfolded in front of her. It was like one you'd see in some kind of John Hughes high school movie.

Melissa, Bree, and Abigail stood on the bleachers, not wanting to join the chaos, but too enthralled with watching it all to move. The massive drove began to move toward the gate as the players made their way to the locker rooms.

Melissa noticed Bree's expression as the people swarmed the players. "Why the grin?"

"Oh," she cooed, "I have got to get me one of those football players."

Webber made his way down to the gate. He had all but begged his friend Logan to go with him to the game. They waited for Nathan to walk by.

Logan was a brilliant mathematician. He'd gotten some special scholarship to the university in exchange for a mathematic formula he'd solved that had only been worked on once before by a professor at Harvard University. So, when the school had found out, they'd offered him a full ride with the stipulation that he assist Professor Jenkins, who was trying to win a grant that would ultimately bring not only funding to the school, but also recognition to the department. This had piqued Webber's interest right off the bat and was just one of the many reasons the two had hit it off when Webber met him in Algebra class. Aside from the time Webber spent in his room, the two of them would hang out, playing video games on Saturday nights or playing chess at the student union when they were both free.

During the football game, Logan had explained all the odds to Webber, broken down the percentages, and boasted about what Nathan had just accomplished in sixty minutes. Because of this, Webber felt almost obligated to congratulate Nathan. Deep down though, he knew Nathan wouldn't be winning a Nobel Prize for throwing a football.

Webber finally spotted Nathan as he hobbled toward them. Just before he got to Webber, a little boy asked Nathan for his autograph. He could tell Nathan was startled by the request. He scribbled on the program and patted the kid on the head.

"Wow, can I have your autograph?" Webber laughed.

"Aw, you came, Spidey," he said sarcastically. "You get to share a room with me. Isn't that enough?"

"Yeah, guess so. Hey, this is my friend Logan." He pointed unenthusiastically to Logan.

"Nice to meet you." Nathan reached out his hand.

Logan feverishly shook his hand. "Mathematically, that was a heck of a game!"

Nathan laughed. "Thanks. I can honestly say I've never had anyone say that to me before."

"Yeah, uh, congratulations," Webber added plainly.

"Hey, I gotta run, but come down to the Ridge house and celebrate with me, will you? I'll put your names on the list, okay?"

Webber just nodded in agreement.

"I have got to go get some treatment on my hip. It's freaking killing me." Nathan started to turn. "Hope you'll come."

Webber observed as he winced while he put pressure on his leg and walked to the field house. The crowd had come and gone quickly. There were few people left lingering in front of the gates, mostly parents and alumni.

"Huh, I have never been invited to a party here. Do you want to go?" Logan asked.

"Really? Go to one of those jock…" His voice trailed off.

Webber caught sight of Abigail walking through the gate with two other girls. The three of them were like straight out of a hot college coed magazine. Webber just stared and said nothing as they headed straight for them.

"Abigail!"

Abigail squinted and then waved to Webber. She spoke something to her friends, and they walked over to Webber and Logan.

"Hey, Webber!"

"Hey." He played nervously with his hands. "How are you?"

"Fine. Just fine. You?" Abigail asked.

"Good. Oh, this is Logan."

"Hi, Logan. These are my floor mates Bree and Melissa." She pointed at them.

Melissa immediately shook each of their hands. Bree gave them a half-smile, appearing thoroughly bored.

"So, what are you guys doing? Did you watch the game?" Abigail asked.

"Yeah, kind of had to." Webber hesitated, unsure of whether or not to reveal who his roommate was.

As it was, Nathan was constantly getting incredibly offensive and crude messages on their answering machine from girls who had been calling left and right. It was very annoying to Webber. Half of the time, Nathan wouldn't even listen to them. At least Nathan wasn't feeding into it. In fact, sometimes, he'd come right into the room, walk over to the answering machine, and just hit Delete All.

"Really?" Bree said snidely. "Doing research?"

Melissa stared at her with wide eyes, as if to say, *Don't be rude.*

"Yeah." Webber knew that she'd be interested in what he had to say if he told her why they had come to the game. "My roommate is Nathan Ryan." He stared directly at Bree. "You know, the quarterback?"

Bree perked up. "Oh, cool!"

"Oh, wow," Melissa interrupted. "What a game he had. Mathematically speaking, it was unreal. Really great to watch!"

"I know. I said the same thing to him!" Logan laughed.

"You talked to him?" Bree asked.

"Talked to him? I live with him, and let me tell you, that guy is really messy." He laughed, knowing full well she was only now interested in what he had to say because of Nathan. He, unfortunately, was used to this by now.

"Anyway," Bree interrupted, "what dorm do you live in?"

He glanced at Abigail and then straight back at Bree with a smirk as he quipped, "It's top secret. The school won't allow me to say."

Webber noticed Abigail's eyes glimmer.

I bet she is wondering why I never mentioned who my roommate was. Jesus, his picture is all over campus. But Abigail doesn't seem like the kind of girl who would care. Her friend, on the other hand, seems way too into it, for my taste. She's just the type of girl I don't want to come over and hang in our room.

Webber also took note of the quizzical stare Bree was giving him. Before she could question him, he added, "But he did invite us to the after-party at the Ridge. I could probably get you guys on the list." Webber knew what he was doing. He never would have gone if it had just been him and Logan, but now, here with three beautiful girls, he was suddenly Mr. Social.

"Great!" Bree flipped her hair to the side.

"Awesome! Thanks!" Melissa chimed in.

Webber held his breath for a brief moment. The only one he really wanted to go was hesitating. He gave Abigail a pleading stare.

She gave him a smile back. "Yeah, sure. I guess it could be fun."

Webber exhaled.

The five of them walked back through campus, talking mostly about the game and what Nathan had accomplished as they maneuvered the downtown streets. The Ridge was on the opposite end of town, so it took them about fifteen minutes to get over to the house.

The Ridge was an off-campus house that sat high up on a large hill. According to Nathan, it was a prime location for parties, barbeques, and such, which was why football players rented it year after year.

By the time they walked up the street to the Ridge, the party was in full swing. They could hear the crowd of people from behind the fence. As they approached, it got louder and louder, and it was a bit intimidating, to say the least.

Webber took a deep breath. *Am I ready for my first college party?*

Nine

Nathan could not have prepared for a game like the one he'd just had. By the time the clock had run out in the fourth quarter, he had been mentally and physically wasted. Despite his injury, he'd played the best game of his life. He had been unstoppable. He'd completed forty-eight passes, and he had thrown five touchdowns.

He sat down on the bench in front of his locker and peeled his pads and T-shirt off of his sweaty skin. The aching that was now settling into his hip and leg was almost more than he could bear. He was in agony, and he tried hard not to cry out in pain as he took his shorts off.

His teammates all yelled and high-fived around him, but he was too exhausted to celebrate.

"Awesome game, Nathan!" Coach Stanfield yelled over the noise of the team.

"Uh, thanks, Coach." Nathan winced.

"You in pain?"

"Yeah, Coach, I am, but I'll be okay. Going to go see Rob."

"Okay, keep me posted. The media is waiting in the conference room, but they'll keep waiting for you if they know you are coming. Hell of a game. Hell of a game." He patted Nathan on the arm.

He got up and went to see Rob in the back room. The training room was crowded with other training staff helping players nurse their injuries from the game.

When Nathan came in the room, Rob stopped what he was doing and approached him. "Wow, what a game. I'm impressed, Nathan."

"Thanks. Appreciate it."

"Let me take a look."

Nathan pulled down his spandex shorts.

"Well, at least we know you didn't reinjure it, but it's gonna be sore for a while. I can offer you some ibuprofen and recommend you ice on and off for the next few days, and rest, rest, rest."

"Yeah, thanks. I think ice and rest are what I need," Nathan said.

Rob went over to the ice machine and began scooping ice into a plastic bag before securing it at the top. He then went to the medical closet, unlocked it, and dispensed two ibuprofens for Nathan.

"Here, take these and use this for now. When you get home later, take a few more ibuprofen and ice again, okay?"

"Thanks, Rob. For all you did to get me ready for the game."

"Anytime."

After undressing at his locker, Nathan walked to the shower. His hip throbbed as he stepped in. He stood in there for fifteen minutes before turning it off and getting dressed. He always left a dress shirt and tie in his locker—Coach's rules. He dressed in his blue button-down shirt, orange-and-blue-striped tie, and dark brown dress pants. He was hoping they wouldn't notice that he was wearing sneakers.

Nathan followed Max into the media room in the field house. He walked up to a long table covered by a dark blue tablecloth. A Big East banner hung behind him with the Hawks logo scattered all over it. A bottle of water was placed in front of him as he took a seat. Lights began flashing as the photographers from the local papers, national media, and the like started taking his picture at record speed. He had a lump in his throat, and his anxiety grew as the reporters began shouting questions at him. He nodded to the guy on his left. He recognized him immediately as Craig Kilborn from ESPN.

"Nathan, how do you feel about your performance today?" he asked.

"I feel good. I mean, we played hard, and we got the results we had hoped for."

"More specifically, what about you? Are you aware that you broke the school record for touchdowns and passing yards for a first-year quarterback?"

Nathan's eyes got a bit wide, but he quickly responded, "No, I was not aware." He sensed his face flush.

Craig, the comedian and sports enthusiast that he was, gave him a smirk as if to say, *Well, now, you are!* "You must have had some sense, no?"

"No. I was just concentrating on getting the win more than anything else," Nathan remarked.

"Nathan!" another reporter yelled.

Nathan turned in the other direction and nodded.

This continued for the next twenty minutes, but to Nathan, it was more like hours. He was asked the same three questions over and over but in completely different ways. He repeated his answers time and time again, yet despite this, they kept asking him questions. Finally, he caught Coach Stanfield's eye, and he stepped in to rescue him.

That was exhausting. He walked away from the table and down the hall to the locker room.

The hallway was filled with parents, alumni, and students all congratulating him as he tried desperately to make his way to where he could be alone.

I need to be on my own for a minute.

His father had not been able to make the game because Uncle Dave had unfortunately experienced a terrible tropical storm near Wrightsville Beach in North Carolina a few weeks back. His father had promised to go down to help try to dig through what was left of Uncle Dave's charter and fishing company. There was no way any of them could have known what a game his father would miss. Nathan was dying to talk to him, and he needed to be alone to call him.

"Dad," he said, standing behind his coach's desk.

"Nathan!" his dad shouted in his ear. "Oh my God, can you believe it? What a game, Nathan. I am so proud of you, so damn proud. Your uncle Dave is furious at himself because I'm here with him and not there with you. I mean, Nathan..." He was barely catching his breath before continuing, "You were outstanding!"

"Thanks, Dad, and tell Uncle Dave not to worry. It was a fluke," he said, half-joking.

"Oh no, Nate. Don't do that. You earned that today. You earned it!"

"Thanks, Dad. Wish you were here and tell Uncle Dave that I hope things are going okay after the storm. Tell him not to work too hard. It will all get rebuilt. I promise I'll come to Carolina as soon as school is over to help him for the summer. But I've got to go. I'm using Coach's phone. I'll call you tomorrow, okay?"

"Sure thing. One more thing. Be proud of yourself, okay? Be proud."

"I will, Dad." And with that, Nathan hung up the phone.

He changed out of his suit, tie, and dark pants and put on his jeans, white T-shirt, and navy hooded sweatshirt. He didn't wear any team gear, just his plain old street clothes, as he'd had just about as much attention as he could take for one day.

He started walking to the double doors when he heard some of the players leaving as well.

"Hey, Nathan. You coming to the Ridge?" Marcus asked.

Marcus was the captain of the team, and for a junior, that was considered a big deal. He was average height but built like a wrestler, and he was the best wide receiver on the team.

"Yeah, sure am." Nathan forced a smile.

"Well, the star of the game rides with us." He motioned in their direction.

"Cool. Appreciate it." He limped over toward them, his ice bag dripping. When he caught up with them, he quickly tossed it in the trash.

He noticed Tank walking with people who appeared to be his parents. They were at the double doors ahead of them. By the time Nathan got outside, they were gone. He hadn't seen Tank after the game, and the two had not spoken a word during all the commotion and celebrating.

Considering two of the touchdowns Nathan had thrown were to Tank, he had assumed Tank would have said something to him. Then again, he wasn't really surprised, seeing the way Tank treated him. There was this strange dynamic to their relationship, and because of that, Nathan was just fine with keeping the talking on the field as opposed to off.

Nathan followed some of his teammates to Marcus's car. He was in a lot of pain and doubted he'd be able to make it more than an hour at the party. He knew showing his face at the party was the right thing to do, and that people, particularly alumni, would be expecting him to come and at least have a hamburger—or in his case, two.

Marcus pulled right up the driveway and parked in his spot. This was Marcus's first year living at the Ridge. It was tradition for the captains of the football team to live together in the house. In fact, it was all he had talked about during Monday's practice—how great it was living there and having the parties literally in his backyard every weekend.

The house was an old Victorian, and at night, it was quite beautiful. During the daytime was another story. It definitely showed its age. The paint was chipping off the sides of the entire house, and some of the shutters were barely holding on. This house had been used and abused over the years but remained an ideal spot for students to rent.

Junior was a friend of the football organization and had been hired by the team to essentially be their bouncer at the gate to their backyard. It was a job he took very seriously. He was the guy holding the clipboard at the entrance. He crossed his gigantic arms over his expansive chest as he glared across the yard before realizing it was Marcus and a bunch of players.

"Killer game, Captain." He unfolded his arms and reached his hand out toward Marcus.

Marcus hesitated and then shook his hand. "Jesus, you are going to have to loosen that grip, Junior. You're going to break someone's hand, ya know." He laughed, and he shook his hand loose. "Have you met my boy Nathan?" he asked with a laugh.

Nathan walked over to Junior.

"Hey, man." Nathan shook his hand. "Nice to meet you."

"Awesome game, man. Awesome."

"Thanks. Appreciate it. We played well."

"You guys sure did," Junior remarked.

"Hey, can I get my roommate and friend on the list?" he asked shyly.

"For you? Heck yeah. What are their names?"

"Uh, Spidey and Logan."

"Spidey, huh? Okay. Any guest of yours is fine by us." He opened the gate to the backyard.

The party was jam-packed. Tons of students, family, and friends of the program stood under and around the tents set up in the backyard.

Nathan walked in behind the other players, too bashful to lead the way. A few alumni and donors of the football program came over to greet him but not before a loud round of applause erupted, much to Nathan's embarrassment.

He could feel his cheeks burn, but he smiled graciously and then quickly turned to an older gentleman who seemed eager to shake his hand.

"Class of '62, cornerback. Great game, son. You made the school proud."

"Thank you, sir."

"Frank," he said, still shaking his hand. "Now, get yourself something to eat. You need to keep that strength up!" He pointed to the line by the back fence.

There was a huge grill and two long tables filled with all kinds of salads, fruits, hamburgers, hot dogs, lobster tails, and steak. It was nothing short of impressive.

Nathan waited in line with everyone else, and as he did, he glanced around at all the people and started to wonder why he had not come before. The party was amazing. All of these people were here to support the team and the program. It was overwhelming. He tapped his empty paper plate in his hand.

Without warning, Jason interrupted his thoughts as he walked up to Nathan in line, "Hey, man."

"Hey."

"Quite a party they put on here, huh?"

"Yeah, I guess I should come more often." He chuckled as they approached the front of the line.

Nathan piled his plate with a hamburger, salad, potato salad, and a steak. He grabbed a Gatorade from one of the coolers on the ground. He walked over to a table of players and sat down with Jason following him.

Nathan ate in silence, not contributing much to the conversations happening around him. He kept his head down.

The sun started to set, and he noticed it was getting darker. He glanced over toward the gate, wondering if his roommate would actually arrive. Surprisingly, he thought he'd feel more at home in this crowd if Spidey were here. He was one of the only people in his life who, if nothing else, treated him as Nathan, the kid who lost his keys a lot and showered four times a day, and not as Nathan Ryan, the quarterback.

Then, he heard a familiar voice.

"Hi, Nathan."

He quickly peeked up and saw Jessica, the girl with the curly, dark hair from the cafeteria, standing in front of him.

"Uh, hey…"

"Jessica. And this is my friend Kelly."

Nathan peered past Jessica to her friend. She stood there in silence, just nodding and glaring at him as though she wanted to eat him for dinner. She made him nervous.

"Why don't you girls join us?" Jason said.

Jason elbowed Nathan on the side. The two girls sat down across from Jason and Nathan. No sooner had Nathan started to eat again than he felt what he assumed to be Jessica's foot sliding gingerly up his leg. He froze.

Ten

Webber's nerves crept up as he approached the huge guy standing in front of the gate. He knew he'd be extremely out of place at a football party. Logan did little to help as he trailed further and further behind him. Webber smiled at the guy, but the guy would not crack a smile back. In fact, he was terribly intimidating.

"Can I help you?" he asked with a rather gruff, deep voice.

"I think I am on the list?" Webber said quietly.

Bree stood right next to him, eager to get into the party.

"Oh, really? Name?"

"Webber."

"Nope, no Webber," he replied, never glancing down at the list. "These girls with you?"

"Sort of," Bree quickly said.

"What's your name, doll?" Junior eyed her up and down.

"Bree." She added a hint of sweetness to her voice.

He glanced down at his list and then back at the group. "How can I help you guys?"

"Oh, well, forget it. Sorry to bother you." Webber turned to walk back down the hill.

Webber could tell Abigail felt sorry for him.

She stepped up and said to the guy, "Well, his roommate is Nathan Ryan, and he mentioned he was putting Webber and Logan on the list, so no biggie." She started to walk away with Webber.

"Spidey?" A huge grin came across his face.

Webber slowly turned around, his cheeks as red as apples. "Yeah," he replied, his head hanging low.

"Shit, why didn't you say so?" He put his arm out toward Webber and gave him a gigantic squeeze on the shoulders.

Webber thought they must look a lot like David and Goliath. Logan, on the other hand, breathed a sigh of relief.

The guy's attention quickly turned to the girls. "You sure you girls are only *sort of* with these two dudes?" he asked, mainly directing his snide remark at Bree.

She smiled. It was fake and nauseating, but he seemed to buy it.

"I don't normally let people in who aren't on the list, but since you're here for Nathan on his big day, I'll allow it this once." He became serious. "Give me your names, ladies."

"Abigail, and this is Melissa." Abigail paused. "And you know Bree…"

"Be safe." And with that, he opened the gate.

Webber could not believe what he was seeing. This party was like nothing he had been to before. There were all kinds of people eating and drinking. The smells were incredible. He hadn't been hungry before, but he could definitely eat now.

The four of them followed Webber into the crowd of the party.

"Spidey?" Abigail chuckled.

"I know. Don't even ask. My roommate's…he's…different." He glanced around the party. "I don't see him. Oh well. Do you want to get something to eat?"

"Sure." Melissa made her way into the line.

Abigail followed along with Logan and Webber.

"I'm not hungry, but I'll wait with you." Bree nervously scanned the crowd.

The line moved quickly as many people there had already had something to eat. The alumni with their kids and some of the older folks started to say their good-byes to one another. The sun was setting, and the players and students were anxious to get the real party started.

The group sat at a table closest to the house. It seemed to be unoccupied on this side, and they all fit nicely at an open table and folding chairs on the grass. The four of them ate while Bree sat there anxiously.

Abigail stood up from the table.

"Where are you going?" Webber asked.

"Just to get a fork. I'll be right back," she said.

She made her way over to the table.

Abigail looks so beautiful today. Actually, she's stunning every day.

A group of guys were standing near the back. He heard one whistle at her, and she quickly grabbed her fork and turned on her heel, coming back to their table. He hoped she wasn't regretting coming.

When Abigail returned to the table, Bree was gone.

"Where did Bree go?" she asked halfheartedly.

"She saw her friend from class or something and went to see her."

"Oh, cool," Abigail said.

It was nice not having her around for a moment.

"Is she always so on edge and anxious at parties?" Webber asked. *Or is it only because it is a football party? Jesus, is it that big of a deal? What am I missing?*

Bree had spotted Jessica through the crowd for just a split second before she was shielded by people walking around. She would recognize that curly brown hair from anywhere.

She sat behind Jessica in psychology class, and since Bree found the class utterly boring, she spent most of her time staring at the back of Jessica's head, following each curl down and down until her hair rested just above her chair. It was just one way to keep Bree occupied in class.

As she approached the table, she noticed Jessica was sitting with football players.

She fluffed her hair as she came upon the table. "Hey, Jessica," she said in a high-pitched, fake voice.

Jessica turned and glared for a moment. "Oh, hey, Bree. I didn't recognize you." She scrutinized her up and down with narrowed eyes.

"Oh, it's me all right," she chimed in, not giving Jessica an opportunity to continue.

Bree waved sweetly to the guys at the table.

"What are you doing here?" Jessica's voice was not so sweet.

Nathan peered up from his plate at Jessica. He was surprised at how rude she seemed.

"Oh, we were sort of invited, I guess." Bree's face turned red. She didn't like feeling unwelcomed.

"Oh, that's cool," Nathan said, breaking the ice.

"Yeah, that's nice." Jason eyed her closely, practically licking his lips.

Bree began to relax a bit. "Yeah, my friend is friends with the quarterback's roommate, so that's kind of how we got in," she announced.

Nathan's ears perked up, and a sly smile grew across his face. "You don't say, huh?" He started to stand up. "Can you point me in his direction?" Nathan glanced around.

Confused, Bree replied, "Yeah, sure. Over there across the way by the side fence. Why?"

"Never mind." He headed in the direction of his roommate.

Everyone at the table seemed to be snickering, except for Jessica and Kelly. Bree watched as he made his way across the party. She noticed how people were patting him on the back and shaking his hand, and then it hit her.

"Oh. Was that Nathan Ryan?" she said to Jessica, who was fuming.

"Yeah. Yeah, it was." She crossed her arms over her chest in obvious disapproval.

Nathan walked across the party through the crowd of people. Most were heading in the direction of the main gate to leave. It was just after dusk now, and the crew was starting to pack up the food. The grill was shutting down, and the rental company was pulling up the driveway. It was time to start loading up all the tables and chairs that had been rented by the booster club for this barbeque.

Every Saturday, after a home game, the same setup and breakdown happened. At least, that was what Nathan was told at practices on Monday. Soon, the band, kegs, and beer pong tables would take their places.

Nathan spotted Webber sitting at a table on the side of the house. Surprisingly, he was with two other girls, and they appeared to know one another. As far as Nathan knew, Webber had done little socializing at school, and honestly, he seemed content with studying and playing Mario Kart on Saturday nights. Nathan knew this because he was there most of the time. He had gone out to a party only once before. He had promised his dad that he would focus on school and football, and that was it. So far, he'd found it easy to do just that.

Webber caught Nathan heading toward them.

"Hey there, didn't think you'd come!" Nathan grinned.

They all looked up as he approached them.

"Yeah, thought we might check it out. Great food," Webber added as he motioned to his plate.

"I know, right? Quite a difference from the cafeteria."

"Hey, guys, this is Nathan. You know Logan."

Nathan shook Logan's hand again.

"And this is Melissa and Abigail." Webber pointed at each one.

He shook Melissa's hand. She blushed and could barely muster a hello.

Then, he walked up to Abigail and shook her hand. As their hands touched, a shiver went up Nathan's spine, and his breath caught. He quickly released her hand. She, much like him, seemed startled and quickly recoiled back in her chair. He waited a moment. He was caught off guard for some unexplainable reason. He stood there, watching her. He didn't want to make her uneasy, but he couldn't help himself.

My God, she is remarkable with those beautiful navy eyes. Wow, what a beauty.

"Nice to meet you," he said, squinting.

"You, too."

He came around the side and sat across from her.

"I met your friend over there. That's how I knew you were here," he said to Webber. "What's her name again?" he asked the girls.

Finally able to speak, Melissa replied, "Bree. She lives on our floor."

"Ah," Nathan said. "So, you guys all know my roommate?"

"Abigail and I are in class together, lab partners," Webber said.

Nathan could see her cheeks flush and her eyelashes flutter.

"Ah, so you're the one he's always running off to study with."

She smiled and nodded. When he caught a glimpse of her spectacular smile, his eyes widened.

Abruptly, Jason approached their table. He walked over to Nathan, bent down, and whispered in his ear. Nathan, appearing agitated, stood up.

He turned to Webber. "You guys are sticking around for the party, right?"

"Uh, sure, I guess," he said.

"Good." Nathan quickly walked away.

He headed back toward the table he had been sitting at earlier. As he neared it, he could hear laughter erupting with a loud voice in the middle. Jason followed closely behind.

When Nathan got close, he could see Tank impersonating someone. He was walking in a circle. He started limping, pretending to throw a ball, and made what appeared to be crying noises. As Nathan got closer, he realized Tank was making fun of *him*. Nathan stopped before anyone could see him. Jason stood next to him and put his hand on Nathan's shoulder.

What Jason didn't know was that Nathan had had enough. All the back-and-forth Tank and Nathan had entertained these past few months was tiring. Some had been witnessed by teammates, but mostly, there had been snide remarks muttered to each other under their breaths. And with the way they played and connected on the field, no one would believe that their mutual dislike for one another had been growing as each day passed.

But this was different. In Nathan's eyes, this was the ultimate kind of disrespect. They were teammates, and the way Nathan looked at it, whatever issues they had should be taken care of in private—with Coach and the team only.

Then, he remembered what his dad had told him about focusing on what truly mattered in life and how we were all accountable for our own actions—in this case, a reaction to others. Nathan knew that his reputation was at stake here, and that was exactly why he chose to walk away.

"Hey, man, this is just crap, and I'm not dealing with it tonight, not tonight. Thanks for bringing it to my attention, I guess. But, yeah, I'm just going to walk away."

"You know what? He's the fool, not you. Just remember that."

Before Tank was given the satisfaction of knowing Nathan had seen him, he turned and hurried off back toward Webber's table.

Nathan didn't break stride as he tried hard to walk, not limp, away. He walked right past Webber's table and out the gate to the side of the house. He leaned up against the house and the old paint crunched as he finally took the weight off his left leg.

He stood there, just staring up in the sky, thinking about the day he had had. As he clenched his fists, he tried not to let his anger overcome him. He took a deep breath and closed his eyes for a second, and then he heard the gate open. He quickly pushed himself off the house, and the throbbing in his leg came back.

"Hey. You okay, Nathan?"

He recognized Webber's voice.

"Yeah, sure, of course. You?" he asked.

"I'm fine. So, I guess the band is coming on soon or something," Webber said.

"Yeah, I guess." Nathan's voice was plain and unaffected.

"Okay." Webber started to turn and go back into the gate.

"Hey, Spidey?"

Webber stopped in his tracks. "Yeah?"

Nathan walked over to him and gave him a quick pat on the back. "Let's have some fun tonight, huh? We both deserve it." He took a breath. "Right? We should have more fun. We both work so damn hard."

This was his way of saying they were just two guys who should have a good time, as friends, not just roommates.

Nathan hoped that their relationship would improve because it was pretty clear to Nathan that Tank was definitely not his friend, not that there had really been any doubt.

Webber opened the gate. "Yeah, of course. It's your night, Nathan." He gave him a sincere smile before walking through.

Nathan followed Webber over to the keg, and Marcus handed him two cups.

"Hey, Marcus. This is my roommate, Spidey."

"Nice to meet you, Marcus."

"Hey, man. Thanks for coming."

Nathan gave Marcus a grin and held up his cup before downing the entire thing in one big gulp. Marcus gave him a sympathetic glance before walking back toward the other players. Webber's eyes widened as he took a sip of his beer. Nathan could tell by the expression on Webber's face that he thought it tasted awful. Nathan tipped up Webber's cup, almost forcing him to drink it down.

"Come on, buddy," he said. "Drink it up."

Webber did and hated every second of it.

Nathan and Webber carried cups of beer back to the table for Melissa, Abigail, and Logan.

Abigail stood up to stretch her legs.

"You're not leaving, are you?" Nathan asked.

Startled, she turned around. "What? Oh no, I'm not. Just stretching my legs. You?"

"Me? No. Why?"

"No reason. We thought you were leaving before." She glanced toward the back gate.

"Just had to take care of something," he lied.

Webber walked up to them and handed her a beer. "So"—he laughed—"funny I ran into you today at the game, and here we are."

Nathan could tell the beer was getting to him, and he was starting to like it.

"You were at the game today?" Nathan asked Abigail.

"Yes, I was. Melissa is a big football fan, so she asked if I wanted to go."

"And you?"

"Me?"

"Yeah, are you a fan?"

"No, not really. Sorry," she said with an apologetic tone in her voice.

Webber laughed. "Don't be sorry. Neither am I!" He laughed again.

"Great. So, on the best game day of my life, I'm here with the only two people who don't like football." He laughed, too.

"Well, congratulations on the game. I hear it was a big deal or something." Not sure of exactly what else to say, she raised her cup to him.

"Oh, thanks. Appreciate it." He raised his cup, as did Webber, and they all toasted.

"But enough about me. You guys met in class? You said, lab partners. What class?"

Webber responded first, "Advanced Bio."

"Nice. What are you studying?" he asked her.

"My plan is to be a veterinarian," she said matter-of-factly.

"You're kidding!" Webber exclaimed. "Me, too!"

"Really, Webber? I didn't know that! That's cool."

"You two should talk more," Nathan joked. He gave his roommate a slight wink.

Webber, feeling good, said, "Hey, I'm going to grab another beer. Can I get you one?"

"Sure. Thanks," Abigail said.

"Me, too," Nathan said.

Once Webber was out of earshot, Nathan turned to Abigail. "So," he said in a hushed voice, "you and my roommate are friends?"

"Yes, sure, we are. He's a nice guy." She was unsure of his questioning.

"Not sure he likes me too much, but I'm hoping that will change. He's a cool guy."

"He honestly hasn't said much to me. I didn't even know you were his roommate until a few hours ago." She hoped her comment did not make him feel bad. She took a sip of her beer.

"I know. See? I think he's embarrassed that he lives with a jock," Nathan said, laughing. "I hate that word—*jock*." He added, "It sounds awful."

"It does, doesn't it?"

Webber came back, carrying three beers. He handed one each to Abigail and then Nathan. "They were free." He laughed.

"Ha-ha." Nathan was surprised to see Webber loosening up so much. It was definitely a change for him.

The band had been setting up for the past hour and was about to start playing. Most of the crowd had migrated toward the stage and the beer pong tables. There was a sign-up sheet on the fence.

Every Saturday, they would have a tournament. Nathan had only heard about it at practice on Mondays. There were ten teams with three players on each team. Nathan could see a few of the players signing up for teams, but he wanted nothing to do with it. He saw Bree, Jessica, and Kelly signing up as well. This was bad news for them. There was no way they could keep up with some of his teammates. It would be impossible. However, the more Nathan scrutinized the situation, the more he thought the girls appeared to be in their glory, surrounded by all boys. But to the players, they were like chum to a pool full of sharks.

Before Nathan knew it, Tank had spotted him. Nathan tried quickly to step away, but it was too late.

"Hey, Two!" Tank yelled before gulping down his beer. "Get over here." He motioned toward the pong tables.

Reluctantly, Nathan excused himself and started walking over toward the tables. The last thing he wanted to do was draw attention to whatever this situation was between the two of them, but quite honestly, he figured he might as well see Tank and move on with his night.

Nathan approached, and without making a big deal of seeing Tank for the first time since the game had ended, he pointed to the pong table. "You guys gonna play?"

Tank just laughed. "So, Two, where you been all night? Doing interviews?" He chuckled.

"Interviews?" Jessica cooed as she walked up to him. She put her arm through his and gazed up at him, batting her eyelashes.

"Yeah. No big deal, just standard stuff." He desperately wanted to change the subject.

Tank scoffed, "No big deal, huh? I guess breaking a school record is *no big deal.*" His voice kept getting louder.

Marcus grabbed his arm. "Hey, man, you ready to play?"

Tank was still glaring at Nathan as he finally responded to Marcus, "Yeah, I'm ready to play." He turned to the end of the table and grabbed a ping-pong ball.

Nathan sensed this was a good time to leave, and he started to back up.

Marcus nodded in his direction, as if to say, *Yeah, probably a good time for you to go.*

Jessica unlinked her arm from his and ran her hand down his back, resting it on his pants just above his buttocks. "You should call me some time," she whispered. She took the pen they had used to sign up for teams and wrote her number on Nathan's hand.

"Sure," he said.

Tank noticed what she had done and called after her, "Hey, come over here, babe, and bring me luck." He winked at her.

She giggled and quickly walked over to him. He put his arm around her while staring in Nathan's direction.

Nathan walked right over to the keg and refilled his cup. He stood by the keg for a bit, talking to some guy who was in his History class. He was obviously drunk and had no idea who Nathan was. This was just fine by Nathan. In fact, if not another word was spoken tonight about football, that would be just perfect. He stood there for a good twenty minutes, talking to…Kevin, maybe. He wasn't quite sure. The conversation had started off as a discussion about the cafeteria food but then turned into what the best video games were before Nathan noticed Webber walking toward him, swaying from side to side. He approached the keg.

"Hey, what's up?" Webber slurred.

"Nothing. You?" He didn't want to embarrass his roommate.

"Nothing at all." The words barely formed on his lips. He reached for the tap and tried to refill his cup but wasn't able to pump and hold the cup and tap all at once.

"Whoa, buddy," Kevin said as the beer started to spray out of Webber's cup.

Nathan stepped back and quickly took the tap. "Here, let me do that."

Webber started to giggle an apology.

Kevin kind of huffed as he mumbled, "See you later," to Nathan.

Nathan filled Webber's cup up just a little bit and put his arm around his roommate's shoulders. "Hey, let's go see what Logan is up to."

"Sure, but I think he likes that girl," Webber slurred.

"I'm sure he does," Nathan said, smiling.

They came close to the table and saw Abigail, Logan, and Melissa all standing around, talking. As Abigail saw them, she gave Nathan a concerned expression. He nodded.

"Hey, guys, I'm going to get going. I've had a really—"

Before Nathan could continue, Webber began to protest, "No, dude, you can't leave…" He could barely stand up.

"You know, maybe—" Nathan started to say before Abigail interrupted, "Yeah, I'm ready to go. You ready, Webber? Come with us."

Webber squinted, trying to see her face better.

"Well…okay then, I guess we're all leaving." Webber turned and attempted to walk toward the gate.

Nathan grabbed Webber's arm and put it around his shoulders. Nathan was much bigger than Webber, as he was about five feet ten inches compared to Nathan at a little over six feet three inches. At this point, Nathan was all but carrying him.

Melissa grabbed Abigail's arm as she started to put her cup down. "Hey, I think I'm going to stay here with Logan."

Abigail took one look at Melissa and then at Logan and just smiled. "Sure, of course. We'll do breakfast tomorrow."

"Sounds good. I'll keep my eye on Bree, too."

They both turned briefly as a loud roar erupted near the beer pong tables. Jessica screeched as Tank lifted her with a tight squeeze. Bree stood there with a player's arm draped around her shoulders. She was grinning from ear to ear.

Melissa turned and shrugged her shoulders. "I'll see you tomorrow."

Nathan let the back gate swing open and then shut as he carefully maneuvered Webber out of the backyard. By the time Abigail got close, they were almost halfway down the driveway.

She whispered, "Can I do anything?"

Webber heard her and picked his head up. "Hey, there you are," he slurred. "Where are the other two?"

Somehow, she knew exactly what he'd said. "Logan and Melissa are just finishing their beers. They'll be right behind us. They said not to wait." She quickly got close to his other side.

Without thinking, she took his hand and draped it around her neck. He was having a hard time walking, and if they both didn't help, it would be a very long walk home.

Nathan, Abigail, and Webber finally made it to the dorm room. Nathan leaned Webber up against the wall as he put his key into the outside door. Abigail grabbed the door once he opened it and held it ajar.

Nathan put his arms on Webber's shoulders and said firmly to him, "Now, be cool. Let's just get you upstairs before anyone notices, okay?"

Being drunk in the dorm could get you written up, and after three violations, you would get thrown out. So, they made sure to try to get in and up to their room, undetected.

They took the elevator to the fifth floor and held Webber up as they walked down the hall. Thankfully, most of the floor was empty, and it was relatively quiet.

Nathan opened the door to their room. Abigail helped guide Webber inside.

He stumbled forward and hit his head on the wall. "Ouch. Damn wall there. Watch for the walls, guys."

Nathan grabbed him right before he almost hit the wall again. Abigail tried not to giggle as Nathan rolled his eyes at her.

"Hey, this is our room?" Webber said, sounding surprised.

"Yes, it is. I think you should lie down, okay?" It was more of a statement than a request.

"Yeah, I guess so, but…" He trailed off as his body sank onto his bed.

He tried kicking off his shoes, but eventually, Nathan had to bend down and take them off for him.

When she saw Webber starting to close his eyes, Abigail whispered to Nathan, "I should go."

"Wait, hold on."

He grabbed a pillow off his bed and propped it up under Webber's head, so he wasn't lying flat. He appeared to really care for Webber. It was nice to witness.

Webber whispered to Abigail in a soft voice, "You're so pretty." Then, he glanced at Nathan with heavy eyes and added, "Isn't she?"

She could see Nathan blush as he responded, "Yeah, buddy, she sure is."

Abigail blushed, too.

She started walking toward the door when she heard Nathan switch off the light.

When she went to open the door, Nathan stated, "Hey, you're not leaving alone."

"What?"

"Well, I don't know where you live, but I'm not letting you walk there by yourself." He grabbed his keys.

"Oh, thanks, but you should stay here with him." She placed her hand on the doorknob.

"Understood, but you don't live on the moon, do you?" He granted her an incredible smile.

Wow, he is so handsome and really seems nice, like genuinely nice.

"No, I live in Willis."

"Ah, Willis. Not too far. Easy, I'll be back before he notices." He peered over at Webber, who was already snoring.

Nathan and Abigail walked down the hallway in silence. They waited for the elevator and got in. When they were alone in the elevator, she noticed Nathan rubbing his neck as he let out a big sigh.

"You okay?" she asked.

"Yeah, just been a long day, hasn't it?"

Before she could answer, she let out a *huge* hiccup. She gasped and put her hand over her mouth. He burst out in laughter, and finally, she did, too.

"I'm so embarrassed. I don't ever drink, and I guess it's catching up to me!"

"Me, too." He laughed just as the elevator doors were opening.

They both snickered as they walked toward the main door. Jokingly, he grabbed her hand as she walked down the stairs, pretending to help steady her. Not even thinking, she played along. They both walked out the door, still holding hands and laughing. A man was standing near the light post closest to the street. He pushed his body off of it as he saw them walking out. He snapped a picture, then another, and another until finally Nathan noticed him.

"Hey," the guy said.

They let their hands go.

Nathan's demeanor became serious, and Abigail started feeling confused, worried even. She remained close to Nathan. This guy was definitely not a student.

"Hey, sorry to bother you, Nathan. I'm Ward Daniels from the *Union Press.*" He handed Nathan his card.

"You always wait for people this late at night?" Nathan asked.

"Just hoping to get a quote on the game today. I had a prior engagement and wasn't able to wait for the press conference. I'm considering running a story about you near the end of the season in the Sunday College Spotlight. You've read my section, right?" he asked, only he wasn't expecting an answer. His tone was as cocky as he seemed with his perfectly gelled hair, his pressed white shirt, and brown tweed sport coat with matching brown shoes.

"Yeah, of course," Nathan said, changing his tone.

Abigail noted how politely Nathan answered the man's questions despite the weirdness of being approached outside his dorm on a Saturday night. But in a small way, she thought he must feel kind of flattered. She could tell he was answering as quickly but as professionally as he could in the moment.

After his questions were done, he tried to excuse them. Abigail had stood there so patiently. "Mr. Daniels, I'm not trying to be rude, but it is late."

"Call me Ward," he said. "Of course, I understand."

Abigail couldn't help but notice that he gave her a once-over.

He started to walk away. "You'll hear from me. Thanks again."

They waited there, as if frozen by the events that had just taken place. Ward climbed into the front seat of his black Audi A6 and drove down the street.

Nathan started laughing. "Like I said, it's been a really long day!"

Abigail beamed up at him, a mere stranger to him just a few hours before. It was *so* genuine.

"What's the smile for?" he asked.

"Nothing. That was just the last thing I could have possibly imagined would happen tonight. You deserve tomorrow off!"

"I wish." He laughed. "Would you mind telling Coach that? Maybe he'll listen to you."

"Doubt it, but I'd be happy to try." She turned now to face him. "Seriously, you do not have to walk me home."

Instead of going back in his dorm, he started walking in the direction of her dorm.

"What are you doing?"

"Come on," he said, motioning to her. "I have to drop something off at Willis."

She quickly caught up with him as he kept walking.

"So, what was he talking about? The College what?"

"The Sunday College Spotlight. It's kind of a big deal—you know, in my world at least. Each season, Ward Daniels picks one athlete to do an entire section on in the paper. It's an honor, particularly as a freshman, to even be considered. I feel kind of flattered."

"Wow, I hope you didn't rush on my account."

"Oh, no. I…well, to be honest, I'm all done with talking about football today."

"Understandable."

They didn't say much on the rest of the walk to her dorm. It was a cool, clear night, and it was nice to just be silent. It had been a hectic night, that was true, and now, they both needed some much-deserved quiet time. They seemed to both feel at ease as they walked side by side.

As Abigail approached her dorm, she glanced at her watch. She was sure James would have called by now, and the guilt of not being there when he did was starting to kick in, but at this hour, she'd have to try him in the morning.

"There." Nathan brought Abigail out of her thoughts. "I'm dropping something off." He motioned to the front door of Willis Hall.

"Funny."

He put out his hand to shake hers. "Good night, Abby."

Huh, no one really ever calls me Abby. "Good night, Nathan." She shook his hand.

His hand was warm and large, and it practically crushed her small hand. A tingle went up her back, and she bashfully glanced away from him. She dropped his hand even though, for some reason, she did not want to.

She started walking to the door. She pulled it open and then turned to wave. He was still standing there, watching her, and as she went inside, she saw him give her one quick wave.

As she pressed the button for the elevator, the strangest feeling came over her, as though she had been in this exact situation before, yet she couldn't place it. It was like déjà vu, and it gave her a funny feeling in her gut. The elevator came and went, and she just stood there, trying to place the memory to another time in her life, but she was unable to do it.

The doors slid open again, and this time, she stepped in. She hit the button to her floor. *Why does he seem so familiar to me?*

As the elevator doors closed, his name escaped her lips in a whisper, "Nathan?" as though she had spoken it a thousand times before, only she knew she had not.

Eleven

SEPTEMBER 26, 1995

Abigail opened her door and switched on the lamp by her desk. The room was quiet. Without hesitation, she went over to her phone and picked it up. There was just an ordinary dial tone, indicating that there were no messages. Her heart sank.

No double beeps. Could that be right? Did James not call?

She dialed her extension and hit pound.

The digital voice stated, "You have no new messages."

She put the phone down and walked to her bed. She tore off her shirt and jeans, and in only her bra and panties, she climbed into bed and pulled her covers up. She always wore pajamas, but for once, she was too tired to care. She had been out all day and night, which was probably why her body sank deeply into the mattress. It was a wonderful sensation.

With her head resting on the pillow, she thought about the past two days and how so much had happened. She wondered when she would see James again. She hoped Webber would be okay. She figured, from what she knew of him, that he didn't drink often, so she guessed he might be a bit embarrassed he had been carried home. Then, she imagined Nathan waving good-bye and how seemingly sweet and unaffected he was by everything that had happened to him in the past twenty-four hours.

Finally, she reflected upon this feeling that she was having, as though she had been here all before. Like she had somehow lived this life and was now on repeat. It seemed like such a strange sensation to have at her age, but it kept coming back day after day, month after month, that she stopped questioning it. Ever since her seizure, she'd had this feeling of déjà vu, and it was starting to make her feel mad, like she was no longer able to live in the moment.

But why? Why can't I just force myself to live in the moment? I am in control of my own mind, right? Her eyes got heavier and heavier.

Thankfully, despite her mind whirling with numerous feelings, she fell asleep with the desk lamp still on.

SEPTEMBER 27, 1995

It was unlike Abigail to sleep so soundly. It could have been the alcohol that had made her night's slumber so deep. So, when she heard a heavy knock on her door, naturally, it startled her. She flew out of bed and ran to the door. She feared she might have locked Laura out, so she threw the door open, rubbing her eyes.

"Oh!" Nathan yelled. "Um, you might want to cover up." He eyed her half-naked body.

Abigail let out a scream and tried to push the door shut, but it quickly swung back open because his foot was partially in the doorway. He yelped as he kicked his foot up and held on to it. Luckily, he was wearing sneakers, so the door only skimmed the top of his toes, but she could tell she'd hurt him. She grabbed a hair towel off the back of her door and tried to wrap it around her body, but it only covered the front of her.

"Oh my God, I am so sorry!" she yelled, trying to hold the towel close to her body.

"It's okay, really. I'm sorry. I thought you'd be awake by now." He tried to balance a bag in one hand while still holding his foot in the other.

"Come in, Nathan. Please, sit down. I'm so sorry. I hope I didn't break it." She started to back up into the room.

"No, no, I can come back." He was trying not to gawk at her as he winced and held tightly to his foot.

"Just give me a second, will you?" She went to the farthest corner of her room, away from his sight. She quickly grabbed her men's dress shirt from off her bed and pulled it over her head. As she did, the phone rang. Without thinking, she picked it up.

As she said, "Hello?" Nathan spoke again, "Really, I can come back. No big deal."

"Who's that?" James sounded irritated.

"What? Who? Oh, nothing—I mean, no one. Hey, can I...can I call you right back? Sorry, I'll explain," she stammered. "I'll call you back, promise."

"Sure. Okay, Abigail, call me back," James said with a hint of sarcasm.

She deserved it. She wasn't always the best at returning calls.

Abigail's heart was beating fast from all the commotion. She took a deep breath and walked over to the other side of the room where Nathan sat, rubbing his foot.

"I'm so sorry." She glanced at his foot.

He laughed and winked at her. "I'm not."

Her face grew another shade of crimson red, if that were at all possible. She held on to the top of her shirt, making sure it was closed.

"I'm kidding. Please, I didn't mean to embarrass you." He placed the paper bag on Laura's desk. "I was out for a run and thought you'd be awake. Spidey asked me to get you this as a thank-you." He pointed to the bag from her favorite bagel shop in town. "He's in pretty bad shape, and he couldn't come himself."

She leaned over her desk and opened it. "Oh, well, tell him this was not necessary, but thank you." She took out the bagel and coffee.

"Sorry about the coffee. I took a hit, and it spilled." He laughed, rubbing his foot.

She put her head down and tried not to feel embarrassed. She'd just opened the door, half-naked, without even thinking about it.

"Anyway," he said, trying to change the subject, "Spidey's having a rough morning, as I'm sure you can imagine, and he doesn't even remember us bringing him home. So, he is quite humiliated, to say the least. I figured I'd help him out and say thank you, from him."

"Again, not necessary." She noticed he'd started to blush a bit—or maybe he was just warm from his run. *Yeah, that's probably it.*

"Do you always sleep this late?" He glanced at the clock on her wall.

"What? No, that can't be right." She sounded utterly surprised as she observed the time.

"Yep, almost noon."

"Well, maybe it's my turn to blame it on the alcohol."

He noticed the running sneakers by the door. "Want to finish my run with me?"

She laughed. "You think I can keep up with you? Aren't you some kind of a professional?"

"I'll go slowly."

For a brief moment, Abigail considered going for a run with him.

"Um—" She was interrupted by her phone ringing. "I'll have to take a rain check, okay?" She walked toward the phone.

"You got it, Abby. I'll see you later."

She waited for the door to close before picking up the phone. It was her mother calling. She exhaled as she heard her mom's voice.

"Hello, sweetheart. How are you?"

"Good, Mom. And you?"

"Your father and I are running out to church, so I'll be quick," she said. "I'm sending a care package to you. Do you need any more shampoo or anything like that?"

"Sure, Mom. That sounds great." She did a quick run through in her head. "Hey, Mom, would you mind sending me some more of that perfume I like?"

"Of course. Anything else?"

Abigail chuckled. "Yeah, I could probably use a bigger towel."

Abigail took a shower and got dressed quickly before sitting down at her desk to call James.

"Hi," she said.

"Hey."

"So, how are you?" She tried hard to sound upbeat.

"Fine, and you?"

"Oh, good, good," she said.

There was silence.

"So, who was that?" he asked.

"Oh, that was just a friend I'd helped last night. I'd had to bring his roommate home because he was drunk, and he dropped by to thank me." She was talking fast.

"Who did?"

"Who did what?"

"Dropped by?"

"Oh, his roommate."

"Oh, what's his name?" he asked plainly.

"Who? The roommate?"

"Yeah, sure," he said, sounding like it didn't really matter.

"Uh, Nathan." Just saying his name made her uncomfortable, so she tried to change the subject. "So, how was your ride home?"

"Oh, fine. Easy."

There was silence on the phone, and Abigail was desperately searching for something to say to fill it.

Thankfully, he spoke first, "I'd like to try to come see you again before the winter break."

"Oh, sure. That sounds great." She began thinking about two nights ago. She had had little time to think about what had happened between her and James. But no one knew Abigail better than herself, and she knew it was best not to dwell on any major thing. She would drive herself crazy. She had to remain calm and cool about all this. "I'd like that."

"Great. I'll call you soon, okay?" His voice sounded more assured.

"Great."

"Oh, and tell Laura I said thanks for giving me the heads-up that she was going away, so I could have some time alone with you for once." He laughed.

Abigail laughed, too, and with that remark, he hung up. She stood, holding the receiver for a moment, and then put it down. She walked over to her desk and sat down. She gazed out her window across the campus. Her coffee was now cold, but she drank it anyway. She took a deep breath and let it out. She reached into her desk and took out her journal and a pen.

Wow, what a weekend this turned out to be. First, James showed up at school. I had been half-expecting him to come, I guess, so when I saw him standing in the middle of campus, I was shocked. We had a nice time and a much-needed talk. I feel so much better about everything that has happened between us over the past year.

But in typical Abigail form, I overthought the situation, and I knew I wasn't ready to have sex with him. There was just something about the timing and, more importantly, how I felt in the moment, so I just decided to wait. I don't think he was too surprised, and he made me feel fine about it. I'm not sure why I have such a hard time with us, but maybe I just need more time to figure it all out, right? Do I need more time?

Then, I went to the football game with the girls and was invited to a party after. It was a cool party, and I met someone. I had such a strange feeling. He amazed me in so many ways. He was much different than I had expected. He was charming and sweet and beautiful. I shouldn't be writing all this, but I don't know…my interaction with him, although brief, was really nice, and I was at ease. Well, until he showed up today. In a bit of a fog, I opened the door in my undies. Boy, was I embarrassed, to say the least. But he was nice about it, even after I hurt him with the door by accident.

So, all in all, it was a busy weekend for me, one of the busiest I've had yet while here at OSU…and I'm kind of hoping I have more like this.

Twelve

Nathan walked back to his dorm with a massive grin spread across his face. He was even happier that he'd come up with the idea of the coffee and bagel as a thank-you. He would tell Spidey about the thank-you gesture once he got back to the room, but he would keep the half-naked reveal to himself. Man, had he hit the jackpot. When Abigail had opened the door, Nathan had thought he was going to have a heart attack. If it wasn't for the pain in his foot, he would have surely hit the ground. She was stunning, and she didn't even know it.

Nathan walked into his room and could hear Spidey moaning in pain. He walked over to their mini fridge and grabbed another Gatorade, and then he got some ibuprofen from the bottle on his desk.

"Take these."

Spidey lifted up his head. "Thank you," was all he could mutter. He took the Gatorade and washed down the two pills before putting his head back on the pillow.

"I just saw Abby. I brought her a bagel and coffee as a thank-you for dragging you home last night." He smirked.

His voice cracked. "Oh God, I'm so embarrassed. But thanks."

"No problem. Get some rest, okay? You'll feel better in a few hours. I'm going to go lounge and watch TV. I'll check on you in a bit."

Nathan walked into the rec room. It was quiet for a Sunday afternoon. He switched on the TV. Then, he sat on one of the couches and put his feet up. He desperately needed to unwind and have some time to himself. No sooner did his body start to relax than he saw Tank and Jessica walking in.

"Well, well, look who's taking the day off." Tank oozed sarcasm.

Tank's appearance was awful—tired, unkempt, and scruffy.

Who is Tank kidding? Nathan knew he had it together better than Tank did. Of this, he was certain.

Trying to seem unaffected by Tank's comment, Nathan replied, "You look good, too." Then, he glanced back toward the TV, and without even giving her his time, he joked, "Hey, Jessica. Have a nice night?"

He could tell she was embarrassed because she answered in a low but firm voice, "Yes. Yeah, I did. You?"

"I had a great time," he quipped, still watching the TV. "Now, if you guys don't mind, I'm trying to enjoy my day off."

Nathan could feel Tank's anger grow, and out of the corner of his eye, he saw Tank clenching his fists. It was really the first time Nathan had said anything back to Tank and in front of a girl, no less. It was perfect timing. He knew Tank wouldn't dare do anything that would jeopardize his spot on the team, and after the game Nathan had just had, he was confident in thinking Coach would side with him.

Tank stood stationary for a moment, glaring at Nathan, who refused to take his eyes off the TV.

Jessica finally spoke up, cooing at Tank, "Hey, want to go grab something to eat?" She touched his stiff arm.

He didn't move, so she pulled on him a little.

"Yeah, let's go," he finally said, still staring at Nathan. As they walked away, he turned and snarled, "Be ready for practice tomorrow, Two." His face was dark and serious.

Nathan nodded his head.

When they were finally out of the lounge, Nathan let out a deep sigh. Not for nothing, but the guy was huge, and if he wanted, he could probably snap Nathan in half. Still, Tank would be crucified by the team and school if he intentionally did anything to Nathan. They both knew this, but that didn't always give Nathan a reassuring feeling. He was a little worried about practice tomorrow. He didn't want Tank to take his frustrations out on him, and he physically couldn't take another hard hit like the one before.

When Tank and Jessica got outside, he quickly turned to her. "Hey, about getting something to eat, I'm gonna pass for right now, okay?" He regarded her with cold eyes.

She tried not to seem affected by this and swiftly responded, "Fine. I guess I'll see you later then."

She began to walk away when he called after her, "Hey, sorry. Just remembered something I have to do."

She just waved halfheartedly, never even turning around to look at him.

Tank walked down the street en route to the field house. His mind was completely blank, but somehow, his body knew where to take him, as if in a zombie-like state. He opened the double doors to the locker room and walked inside. It was dark, and all he could hear was the dripping of the faucets in the restroom. He walked over to Nathan's locker and stood in front of it for a moment before he sat down and put his head in his hands. The memories began to play again.

"I have something to tell you," Jonathan said.

He looked serious. He never was solemn. He was always clowning around, telling jokes, laughing. He wasn't named the Class Clown our junior year for nothing.

"Okay, sure. What's up?" I sat down at his kitchen table.

I had a feeling I knew what was coming. In the past few months, Jonathan had gone to Boston over several weekends. He had been quiet about the trips, which made me believe he was visiting other schools and didn't know how to tell me he was not going to go to Onondaga State University with me as we had planned.

"You know how I have been going to Boston?" he asked.

"Yeah." My heart began to pound as I anticipated my friend's news.

I glanced over at Mrs. Higgins, who was abnormally quiet.

Mrs. Higgins was standing in front of the kitchen window, staring out into the backyard. Her face seemed different, somber almost.

She always greeted me when I came in the house. In fact, she usually had a ham and cheese sandwich with mustard on a bulky roll with a big side of potato chips and a glass of milk ready for me. No kidding. She had done this for years. She always said I needed to get bigger—joking, of course. She called it my snack. She had one every time I came over, which was just about every day, except for today.

"I'm just going to say it because that is the only way I know how," Jonathan said.

I looked at my best friend, but then he glanced away.

When he did, I peered up at Mrs. Higgins, as if to say, What the hell is going on here?

Instead, she remained frozen, and a single tear streamed down her cheek. It was then I knew this did not have anything to do with college.

Finally, Jonathan continued, "I have an inoperable brain tumor."

Mrs. Higgins came over and put her arm around Jonathan. When I saw Mrs. Higgins's face up close, I knew the answer to the one question I would never ask.

Jonathan was going to die.

I did not cry that day. Instead, I stood up and embraced my one true friend.

I had known Jonathan since I was five years old. We had ridden the bus together and played every day after school while my mom put herself through college to become a registered nurse. We'd studied together and shared a limo to the prom. We did just about everything side by side. We were the definition of best friends, and we both, without a doubt, loved football.

Jonathan didn't cry either.

As I squeezed his body, Jonathan yelped. "Hey, Tank, you're going to kill me."

We laughed so hard that my stomach started to hurt. This incessant laughter was the only way we knew how to cope. We were only seventeen. We didn't know the right or wrong way to handle news like this.

Mrs. Higgins wiped a few tears from her eyes before standing up and saying, "Would you boys like a snack?"

We both laughed.

"Of course, Mrs. Higgins, and thank you." I smiled at her.

She barely smiled back as she walked to the refrigerator and took out the ham and cheese.

Tank finally sat up and stretched back his arms as he let out a huge sigh. He was mentally exhausted from the past year. He missed his friend so badly. Thinking back, he remembered a few occasions of Jonathan complaining of a headache, but never in his wildest dreams had he thought an athlete like Jonathan would be so sick. Tank wished he had asked Jonathan about his trips to Boston. Maybe Tank could have had more time with him, and maybe Jonathan would have had a friend to help him along the way. They had dreamed of so many things together. But it had all been taken away, and Tank didn't know how to deal with it.

He took out the newspaper clipping from his wallet and opened it. It was starting to fade. He had opened and closed it so many times that the edges were now frayed, and the creases were getting deep. He looked at the picture of Jonathan. The newspaper had used his school picture from junior year because by the time senior pictures had come around, Jonathan hadn't wanted to be photographed. There was a picture of him on the football field, and above it read, *Community mourns the loss of football star Jonathan Higgins.*

Tank stared at Nathan's locker and at the number twelve on the top center of the locker. His eyes began to well up. He tried desperately to fight back his tears, but they came flowing out. He began to sob. It was the kind of sobbing that took over your entire body, and he couldn't stop, no matter how hard he tried.

"You should be here!" he yelled as he pounded his hand on Nathan's locker. "It should have been you!" He stared up in the air, as if by speaking out loud would somehow make Jonathan answer him. But all he could hear was his breath as he drew air in. His anger toward Nathan began to grow, and he beat his fist again and again on the number twelve.

"Hey, hey!"

Tank whipped around and saw Coach Bromley hurrying toward him. He grabbed on Tank's arm. Without thinking, Tank yanked it away, forcing Coach into the lockers. He hit the locker with a thud and winced.

"Oh crap! I am so sorry!" Tank yelled.

Coach steadied himself as Tank went to grab his shoulder to help. Coach scrutinized him and knew Tank had been crying. Quickly, Tank wiped the tears off his cheeks.

"Slow down, will you?" Coach grabbed his arm. "Take a deep breath. What's the problem here?"

"Nothing, Coach. I'm so sorry. I didn't know anyone was here, and it…" He let his thoughts go.

Coach observed the dents on Nathan's locker. "Jesus, son. Come on." He motioned for Tank to follow him.

He walked back toward his office. Tank stood there for a moment before following. He folded up the newspaper. He noticed it was ripped. It must have been during his unintentional scuffle with Coach. Tank cursed himself as he put it back in his wallet.

He entered Coach's office and immediately sat down on the chair across from him. He couldn't look Coach in the eyes.

"Son."

Tank peered up. His eyes darted back and forth.

"Son, I am not going to pretend that I know how you feel. Hell, no one does." He paused for effect. Then, he said with a loud, clear voice, "But you have got to get yourself together. Do not blow the opportunity *you* have." He stressed the word *you*.

It struck a chord in Tank. His eyes started to well again. They both sat in silence for a moment while his words sank in.

"Okay, Coach."

"When we spoke over the summer, I told you I would do whatever I could to help you through this while you were here, but you have got to let me in, let someone in. Heck, did you ever talk to Marcus about all this? He is your captain, and he wants what is best for you and the team."

Tank just shook his head.

"Well, you have to trust that those guys, your teammates, will understand that this is hard for you. If you don't let them in on your pain, son, then you can't expect anyone to know how you feel."

"So what?" he quipped. "You just want me to get together with them, like some kind of therapy session, and talk about my feelings?"

"Well, yes. You need to at least talk about it. You can't be in here, banging on Ryan's locker, and just expect people to get where you are coming from."

"No. But, Coach, you know Jonathan is better."

"Son, maybe he was better. But I can't say that for sure. You understand what I'm saying, don't you? I can't live in the past, the what-ifs, forever. I have to focus on the here and now. I'm telling you, you should do the same."

Tank had a lump in his throat, and it took all his might not to burst into tears.

"If it's too hard to talk to them, then I can recommend someone here on campus for you to talk to." He pulled out a piece of paper from his desk drawer and began writing on it. He handed the paper to Tank. "At least tell me you'll consider it. She has helped many of my players over the years. She is very good at what she does, and I believe she can help you."

Tank started to get up.

Coach stopped him by saying, "What would Jonathan want you to do? Think about it."

Tank stood the rest of the way up and walked toward the door. He stopped in the doorway, and without turning around, he said, "Sorry I pushed you, Coach."

"I know, son."

With that, Tank headed out the door, through the locker room, and out to the parking lot.

As he began to walk back toward campus, his hands shoved deep in his pockets, an unsettling feeling burrowed deep within him. He stopped dead in his tracks. He viewed the beautiful campus that lay before him. In his heart, he knew that he had worked too hard to get here to let anyone stand in his or Jonathan's way.

"What would Jonathan want me to do, Coach? I'll tell you," he mumbled. "He'd have wanted the world to know that he deserved to be here, not Nathan Ryan, and I'm going to prove it."

Thirteen

OCTOBER 21, 1995

"Can you believe it's already late October?" Abigail pulled open the door to the student union.

"I know. Hard to comprehend," Laura said.

The student union had quickly become Laura's and Abigail's favorite place to get away to. The library served its purpose for studying, but the union was the best place to grab a coffee, a snack, get your mail, go to the bookstore, and just hang out, all while getting a little studying in, too. They both loved coming here and spent almost every day together.

"Hey, you mind grabbing me a pumpkin spice latte while I run into the bookstore and see if my new lab book is in?" Abigail asked.

"Nope. I'll meet you at our table near the fireplace."

"Cool. Thanks!" Abigail walked out of the coffee shop and toward the bookstore.

When she walked into the store, there, smack dab in the middle, was a huge display of football merchandise, but what was even more alarming was the huge poster displayed on the post. It was of none other than number twelve, Nathan Ryan.

Abigail's heart skipped a beat. *He looks really good.* She glanced down at all the T-shirts, sweatshirts, and such that had the Onondaga State football logo plastered all over them. For a brief moment, Abigail considered buying the navy women's sweatshirt in the front. She held it up to herself, but then she quickly thought about how embarrassed she'd be if Nathan—or even Webber, for that matter—ever saw her wearing it. She didn't want to seem like some kind of groupie-stalker girl. According to Webber, they already had enough of those calling their dorm room every day.

"Looks good on you."

Abigail whipped around, her cheeks apple red. "What? Oh..." she stammered.

"No, seriously, it suits you," Nathan said.

"Oh God, well, I saw your nice face—I mean, the poster of you. I had to...I was just looking at this. I need a new sweatshirt." *Oh my God, Abigail, get it together!* she screamed in her head. *You are making such an ass out of yourself.*

"Well, glad you like my poster."

He grinned at her, and she thought she might melt.

Does he really have to be so freaking handsome? Like, all the time?

She started to fold up the sweatshirt.

"So, you're not going to get it now?" he asked, sounding a bit hurt. "You know, it does support the team."

Oh God, I screwed up again. "Oh, of course, I'm getting it." She laughed, trying to recover from her obvious insult.

"I'm just kidding, Abby."

Feeling a little slighted that he'd made such fun of her, she picked up the sweatshirt, and with the sweetest voice, she said, "Oh no, now, I'm certainly getting it, and I'm going to wear it every day. Don't want to be accused of not supporting our athletic programs."

She started to walk over to the counter, and much to her delight, he came with her.

"Can I help you?" the girl behind the counter asked.

"Yes, are the lab books for Rhodes Biology two-oh-one in yet?" she asked.

"Yes," the girl said. She walked back into the supply area.

Nathan stood quietly next to Abigail for a moment. "So, what have you been up to?" he asked.

"Oh, school and all that. Really just school stuff. You?"

"Yeah, same but football stuff, too."

The girl came back and noticed Nathan. "Hey, is—that's you, right, on the poster?"

Feeling an opportunity to get a jab back, Abigail said, "Yes, and can you believe he is forcing me to buy this sweatshirt?"

He loudly burst out in a quirky laugh as he regarded Abigail.

Ha, got you back, she thought as the girl rang up her purchases.

The girl didn't quite see the humor in what Abigail had said. In fact, she just kind of sneered at the both of them before she punched the numbers into the cash register.

"That will be thirty-one sixty-seven." She started to put Abigail's items in a bag.

Abigail reached into her backpack for her wallet.

"Oh, she doesn't need a bag—at least, not for the sweatshirt. You were planning on wearing it, right?"

Abigail squinted her eyes at him and tried hard not to laugh. "Yes, obviously, I was planning on wearing it."

She handed the girl two twenty-dollar bills. The girl gave her the change and a receipt. Abigail then grabbed the sweatshirt off the counter and put it on, zipping it up all the way to the top. She took her new lab notebook and put it into her backpack and started to walk out.

"So, you want to grab a coffee or something?" he asked.

"Actually, I'm here with Laura, my roommate. She already got one for me. I'm supposed to meet her by the fireplace."

"Oh, okay."

You jerk! What's your problem? It's rude not to invite him. "You are welcome to join us."

"Nah, it's okay. No worries. I'll just say hi. I haven't met her yet." He walked alongside her.

"Oh, right, of course."

Abigail and Nathan approached the tables near the fireplace. Laura was sitting near the back, thumbing through one of her textbooks. She glanced at Abigail, then at Nathan, and then back to Abigail as she smiled awfully big for the occasion.

Please don't embarrass me, Abigail thought.

"Hey," she greeted them both. Then, she said to Abigail, "Nice sweatshirt," with a terrible smirk.

Oh, you'll pay for that. Abigail sat down.

"Laura, this is Nathan…Nathan Ryan."

"Yes, I recognize you from your pictures."

"Hey, Laura. How are you?"

"Great. Nice to meet you. How's the team doing?"

"Oh, good. We're doing pretty well."

"Awesome. You're welcome to sit." Laura gestured to the chair next to Abigail.

"Yes, sorry. Please join us," Abigail chimed in.

"Really, thank you both, but I just wanted to say hello. I gotta grab a coffee myself and get to studying. But I'll see you guys soon." For some reason, he turned to Abigail and had this beautiful grin. Then, he nodded and said, "Abby," before walking away.

She couldn't help but watch him as he walked toward the coffee shop. It was the way he carried himself with his long, lean, muscular legs, his broad shoulders, and his beautifully chiseled arms.

My, he is really something to behold.

He finally disappeared into the shop.

"Hello?" Laura cooed. "Stare much?"

"What? No!" There was far too much protest in her voice.

"Sure, okay. Whatever. You're such a big supporter of the team now." Laura pulled on the arm of Abigail's new sweatshirt. "Did he autograph it for you, too?"

"You're terrible! Stop trying to embarrass me!"

"Well, I don't see you blush like that when you talk about James, do I?"

"I'm not answering that. Just stop it."

"Okay…if you say so."

"I do say so. Now, let me drink my latte in peace."

Laura flipped through her textbook but not before an obnoxiously huge smile spread across her face. Abigail stuck her tongue out at her roommate before she took a sip of her latte that was, at best, room temperature now.

After about an hour of studying and two pumpkin spice lattes later, Abigail and Laura decided to take a little study break.

"I'm going to check my mail. I'll be right back." Laura got up and walked back toward the mailboxes.

Laura came back with an orange piece of paper from her mailbox. "Check it out! The flyers are out, and there is no turning back. This party is happening!"

Abigail glanced at the flyer. "You sure you still want to go to the Halloween Party at Delta Chi?"

"Of course. It will be a blast. The fraternity is known for this bash and costume contest. It's the place to be on Halloween night."

"Really? Who did you hear that from? Bree?" Abigail asked.

"Yes, and tickets are hard to get, but you know Bree and Melissa waited in line last Saturday and were able to get enough for everyone on our floor. The tickets are only five bucks, which is pretty darn cheap. Besides, Bree insisted we all sign up for the costume contest, so I guess this is my way of saying, if I'm in, you're in!" Laura laughed.

"The things I do for you. You owe me one for this. You know that, right? You did see the costumes we have to wear. Laura, there is barely anything to them."

"Well, define *barely*," she said with a smirk.

"Ha, funny. We'll see how you feel when you actually put it on."

The girls had had only a short time to think about their costumes last week. Once Bree had secured the tickets, they had gotten together at a floor meeting to talk about ideas. Bree had shown little enthusiasm for the girls' suggestions and finally proposed they all go as the Ten Little Indians.

"I got it! Brilliant. We are going as the Ten Little Indians. Oh my God, I can't wait to pick out our outfits. We are going to look so hot!" she'd yelled. She'd then run into her room and started calling costume places in New York City.

Unfortunately for Abigail, what she hadn't known at the time was that Bree really meant they were going to go as scantily clad Little Indians.

"It will be fun, and the costumes are not that bad. You're exaggerating!" Laura scoffed.

"We'll see, won't we?" Abigail rolled her eyes at her friend. "Let's get out of here. I think I've had enough studying for one night."

Halloween night, Abigail and Laura were in their room, getting ready for the party. Abigail was hesitant while putting on the outfit Bree had picked out for them. It wasn't so much the low-cut shirt that barely covered her breasts; it was the extremely short pseudo-suede skirt that had Abigail wanting to run away and hide for the night. When she walked over and stood in front of the mirror, Abigail could feel her cheeks burning as Laura's eyes lit up.

"Wow! You look unbelievable," she gushed.

Abigail viewed herself and tried to pull down the skirt.

"Oh, leave it alone." Laura laughed. "It's no use!"

"You're right. I don't know if I can go out to a party like this," she stated, turning toward Laura.

"Oh, yes, you can, and you will!"

"You look great, too, Laura. You really do."

Laura just laughed and smoothed down the miniskirt. "Now, let's get some makeup on and go show Bree how hot we are!" She winked at Abigail as she leaned over her dresser toward the mirror with a mascara wand in her hand.

After putting on the finishing touches of their makeup, they went to Bree's room to get their headbands and feathers.

Bree's eyes lit up as the girls walked in the room.

Melissa cooed, "Oh, you guys nailed it!"

Bree didn't say a word but just politely handed them their headbands and feathers.

"Thanks, Melissa. You guys did, too. Hopefully, we'll win," Abigail said.

"Of course we will win," Bree interrupted. "As the head of the group, I'll make sure of it!" She adjusted her headband in the mirror. "Everyone ready?" she shouted over the music. She started to count all the girls.

Melissa, Abigail, and Laura walked into the hallway.

"I told Logan we were going to this party tonight." Melissa grinned.

"Oh, really?" A sly grin grew across Laura's face.

"Yes, *really*," Melissa said dramatically.

"That's cool." Abigail and the girls headed for the stairs.

Since the football party last month, Melissa and Logan had been hanging out more and getting to know each other. Melissa wouldn't say they were dating, but she did see him often.

"Did Nathan and Webber mention to you that they might try to get tickets?" Melissa said.

"Not exactly. When I saw Webber in class, he didn't say too much, other than stuff about our Bio lab midterm. He said the football guys at the Ridge are having a small party and that he might go there."

"Oh," Melissa said.

"You never know," Abigail quickly added. A part of her was hoping they would come, too, although she hated admitting it to herself that she wanted to see Nathan.

They could hear the loud music coming from the basement as they approached the fraternity house on Russell Street. The backyard was dimly lit, and each girl made her way off the street and down the grass toward the back door. There were two guys in costumes. One was dressed as a doctor, and the other was dressed in a skeleton suit with a scary skeleton mask on. The doctor was taking tickets and handing out red plastic cups for beer, and the other was taking names for the contest.

Bree quickly snuggled up to the skeleton. "We're the Ten Little Indians."

"I can see that." Sarcasm dripped off his tongue.

Bree frowned.

"What's your name?"

"Bree."

"Well, Bree," he said, eyeing her up and down, "you girls look hot. Good luck."

Bree beamed as she took her cup from the guy dressed as the doctor.

"Thank you, Doctor," she cooed.

The door to the basement swung open. All ten of them walked down the stairs lined with glowing, carved pumpkins. The party was roaring and completely decorated like something you would see in a movie. Spiders and cobwebs hung in the corners. A fake zombie stood by the back wall, eyes shining in the darkness. A coffin was lying across the pool table and would pop open every so often, revealing the vampire inside. The walls were covered with glow-in-the-dark paint, and the fraternity had placed black lights in the corners, giving the room a dark and eerie feeling. Skeletons hung off nooses from the ceiling, and witches were standing over huge black pots filled with smoke.

This is amazing, Abigail thought. It was even a little scary.

The girls made their way to the back room where the kegs and punch were. Bree, Laura, and Abigail shimmied their way up to the bar covered with cobwebs and waited to be served. It didn't take long before people started to notice all the Indians and their short little outfits, and that included the bartender. He quickly went over to the girls.

"What can I get you, ladies?"

"Four punches, please." Bree handed their cups over.

"Anything for you." He then winked at Abigail.

Her skin prickled. He took their cups and walked over to a gigantic tub. It resembled a huge container you'd pack clothes or books in and put in the attic. He took each cup and dunked them in the tub and then handed the cups, one by one, back to them.

"Four Witch's Brew. Come back soon."

Bree grabbed two cups. "Creep," she said to Abigail as she grabbed the other two cups off of the bar.

"Really," she said dryly. "Ugh."

They both started to laugh. They were turning a lot of heads as they walked back toward the other girls.

"Here you go." Bree handed Laura the cup of sticky red punch.

Abigail noticed more and more people watching them, and she began to feel self-conscious.

She handed a cup to Melissa.

Abigail took a small sip off the top. It was strong and sweet. She swallowed hard.

"Drink up. Soon enough, you'll forget how revealing your outfit is!" Melissa laughed.

Abigail leaned into Melissa. "Is it obvious that I hate this costume?"

Melissa leaned back and said loudly over the music, "Yes!"

Seeming somewhat annoyed that she was not the center of their attention, Bree announced, "I'm going to find the other girls. I'll be back." She grabbed Laura's arm. "Come with me."

It didn't bother Abigail that Bree and Laura had started to get close. She knew Laura was smart enough to see that Bree liked everything to be about her. As long as Bree didn't take advantage of Laura, Abigail would stay out of their way.

Bree and Laura disappeared through the doorway and into one of the other larger rooms. Melissa and Abigail started laughing even harder once they walked away.

"This is the last time I let her talk me into any outfit!" Abigail laughed.

"Me, too!" Melissa said with a chuckle. "We'd better drink these."

Abigail took another sip and then another and another. As she drank the red punch, she thought that it couldn't hurt her to occasionally have some fun.

The DJ announced that the contest would be starting in five minutes. By that time, Abigail was on her third glass of punch, and she had forgotten that she was merely wearing a few yards of material. The girls had all gathered in the back room near the DJ. He'd told the contestants that they each had to walk in front of the crowd, and whichever contestant or group got the loudest cheers would win. The grand prize was one hundred dollars. For an individual, it was huge, but for them, it was merely ten dollars each.

Oh well, Abigail thought.

Bree scanned the group of contestants and then grouped the girls. "Now, girls, we are going to win this. Understood?"

She gave one of those mean-mom smiles, like the one where your mom told you something but wouldn't accept anything less from you than to say yes. So, they all nodded their heads.

With that, Bree quickly grabbed Abigail's hand. "You're up front with me."

"Me? What? Why?"

"Oh, come on, Abigail." Bree rolled her eyes. "You know you're the next best-looking one, and if we want to win this, you cannot be stuck in the back, next to Casey."

She was referring to one of their floor mates who was not unattractive. Sure, she wasn't a model, but she was pretty. Abigail was about to protest when the DJ made the statement that the contest would be starting in one minute.

Bree held tight on to Abigail's arm.

The DJ introduced each person or team as they walked through the room. A total of fifteen sets or individuals had entered. The girls were the last to go, and as the broadcast was made, the rooms erupted in a painfully loud cheer. The fraternity guys hollered at the top of their lungs. Finally, the DJ had to cut them off, so he could say that the Ten Little Indians were the 1995 Delta Chi Halloween contest winners.

Who could have predicted that? Abigail rolled her eyes.

Bree shrieked and ran up to the DJ to grab the prize. The DJ asked the girls to take a bow one more time. Abigail's face began to burn red, and she quickly grabbed Melissa and headed back to the room with the bar. She had to get away from all the noise, and besides, this was really Bree's moment.

As the girls snuggled up to the bar, Abigail was more than relieved that it was all over. "Oh my, I'm so embarrassed," she said loudly to Melissa.

"No, no," someone interjected in a deep voice. "I'm pretty sure I can top that."

Abigail turned around to see Webber standing there, dressed as Luke Skywalker.

"Webber!" she shrieked and threw her arms around him.

He hesitated at first but then hugged her back.

"You girls look amazing." Logan stepped around from behind Webber. He was dressed as Han Solo. He gazed at Melissa.

"Oh, Logan, you're too funny." Her skin pinked with approval.

"Well, I'm not trying to be."

"You guys decide not to go to the Ridge?" Melissa asked.

"Yeah." Webber glanced over his shoulder. "Nathan didn't feel like going and heard this party was better."

They all turned in the direction Webber was and saw Nathan, dressed as none other than Clark Kent. He was making his way through the crowd toward them. He was getting the usual handshakes and acknowledgments from students. He spotted them, and within a moment, he locked eyes with Abigail. He pushed up the black-framed glasses on his face. Abigail turned a thousand shades of red as he walked right toward her.

"Hey, guys," he greeted everyone.

"Hey, Nathan," Melissa said. "Clark Kent?"

"The one and only." He grinned.

It was amazing. He actually did resemble Clark Kent. He opened his white button-down shirt a bit and revealed a Superman T-shirt underneath. It was quite charming, to say the least. He went over the bar and asked for a beer. He took it and walked back over toward Abigail. He leaned down closer to her, but she nervously moved away.

"Hey." He tried to bring her within earshot.

She peered up at him as he came even closer.

"Hey."

He started to say something, but she couldn't hear him over the music.

So, he whispered loudly in her ear, "You shouldn't be dressed like that."

Embarrassed, she just gawked at him. At first, he seemed serious, and then he slowly lifted his eyebrows and smirked.

"I have X-ray vision, you know."

She merely choked, as she had been taking another sip, trying to avoid his eyes.

"Although I'm not sure I'd need it." He eyed her up and down.

She wanted to crawl into a hole. At this point, he had already seen her half-naked in her dorm room, and now, this outfit.

Ugh, I wish I could just disappear.

"Well, it wasn't my idea," she said flatly, trying not to expose herself even further.

"Let me guess. The girl who pulled you to the front—what's her name again?"

"Bree. Oh God," she moaned. "You saw that?"

"Yep!" He laughed. "Every bit of it. Not that it was a bad thing, believe me. You guys won for a reason. Did you see the guy dressed as Pee-wee Herman? No way was that guy going to win. No way."

"Well, I don't think it's too hard to impress this crowd." She scanned the crowd, getting a glimpse of all the people dressed in their silly costumes.

"You impressed me, if that means anything. But, last time I saw you, you were wearing a football sweatshirt, and you impressed me then, too."

Oh my God. Is he flirting with me?

"Oh, well, thanks, I think." She stumbled over her words. She wasn't usually at a loss for intelligent things to say, but she was all shy and mushy around him. *Come on, Abigail, say something smart.* "Hey, I saw that Emmitt Smith has, like, a lot of touchdowns already."

"You saw that?" He was clearly smirking.

She felt even stupider because she'd brought up football. *Really, Abigail? Now, you've resorted to talking about football. Who are you?*

Noticing her squirm, Webber came over. "You guys okay?"

"Yeah, sure," Abigail said, clearly not willing to make eye contact with Nathan.

"Abby was just telling me how she picked out the outfits for all the Indians." Nathan laughed.

Horrified, she yelped, "I did not!"

Abigail blushed as Webber let out an uncomfortable laugh. Still, he stood there, glancing back and forth at Nathan and Abigail.

What is Webber thinking about? And why is he looking at the two of us like something is wrong?

She observed him as he stared off. A glum expression came over his face.

"You okay?" she asked.

Webber looked between her and his roommate. With a serious expression, he said, "I wonder what her boyfriend would think of her dressed like that. Huh, Nathan?" His laugh was deep and cold. He barely made eye contact with Abigail as he took a long sip of his drink.

Abigail was paralyzed by his comment. Worse, she felt like a complete idiot for standing there, dressed the way she was, while flirting with someone—or at least, it'd seemed like flirting.

She glared at Webber, but her mind was absolutely blank.

Nathan was about to say something when, suddenly, a beautiful girl dressed as a sexy nurse with long, wavy brown hair and bright red lipstick pulled on Nathan's arm. He spun around, and without even a bit of hesitation, he threw his arms around her and gave her the biggest hug

Abigail had ever seen. The beautiful girl squealed as he lifted her off the floor.

"Whoa, Superman!"

Nathan put her down. He turned to introduce her to the group with his arm draped over her shoulders. He was grinning from ear to ear.

Before he could make his introduction, Abigail quickly slipped past them.

I can't stay here. I can't endure any more humiliation. I think I've had just about enough. She made her way up the stairs and out into the night. *I knew this party would suck.*

Abigail walked home alone. She would have preferred not to be alone on Halloween night while dressed like this, but she was too angry and, quite frankly, embarrassed to stay at the party. She stuck to the main walkways, each one lit with an emergency button, should she need it. This gave her a false sense of safety, but regardless, she hurried home.

She couldn't believe what a terrible night this had turned out to be.

Why did Webber turn so quickly on me? When he saw me that day, he must have just assumed that James was my boyfriend. Still, to never ask me and then to say it the way he did is just wrong. I thought we were friends. So, was he just saying that to be a jerk? Do I give off the vibe that I'm trying to hide the fact that I do have a boyfriend?

And Nathan…I didn't know he had a girlfriend. Then again, why would I? She huffed her way back toward her dorm. She didn't care that it was freezing out, and almost every inch of her body was exposed to the air.

I don't talk about James, and Nathan doesn't talk about…what's her name? It's not as if he owes me some explanation for it. After all, we hardly know one another, she thought, still moving full speed ahead.

But why did he always seem to flirt with me or ask me to grab coffee. Is that just how he is? Maybe he is a typical athlete, thinking he can get whatever girl he wants, whenever he wants. Ugh, I don't envy his girlfriend, not one bit.

Abigail keyed into the main door of her dorm and ran up the stairs to her floor. As she passed Melissa's room, she wrote a note on the white board on her door.

I'm home. Going to bed. Abigail.

She hurried into her room, closed the door, and turned out all the lights, except the small light that hung over her bed. She literally tore off her costume and left it in a heap on the floor. She picked up her phone and dialed James's number. It rang and rang until his answering machine finally picked up. She contemplated hanging up but decided to leave a message.

"Hey, it's me. Happy Halloween." She tried desperately to come up with something clever to say next. She didn't feel like talking, even to a machine. "We won the costume contest. Big deal, right? Well, I'll see you soon during Thanksgiving break. Good night."

With that, she hung up, climbed into bed, and pulled her covers up to her chin. She closed her eyes, wishing she could just erase this stupid day from her memory.

An overwhelming sense of disappointment and hurt washed over her. She was confused and sad. *Or is this jealousy?*

Am I jealous that Nathan Ryan has a girlfriend? Maybe Webber was just trying to protect me? Maybe Nathan flirts with everyone, and Webber knows it, so he was just trying to keep me out of harm's way. Did I just overreact, or is there something more to how I'm feeling?

Am I so bothered because Webber called James my boyfriend? That seems really stupid at this point. We've been dating for, like, a year. But why am I not shouting it from the rooftops? Why do I keep feeling like I am just going through the motions with James? Ugh, what should I do?

Why can't I feel the way Nathan seemed to feel when he picked up what's-her-face? He was so excited to see her, and her, him.

Why am I always feeling like I'm two steps behind? I am capable of love, aren't I? God, I hope so.

Fourteen

NOVEMBER 5, 1995

"Abigail, wait, will you?" Webber shouted, sounding desperate.

She hesitated before she got to the back door of the lab. Then, she waited for the class to clear out before she turned around to face him.

"Look," she began.

He stopped her immediately "No, let me talk. I have something to say." He was incredibly nervous as he took a deep breath. "I'm sorry, Abigail. I am. I don't know why I said what I did."

"Really? You have no idea why you said that?"

Only he did know. *Oh, Abigail. Don't you know? You are intelligent, sweet, and absolutely beautiful. Only you don't seem to know just how gorgeous you are. Unfortunately for me, that makes you even lovelier.*

And what's worse is that you became my friend long before you knew Nathan existed. So, I've never had to question your motive for being my friend. Besides, no girl who looks like you even glanced at me in high school, let alone spent time with me.

When you hugged me at the Halloween party, I stupidly thought, just maybe, I had a shot with you, but then I saw you and Nathan, and I just knew I'd never stand a chance. He's always asking me if I've seen you. Jesus, I can't blame the guy!

But the thought of not being your friend is worse, far worse.

In a perfect world, he would, right here and now, profess his adoration for her, but regrettably, if he did, he might ultimately risk the friendship they had.

So, instead, he simply admitted, "I'm an idiot. Can we please just be friends again? I promise you, I'll never be a shithead like that again. You know I can't handle my alcohol."

Her features softened, and he started to feel like maybe he was getting a second chance.

Her shoulders dropped as she let out a big sigh. "Oh, Webber, I have no idea why I reacted the way I did. I was so embarrassed in that costume to start with, and I was such a lemming for going along with Bree's stupid idea anyway. So, half of me was already in a mood. I guess I owe you an apology, too."

"No need to apologize to me. I get it. I was a jerk, and I'm sorry, truly."

"Me, too. Yes, of course we are still friends. I could never stay that mad at you."

She walked back over toward their lab bench, and they both sat down in their stools. Inside, he was brimming with happiness.

"Good, I'm so glad. These past few days have been killing me." He gazed at her with puppy-dog eyes.

"Killing you?"

"I know; I know. What I mean is, we didn't have class Tuesday, and here it is, Friday. I didn't want to bother you. Nathan said—"

She cut him off, "Nathan said what exactly?"

"Uh, well, he thought I should just give you some space and that maybe because you have a boyfriend, you didn't need us bothering you."

She was about to speak but stopped.

Maybe Nathan knew her better than she'd thought, or then again, maybe he didn't know anything about her.

"What? Did I say something wrong again?"

"No, I guess I just didn't know your roommate was such an expert."

Webber snickered. "Yeah, I know, right? He'll be the first one to tell you he has no clue."

Abigail laughed, too. She started to get up from the bench and head to the door. "I guess, if you think about it, who does, right? Who says I know any better?"

As she stood there, Webber noticed a touch of sadness in her expression. He decided not to press her. He was just getting back on her good side, and that was one place he always wanted to be.

"Hey, I'll see you soon, okay? I gotta run and check my mail."

"Yeah, of course." He tried to sound casual. Then, he added, "Pretty cool about Melissa and Logan, huh?"

She stopped in the doorway and turned. "Yeah, it is pretty cool. They are cute together. I'm happy for them. I guess something good did come out of Halloween after all."

A lovely, genuine smile came across her face, almost melting his heart in the process.

"See ya." He put his notebook in his bag.

"Bye." Then, she was out the door and up the stairs.

Once he knew she was out of sight, he let out a huge sigh of relief. This past week, he had repeatedly played that conversation in his head in agony.

He had been so worried that she would tell him to kiss off, that she didn't want to be friends with him anymore. The thought of it had been killing him, but Nathan was right after all. Maybe she had just needed some time to cool off. As long as she knew he was sorry in the end, that was all that truly mattered to him.

Webber walked out of the lab and back to his dorm room. When he opened the door, Nathan was on the phone.

"Great. Yes, that sounds awesome. Thanks, Dad. I appreciate you saying all that." Nathan listened to the rest of what his father had to tell him. Then, he said, "Yes, of course. Love you, too, Dad. Talk to you soon. Bye."

He greeted Webber as he put the receiver down, "Hey."

"Hey, what's up?"

"Oh, nothing. That was just my dad telling me that Ward Daniels is finalizing the feature on me that the paper plans to print over the holidays." His eyes were wide with excitement.

"Awesome news!"

"Yeah, Mr. Daniels called my father a few days ago and asked if he could stop by for an interview and photos. He wanted to pay a visit to my house and ask some questions about my childhood. He took pictures of the house and town—the places I used to hang out. I'm sure my dad was so eager to tell him all about me. Oh, to be a fly on the wall during his visit!" A smile crept across Nathan's face as he reflected upon all his father had just told him.

"That's great, man. Congrats."

"Thanks, Spidey. I appreciate it." He plopped down on his bed and kicked off his sneakers.

Webber walked over and put his lab book down on the desk. He seemed wiped.

"You okay?" Nathan asked.

"Who? Me? Yeah, sure." Webber then professed, "I finally talked to Abigail."

Nathan perked up. "Oh, yeah? What did she have to say?"

"Nothing really. We're still friends, so I guess I'm back on her good side." Deep down inside, he knew that was all they were meant to be—just friends. But it stung all the same.

"Good. I figured she would forgive you. You didn't mean anything by it." Nathan was trying to reassure him that all was well.

"I know. It was just stupid."

Abigail walked to the student union to get a cup of coffee. She entered the main doors and walked into the coffee shop. It was busy for a Friday afternoon. She placed her order at the counter and waited for the girl to give her the cup of pumpkin spice latte. It was her favorite.

Once she paid, she left and walked past the bookstore, the help desk, the radio station, and finally reached the fireplace where she usually sat with Laura. She went behind the tables to the hallway where the mailboxes were all lined up in numeric order. With her book bag slung over one shoulder and the cup of hot coffee in her hand, she went up to number thirty-two forty-eight. She could see through the slit in the mailbox that she had a small package. She put her bag down and took out her mailbox key. She opened it and retrieved the two pieces of mail and the small package. One was a card from her grandmother. She was excited to see it, as she knew there was probably money inside, but what really grabbed her attention was the small package postmarked from the University of New Hampshire. It was from Rebecca, her best friend from back home.

Balancing the hot coffee and her mail, Abigail walked over to a small table near the mailboxes and put her coffee and bag down. She tore open the small package. She read the note first.

Abigail,

All is well here at UNH. Classes are going great. I met a guy named Connor. He is awesome, and you'll love him. I can't wait to see you over Thanksgiving break to catch up. I miss you terribly. Made this mixed tape for you with all the songs we love. Hope this tides you over until we are home again.

Love you,

Rebecca

P.S. See James at all lately?

Abigail browsed the inside cover, and all their favorite songs from Alice in Chains, Bruce Springsteen, U2, Pearl Jam, The Pretenders, Sarah McLachlan, Beastie Boys, and Tom Petty were listed. She took her Walkman from her bag and put the mixed tape in. She put on her headphones and instantly began to feel better when the harmonica came through the tiny speakers in her ears as "Thunder Road" began to play.

She put her bag over her shoulder and grabbed her coffee and the rest of her mail. She headed for the back door of the student union. She wasn't quite sure where she was going, but it was Friday afternoon, and she was through with classes until Monday. She started quietly singing the song to herself as she reached for the door. The card from her grandmother slipped out of her hand. As she bent down to get it, the doors swung open, and a group of guys came barreling in. She didn't miss a beat as she swiped the card off the floor and steadied her latte.

She kept singing. She had her head down as she squeezed past them.

She started to walk in the opposite direction of her dorm room, just listening to the loud music. For once, she didn't have a care in the world. It had been a long time since she felt that way, and she had her best friend, Rebecca, to thank.

Tank walked out of his Economics class with Jason and Marcus. A few other players joined them as they walked down the stairs and toward the student union to grab a bite to eat before their team meeting. The campus seemed quite busy for a Friday afternoon, and in the distance, Tank could see that the union was packed.

"Hey, guys, I gotta check my mail before we grab a bite, okay?" Tank announced.

The others followed him as he started to walk in the direction of the side doors, mumbling in unison about their mail.

Jason yelled to Marcus, "Hey, Marcus, go long!"

He drew his arm back and tossed his empty water bottle in Marcus's direction. He caught it and tossed it back.

"Now, see if you can catch it with me on you!" Tank yelled as he caught up to Marcus.

Jason again drew his arm back and yelled in their direction, "Ready?"

Marcus took off toward the union with Tank only feet from him. Jason tossed the bottle in the air. It launched about twenty feet toward the doors, and with a slight push off Marcus, Tank jumped up and caught it. Steve, one of the other players, and Jason came running toward him for a round of high fives.

Steve jokingly tried to push Tank over. Steve was considerably smaller than Tank, so Tank pretended to fall back as the others pushed their way through the doors and toward the mailboxes. Jason grabbed Marcus and pulled him to the side. They nearly missed a girl as she bent over to pick up mail she'd dropped. It appeared as though she never heard them coming.

Steve pushed his way through, but Tank held the door as the girl, still not noticing them, ducked past them and out the door. She had her headphones on and never even acknowledged they were there.

As she moved past Tank, an ache settled in his chest. She was singing a song, and it reminded him of something, but he couldn't quite put his finger on it. *I feel as though I've lived through this moment before.* He stood there for a second as she walked away. With her long blonde hair, her tan skin, and her voice, he recognized her, but he could not for the life of him remember from where. A chill ran up his spine.

He felt a slap on his arm.

"Quit drooling, dude." Jason chuckled.

"What? Huh? Uh, no." His voice started to fade as he kept his eye on the girl.

"You see a ghost or something? Come on!"

"No—I mean, I think I know her," Tank said finally. *Did I meet her at a party? Is she in one of my classes? No, it's something more. Something much more.*

She disappeared around the corner. For a moment, he considered chasing after her but then quickly shrugged it off.

"Okay, well, I'm heading in." Jason entered the student union.

"Sorry, I'm coming." He started to follow Jason in. "I'm coming," he repeated but not before squinting in her direction one more time just in case he might see her again.

Fifteen

Abigail stuffed her laundry into her bag, and as she tried desperately to zip it, she had Laura pull the sides together.

"You sure you don't just want to use my laundry bag?" Laura asked.

"No, but thanks. You'll need it." Abigail pulled the zipper closed. "See? All set!"

Laura chuckled as she let go of Abigail's bag. "What time are your parents coming to get you?" she asked, glancing at the clock.

"In about an hour. You?"

"I think they'll be here sooner. Probably by eleven." She sat down on her empty bed.

Their room was bare. Both girls had stripped their beds and packed up as much laundry as they possibly could. They had emptied out the mini fridge as well. They wouldn't be back for about a week.

"It doesn't take long to get to Stockbridge, right?" Abigail asked.

"Not too long. Three and a half hours or something like that."

"About the same time to Glens Falls. Easy ride." Abigail walked around the room, straightening up a little here and there.

"You planning on seeing James when you're home?"

"Oh, yeah. We are getting together this weekend."

"Great. And Rebecca?"

"Of course. I can't wait to see her!" Abigail exclaimed.

The phone rang, and Laura leaned over to pick it up.

"Hi! I'll be right down. Nope, don't need any help," she said.

Abigail picked up one of her bags.

Laura hung up the phone. "Thanks. Appreciate it." She hoisted her bag on her shoulder.

"Of course. I want to say hello to your parents, too." Abigail headed toward the door.

Abigail and Laura walked down the hallway to the elevators.

"Hang on one second." Laura approached Bree's door.

It was partly open, and Laura could hear music playing, so she knocked.

"Come in!" Bree yelled in a sickly-sweet voice. "Hello, girls," she said as they entered the room. "You both leaving?"

"No, just me. I wanted to say good-bye and happy Thanksgiving." Laura put down her bag to give Bree a hug.

Bree leaned over and patted Laura on the back, the kind of no-body-contact type of hug. It was one of the fakest hugs Abigail had ever seen, but still, Laura hugged Bree back.

"My father is driving from Manhattan and should be here soon, too," Bree said as she let Laura go.

"Have a great Thanksgiving, if I don't see you before you leave," Abigail said politely.

"You, too." Bree didn't lean in for a hug with Abigail.

With that, the two girls walked out of Bree's room.

The lobby of their dorm was filled with students waiting for their parents to arrive. Many stood by mounds of luggage and laundry bags, appearing exhausted and in much need of sleep and real home-cooked food. Laura waved anxiously to her parents, who were waiting in the lobby, as she stepped off the elevator. Her mom seemed as though she might burst into tears at the sight of her. She ran to her mom and gave her a huge hug.

"Girls!" Laura's mom boasted. "You both look well!"

Over the past months, Abigail had gotten to know Laura's parents well. Each time they'd called, they had been friendly and engaging on the phone. They always asked about school, classes, friends, and so on. They were kind, and Abigail was really starting to like them.

"Thank you, Mrs. Chase. So nice to see you again."

She gave them both a hug, too, before Laura's dad grabbed the heavy bag of laundry from her.

"You tell your parents we said happy Thanksgiving," Laura's father added.

"Of course. I hope you all have a nice Thanksgiving as well. Laura was telling me about the great tradition you have with her cousins, aunts, and uncles each year. Sounds like so much fun!"

"It is. Hey, maybe you can come home with Laura next year and partake in our annual family board game competition." Her mom laughed.

"Oh, Maureen, you make it sound so formal," her dad said. Then, he turned to Abigail. "I wouldn't say it's a competition. It's more like a bunch of siblings trying to see whose college education is actually worth the money."

"Dad, you shouldn't say that here! I am at this school, you know." Laura chuckled.

"Obviously, this school is worth it," her dad responded with a roll of his eyes.

"Oh, Rick, cut it out." Mrs. Chase playfully tapped him on the arm.

"I sure have missed you guys." Laura gave her parents a loving smirk.

Then, she turned and gave Abigail a hug. As she did, Abigail could see the front doors over Laura's shoulder. She thought she was mistaken as she saw Nathan walking through the door. Her cheeks flushed as he caught her eye. He waved. He was wearing jeans and a navy sweater. The sweater fit nicely, outlining his chest muscles. He must have just gotten out of the shower because his hair was wet and slicked back. It wasn't often that Abigail saw him in regular clothes. In fact, most of the time, he was in sweatpants or running shorts.

He looks nice. Actually, nice *is too common a word for him. More like awesome.*

Laura stepped back and could see Abigail's red face. "What is it?" she asked with a look of concern.

"Nothing, nothing," she whispered.

Following her eyes, Laura turned in the direction of the doors and saw Nathan.

"Ah," she said under her breath.

Nathan approached them. "Hey."

"Hey, Nathan," Laura said.

Her father turned and instantly recognized him. "Oh, Nathan Ryan, right?" Mr. Chase reached his hand out to shake Nathan's.

"Yes," he responded politely. "Are you Abigail's parents?"

"No, Laura's," Mr. Chase said, pointing to her.

"Yes, these are my parents, Rick and Maureen," Laura said.

"Ah, great. You all heading out soon?" he asked. He glanced at Abigail, who still had not said a word.

Abigail noted how comfortable he seemed with meeting strangers.

"We are right now." Laura stared at Abigail and then slightly nudged her in the ribs.

Abigail finally spoke, "Yes, hi."

"You ready, honey?" Mrs. Chase asked.

"Yeah. Have a great Thanksgiving, you guys." Laura waved to Nathan and Abigail.

"You, too. Nice to meet you."

"You as well, Nathan. Great season," her father said.

"Thank you, sir. We've done all right this year."

"You sure have." Mr. Chase picked up the laundry bag and swung it over his shoulder.

"Bye," Abigail said.

With that, Laura and her parents headed to the side doors that led to the guest parking lot. Abigail and Nathan stood there, watching.

Once out of earshot, Mrs. Chase asked, "So, is Abigail dating him?"

"Oh, no. Nope, not at all," Laura said in protest.

"Could have fooled me," Mr. Chase said with a sarcastic tone.

"Why do you say that?" Laura asked.

"Oh, honey." Mrs. Chase gave her daughter a slight smile. "He's smitten with her, and she…well, she doesn't even know what hit her."

"Cat got your tongue?" Nathan asked.

Abigail blushed when he glimpsed at her.

I must be making her uncomfortable.

Only he couldn't stop doing it. He had to look at her. She had on a tight, long-sleeved white shirt and a pair of gray corduroy pants that fit her perfectly. He had not seen her since Halloween night, and he just knew he had to lay his eyes on her before she left for the holiday even if it did seem to make her uneasy. Nathan knew he could no longer keep asking Webber about her. He worried it might become too obvious to Webber that he was interested in her.

"Sorry. No—I mean…" She searched his face. "What are you doing here?"

"Just making my rounds," he lied.

"Oh, yeah, of course." Somehow, his comment disappointed her.

"You leaving now, too?" he asked, knowing full well that she wasn't.

According to Webber, who got the privilege of talking to her in class, she would not be leaving for at least another hour.

"Nope. Just came down to help Laura and to say hello to her parents."

"Cool, cool." Then, he said sarcastically, "Since you asked, I'm not leaving for a few more hours."

His white teeth gleamed, and she couldn't help but laugh.

"I'm sorry. And you? You're leaving in a few hours, I assume? I hope you have a great Thanksgiving."

"Thanks."

"I've got to finish packing." She glanced toward the elevators.

"Oh, great, I'd love to help."

She blushed a thousand shades of red. She didn't say a word as he followed her toward the elevators and got in. They rode up in silence. When they got off on her floor, they walked down the hallway to her room.

"So, what ya got planned for the holiday?"

"The usual, I think." She struggled to get her key in the lock. "Come on," she said in frustration to the door.

She couldn't open her door.

He scrutinized her for a few more seconds. "Could that be the wrong key?"

"No, of course not." She tried again to force the key.

It wasn't until she noticed him staring at the key and laughing that she realized she was in fact trying to use her much smaller mailbox key in her door lock. She burst out in the most uncomfortable yet sense-of-relief kind of laugh. Nathan noted her incredible, silly laugh, and he began to chuckle. They began to laugh harder, so much so that a few of the girls on their floor stuck their heads out, wondering what was happening in the hallway.

Just as she finally got to the right key and opened her door, Bree peeked out her door. She observed with a frown as Nathan and Abigail went into her room, laughing hysterically.

"I'm so embarrassed." Abigail wiped the tears from her eyes.

"Ha! Well, at least I was here to help." He sat down in Laura's desk chair.

Hesitating a moment, Abigail sat down in her desk chair and faced him.

"So, I hear everything is okay with you and Webber."

"Yeah. We're fine, of course."

"I just wanted to be sure you guys smoothed it over."

"Water under the bridge."

"Good. Hey, for what it's worth, I hope I didn't upset you in any way. I guess I just wanted to say I'm sorry if I did, and…" He hoped it wasn't too obvious to her that he wasn't making his rounds. He'd come here to see her. He had something he wanted to say.

But why do I care so much? After all, she is seeing someone else.

But it had been bothering him for weeks, and he needed to say he was sorry, just in case.

She intently gazed at him. He began to squirm in his seat. Her navy eyes, the way they appeared right now, were so beautiful and warm that he was completely drawn to her. He wanted so desperately to ask her what she was thinking. But something stopped him.

She is not mine. I can't ask her for her thoughts. She hardly knows me.

Up until now, their conversations had been so light and carefree.

"Anyway"—his eyes shifted back and forth—"I just wanted to say that."

She finally let him off the hook. "Well, I appreciate that, but I'm fine. It was no big deal."

They were silent as they both peered out on the west end of campus. Cars drove by with backseat windows packed with suitcases and laundry bags. For the first time, Nathan was surprisingly sad about leaving for the week.

Am I sad perhaps because I know I'll have to exit this room and leave her?

He viewed her out of the corner of his eye for a few moments. She was deep in thought, and he wasn't about to interrupt. She turned back toward him and smiled.

"So, are you happy about going home?" he asked.

"Yeah, I guess. Mixed feelings."

"Where is home, by the way?" He realized he had never asked her that.

"Glens Falls, north of Albany."

"Oh, yeah, I know where that is. I played in a football tournament there a few years ago."

"Oh cool. I love where I'm from. Lots to do around Glens Falls and Lake George in the summer. I'm also close to Saratoga Springs, which is just the best place to see concerts outside and..." She realized she was rambling. "I'm sorry. Where are you from?"

"No, don't be sorry. Sounds like I'll need to go back again. But I'm from Halifax, Pennsylvania," he said.

"Nice."

"I like it. I'm looking forward to going home. I *need* the rest."

"I bet. You've had a great season so far, right?" she asked, only half-guessing that he had.

"You still don't follow football, huh?" He chuckled.

"Sorry, not really, but I did go to some games." She shrugged. "I even went to that game in the rain."

"You did?"

"Well..." She considered her words. "I am friends with the quarterback."

As the words moved from her lips, he saw her cheeks flush with heat.

"Yeah, I guess you are."

He regarded her, trying desperately to read her. She was a mystery. Then again, he was glad that she thought of them as friends. Maybe he had tried too hard this past month not to seem like her friend because he knew she had a boyfriend. But he was starting to feel silly about all that now. They were friends. So, he figured this would be a good time to ask.

"Is your boyfriend from back home?"

He noticed how her reaction switched. The color moved from her face, and she grew a bit somber.

"Yes. He goes to SUNY Albany."

"Ah, I see."

"You see what?"

He leaned over, put his elbows on his knees, and regarded her square in the eyes. "That's why you're having mixed feelings." Before she could protest, he added, "I get it. I do. You're not sure if things are going to be the same. Who knows? Sometimes, they are, and sometimes, they aren't. Just go easy on yourself. Don't think too much about it and see how it goes."

He even surprised himself that he'd had the gall to bring up her boyfriend. If nothing else, he had hoped she would say it wasn't true, that Webber was mistaken. But she didn't. At a minimum, he wanted her to feel more comfortable around him, so they could be better friends, if that was all that was in the cards for them.

Nathan wanted her to leave for Thanksgiving, thinking he was thoughtful and easy to talk to. Despite the fact that she barely spoke around him, he wanted to make her feel a bit at ease.

She leaned back in her desk chair and again gazed outside. She let his words soak in. Her face softened. "You're right. Thanks. I needed that."

"You're welcome, Abby."

She turned and smiled at him. A warm rush came over his body. It was the first time she was viewing him with a totally relaxed expression, and all he could think of was how much he wished she'd go home and dump her boyfriend. But he knew he didn't have the courage to say that to her.

He started to stand up.

"You're leaving?" she asked, sounding disappointed.

"Yeah, aren't you?" He glanced at the clock on her wall. *Wow, an hour has passed already.*

"Yeah, I guess I am." She also stood up.

"Oh, hey, keep an eye out for the article this week. It's coming out over Thanksgiving." He was grinning ear to ear.

"Oh, that's great news. Good for you. I will definitely do that."

"Cool, well…have a good one."

"You, too."

With that, he turned and opened the door. "I'll …" he said, hesitating. "I'm sure Webber and I will see you when you get back."

"I'm sure. Happy Thanksgiving, Nathan."

Tank drove down the street near the dorms. So many students and parents were milling about that it was almost impossible to maneuver between all of them. He had been driving around for the past hour, getting gas and snacks and saying good-bye to some of his friends. He knew he was avoiding getting on the road and heading home. He hated the thought of going home to see all his old friends without Jonathan being there. Right now, it would have been him and Jonathan packed up in the truck, driving back home together. Instead, he was alone, just him, and hating every minute of it.

As he drove past his dorm for the third time today, he saw Nathan walking from Willis Hall toward Boyd Hall.

He pulled over and yelled to him out his window, "Hey, Two!"

He could see Nathan's shoulders sink in disappointment as he noticed Tank sitting on the side of the road in his truck. He took his time crossing the street.

"What's up?" Nathan said halfheartedly.

"Nothing. Getting ready to head out. You?" Tank stared straight ahead.

"Yep." Nathan's patience was tiring.

"Cool. Where are you coming from?" he asked.

Nathan hesitated. He wasn't in the mood for an argument but was curious why Tank even cared. "Not that I need to report to you, but..."

Tank turned, an annoyed expression on his face.

"From a friend's room." He glanced in the direction he'd just come from.

Tank could see over toward Willis Hall, and that was when he spotted a girl pulling the glass door open, balancing her laundry bags. A black Jeep Cherokee was parked by the entrance with an older blonde woman in the front seat. The girl glanced up and waved, and Nathan gestured back.

Tank caught sight of her for only a moment before she disappeared on the other side of the Jeep. A strange feeling came over him, and he squinted to see her, but she was too far away to make out. He was sure she was the girl he had seen before.

Why does she seem so familiar?

"Who is that?" Tank asked, still staring ahead, hoping she would come around to the other side so that he could see her better.

"A friend." He tapped on Tank's door a few times before saying, "Happy Thanksgiving," and walking away.

Tank started to yell after Nathan, "Hey, wait!"

But Nathan was already in a slight jog, crossing the street and heading back toward his dorm.

Tank turned back toward Willis Hall and saw the Jeep was gone. He went to put his car in drive when a group of students started to cross in front of him, carrying bags and boxes. He had no choice but to wait for them.

"Damn it!" He pounded on the wheel.

When they were finally gone, he took off down the road. By then, the Jeep was long gone.

"Calm down, Tank," he mumbled. "No need to stalk some girl's parents' car. Jesus, get a grip," he barked to himself.

Frustrated by his own feelings and longing for a break, he decided it was time to get on the road and head back home. His plan was to drop by the Higgins' house before he went home, and he didn't want to show up too late.

A little less than an hour later, he pulled off his exit in Fairmont and took a deep breath. He held it for a moment before letting it out. He drove down Main Street, eyeing all the shops, taking note of any changes. He saw a few kids he knew from high school, but he just beeped and waved as they yelled after him.

Finally, he pulled down Cross Street and then made a left onto Poplar Drive. He parked in front. He sat in his truck, took a deep breath, and then turned off the ignition. He walked up to the front door, nervously swinging his keys around his finger. He knocked. He waited a few minutes before he heard footsteps. He took a step back.

Mrs. Higgins seemed tired, even as her face lit up at the sight of Tank standing on her doorstep. "Thomas!" she cried with sheer excitement. "Come in, come in!"

She held open the door as Tank stepped in.

"Hello."

"Oh my, let me take a look at you!" She laughed. "You are bigger than before, if that is even possible. So handsome, my Thomas. Now, give me a hug."

He bent down and gave her a big hug. She patted him on the back a few times. He could feel her beginning to weep, so he squeezed her tighter. She finally let go and wiped a few tears from her cheeks.

"Can you stay for a bit?" she asked as they walked down the hallway.

"Of course." He took his usual seat at their kitchen table. "How's Will?"

"Oh, doing well. He's out tonight at the movies. He's got a girlfriend now. The Downing girl. Do you know Claire?"

"Nice." Tank's eyebrows went up and down. "Pretty girl, if I remember her correctly."

"Yes, very nice girl, too."

"Good. And Mr. Higgins?"

"Fine. Things are hectic at work for him. He won't be home until later, unfortunately, but you'll come back, right?"

"Yes, I'm sure my mom will be stopping by with a pie this weekend. I'll be sure to come then."

"Wonderful. Yes, I saw your mother last week. We met at the Zonta Club for a scholarship event. They mentioned you were doing well at school and…" She paused.

Tank knew what she wanted to say. He tried quickly to pass it over. "Yes, school is great, and classes are going well." He mustered a smile.

"They'd better be." She laughed as she poured Tank a glass of milk. She walked over to the table and sat down across from him.

There was a brief silence.

Tank glanced around the kitchen. Everything was exactly as he remembered it. He noticed a picture of Jonathan still sat on the windowsill next to a football trophy and a game ball he had won his junior year. Tank's heart sank as he saw the picture of his friend.

"So…" she finally said.

"So…"

She grabbed his hand, and her eyes softened. "It is so good to see you, Thomas."

"You, too. You look good."

She laughed and smoothed down her wavy brown hair. She was tall, a little over five feet eleven inches, and always had just a touch of makeup on because she was naturally beautiful. She never seemed unkempt, except for this past year after Jonathan's passing. Of course, that was understandable.

"Oh, Thomas, you always did try and flatter me."

"I did, didn't I?" He chuckled.

She stared at him. It made his eyes well up, but he fought back his tears. Being here was hard, but it was important. Just by looking at her, he knew how much it meant to her, and that was why he had come right here.

Mrs. Higgins had treated Tank like a son for most of his life, so it wasn't that he felt obligated to visit her. He loved her like a second mother.

"Sorry we haven't come up to see a game this year."

"Don't worry about it," he said sincerely. "Maybe next year."

"Yes, absolutely. Next year, we will come, promise."

Tank and Mrs. Higgins chatted briefly about school and his classes. She even asked if he had a girlfriend.

Tank replied with a cocky tone, "A few."

He got a laugh.

She never brought up football or the season again, and he didn't feel compelled to talk about it either. The conversation was much easier for both of them to handle. It was too painful for them to talk about Tank being at OSU and playing football without Jonathan.

After a few breaks here and there in the exchange, Tank glanced at his watch. It was half past six.

Mrs. Higgins noticed the time. "Well, your mom will be wondering where you are."

"Yes, I should get going, but I have a feeling she knows I'm here."

"So good to see you. We've missed you around here."

"I've missed being here."

He got up from the table and started to walk toward the front door. He turned to her with his hand on the doorknob. A strange sensation, something he couldn't quite place, kept him from opening the door.

"Mrs. Higgins, can I ask you something?"

"Of course. What is it?"

"I hope this doesn't sound weird."

"You have my attention now." She chuckled.

"Or this doesn't upset you."

"Go on." Her tone was much more serious.

"Do you remember if Jonathan mentioned anything to you about a girl, or do you know a girl who is kind of tan and pretty with long blonde hair? Maybe someone close to the family, a friend?"

She stood there. The mere mention of his name changed the air in the room.

"Well, I don't know, Thomas. Not that I can remember. Why do you ask? Something wrong?"

"No. Nothing is wrong. I was just curious; that's all. He mentioned that he…" Tank trailed off. He didn't want to say that Jonathan had mentioned a girl while he was dying. He definitely didn't think that would get him anywhere.

Sensing where Thomas was heading with this conversation, Mrs. Higgins quickly cut in, "Oh, okay. Well, there are a lot of people on my side of the family. Maybe I'm just not thinking of someone. If it comes to me, I'll let you know. Did he say her name?" She cocked her head.

"Abby. He said her name was Abby."

"No, I don't know anyone with that name."

Seeing the pain in her eyes, he decided it was time to go.

"Okay, no biggie." He leaned over and gave her a kiss on the cheek. "I'll see you in a few days."

She patted his arm. "Tell your mom I didn't give you a snack on purpose. Didn't want to spoil your dinner." She laughed.

"I will." He pulled open the door and walked to his truck.

As he drove onto Poplar Drive and headed toward Dixon Avenue, he couldn't help but feel a pang in his heart.

Why am I so concerned about this? Why do I feel compelled to ask about some girl?

When Jonathan had been lying in his hospital bed, dying and obviously hallucinating as he went in and out of consciousness, he could have said any name, but he hadn't. He'd kept saying Abby over and over again.

Tank just wasn't able to let it go. Something told him he wouldn't be able to even if he tried.

Sixteen

NOVEMBER 28, 1995

Abigail woke up late on her last day home. Her dog, Skyler, was still lying at the end of the bed. She was glad Abigail was home and hadn't moved from her side the entire time.

Tomorrow, Abigail would have to head back to school, so she was determined to take full advantage of the solitude. In fact, she was in no hurry to do anything today. It felt so good to sleep in her bed that she actually had to force herself to move. She swung her legs over and let her feet dangle off the edge for a few minutes. She scratched Skyler's head as she stretched her legs out to the side and let out a groan of approval.

Abigail stood and yawned. *Oh, how I'm going to miss my room.*

It was so nice to be home again. She dreaded the idea of packing up all her stuff to return to school tomorrow, so she tackled a few things before she got in the shower.

During these past few days, she had loved taking showers without shower shoes on. She let the hot water run down her skin as she shaved her legs, scrubbed her body, and washed and conditioned her hair. After she toweled off, she pulled on a pair of jeans and a navy T-shirt, and then she put a flannel shirt over it. She ran a comb through her hair and then piled it on top of her head before securing it with a few bobby pins. She viewed herself in the mirror as she applied face lotion, mascara, and a touch of blush and eye shadow.

The clock next to her bed read two o'clock. She had promised James that they would spend the night together before they both went back to school. She'd had a chance to see him a few times before Thanksgiving. The night they'd gotten back home from school, a lot of their friends had gotten together at Chet's Diner for their fish fry. It was where they'd always met on the weekends to hang out and eat.

Abigail and James had spent some time together afterward, but it had been limited. It wasn't on purpose. It had just worked out that way. When they'd first seen one another, Abigail had had butterflies in her stomach, as it had been over a month and a half since they last laid eyes on each other. There had been a lot of bashful smiles and tension, all rolled into one. He'd tried to grab her for some time alone, but all their friends had been so busy asking questions, talking, and laughing that they barely had a moment to say hello. It wasn't until he had taken her home later that he even got a chance to kiss her. So, they'd made a promise that they would spend the rest of their time together.

As she started to walk down the stairs, she could hear her mom and dad talking in the kitchen.

"I don't know, Natalie. She didn't say anything to me."

"But I thought she was dating James," her mother said.

"Maybe she is trying to figure this all out. I don't know. Isn't this your department?" He snickered.

"What's your department?" Abigail reached the bottom of the stairs with Skyler right behind her. "What are you guys talking about?" she asked.

"Uh, well, honey..." her mom began. "We were just curious about—" her mom stammered.

"Oh, Natalie, just show her," her father quipped.

"Show me what?"

"Okay, Edward." She glared at him a bit before turning to Abigail. "This." Her mother handed her the newspaper.

Hastily, Abigail grabbed the newspaper and noticed it was the Sports section.

"And?" she said.

But her mom just stared at her, so she peered back down at the paper, and that was when she noticed the title.

FRESHMAN FOOTBALL STAR TAKES ONONDAGA STATE BY STORM

Oh, so what? She already knew about this, so it was no big deal. She started to glance at the article. "And?" she said again.

"Turn the page," her father encouraged.

Abigail turned the page, and her face turned snow white as she gasped. There she was, on the center page, holding hands with Nathan as they walked out of his dorm room. She sensed fear and disbelief wash over her as the paper slipped from her grasp and hit the floor. Her mother quickly grabbed it.

"What is it, honey? I mean, what a nice picture of you two. You look happy…" She trailed off, seeing her daughter's expression. "Your father and I were just wondering why you hadn't told us you were dating the quarterback."

Her father added, "*Star* quarterback."

Abigail was stunned, unable to make a peep or do anything, as her mother and father spoke. She could not believe that she was in the paper, something the whole world could see. But worst of all, she was holding hands with him.

How the hell did this happen?

"Honey?"

"Abigail, say something. You seem terrified. What's going on?" her father pleaded.

Abigail sat down at the breakfast bar and put her head in her hands. She took a deep breath. The room began to spin.

"What does it say?" Abigail asked flatly.

"What do you mean?" her mom asked.

"What does it say under the picture?"

"Um…" Her mom opened the page again. "It says, *Nathan Ryan celebrates with girlfriend after record-breaking game.*"

"What the hell!" she cried.

"Honey, please tell us what is happening."

"Nothing, Mom. That's just it. He's a friend, and we were only joking. It was late, and he was walking me home because his roommate, who is also my friend—oh God, never mind. What am I going to tell James?"

"Tell him the truth. I'm sure he'll understand," her mother said.

There was a long silence.

"Maybe he didn't see it. He hasn't called, right?" she asked, desperately searching their faces for an answer.

They both just shrugged and mumbled, "No."

"Okay." She took a deep breath. "I'll just have to see what happens, and then when I get back to school, I can figure this all out. If I have to, I can explain to James then, right? Once I know how this happened," she said, sounding frantic.

"Of course, honey. If you say this is just a misunderstanding, then—"

Abigail quickly cut in, "It is. I mean, that is me, obviously, but it's not what you think."

"Okay, honey, we believe you. But just understand how it might seem to others. Does Nathan think you are his girlfriend?"

As she stared at her mom, confusion, embarrassment, and anger all rolled into one ball in her stomach.

Boy, when I get back to school, he is going to have some explaining to do to me. I'm pretty sure he wouldn't have done this on purpose. Then again, didn't he have any say in the article and the photos that were used? How could he do this to me? Did he do this to me? Her mind began to race with a thousand different scenarios. *The worst would be if he were horrified with the picture, if he were mad that it was me in the photo with him. What if his girlfriend sees it? Duh, of course she'll see it. His girlfriend and family were probably all sitting around his kitchen table, waiting to open the newspaper, excited that he had been chosen for the article, and there I was, smack dab in the middle with him. Oh God, she must be furious. What if she comes back to school, and I see her like I did at the Halloween party? Only, this time, she'll want to kill me. What will I do if he's so mad at me that he won't want anything to do with me? This is just awful.*

Tears began to well in her eyes. She regarded her mom and then her dad. Finally, she pointed at the picture her mom held in her hand. "I know exactly how this looks."

She got up, took the newspaper from her mom, and went to her room. She closed the door and then heard a scratch, so she opened it to let Skyler back in. Her parents knew better than to come knocking on her door.

She stayed in her room the rest of the afternoon, packing and just trying to keep her mind off of the potential situation brewing around her. She stared at the picture in the paper of the two of them over and over, playing every possible scenario in her head.

What are the chances of James even seeing it?

On a few occasions, she picked up the phone to call him and just bite the bullet, but she couldn't dial the numbers. She wasn't ready to face the music, and she just didn't know how to explain something so innocent. No matter how she might explain it, she was still holding hands with someone else, and she knew the visual of them would sting James more than anything.

Shortly before five o'clock, the phone rang, and she grabbed it. She let out a deep sigh because it wasn't James. It was Rebecca.

"Oh, good, it's you." Abigail's voice started to quiver.

"Oh, Abigail. I saw the article. What happened? Why didn't you tell me?" Rebecca asked.

"I didn't know anything about it. I have no idea how I got in the article to begin with. He's my friend. I guess it just looks bad. I don't know why he would say I was his girlfriend." Tears formed in her eyes.

"Okay, calm down. You didn't do anything wrong here. It's a mistake."

Abigail cut her off, "But we are holding hands, laughing! How do I explain that?"

"I don't know. Maybe you just don't," she said, her voice sounding defeated.

"What do you mean?"

"Maybe you just tell James the truth and see where it goes. I guess you have to ask yourself what you want."

There was silence on the line.

Finally, Abigail spoke, "I know you're right."

"When is he coming over?"

"Any minute."

"Good luck. Call me later."

With that, Abigail hung up the phone. She got up and crossed the room. She untied her hair and ran a brush through it. She touched up her makeup a bit. If nothing else, she wanted to make herself appear like she had not been crying. She took a deep breath and waited.

Within moments, she heard her mom yelling up the stairs for her. James had arrived.

She took a deep breath, shoved the newspaper into her top drawer, and practiced a smile in the mirror. She was exhausted, but she opened the door anyway and went down the stairs.

A huge sense of relief flooded over her when she saw him standing in the kitchen. He had a pleasant expression on his face when he saw her. He seemed happy, so that made her happy.

"Hey!" he said.

"Hey. Ready to go?"

"Sure am. I won't have her back late." He nodded toward her parents.

"Good to see you, James," her mother said.

"You, too."

Abigail headed down the hall to the mudroom. She grabbed her winter coat off the rack in the corner and slipped it on. *It's getting colder out,* she thought as she buttoned it up. She would have to remember to bring this jacket back to school with her tomorrow.

They walked out the side door and down the driveway to his car.

"What would you like to do? See a movie or—" she asked.

"I have something better in mind, if that's okay."

"Sure, sounds good to me." She was trying to keep her voice light.

She walked over to her side as James said, "Go ahead and try it."

"No!" she said with a laugh. "You got your door fixed?"

He nodded toward the door with a grin.

She gently pulled, and there was no resistance as she swung it wide open. "Never thought I'd see the day."

"Me neither."

He drove for about twenty minutes and turned down the road toward Prospect Mountain in Lake George. She loved it here. It was one of her favorite places to come during the warmer months. Even though the trails were closed, you could still drive up to the summit parking area in the cooler months and take in the panoramic views of Lake George and the entire Adirondack Region.

"Ah, the Adirondack Mountains. I sure have missed being here."

"I know. Me, too. It truly is spectacular up here. I feel sorry for anyone who hasn't experienced this view." He laughed.

"Agree. They don't know what they are missing."

James parked the car. He reached behind him and grabbed a bag. Inside was a large thermos of hot chocolate.

"Great idea."

"Before we have some, you have to give me a kiss." He leaned over toward her. With his free hand, he touched the side of her face and then moved his hand to her neck. He drew her in and softly kissed her. Before letting go, he rested his forehead on hers and then quickly kissed her on the nose. He closed his eyes and took a deep sigh. "Okay." He moved away. "Hot chocolate, coming right up." He grabbed two disposable cups from the bag and poured a little in each cup. He handed one to her.

She took a sip. "Mmm, this is good."

"Compliments of my mom, of course." He took another taste.

He seems to be in a good mood.

Every once in a while, she'd glance at him out of the corner of her eye while he drank the hot chocolate.

He chatted a little about his classes and a few of the friends he had met, but mostly, he sat there, just staring out into the darkness. She hoped that the article wouldn't come up. Once she talked to Nathan back at school, she might be even better equipped to explain how the picture had gotten in the paper.

"You want to get out for a bit?" he asked as they finished their drinks.

"Sure."

"Here, take this blanket." He handed her his car blanket. "Wrap it around you."

She got out of the car and walked to the front. He met her in the middle and grabbed her around the waist. He tightly held on to her before releasing just a bit to gaze at her. He didn't say a word as he leaned down and kissed her. It felt different, only she couldn't explain why. It just did.

He pulled back.

"What is it?" she asked.

He grabbed her face, and with everything he had, he gave her the longest and sweetest kiss she had ever felt. Then, he stood back and took her hand. She could just make out his face by the light coming down from the parking lot posts, and she saw that he was crying.

"James?"

"Don't think I'm a jerk, okay?" he finally said in a barely audible, low tone.

"Okay."

He took a deep breath in and let it out. "I'm breaking up with you."

His words stung like a thousand bees. After all they had been through, *he* was finally ending it.

"What? Why?" Deep down, something about what he'd said wasn't coming as a surprise to her.

His eyes were filled with sadness.

She never saw it coming as he finally admitted, "I saw the article, Abigail."

The past few years began to drain from her body. *This is it. It is finally ending.*

She saw the pain she was causing him, the pain she had caused him, and realized to herself that this was definitely happening. It was over. She knew he was not her meant-to-be. He never was. She couldn't articulate why she'd hung on for so long. She just had.

Now, it was her turn to take a deep breath in and slowly let it out. She owed him an explanation regardless of the outcome. She owed him the courtesy of not clamming up and speaking to him as though he was someone who meant something to her.

"I'm so sorry, James. I never meant to hurt you, and I will forever be sorry that you had to see that. But if you would just allow me the chance to explain…" She felt desperation settling in.

He didn't say a word. She reached out her hand toward him, and surprisingly, he took it.

"It was a fluke thing. We were joking. I had helped him with his drunken roommate, and as we were leaving, the guy took our picture. I didn't think anything of it at the time. I never would do that to you, to anyone. I can only hope"—she pulled on his hand to keep his attention— "that you know me well enough to know that I wouldn't do that to you."

"I'm humiliated, Abigail. Everyone saw the picture of the two of you. All our friends know we've been dating, but there you were, front and center in the paper, holding hands with him!" His voice sounded angry. He took a step back.

"I know; I know. How do you think I felt? It wasn't like I asked for this either."

"Well, did you? You were with him that night, and you looked so happy."

She started to cry. She couldn't help herself. It just hit her like a ton of bricks. All of this was out of her control. There was nothing she could do to stop this. And on top of it all, she had been happy that night and every time she had been around Nathan.

"He was the guy in your room when I called that day, right? What am I supposed to think?"

"I know how bad it seems. My parents were the ones who saw it first. Now, I have to go back to school tomorrow, and I just don't know what to say or do. I mean, it's there for everyone to see!"

"Oh, Abigail, how did you end up in all this? You of all people. I guess I just always wanted us to be perfect so badly, and I should have seen the signs better."

"What signs? What did I do?"

"Nothing," he said. "You did nothing. It's just you. You make people want to be with you, and you don't even know it. I can't blame the freaking guy. Jesus, what did I think was going to happen when we went to separate schools?"

"I'm so sorry. You know I am not like this. This stuff is not me. I just wanted to go to school and study and do well and..." She lowered her head.

She thought of Nathan. She was so angry with him but felt sympathy toward him. It was weird. She knew she'd have to confront him when she got back. She wondered if he was having the same conversation with his girlfriend. She imagined the pain she was causing them. She was so mad at herself for that night. She'd do anything to take it back.

"Did you call him?" James asked.

"What? No, I don't have his number. I don't even...I mean, he has a girlfriend, I think. So, can you imagine..." She trailed off.

"Oh, Abigail."

She couldn't stop crying, so he just put his arms around her and held on tight. It made her cry even more. They held each other, knowing it might be the last time.

She finally asked, "Why did you bring me out here tonight? Why not just call me, yell at me, and tell me you never wanted to see me again?"

He let go of her, searching her face. There was a feeling of sadness in the air as he reached up and wiped away her tears. Then, in a quiet voice, he whispered, "Because I wanted you to be mine one last time."

Seventeen

NOVEMBER 29, 1995

Abigail opened the door to her dorm room. Laura sat at her desk with an open book and her headphones on. She turned as the door shut.

"Hey." Abigail released her laundry bag on the floor.

"Hello. I'd ask how your Thanksgiving went, but by the look on your face, I won't."

"Just great," she said sarcastically. She put her book bag on her desk and slumped into her chair.

Laura turned off her music and turned to her friend.

"James and I are through." Tears welled in her eyes.

"Oh, Abigail, I'm so sorry."

"Yeah, me, too. I really made a mess out of everything. I wrote all about it in my journal. About what a heel I am." She pulled her journal out of her bag and tossed it onto her desk. "God, I just…"

"I know; I know," Laura said.

Then, Abigail noticed the blinking light on their answering machine. "What now?"

"Don't freak out," she said, preparing her friend. "We had eighteen messages."

"What?" she gasped and placed her hand over her mouth.

"Yeah, half of them were just people being rude, telling you not to distract Nathan, he has a job to do as QB1 and the others where just boys being pigs! Such perverts."

"And?"

"Well, you might want to listen to the first two."

She got up, went over to the dresser, and hit the red blinking button. She waited for the message to play.

"Sunday, 3:23 p.m. 'Abby, it's me, Nathan. Please call me when you get in.'"

She could hear the worry in his voice.

"Sunday, 4:38 p.m. 'Abby, it's me again. I'm not trying to bother you, but I have to talk to you. Can you please call me?'"

She hit Delete All and turned off the machine. The clock on the wall said it was almost five thirty. She turned back to Laura.

"Hey, I was going to go to the cafeteria with Bree. Want me to bring you a sandwich or something?"

"Thanks. I'd appreciate that."

"Great. I'll be back in an hour." She grabbed her badge and opened the door. "Everything will be okay."

"Hey, thanks. And don't mention this to Bree, okay?"

"Of course not."

As the door closed, Abigail picked up the phone and dialed Nathan's extension. She half-prayed he wouldn't be there, and the other half prayed Webber wouldn't answer either. Her heart seemed like it was going to beat out of her chest.

He picked up on the first ring. "Hello?" Nathan sounded anxious.

"Hi, Nathan. It's Abigail. I'm back now."

Before she had a chance to speak, he said, "I'll be right over." Then, he hung up.

She put the receiver back down and sat in her chair.

She didn't have to wait long even though it felt like ten of the longest minutes of her life. There was a slight knock on the door.

Nathan pushed the cracked door open. "Hello?"

"Come in."

He walked in, looking frightened as hell. When they finally locked eyes, she could see the pain in his.

"Hey there."

"Hey," was all she could muster.

As he got closer, she couldn't help but turn and stare out the window. The sight of him made her heart race, and she hated him for that. He sat down and then pulled Laura's desk chair closer to hers.

"Will you look at me, please?" he asked.

She wanted to, but the tears were coming, and she was embarrassed.

Trying to break the ice, he commented, "Feels like we were just here, right?" He chuckled a bit.

She nodded, still staring out the window.

He gave her a moment before saying, "You're upset, I can see that, but tell me how to fix this, and I will." His voice was low and sincere.

She didn't move.

Finally, she asked, "You can't fix it, right?"

"Look at me, Abby," he said with sheer desperation.

"I'm afraid, if I do, I'll cry." Her voice trembled as she turned her head.

"Yeah, and?"

"Easy for you to say. You're not the one who feels like crying." Her eyes welled with tears.

"Please," he said. *"Please."*

She could hear the need in his voice.

She turned as a tear dropped on her cheek. She wiped it away.

He appears as though he hasn't slept in days. It made her feel worse, but she knew there was nothing she could do about it.

Even though he'd said he would fix it, they both knew the damage had been done, and they would just have to deal with it.

He tried to make her smile by saying, "I see you still have your good looks!"

She scoffed at his remark. "Please don't."

"Sorry, sorry. I just…I've made things hard for you, and I guess I just didn't know how badly until now. I didn't know how to get in touch with you, so I wasn't sure what to do and—"

"How did this happen?"

"Not sure, but my dad asked a friend who is a lawyer. The best the newspaper can do is publish a retraction, saying you are only a friend, not my girlfriend. You remember when Ward Daniels spoke to us that night and snapped our picture? I never said you were my girlfriend, but I'm sure he just assumed. If they do put something in the paper, it will be printed on the last page, hidden somewhere. Writers don't like to admit they made a mistake, especially Ward Daniels. It is kind of a big deal when he does these spreads on athletes, and I'm not sure he's ever had to recant anything."

"It would probably make you look bad, too," she thought out loud.

"I don't care about that," he said firmly.

"Well, I do. I don't want to be the one to—"

He cut her off, "You just tell me what you want me to do, and I'll do it. We are in the picture, holding hands, so it might be difficult to say that we are not friends or don't know each other. I guess I could just tell him to say we're not dating." He eyed her, trying to gauge her reaction.

"The damage has already been done."

"What do you mean?"

She didn't know why she had said anything. It hadn't been her intention to make him feel worse. She knew it wasn't his problem and that it would only make him feel lower if she told him her boyfriend broke up with her over the picture in the paper.

But I want him to know.

"Well," she stammered, "James wasn't too pleased."

"James?"

"Yeah." She realized she had never told Nathan his name. "He broke up with me," she blurted out.

Nathan was horrified as he sat back in the chair. He ran his hands over his face, and with an exasperated tone, he said, "Oh my God."

"Nathan, it's not—"

"I am so sorry, Abby. I can't say that enough. Is there anything I can do? Can I talk to him?"

What? Why would he want to talk to James? "No. I know that won't help. Nothing will. It's over." She stared out the window. "No going back."

He put his head in his hands and moved from side to side. By the way he shook his head, she could tell that he felt terrible. It dawned on her again that he, too, had probably gone through a similar situation with his girlfriend, and she was making this all about her. Without thinking, she reached forward and touched his arm. He froze for a moment and then glanced up at her.

"Nathan, I'm sorry, too. I'm just as much a part of this, and I can only tell you how sorry I am. I hope I didn't cause you and your girlfriend any issues. I'm sure she was pretty pissed," she said softly.

With a confused expression he asked, "Wait, what?"

"I'm sure she saw it."

"Who?"

"Your girlfriend."

"Wait, am I missing something, Abby? Did someone say something to you?"

"Huh? Who said what?"

"I don't have a girlfriend, Abby. I'm not sure what you're talking about."

"Really? But I thought that girl on Halloween…I just assumed you had a girl…" She trailed off.

She saw the expression on his face. He was telling the truth.

He laughed. "Who? Lexi?"

"I don't know." She suddenly felt defensive.

"Oh, no. Lexi's brother and I were, like, best friends in high school. They're twins, and she was visiting another friend here; that's all. I hadn't seen her in months!" He chuckled, only Abigail did not see the humor.

"Oh, sorry," she said, "I just assumed."

He took a long, hard look at her before saying, "Well, I guess we both know what that feels like, don't we?"

He pulled his chair closer and leaned forward on his elbows. Now, this time, he grabbed her hand. She didn't move a muscle. He reached forward to wipe the wetness from her cheek. Since she still didn't move, he brought his hand up toward her hair and smoothed a strand that had fallen over her face behind her ear.

Finally, he rested his hand on the side of her face. Her cheek was warm, and his hand was surprisingly soft against her face.

"You know," he said with a smile, "of all the girls to be mistakenly linked to, I'm sure glad it was you."

He still hasn't moved his hand, she noticed.

"Really? How come?"

His appearance turned serious as he moved closer to her. He was now on the edge of the chair, and their knees were touching. Her face filled with heat as he kept his gaze on her.

"Because, here you are, right after your boyfriend broke up with you, and you're still allowing me to talk to you." He tried to get a read on her, but it was no use. "I'm sorry, Abby. I don't know if I should stay or go or what. But I hate to see you upset. Is there anything I can do?" He finally let his hand go and rested it on her knee.

"I know it's not your fault. I guess I'm just in a bit of shock from all of this. It was only yesterday this all happened. I just need some time." She sniffed and wiped a tear from her eye.

The exhaustion began to set in. It had been an emotional two days, and it was starting to catch up to her.

"Then, time is what you will get." He got up from the chair and pushed it back to the desk. He stood in the room for a moment.

He walked over to the door and hesitated before he pulled the door open and closed it behind him. He hurried down the hallway to the stairwell where he passed Laura and Bree.

He quickly said, "Hello," and then bounded down the six flights of stairs.

Abigail's head was spinning as she heard the door close.

What have I done?

She felt even worse after he was gone. She knew he was hurting, too, but she could barely help herself, let alone Nathan. Then, James came to her mind as well as all the pain she had caused him. She wanted to call him just to hear his voice, for him to tell her he forgave her and that they would always be friends. Sadly, she knew that was false. She knew he was angry and embarrassed on top of it all. In many ways, she was, too.

Her body ached as she got up from the chair and walked over to her bed. She grabbed her comforter and lay down with it on top of her. She closed her eyes. The salt from her tears stung, and she squeezed her eyes shut. She needed to sleep. She needed to drift off somewhere all this didn't exist. She heard the click of her door open and could hear voices.

"I think she's sleeping," Laura whispered.

"Must be exhausting to be the center of all this attention." Bree snickered.

And with that, Laura closed the door.

Abigail rolled over to face the wall and began to cry.

After class on Monday, Tank headed down to the field house for an optional team workout. He opened the double doors to the weight room and went over to the free weights to do some curls. He bent over and picked up the fifty-pound weights. He stood in front of the mirror, alternating arms as he pulled each dumbbell up toward his shoulder. His biceps bulged with each rep. He'd continued to get bigger, and he loved feeling so strong.

The room was practically empty, so he went over to the stereo and turned up the music.

After about forty-five minutes of arms, he moved over to legs. He sat on the bench and did fifteen reps of quadriceps curls. He was focused today. He needed to get back into the swing of school.

Being home this past week had been difficult. It'd brought back a lot of unwanted memories of Jonathan and him. It had been such a bittersweet week for him.

So, he wanted to push himself through this workout. He was so glad no one was around to talk to. He wanted to just be alone.

Unfortunately for Tank, Jason and Marcus came into the weight room with three other players. At first, Tank tried to ignore them, but he knew he'd have to talk to them. He nodded in their direction as they walked over toward him.

"Hey, dude. How goes it?" Jason said.

Tank got off the bench, grabbed a towel, and wiped his forehead. "Fine. You?" He had a slight edge in his voice.

"Good," Marcus said.

"Have a good break?" Jason asked.

"Yeah, sure." Tank wrapped the towel around his neck.

Pausing for a moment, Jason finally said, "So, did you see the article about Nathan? Nice mention of the team."

"I didn't read *that*," he said, sounding disgusted.

"Oh." Jason turned and picked up some free weights. "Well, it was pretty good."

Tank slammed down the free weights he had been using and stormed out of the weight room and into the locker room.

"What did ya do that for?" Marcus asked.

"What? The guy has always had some problem with Nathan. I mean, you can't be freaking happy for your own teammate?" Jason quipped back.

Marcus's face softened. "I know; I know. It is kind of weird, right?"

"Yeah. Strangely, Tank makes fun of Nathan and doesn't want to work with him. This is coming from me as the backup. I wish I were in there each week, but then again, I wouldn't want to deal with Tank's crap, day in and day out. Sorry, man, but it's not worth it. Tank's got a lot to prove himself. He's only been on the team a few months."

Marcus put down the weights. "I know. If he keeps this up next year, we should tell Coach he's an issue, right?"

"Definitely. Who knows what we could have done this year if he wasn't always giving Nathan a hard time? Enough is enough."

"Yeah, but I guess at least we owe it to Tank to figure it out first, no?" Marcus asked.

"You're the captain of this team, and I'll go with what you say. If it were me, I'd give him a few months, and then I'd be done." Jason turned toward the mirrors again. "Agreed?"

"Agreed."

There were about ten players hanging out in the trainer's room. Tank walked by in a huff but then slowly backed up as he saw a bunch of the players gathered around the back table.

Tank squeezed his way in. "What are you all staring at?"

"Nathan's article," one of the players said.

"Jesus, what's the big deal?" he asked angrily.

"Dude," another player said, "did you see the babe he hangs out with? Smoking hot!"

"What? No. Whatever." He started to turn and walk away, but then he stopped dead in his tracks.

The newspaper was lying on the trainer's table, and he could see the picture of Nathan and a girl. He reached over and grabbed the paper. He froze as he saw her face.

Is that the girl I saw on campus? Is that the girl I saw the other day, getting into the black Jeep?

Under the caption, all it said was *girlfriend*, no name. He knew he recognized her, but he didn't know from where. He took the paper and stormed off into the empty locker room.

Tank sat on the bench in front of his locker and started to read the article. *Maybe, just maybe, her name is mentioned somewhere.*

Nathan had barely slept last night.

Webber had tried on numerous occasions to get information out of him about what had happened between him and Abigail. Nathan had finally just told him straight up that he didn't want to talk about it. He knew he owed his roommate an explanation, but he just couldn't find the words to sum up the events of the past few days.

In the morning, he got up before Webber and went for a run. He needed to clear his head. He ran for at least five miles until he realized that if he didn't turn around soon, he'd be late for his first class.

He showered, grabbed a protein bar from his room, and headed off to class. He had a terrible time concentrating. All he could think about was her.

What is she doing right now? Is she still sad, angry, and maybe even crying? It was killing him.

As soon as his last class was over, he jogged back toward his dorm, hoping that with a stroke of luck, he would run into her.

"Nathan!" a high-pitched voice yelled.

He came to a stop and whipped around.

Damn it. "Hey, Bree," he said halfheartedly.

"I saw your article."

"Great." He wished to God this whole thing would just go away.

"It was awesome. I loved it." Her tone was sickly sweet.

"Thanks, Bree."

"Hey, uh, so you and Abigail?" she pried.

"Oh, no, it's nothing like that," he stammered.

"Ah, I see. So, what about your girlfriend then?"

"What?" He was trying desperately to get away. "I don't have one. I mean, nothing to worry about there!" He wasn't trying to be rude, but he didn't feel like hashing it over with her either. He peered past her toward Willis Hall, hoping to catch even just a glimpse of Abby. Nothing.

"Oh, really. How interesting."

"How so?" he asked.

"Well, I was wondering if you wanted to go out sometime."

Is this girl serious? Does she think I'm interested in her? With a chuckle and some serious sarcasm, he said "Yeah, um—"

"Great!" she said before he could protest. She grabbed his hand, and with a black pen, she wrote her extension on his palm. "Call me, okay?"

Then, he saw Abigail walking into her dorm. *Darn, I missed her.*

"Wait, what?" he yelled as Bree walked away.

He was still staring straight toward the dorm, and within moments, Bree was in his view in the distance. He tried rubbing her phone number off his hand. Then, he noticed the time. There was an optional practice that he wanted to get to. He'd hoped to get down there sooner. He started to jog again, but this time, he went straight down the hill and toward the field house.

He walked into the locker room and noticed it was empty. *Everyone must already be in the gym.*

As he turned the corner to head toward his locker, he noticed Tank sitting on the bench, his head down, reading.

"Didn't know you could read." He laughed.

Tank's muscles became tense. He had an expression on his face that Nathan had never seen before. It was part concern, part anger. Then, he turned and stared straight toward the lockers.

"Ah, reading my article. I won't disturb you." Nathan started to turn the dial on the lock to his locker. He popped open the door and put his keys on the top shelf.

"Who is she?" Tank asked in a low voice.

"What? Did you say something?" Nathan asked.

"Who is *she?*"

"Pardon me?" He wasn't trying to be difficult, but he was confused by Tank's demeanor and line of questioning

"Are you deaf? I asked you, who is she?" Tank started to get up.

For the first time, Nathan was a bit nervous around Tank.

"The girl!" Tank barked in an ungodly loud voice. "The girl in the picture!"

He was angry, and Nathan could not figure out why.

"Dude, you need to chill a bit." Nathan glanced over his shoulder toward Coach's door.

By Nathan's expression, Tank could see that he was serious, and he started to back down.

"Sorry, man. Sorry. Just tell me who the heck she is."

Nathan reacted quickly. There was no choice to be made. For some reason, Tank was interested in knowing who she was in the picture, and it was Nathan's duty to avoid putting her further in harm's way. He had already caused Abigail issues with the photograph. He knew he would anger Tank even more, but he had no choice.

"Sorry, dude. She doesn't want anyone to know." He turned toward his locker.

Tank didn't move, but he could feel his face begin to grow a deep crimson color. His fists clenched, and he took a step closer to Nathan.

Tank laughed, but it was dark. Then, he pointed his finger toward Nathan's face. "Let me tell you something. We're through. You hear me? Done. I'm gonna make sure Jason is our quarterback next year even if I have to take you—"

Tank is taking this too far.

"What? You'll what?" Nathan's voice was raised to a decibel it had never been before, except for on the field. He had never yelled at anyone his entire life, let alone another teammate. "You're gonna take me out? Huh? Is that what you're saying?"

Tank just grunted, "Yes."

"Dude, you need—"

"Hey! Hey!" Coach Bromley yelled. "What the hell is going on in here with you two? Tank, move back now!" he yelled. "Get your crap and get out!"

Tank slowly stepped back, never taking his eyes off Nathan for a second. Before leaving, he crumpled the article and threw it on the ground.

As he walked past Coach, he mumbled, "Sorry, Coach."

"Yeah, I know. You've been saying that a lot these days!" he yelled after Tank.

He turned toward Nathan. "Now, what's the problem?" he asked.

"Nothing, Coach. Sorry. It won't happen again."

"You're damn right." With that, he turned and walked into his office before slamming the door.

Nathan let out an exhausted breath and rested his head on the door of his locker. *Jesus, that was close.*

Abigail rushed out of her English class and walked toward her dorm. It was cold out, and she was ready to get back to her room to take a shower. She was getting sick of the whispers and mumbles as she walked in and out of buildings. She was anxiously searching for some solitude away from all the gossip.

As she walked with her head down, she heard someone yell, "Nathan!"

She noticed Bree jogging toward him. Without consciously realizing her actions, she ducked toward the back of the building and observed them for a moment. She was hoping they wouldn't see her.

As she peered around the corner, she could see Bree dip her head from side to side, laughing and cooing. When Nathan glanced down at her, Abigail decided to sneak through the back road toward her dorm. She had seen all she needed to see. But before they were completely out of her sight, she turned one last time to see if they were still talking, and that was when she saw Bree write something on Nathan's hand.

Abigail pulled open the door to her dorm and went inside. She rushed up the stairs two at a time to her floor. She hoped that if she hurried, she would make it to her room before Bree came up in the elevator. She had a knot in her stomach as she thought about the two of them standing there, laughing and smiling. She couldn't blame either one of them. They were both good-looking, and it would be only natural if they were attracted to each other, but still, it made Abigail feel worse even though she'd assumed that was impossible to do at this point.

She opened the door to her room, and Laura was sitting at her desk, studying.

"Hey there. How was class?" she asked.

"Oh, fine." As she began talking, her bottom lip trembled. She had an overwhelming sense of sadness wash over her, and she started to cry.

"Oh my, what is it?" Laura's face twisted with concern.

"I don't even know anymore. That's the problem." Tears began to fall down Abigail's cheeks.

"Sit down. Tell me, please." Laura pulled her chair close to Abigail.

"I don't know. A part of me thought I'd be sadder about James. To be honest, I didn't want it to end the way it did, but I did little to stop it. I was almost relieved that he broke up with me. Is that horrible or what?" she said quietly.

"Of course not. It doesn't make you a terrible person. Abigail, it is not often you meet the love of your life in high school. You have to give yourself a break on this." Laura grabbed her friend's hand and squeezed.

"I guess, but I feel like a jerk. Everyone saw the picture, and…" She trailed off, not wanting to admit what she was about to say.

"And?"

"Even my mom said I locked so happy in the picture, and I was. I was happy, and I didn't really feel that way with James."

"Well, there is nothing wrong with feeling happy, Abigail." Laura handed over a tissue.

"I know, but I shouldn't feel this way, right?" she asked with desperation in her eyes.

"Wait, what are you saying?" Laura's eyes widened.

"Nothing. Just forget it. I have to just let this go."

"Let what go, Abigail?" She looked intently at her friend. "Are you saying that you have feelings for Nathan?"

Suddenly, there were two loud knocks on the door, and Bree opened it. "Knock, knock," she said sweetly.

Quickly, Abigail moved to the other side of the room to where Bree could not see her.

"Hey there! You're never going to believe what just happened to me!" Bree gasped.

"Uh, hey can you—" Laura started to say.

Bree cut her off, "Nathan just asked me out! Ah! I'm so excited. He's so hot, right?"

Laura quickly shuffled her friend back toward the door. "Hey, cool. Come get a soda with me, will you?" She opened the door and pushed Bree out. Then, she quickly closed the door.

Abigail sank down on her bed. *I guess that answers the question about Nathan and me. He isn't interested in me after all.*

Eighteen

DECEMBER 12, 1995

Abigail spent almost every free moment she had at either the student union or the library. She avoided her floor, for fear of running into Bree. It would kill Abigail to have to hear how happy she was. This unfortunately meant she also had to avoid Laura. Abigail had convinced herself that Laura probably felt caught in the middle of her two friends and over a boy, making it impossible to pick sides. This made Abigail feel terrible for Laura. So much like her relationship with James, she began to avoid her friends, her problems, and her feelings.

So, in typical fashion, she would return to her room late when she knew everyone was sleeping.

Even her chitchat with Webber was limited. From time to time, during class, he'd ask her how she was doing, and each time, she would say, "Great," even though she was not.

She had wanted to ask him about Nathan, but she never got the courage to do so. She had not seen him at all these past few weeks, except one time when she ran into him when she was getting a cup of coffee in the student union.

"Hi!" Nathan said.

"Hello." My God, is he handsome.

"How have you been?"

"Oh, just great. Yeah, really great," she lied straight through her teeth.

"Oh, great. Yeah, me, too." Only his voice had this sadness to it.

She wasn't sure what to make of it. He shifted from one foot to the other as he gazed toward the ground.

Ugh. He can't even look at me. He must know that I know about Bree by now. Well, I'll show him that it doesn't bother me one bit!

"Off to somewhere special?" Abigail asked.

With confusion in his eyes, he responded, "Well, no. Not exactly. Why?"

"Oh, just wondering."

Coward. At least have the decency to tell me to my face. Tell me that you asked out a girl who lives in my dorm, on my very floor. Is that what you meant by giving me time? What? You gave it a few days, tops, and when I didn't come running to you, you asked out Bree, of all the girls.

She wanted to scream, but instead, she simply said, "Well, it was great to see you. Good luck on your finals."

As she started to turn, he said, "Abby, wait."

Good. *She turned back to face him.* He is finally going to tell me the truth.

He stepped closer to her. His brow bent, and his eyes, although incredibly beautiful, seemed concerned.

She tried hard not to envision him and Bree lip-locked and pining all over one another. She had known it was inevitable that he would find someone at college. She'd just hoped she wouldn't be around to see it. She braced herself for the terrible news.

Much to her surprise, he said, "Good luck on your finals, too."

She was let down that he couldn't tell her. She had never seen him pay any attention to Bree. Not even three weeks ago, he had been in her room, telling her they were friends, and now, he was lying right to her face. Then, as she turned to walk away from Nathan, she was relieved that she could live one more day not knowing for sure if he were in fact dating the most beautiful girl at school.

Abigail couldn't believe it was the week of finals.

I need to focus. I need to take all the study time I can mentally handle. It's not like I haven't found time alone these past weeks. I've all but made sure that was the case. But now with my Biology final in two days, I need to meet Webber at the library. If we are going to hand in our lab notebooks as a team, I'd better start pulling my weight. I have to stop being preoccupied with all my ridiculous drama.

With a renewed sense of focus and an eagerness to socialize with the human race again, she went back to her room to get her stuff for the library. As she went to leave, she noticed there was a note on the door.

Last Goodbye

In desperate need of a science tutor. Can you meet me on the second floor of the library at 7 p.m.?

P.S. Miss you.

Laura

Her heart sank as she read the note. It wasn't fair that she had been dodging Laura. It wasn't her fault that Bree had come in the room and told her that Nathan had asked her out. They were friends, and that was what friends did.

Abigail glanced at her watch. If she left now, she could get there in time to help Laura. Now more than ever, she owed Laura this one-on-one time. She had not been a good friend these past few weeks.

Abigail knew better than anyone that she could easily get wrapped up in her own mind, much like the months after her seizure. It could be perceived as being self-involved by avoiding those who cared the most about her.

Because I don't want to burden them with my problems. Keeping things inside is what I do best.

She locked the door and took the back stairs down to the side door and exited into the chilly evening. She pulled her jacket tight up around her face and briskly walked to the library. It was about thirty-five degrees out, but the wind made it feel colder. She hugged her body as she fought the gusts blowing across campus.

Her eyes watered from the cold as she pulled open the library door. She showed her ID to the monitor and took the stairs to the second floor. She didn't see Laura anywhere. She took a seat at a table near the windows, so she might see Laura coming in. She shivered as she unzipped her coat. She smoothed down her windblown hair and tucked it behind her ears.

Webber came walking up the stairs and immediately spotted Abigail by the windows. He walked over and plopped his bag down on the table. She jumped.

"Sorry about that. Daydreaming?"

"Oh, yeah, sorry. I'm meeting Laura here, too. She said she needed some help with her science class."

"Ah, you're a good friend."

If he only knew.

She glanced around the second floor again. The library started to fill up with students. The last few days had been particularly busy, but it was not uncommon for this time of year.

"I guess, but I haven't been much of a friend to anyone these days," she said, nose buried deep in her book.

"It's okay. It happens. So, we just need to review the last fifteen pages or so. Then, we sign the book, and we're done, right? I feel pretty good about handing this in."

"Yeah, definitely. I think we'll do great." *Because of you.*

They skimmed through each page of their lab notebooks, reviewing the processes and data, and then initialed each page once they were satisfied. Again, Abigail glanced at her watch. It was twenty past seven.

Huh, maybe Laura is just running late.

She peered out the window across the street toward the campus, and that was when she spotted Nathan and Bree walking together toward the library. The very sight of them made Abigail's heart sink.

They stopped before crossing the street and appeared to be having some sort of lovers' quarrel. Bree seemed somewhat annoyed as she tossed her hair to the side, and Nathan seemed different. His shoulders hung low as he shifted back and forth from one foot to another.

Oh no. Please don't come here!

Seeing the expression on her face, Webber asked, "What's wrong?"

"Nothing," she said in a huff. "It's nothing."

Laura and Bree left the cafeteria. It was ten until seven, and Laura had asked Abigail to meet her at the library at seven. She knew if she didn't hurry, then she might miss her.

"I need to grab my keys from the front desk in the dorm," Bree said. "I dropped them on my way to class, and they left a message, saying they were waiting for me at the desk."

"Hurry up. It's freezing out!" Laura's teeth chattered.

Nathan noticed the two of them leaving the cafeteria. He was trying to avoid Bree at all costs but wanted desperately to talk with Laura. He had to know how Abby was doing. As soon as the door closed, he got up, put his tray on the belt, grabbed his bag, and ran out after them. He couldn't believe his luck when he saw Laura standing there alone.

"Laura," he said.

She quickly turned around. "Hey, Nathan. How are you?"

"Good. Hey," he said, getting right to it, "how is Abby? I haven't seen her in over a week, and I need to know how she is."

Laura could see the deep concern in his eyes. Surprised by this, she said, "Well, she's okay, but I'll be honest, Nathan. I think she's hurt that you asked out Bree. And you know what? As someone who is friends with both, I wasn't—"

He cut her off, "What? I did no such thi—"

"Nathan! Hi! So good to see you!" Bree squeaked as she came rushing back. "We're on our way to the library. Walk with us, will you?" She cozied up to him.

"Hey, Bree," he said.

He gave Laura a look, as if to say, *Please believe me that I did not ask Bree out.*

They started to walk when, all of a sudden, Laura stopped. She patted her bag. By the feel of it, she knew her book was not in there. "Oh crap, my science book is on my desk. I can't believe I forgot it!"

"Oh. Well, it's cold, so we'll meet you there, okay?" Bree gave Laura wide eyes, as if to say, *Leave us alone.*

Laura hesitated as she noticed Nathan give her the same eyes, only his were saying, *Please don't leave me with her.*

Bree tugged on his arm.

"I'll hurry and catch up, okay?" Laura started to jog back to her dorm.

"Okay!" Bree pulled Nathan in her direction.

They walked across campus toward the library. Bree did virtually all the talking while Nathan just nodded his head.

He said a few, "Oh, yeah," and, "Yep," from time to time.

They stopped before crossing the street to the library.

Bree turned to face him. "So, I thought you were going to call me," she quipped. "I'm not used to waiting for guys to call me." She batted her beautiful eyes at him.

"Listen, Bree." He didn't feel like dealing with this right now, but after what Laura had said, he knew it was best to address it straight on. "I think maybe you got the wrong idea somehow." he stammered.

"How so?" she said sweetly through gritted teeth.

"Well, I'm not sure exactly, but to be honest..." He wondered how best to say this. "I, uh...I like someone else," he blurted out. "Don't get me wrong. You're—"

"It's Abigail. Oh, please," she scoffed. "You do realize, all she does all day is cry about James. James this, and James that. Just ask her. She'll tell you. I hear about it all day long. It's annoying."

With that, she turned on her heel and began walking across the street. Nathan jogged to catch up.

"Wait, what?" he asked.

"I said what I said, and I stand by it, so if you change your mind"—she touched his arm—"just let me know, okay?"

He stood practically in the road as she started walking up the steps to the library. He felt like he had been punched in the stomach. A car beeped as it drove past him. He turned and hurried up behind her.

They waited by the door for Laura, who was now close behind. Nathan leaned over and pushed open the door as Laura approached.

"Well, that stunk," he remarked to her under his breath.

Laura gave him a concerned expression, and he rolled his eyes in Bree's direction. She didn't have to ask once she saw that Bree was visibly upset. She had a feeling she knew why.

Nathan followed them to the front desk. Bree fumbled in her bag for her ID as the monitor patiently waited.

"Where is my stupid ID?" she mumbled.

Laura took this as her moment to ask, "What happened?"

"She told me Abby still has feelings for James," he whispered back. His expression was so sad.

"You didn't ask Bree out, did you?"

No, he mouthed. He showed the monitor his ID now that Bree had gone through.

Laura showed her ID as Nathan stood close. "She doesn't like him. I think she likes you."

Laura walked past him, leaving him speechless.

By now, the library was packed. There was a large part of Nathan that just wanted to excuse himself and walk right back out the door. But he knew his grades were keeping him here, and so far, he was doing great. He had no plans to let that change.

"Let's go to the second floor," Laura said.

They followed her in silence. Laura spotted Webber first, and then she noticed Abigail hunched in the corner, biting on a pen.

Nathan's heart sank as he soon realized who was at the table they were walking toward, but considering how packed the library was, he had no other alternative. "Great," he mumbled under his breath. He never took his eyes off Abby as he approached.

She looks tired but still as striking as ever.

She didn't notice him coming until the very last moment. By then, it was too late for either one of them to bail.

Her face gave it away. She was not at all happy to see him, but he wondered why.

"Hey, guys." Laura scooted into the chair next to Abigail.

"Hey, guys," Abigail and Webber both said at the same time in hushed voices.

Nathan noticed that Abigail could barely acknowledge Bree and him as they sat down next to each other. Bree leaned in toward Nathan as she opened her book bag, exposing the top part of her bra. She pulled out a textbook. She brushed up against his arm as she placed her bag down. Nathan blushed as he waited for her to get settled before he took out his own book and began to read.

162

Occasionally, Nathan would try to catch Abby's attention. But she never glanced up from her notebook. It was killing him. He had to see her eyes again. He wanted her to pay some sort of attention to him, but she hardly moved or spoke.

Why is she not acknowledging me? Does she really think I asked out Bree, or is she still upset about the picture in the paper? Or worse, is she still hung up on James?

"Anyone have a pen I can borrow?" Bree asked.

Almost everyone held up a pen, but she waited for Nathan to volunteer his.

She quickly took it. "Thank you. You're so sweet."

He kind of muttered something and just kept his head down. He tried to read, but he couldn't concentrate one bit.

They sat there for another thirty minutes. Abigail and Webber both helped Laura with her science paper. Nathan watched Abigail as they reviewed each chapter, one by one. Abigail reviewed the definitions to Laura and explained in detail about how there was a need for the basic understanding of natural hazards. He could see how passionate she was about science. It came so naturally to her. As time went on, he watched her, trying not to be obvious as she talked about how assessing the earth's climate could possibly predict global change.

With ease, she would slide into the next topic in great detail. "With all the man-made pollutants, it's certainly the duty of science to explore alternatives for energy and mineral resources. The world will depend on it, which is why in chapter five they start talking about…"

And on and on, she spoke with such simplicity.

She even expressed her opinion about certain pollutants and how they could affect wildlife and domestic animals. She seemed relaxed and in her element, particularly when talking about animals.

This was a new side of Abigail. He had rarely spoken to her about school. He knew what she wanted to major in, but he never got the chance to ask her more about it.

She leaned over the book as she showed Laura a diagram. Her hair fell from behind her ear, and he *knew* right then and there that he couldn't take it anymore. He could not let someone like her slip through his fingers. He knew she was beautiful, anyone could see that, but he'd had no idea that she was so intelligent, too. She was the total package.

Even Webber had stopped talking and was listening to her, hanging on every word she spoke.

Nathan decided that he was going to fight for her. She'd wanted some time, and he had given it to her. He hadn't spoken to her in almost a week, but he wasn't going to sit back anymore and let James win her back.

Nathan slammed his book shut. Abigail stopped talking, and they all turned toward him. He stood up, put on his coat, grabbed his book, and shoved it into his backpack. He let out a deep sigh, closed his eyes, and then opened them.

He stared directly at Abigail when he spoke, "I've had a crappy few weeks, some of the worst of my life, and that's saying a lot. So, I'm asking you—no." He paused. "No, I'm telling you as politely as I possibly can to please stand up, put your coat on, and come with me." He knew everyone was watching him, and he didn't care.

Abigail's face flushed crimson. She swallowed hard, unable to speak or move. Bree's jaw dropped as she watched him walk over to Abigail's seat, grab her coat, and hold it for her to put her arms in.

"Please," he said.

Concerned, Webber whispered to Abigail, "What's going on?"

She couldn't say a word but found herself standing up. She put one arm in her coat and then another. Nathan pulled the chair out from behind her to give her room to pass behind Laura. She grabbed her bag, trying desperately not to make eye contact with anyone even though they were all staring at her. Nathan motioned for her to go ahead of him, and in silence, she headed toward the stairs to the main floor. She stopped. Nathan's face was marked with apprehension, but instead of speaking, he motioned again for her to go outside, so she did.

His mind was racing as the cold air hit his face. He gestured for her to walk down the stairs in no particular direction. His heart swelled as her eyes finally met his.

"Where are we going?" she asked.

He didn't say a word to her. He grabbed her hand, and with a slight jog, they crossed the street. She tried to keep up with his much longer strides, running alongside him. He had a firm grip on her hand, and he wasn't letting go.

They passed the science building and labs before he stopped at the back of the English building and pulled the door open. It was barely lit in the stairwell.

"Wait here." He walked down the hallway and opened another door, glancing down the corridor to make sure there was no one around. He closed the door and walked back to her. Halfway back, he dropped his book bag on the floor without breaking stride and kept coming closer to her.

She swallowed hard. She seemed incredibly nervous, and he had a knot in his stomach. He was thoughtful but determined as he came near her. On instinct, she backed up against the concrete wall. He towered over her. She was much smaller than he remembered. She didn't say a word and appeared as though she couldn't move. It was as if she were stuck in quicksand.

He put one arm on each side of her, his fingertips gently touching the wall.

"Nathan, I—"

"Abby, let's not pretend this isn't happening, okay?"

"What's happening?"

"This—me and you. Unless you still have feelings for…" He pulled her book bag off her arm and let it drop to the floor.

"My feelings? What about you and Bree?"

"Bree?" He shook his head. "How could she not see and how could you not know that I've only had eyes for you? God, the day I met you, when I touched your hand, I knew then that…it's been driving me crazy. And you know what?"

Her eyebrows were bent in concern as she stared up at him with those beautiful navy eyes.

"Oh, forget it," he said quickly. "I just have to kiss you."

She started to say something when he leaned over her and gently pulled her face to his and kissed her.

A wonderful sensation tore through his entire body. Her lips were softer and warmer than he could have ever imagined. He held on to her face as his lips moved over hers, his tongue gradually entering her mouth. It was the best kiss he had ever had.

Then, with tremendous strength and as though he could not get close enough to her, he grabbed her around the waist and slid her body up against the wall. He pulled her legs around his waist and her arms around his body. He kissed her harder as he pressed his body on hers. She kissed him back. He could feel his heart beating in overtime. She was so confident and sexy right now that he wasn't sure he'd be able to control himself. Her body was even more amazing than he could have dreamed. She grasped on to his shirt. He moaned as she ran her hands up his skin, gently caressing the muscles along his back. She gave him goose bumps as she touched him. He wanted to be closer to her, too, to feel every part of her.

"Nathan," she said in a breathy voice.

He didn't want to stop kissing her, so he just mumbled an, "Uh-huh?"

"Nathan," she said again.

He stopped and rested his forehead on hers. He closed his eyes and took a deep breath. He was seriously breathless.

"Yes, Abby?" He opened his eyes. He lowered her back down to the floor. His body stayed pressed up to hers. Finally, he took a step back.

"I-I thought you weren't…" she stammered.

"What? Totally into you and only you?" he quipped. In doing so, he stopped her from having to say anything to the contrary.

"Well, yeah, I mean…" She gazed up at him.

He took a step back toward her and leaned his head closer to her. "Why do you think I needed you to leave with me? I couldn't be away from you anymore. You said you needed time, and I gave it to you, but I'm not waiting anymore. If that upsets you, I'm sorry. But I'm not wasting another day."

For the first time in weeks, Abigail smiled. Granted, it was a small one, but it was there nonetheless. He caught it, too, and smiled.

"Okay, so when you and Bree came into the library, what was that all about?"

"I had tried to get Laura alone to ask her about you. I needed to know that you were doing okay, and that was when Laura told me you thought I had asked out Bree. I felt terrible."

"You felt terrible? When I saw you in the union last week, I thought for sure you'd tell me, knowing that I probably already knew. When you didn't say anything to me...I don't know. It seemed like before I knew it, I was out of the picture."

"Out of the picture? You've never even been out of my mind, let alone out of the picture."

"Oh, well, now, I feel even more foolish." She lowered her eyes.

"Please don't. Please don't feel anything but great right now." He then asked, "You do feel great, don't you?"

She gazed up, searching his face.

She is so gorgeous. I almost can't believe she is here with me.

"Nathan," she said sweetly, "I do feel great. I honestly do."

Relieved, he reached for her hand.

"But before we get kicked out of here, will you kiss me again?" she asked.

He laughed. "Trust me when I tell you that there is nothing else I'd rather do."

And he did. He put one arm around her neck and the other around her waist. He then held the back of her head and cradled her into his arms. She was weightless. With his pouty lips only inches from hers, he planted a passionate kiss on her jawline, her cheek, noting the warmth in her flesh, and then finally on her waiting lips. He didn't want to, but eventually, he leaned her back up and smiled at her.

Since the moment he'd laid eyes on her, he had wanted to kiss her. Granted, he never let her know that, but secretly, that was all he'd thought about each time he saw her. The picture of the two of them in the paper had been stuck in his mind. He would stare at it every day, wishing for the days to go by until he could see her again. It was what had gotten him through these past few weeks. He knew it had caused them both issues, but being here with her now, he knew it was the best thing that could have happened to both of them. He wanted to stay here all night, away from everyone, and just kiss her over and over again, but he knew they'd have to part.

He reached up and lightly touched her hair, the golden tendrils that surrounded her beautiful sun-kissed face. "So, did you really think I would want anyone but you? Was I not obvious enough? Because I thought I was too obvious."

"Not to me. I've been so confused and hurt, thinking you had asked her out. I was convinced I'd just missed my moment. I had pushed you away. I didn't want time. I wanted you." She even surprised herself as the words came flowing out of her mouth, like a stream of consciousness, revealing all of the thoughts that had been bottled up for months.

He kissed her again. *Could she be the world's best kisser?* He released his embrace.

"I wish I didn't have to leave on Saturday for Christmas." Her cheeks blushed a beautiful pink hue. In reality, she wished she didn't have to go anywhere that he wasn't.

"Believe me, me, too. But what's next? I'll do whatever you want me to do."

"Let's wait until after the break to tell people about this. Is that okay?"

"Couldn't agree more. Let's just get through finals and vacation and come back. By then, you and I might actually get to spend some time together, just us…"

"I know. I hope by then…" She trailed off, thinking about all that had happened since Thanksgiving between her and James and Nathan and even Bree. She didn't want to hurt Bree either. "Thank God I'm meeting my parents in Florida. I'm so glad I won't have to go to New York."

Feeling incredibly relieved that she wouldn't be home and around James, Nathan said, "Oh, great. That will be nice for you. You leaving from here?"

"Yeah, on Saturday morning. I'm taking a cab to the airport. I'm meeting them in Florida."

"I'll take you. I mean, I'd like to take you."

"Thanks. I'd like that."

He walked over and picked up his book bag. She bent over and got hers. When he was back next to her, he grabbed her hand.

"Let's go get a hot chocolate or something in the union. Whatever you want."

"Sure." Inside, she was screaming like a fourteen-year-old girl.

He kissed her again, making it almost impossible for either of them to part. But, finally, they did. He pushed open the door and led her back out into the cold.

They crossed campus to the student union and went inside. They each got a hot chocolate and sat down at a table near the window.

For once in his life, off the football field, Nathan was excited and completely sure of himself. He was always confident when it came to sports, but that was about it. He never felt assured with girls. But he knew this was different. Abigail was different. He'd finally found what he was searching for.

Webber, Laura, and Bree finally left the library. They barely spoke to one another after Abigail and Nathan had left. Laura knew Bree was fuming but didn't say anything to try to make her feel better. She knew nothing would.

As they walked back across campus, Bree finally said in a dry, sarcastic tone, "I wonder where the star quarterback and the damsel in distress went."

Webber and Laura ignored her comment, and both kept walking to their dorms. As they passed the union, Laura noticed Nathan and Abigail sitting near the window. They were smiling and talking. She had never seen Abigail look so happy—well, maybe once before, in the picture in the newspaper.

Nineteen

DECEMBER 16, 1995

By Friday, Nathan might as well have been walking on a cloud as he stepped out into the cold afternoon after he aced his last exam. He was pumped because he was sure he had done well on *all* his finals. He was confident that he would end up with a GPA of at least 3.5.

Nothing bad could happen today. He was convinced of it. He glanced at his watch. It would be just a few more hours until he and Abigail would be alone for the first time since that night after the library. Most of the students had either already left for the holidays or were leaving this afternoon but not them. Nathan was going to drive her to the airport first thing in the morning, and with both their roommates gone, they would have the night to themselves.

As he unlocked the door to his room, he saw a note on the board.

Have a great Christmas and happy New Year. —Spidey

After Nathan took a hot shower, he got dressed and then inspected himself before he sat down on his bed and waited. His eyes became heavy as the sun began to fade.

He was startled when the phone rang. *I must have dozed off.* He grabbed the receiver.

"I thought that Laura and the girls would never leave," Abigail said.

"What time is it? I must have fallen asleep." He sounded groggy.

"It's six thirty. I'm sorry. You must be starving!" she exclaimed.

"Yes, I could definitely eat. What would you like to eat? Feel like Chinese?"

She laughed, thinking about the time James had visited campus and he wanted Chinese.

"What? You don't like Chinese?" Nathan asked.

"No, I do. I love it! I'll meet you outside my dorm, say, in ten minutes?"

"I'm on my way!" Before he left his room, he stuffed a clean pair of shorts, a T-shirt, and a long-sleeved flannel shirt inside his bag. He sprayed more cologne on. Then, he tucked his wallet into his back pocket, took his keys and coat, and turned off the lights before shutting the door.

As he walked out of his building, he took a deep breath in and out as a sense of happiness washed over him. He hoped this feeling would last. He walked to Abigail's dorm with his hands shoved deep into his pockets. It was much colder than he had expected. As he got closer, he could see her standing under the post near the front of the building. She was wearing a navy wool coat and a green knit hat, her hair cascading down the front in thick rings. He no longer was cold as he observed her walk down the walkway to meet him. His body was warm all over.

"Hey there."

He leaned over and kissed her on the cheek and then anxiously pulled back, longing to take her in. He had not laid eyes on her since they parted ways that night in the student union. She seemed to be glowing.

"What?" he asked nervously.

"Oh, sorry. Nothing. Just good to see you; that's all."

"It's good to see you, too."

"So, food?"

"Yes, yes, let's get some. I'm starving. What place do you want to go to?" he asked.

"Let's try Flower Drum Song. I hear it's better than Panda Palace," she lied. She had heard nothing of the sort but would do whatever it took not to go there tonight on her first night out with Nathan. The last person she wanted to think of was James.

"Sounds good to me. It's closer, too, right?"

"Yeah, we can walk there. It's just down the street."

"Perfect."

As he started to turn, he shoved his hand in his pocket, motioning for her to link her arm through. She quickly did and cozied up next to him.

This just feels right. He pulled her in closer. *It's so easy to be with her.*

He opened the door to the restaurant and allowed her to go in first. They were immediately greeted by what appeared to be an older couple, possibly the owners.

"Hello. Two?" the woman asked.

Abigail noticed the man tap his wife on the shoulder and pointed to the wall.

"Oh, you're the quarterback, right?" she asked in a thick accent as she motioned to the framed article.

The wall was lined with photos, cutouts from newspapers, and other Onondaga State football stuff. Nathan reddened. Abigail quickly pulled off her knit cap. The woman immediately noticed Abigail as well.

"And you, pretty girlfriend. How nice. This way, right here." The woman eagerly showed them to the table.

"Thank you so much." Abigail's face was now a fierce shade of pink.

It had been a few weeks since she thought about the article. She had distanced herself from it merely because the students on campus were finally allowing her to. She was no longer hearing whispers or seeing them point at her. Sure, she would get the occasional stare, but those she could handle.

"She is, isn't she?" Nathan slid into the booth across from her.

He didn't take his eyes off of her. She put her head down in embarrassment as she tried to pull off her jacket. She was wearing a tight, long-sleeved black knit top with gray pants, a bit different from her usual jeans and T-shirt. The shirt hugged her in all the right places, and Nathan couldn't help but notice it as he pulled his jacket off as well.

"Wow, Abby. You look spectacular." His eyes widened.

She quickly smoothed down her hair and tucked one side behind her ear. "So do you," she said quietly as the woman filled their water glasses.

She nodded at them both before she walked away.

Abigail scanned the menu and then waited for Nathan to put his down.

"Do you know what you want?" he asked.

"Yep. I'm going to get the number eight—chicken and broccoli, crab rangoon, and rice. Sorry it's so late. I'm starving. You must be hungry, too!"

"No worries, but yes, I am hungry. I think I'll get orange chicken—spicy, of course—an egg roll, and rice. Maybe even a side of boneless spare ribs. Yeah, I think I will."

The woman came back over once she saw them put their menus on the table. They ordered, and she took the menus and promptly left. They were the only ones in the whole restaurant, so it was quiet and surprisingly relaxing.

Nathan leaned over the table toward her. She began to fidget in her seat.

"Sorry, I don't mean to make you uncomfortable."

"No, no. You're not at all," Abigail said in protest.

It was just, every time he gazed at her with those intense steel-gray eyes, she wanted to jump up and kiss him a hundred times. But she knew she had to control herself. She didn't want to seem desperate.

"Good, because, man, I just have to lay my eyes on you."

"See? That's why I get shy. You say these wonderful things, and I'm not sure how to answer," she explained, her cheeks filling with heat.

"I don't want an answer…" He trailed off as he gave her a slight wink.

She could feel her heart race.

"Can we, um …" she stammered.

"Change the subject?" He laughed.

"Yes, *please*," she begged.

"Of course. You pick!" He leaned back in his seat.

"Great. Thanks a lot. You're not going to make this easy, are you?"

"Nope."

"Okay, so any topic I choose?" she asked.

"Anything. Anything at all."

"Okay, where does your dad think you are tonight?"

"Oh, good one," he said quizzically. "Here at school"—he stopped—"helping a friend."

"A *friend*."

"Yep," he answered with a big smile, "a friend."

"Okay, did you think about this friend during the week?"

"More than I'll admit," he quickly shot off.

"Did you tell anyone you were helping this friend tomorrow?"

"Nope, no one."

"So, you have any ex-girlfriends to speak of?"

"Diving right in? Good."

"Well, I figure you know about my ex-boyfriend."

"True, true. Yeah, one. We dated for about a year or so until our junior year. Once football and school got more serious, I just couldn't make the time."

"She must have been crushed." Abigail grinned.

He laughed. "Of course she was."

"I'm sure. I assumed she was. I mean, look at you!"

"Oh, I see. Now, it's your turn to make me blush."

"Exactly." She giggled.

"How is James holding up these days?" Nathan said, firing back.

"Oh, lowball," she scoffed. "Fine, I guess. I haven't heard from him."

"Really? Not at all?"

"Well, I heard he was upset that I was going to Florida for Christmas. At least, that is what Rebecca told me, but there's nothing I can do about it."

"Rebecca?"

"Yeah, she's my best friend from home. I've known her since I was six."

"Wow, cool. Well, you can send him a postcard." His tone was cocky.

It was different for him, and she liked it.

"But only after I've gotten mine," he added.

"Ha! I'll make sure you get yours first. So, how did you do on your finals?"

"Aced them. I'm guessing a three-point-five GPA."

"*Really?*"

"Yeah, really, Miss Smarty-Pants. You're not the only one with brains in this relationship."

"Relationship?"

"Yeah, relationship. Unless you…" He trailed off.

"Unless I…" she cooed, turning the tables on him.

He hesitated, trying to read her. Then, a smile crept across her face.

"Good one. I see what you're doing. Yeah, you, me…you know." His expression quickly softened. "That's if it—" He cut off as the woman approached with two plates.

They both leaned back in their seats as she placed the hot plates in front of them.

"Can I get you anything else?" she asked sweetly.

"I'll have more water, please."

"Me, too, please," Abigail said.

Abigail picked up her fork and moved some of her food around to try and cool it down before taking a bite. It was steaming hot, but she could only wait so long. By now, it was after seven, and she had not eaten since this morning. They spent the next five minutes or so eating in silence, commenting only from time to time on how the food tasted. Nathan was enjoying the quiet with her. He felt relaxed, as if they were the only two people left on campus. Watching her, he imagined how the two of them would be once everyone was back. To be honest, he thought it would be the same. There was something so laid-back and natural about being around her.

He smiled.

"What's that for?"

"Oh, nothing."

She laughed quickly. "You're generally a happy person, aren't you?"

"I am now. I feel happier now."

"I'm glad, Nathan."

He eyed the room for the woman and called her over. "I'll take the check, please," he said.

"No, no. On me. We insist." She put two fortune cookies down on the table. Then, she moved one in front of each of them.

"What? No, I can't, ma'am, but thank you."

"My husband insists. Thank you so much for coming in." She walked away.

"But, ma'am, I can't—" He tried to yell after her, but she was gone behind the door leading into the kitchen. He shrugged his shoulders. "You won't tell, will you? I can get in a lot of trouble for that—NCAA violation."

"Your secret is safe with me. I'll tell everyone you made me pay!" She laughed.

"Cute, really cute, Abby." He glanced down at the fortune cookie.

At the same time, they both moved theirs in front of the other. "Switch," they said in unison.

Nathan reached for his. Abigail did the same. They opened them at the same time.

"You go first."

"Okay…" He read it to himself first. "*If you have something good in your life, don't let it go.*"

Wow. He hoped that something good was her.

He winked at her. "Now, your turn."

"*An upward movement initiated in time can counteract fate.*"

Huh. She sat back and contemplated what that could possibly mean.

He could see her mind racing, and he reached across the table to touch her hand. He squeezed it and then said, "Fate, huh? Okay, something to think about. Ready to go?"

He stood up and put on his jacket. He slung his bag across his body, over his chest. She stood up as well, and he grabbed her jacket to help her put it on. She put her arms in, and as he pulled the coat onto her shoulders, he put his arms around her and drew her close. With her back against his chest, he squeezed her. She didn't resist in the least, and they just stood there for a moment. She didn't want him to let her go. Finally, he kissed the top of her head. Then, with one arm on her shoulders, he moved to the side of her, and they walked to the door together.

Abigail and Nathan walked together the entire way back to her dorm, and never once did Nathan take his arm off her shoulders. At one point, she even reached up with the same hand and grabbed his hand that was draping down.

When they got to the door, Abigail unlocked the main door, and they both went inside. They walked up the six flights to her floor and strolled down the empty hallway to her room. They had not spoken about whether or not Nathan would be staying in her room, and Abigail assumed that not saying anything implied that they were both okay with the idea. She was *more* than okay with the idea.

She unlocked her door and pushed it opened. She had left a small lamp on near her bed. She pulled off her coat, and he did the same before tossing it onto Laura's desk chair. She took the fortune out of her pocket and tacked it on her corkboard near her desk.

Her heart began to pound inside her chest, and she thought for sure that he would be able to hear it. She turned toward him. He seemed so calm and collected as he dropped his bag on the floor near her desk, like he had been here a thousand times before. She noticed again how handsome he was. His hair was pushed back with slight curls on the sides, and the red sweater was just the perfect color for him. He was almost too good to be true, like something out of a magazine. She got the sense that he didn't think that way, and that, of course, made him even more desirable.

"What is it?" he asked. "Everything okay?"

Rattled by his question, she quickly snapped out of it. "Oh, yeah. I mean, nothing's wrong. You?" She turned to face the other way, pretending to search for something on her dresser.

"Abby? Look at me, will you?"

She swallowed hard and turned back to him.

He stood before her, trying to gauge her reaction. Noticing how nervous she seemed, he took a seat on top of her desk and asked, "Hey, what's on your mind?"

"Nothing," she lied. "Just thinking about my flight tomorrow. I'm a nervous flyer."

"Oh, you are, huh?"

"Yes, I am, so don't make it worse, okay?"

"Sorry, I was only playing."

His smile was drawing her in, and she blushed again. She reorganized a few things on her dresser. She had already packed but pretended as though she were still getting ready for her trip.

"What are you listening to?" He switched on her CD player.

"Mazzy Star," she said with a hushed voice. "Fade into You" played sadly through the speakers.

Nathan turned from her and faced the window, staring out across campus, as the music became their background filler.

"Abby, come here." His voice was quiet yet excited.

He leaned over and switched off the light on her desk. It was dark in her room now, but as she approached him near the desk, she could see why he wanted her to come over.

"Oh," she gasped, "it's snowing!"

He moved his legs over and allowed her to walk through the two desks to the window to get a better view.

"It's so—"

"Beautiful." He put his arms around her waist, resting them across the front of her stomach.

He pressed his body up against her back. She could feel how big and strong he was as his arms seemed to envelop her entire body.

"Yes, beautiful," she whispered.

They stood there together in the dark, watching the snow fall across the ground of the deserted campus. This time, it wasn't as though they were the only two people on campus. It was like they were the only two people in existence.

She leaned her head back onto his chest as he began to sway slightly to the music. Her heart beat loud and heavy. He leaned down to one side of her face and kissed her on the cheek.

"I'm so happy to be here"—he breathed—"with you."

"Me, too."

"Good. I'm glad you feel the same. I've been looking forward to some *alone* time with you since the day I laid eyes on you." He started kissing her neck, and she could hear his breath deepen. He ran his hand up her body.

Alone time. Oh boy, I think I know what that means. God, just being alone with him makes me nervous.

She turned toward him.

He never let his arms go as she moved to face him.

"I almost feel like it's—"

"Too good to be true?" he whispered, finishing her thought.

"Yes, like it's too good. You're too good to be real, I guess." She bent her head as the intensity of gazing at his beautifully chiseled face was almost too much to handle. Then, she whispered, "I mean, it's you. You could pick anyone you wanted here—"

He cut her off, "Now, wait a second." He dropped his arms and backed up. His eyebrows bent in disappointment. "Don't you go there with me, Abby. I don't know what you're thinking, but whatever it is, it just isn't true. No one can have anyone they want. Not me, not anyone."

"You know what I meant. You're popular—"

"Abby, stop, please. Think about what you're saying."

He seemed upset, and the more she tried to make it right, the worse she made it.

"Well, just because you're a football player. Your pictures are all over campus and—"

"Ugh," he said in frustration. "You went there."

She started walking toward him, but he put his hand up to stop her.

"Listen, and I only want to say this once. The first day I saw you, I never once thought a girl like you would be interested in someone like me. A jock, remember?" he said, sounding hurt. "So, the next time you look at yourself in the mirror, just think that you are someone that people—boys, guys, whatever—desire, Abby. And I'm not going to screw this up because I play football, understand? One has nothing to do with the other. So, if you have issues with dating a football player, you'd better speak up now."

"Dating?"

"Yeah, of course."

"I just assumed—"

He let out a frustrated sigh. "Abby, are you doing this because you want to push me away?"

She didn't have a clue as to why she was making this so hard, why she was asking him so many questions. She was nervous—she knew that much—but she didn't want to push him away. She didn't want him to leave.

When she didn't respond, he said, "I'll still drive you to the airport, but I'll leave if this is making you feel uncomfortable. It's not something we need to decide right now, next week, or…"

She was hurt when he spoke those words. *Or what?*

Finally, she asked, "It would be that easy for you?"

"Easy? No, not easy. It would be agonizing, distracting, and painful to wait to be with you. But I would wait." He leaned up against the wall.

She tried to read him, but she was barely able to see his face in the darkness. There was the glow of light from the campus buildings outside. It lit his expression enough for her to see the anguish on his face.

"I'm sorry, Nathan. I don't know why I assumed anything. I feel a connection. Stupid, right? We hardly—" She broke off, hanging her head.

Before she knew what was happening, Nathan pushed off the wall, and with one long stride, he was in front of her with his arms around her waist.

"Look at me, Abby, please."

She did. She gazed right up at him and straight into his beautiful eyes.

"I feel it, too, I swear." His voice was so sincere and serious.

She swallowed hard. "I want you to stay with me, but I need to tell you something."

"You can tell me anything."

She couldn't believe she was about to say the words to him, but he needed to know. She wanted him to fully understand why she had been acting so strange and so obviously nervous.

"I'm, um…well, I guess what I wanted to say is that I'm a virgin. So, I'm feeling anxious, and I thought you should know."

"Oh, really? But what about James?"

She recalled the night James had come to stay with her. They'd fooled around a lot that night, and he never pressured her in the least. At one point, she'd imagined that she would go through with it, but something had told her to wait, that it just wasn't the right time. In hindsight, it just wasn't the right person.

"I know. I guess when it all came down to it…it just wasn't meant to be."

A smile came across his face.

"What? Say something, please."

He didn't say a word. He didn't have to. He lifted her face with his hand and kissed her. A surge of excitement entered her body. He pulled her closer and kissed her again—harder.

"How could that guy ever let you go?" he said as their lips parted.

"I suppose I was never really his, Nathan."

"Abby, the last thing I ever want you to feel is uncomfortable or as if I'm pressuring you. I would never do that. I meant what I said about waiting for you. You have to be ready, and besides, there are so many things we can do outside of having sex, you know."

She swallowed hard. *Oh my, how I want to do all of those things with you.*

"Have you—"

"No, I haven't, but I plan to stick this out with you. So, when the time is right, we'll both know." He was so sweet and sexy that it nearly melted her heart.

The sense of relief she experienced was overwhelming. She didn't want to think of him being with anyone else. She was more at ease than before, just knowing they would be going through this together.

"So," she said softly, "you mentioned doing other stuff…"

Abigail surprised herself with her forwardness, but with him standing in front of her, looking the way he did right now, well, she'd do just about anything he wanted. No questions asked because he was that damn hot.

"Well, there are lots of things we can do," he said with a suggestive grin as he came closer to her.

He pulled her in, and then he spun her toward the desk. He picked her up and set her on top. Spreading her legs, he moved in between them. He leaned down and kissed her. His mouth was all over hers. He used his tongue to twirl around hers, and he pressed his lips deeper and harder onto her lips. A rush went up and down her entire body. His lips told her how badly he wanted her, and the feeling was incredible—to be so wanted and so desired with no words spoken. She almost immediately knew the difference between Nathan and anyone else she had ever kissed, including James. She moaned, and she could feel his body harden as he pushed himself on top of her. She wrapped her legs around his waist, and he pulled back to gaze at her.

He couldn't help but pull her legs off. "Stand up," he said with a heavy breath.

"What?"

"Just stand up." He took her hand, leading her off the desk.

She followed his request and stood in front of him. He pulled off his sweater and tossed it on the chair. He was wearing a tight T-shirt that showed the outline of his perfectly chiseled chest. She bit her lip.

"Come here."

Her skin blushed. He put out his hand, and she took it, following him toward the bed.

He pulled her along with him softly onto the bed, and she eagerly let him. He lay halfway on top of her, cradling his body on one side of hers. He slowly ran his hand up her leg, thigh, hip, and breast until he gently pulled her hair back, all while watching her with intense eyes. Then, he began kissing her newly exposed neck. She let out a sweet moan. He ran his hand back down her body and then up under her shirt, feeling her skin.

Oh my God. His hand feels so good. Touch me more, Nathan, please.

"You feel amazing," he whispered.

He reached up again and ran his large hand over her breast. She moaned, as the feeling was almost more than she could handle. She thought she might explode from only his touch.

Oh, I'm in trouble. I'll never be able to control myself.

She stretched her arm around him. "Nathan, kiss me again, please," she begged.

He obliged her. This time, he slid down and began kissing her stomach. Moving his way up, he pulled her shirt up. She grasped it and pulled it over her head before tossing it on the floor next to her bed. His eyes were wide as he took her in, lying there, in a sexy pink lace bra. She noticed his cheeks flush, and she knew he liked what he saw. He leaned up a bit and pulled his T-shirt over his head.

Wow, he is in perfect shape, so fit and muscular. His body is amazing.

She ran the tips of her fingers over his chest muscles. His body twitched a bit, and she liked that she could make him feel excited just by her fingertips.

"You're beautiful," she said.

He laughed slightly. "You're the beautiful one, Abby."

She put her hand on the side of his face. He moved his body up, bringing his face in direct line with hers, their lips only centimeters apart. His body was now resting totally on hers. Their eyes locked on each other.

"I've never felt this way before, Nathan," she said.

"Neither have I." He leaned in and softly placed his lips on hers.

The sound of the alarm startled Abigail. She and Nathan had stayed up most of the night, talking and then fooling around, fooling around and then talking. It was the most comfortable Abigail had ever been. She shot out of bed and ran to the dresser to hit the button. The noise had to stop. She quickly realized she had no clothes on. She spun around, and with deep embarrassment, she noticed Nathan was propped up in bed on one elbow, eyeing her with a grin.

"Good morning." He granted her a devilish stare.

"Morning." She leaned over, desperately trying to find her nightshirt.

"Don't cover up on my account."

"Nathan."

"No, I'm serious."

"I know you are." Still, she tried to find something, anything, but she came up with nothing she could quickly grab. So, she just put her hands up in the air. "I give up. Here I am!" She twirled around once.

His eyes lit up as he reached out his arm to her. "Come here."

She walked over to him, leaned over him, and kissed him. "I have to shower, or I'll be late."

"I know." He kissed her deeply anyway. "Go ahead."

She grabbed a towel off the back of her door, wrapped it tight around her body, took her shower caddy, and walked down the hallway to the showers.

She pulled back the first curtain to the showers. The dorm was completely empty. She let the water warm up a bit before stepping in. The water trickled down her hair and skin, and she let out a deep sigh. The hot water was a welcome sensation on her skin. She grabbed the shampoo bottle and poured a small amount in her hand. She lathered it up and then began to rub it in her hair. She rubbed and scratched her scalp as she piled more and more hair on top of her head until she was satisfied and knew it was clean. The soap began to run down her face, and she closed her eyes as she stood back under the water. With her head immersed in water, she didn't hear the bathroom door creek open, and without warning, the curtain pulled back. She nearly leaped out of her skin.

"Move over." Nathan hung his towel up on the peg.

"Nathan!" she screeched. "What are you doing?" She scrambled to cover herself.

"Hey, I gotta shower, too, and I'm not in my dorm." He ducked his head under the water. He wiped the water from his face. "Continue," he said with a smirk as he handed her the body wash.

He had some nerve, coming in here and scaring her half to death, but in the same sense, she liked and appreciated how comfortable he seemed around her. And, for the first time in her life, she was comfortable around a boy.

Nathan quickly washed his hair and body. She tried not to be obvious, but it was hard not to stare at him as he ran his hands over himself, soap lathering perfectly. An excited feeling came over her. With ease, he let the water rinse him clean.

He stepped out. "Being an athlete means you're quick in the shower. I take a lot of showers." He winked at her.

She blushed as she poured conditioner in her hand and ran it through her long hair. "Maybe next time, you shouldn't be so quick with me," she teased as she turned her back to him.

He stood there, gawking at her, his mouth dropped open slightly. He wrapped the towel around his waist. "You flirting with me, Abby?" He secured his towel.

She glanced over her shoulder. "Yep."

He noticed a birthmark on her upper left shoulder. Playfully, he asked, "What's with the tattoo?"

"Huh?" she said, still not turning. "Oh, this?" she said, pointing to her shoulder. "It's a birthmark. Resembles a moon though, doesn't it?"

"Yeah, clearly."

"That's why my middle name is Luna. But don't tell anyone, okay?"

"Why not? It's beautiful."

"I don't know. I guess it's just something I keep to myself. Sometimes, my dad still calls me his little Moon Pie. Embarrassing, I know."

"I think it is adorable. It suits you."

She gave him an incredibly sexy smile as she washed her shoulders and back. He stood there for a moment, just watching her. He wanted so badly to get back in the shower with her, but he knew if he did, he'd never want to let her go.

"You're killing me." He started for the door. "Killing me, Abby Luna Price!" he hollered before the door swung shut.

Abigail stood in the shower a moment longer, smiling, as she rinsed her hair, and then she stepped out to dry off. She couldn't wipe this smile off her face if she tried.

When she got back to her room, Nathan was in the desk chair. He was wearing a white T-shirt and jeans, and he was leaning over, putting on his sneakers. He glanced up at her as she walked in. He was so gorgeous with his still-wet hair pushed back. Feeling flirty, she dropped her towel on the floor and walked over to her dresser.

He saw it drop and leaned to the side to watch her. "You're terrible. You know that, don't you?"

"Only with you," she said. She got dressed and glanced at the clock.

She had about ten minutes before they absolutely had to be on the road.

"How does it look outside?" she asked.

"Roads appear to be plowed. It should be fine."

"Good."

She blow-dried her hair a bit and then secured it back in a bun. She decided to leave her winter coat behind since she was positive she wouldn't need it in Florida. She went through her bag again, making sure she had everything she needed.

"We'd better hit the road, Abby," he finally said.

"Right, I know. I'm ready."

He grabbed her suitcase, and they walked out her door and down to the car.

It was beautiful outside. The snow was so pure and untouched. The bright sun reflected off every flake, almost blinding them as they walked to the car. Abigail pulled out her black sunglasses and got into the passenger seat.

It was only a short drive to Syracuse Hancock International Airport.

Nathan pulled the car in front of the drop-off zone and put it in park. Abigail let out a big sigh as she reached for the door handle.

"Quick flight. Just remember that," he said, putting his hand on her leg.

"I know, but it doesn't help."

"Let me grab your bag." He climbed out and went around to the trunk. She got out and followed him.

"Hey, I have been meaning to ask you," he said. "There's this banquet thing happening in a few weeks, and I guess I'm up for Rookie of the Year or something." He shoved his hands deep in his pockets and stared directly at his feet.

"Really? Oh, Nathan, that's great news! Congratulations!" She beamed. This was just the sort of chitchat she needed to take her mind off flying.

"Well, I haven't won anything yet."

"It's a big deal just to be recognized. You should feel proud of that. I mean, especially for a quarterback."

"Thought you didn't know much about football?"

"Well, I did a little digging, I guess," she said, blushing.

He grabbed her around the waist, and she let out a small giggle. He bent down and kissed her.

"Come with me to the banquet, will you? Please?" he said softly in her ear.

"Really?"

"Of course. They're going to want to see the girl from the article," he said with a deep laugh.

"Funny. Really funny."

"You'll come, right?"

"But what about your dad?"

"I told him I was going to ask you today."

"Wait, what? But I thought you told him…" She trailed off.

Still clutching on to her waist, he replied, "Of course I told him about you. I tell my dad everything. He said I should absolutely take you. Hey, he saw your picture after all." He laughed. "He said I'd be a fool to take an ugly guy like him over you!"

"Oh, gosh, please. Don't embarrass me. You should take your dad."

"Come with me, please," he said again.

"Well, if you're asking and your dad is okay—"

"Come with me," he said again, cutting her off mid-sentence.

"Of course I will. I'd like to see you win!"

"Good," he said, letting out a sigh.

"I gotta go," she said, glancing at her watch.

"Hey, next time, don't make me ask so many times, okay?"

"That's fair."

She leaned over and pulled the handle up on her suitcase. She grabbed her carry-on backpack and slung it over her shoulder. Standing on her tippy-toes, she kissed him on the cheek. He gave her a tight squeeze. She wished he would never let her go.

"You took my home phone number, right?"

"Yes. I'll call you but not on Saturday," she said with a smirk. "I know you'll be out with all your old teammates."

"You can call me anytime."

She quickly turned and stepped onto the curb. Her heart beat pounded, and her stomach was doing cartwheels. She was going to miss him, and after last night, all she wanted was *more* Nathan Ryan. She didn't know if she could wait until January.

He kindly stood on the sidewalk, waiting for her to get inside the gate. She waved bashfully.

"Merry Christmas, Abby Luna!" he yelled after her.

"Merry Christmas, Nathan!" she yelled back.

Twenty

JANUARY 4, 1996

Abigail walked into her room and put her backpack on her desk. "Hey, Laura. Have a good Christmas?"

"I did. And you?"

"It was nice. Great weather and very relaxing."

"Yeah, I bet. You didn't have to suffer through this cold spell we've been getting hit by."

"Well, I'm in it now!" She winked at her roommate.

"Good. About time you joined." Laura laughed.

Abigail noticed a note on her desk.

Nathan called.

Laura had drawn a heart under his name. Abigail blushed.

"Something you want to tell me?" Laura asked.

"Yeah, well…" she stammered, like a child searching for an answer to get out of trouble.

"I'm going to make you say it," Laura interjected.

"I expect that you would enjoy watching me squirm."

"So, spill it!"

"Okay, okay!" She smiled. "We were planning to tell everyone when we got back, so I haven't been keeping anything—"

Laura cut in, "We?"

"Yes, we—I mean…" Her face was crimson.

Laura crossed her arms over her chest, waiting patiently.

"Nathan and—"

"Aha!" Laura screamed. "I knew it! Ha!"

"Shh, please keep it down."

"I knew it," Laura whispered. "I saw you guys in the window of the student union, and I just had a hunch. You two are meant for one another. Oh, Abigail, he's so cute!"

"I know," she said. "Honestly, he is so nice and sweet and just a regular guy, I think. Despite all the football stuff. We just get along, and I feel comfortable…" She trailed off, realizing she was spilling everything all at once.

"You're gushing, my friend!"

"I know. I can't help it."

"Oh, Bree is going to be so jealous!"

"Laura, stop that. She will not."

"You wait. This will eat her up." She laughed.

Regardless if it were true or not, Bree was not one to take kindly to a romantic defeat even if she was never really in the game to begin with.

"Well, that was never my intention."

"Of course not. How could it have been? So, are you going to see him tonight?"

"I hope so. I'm sure he's busy and all, but…"

"Oh, please, he's dying to see you, and you're dying to see him!"

She laughed. "I am. I *really* am."

Webber walked in the room and dropped his duffel bag on his bed.

"Hey, Spidey," Nathan said. "How was your holiday?"

"Awesome. And you? Get some rest?" he asked.

"Yeah, it was nice and relaxing. Good to see my buddies, too. We had fun."

"Cool. Yeah, it was a nice break." He peered over at the phone as it rang.

Nathan lunged toward it and grabbed the receiver. Webber was alarmed at how fast he'd moved.

"Hello?" he said.

"Hey, it's me, Abigail."

"Hi!" he said, his voice rising an octave. "How was the rest of your holiday? Good, I hope?"

"Yes, yes. And yours? You see your friends on Saturday night?"

"Yes, it was tons of fun. Great to see all my old teammates. Sorry I didn't get to call you back last night. The night kind of got away from us."

He noticed Spidey had left the room. "So, your flight was on time. That's good."

"Yes, got in about an hour ago. I had to unpack and catch up with Laura."

"You get my message then?"

"Yes, I did."

"Yeah, wish I could have picked you up at the airport."

Abigail could sense his hesitation.

"So, did she figure it out?" he asked.

"Yep!" She laughed. "Nothing gets past her."

"I was planning to tell Spidey, too. He just left for a bit, but he should be back soon. More importantly, can I see you?"

Her heart raced as the words came through the phone. "Yes," she cracked out. "Why don't I come over to your room? I'd like to see Webber, too. Hopefully, he won't feel weird about us, ya know."

"You're so thoughtful, Abby."

"Well, it's not like—"

He cut her off, "You are, Abby. You're sweet."

Her cheeks flushed. "Thank you, Nathan. So are you."

"Good. Now, get over here, will you?" He laughed.

"On my way." She hung up and grabbed her jacket as a wave of excitement came over her body. She couldn't *wait* to see him.

Abigail walked out into the cold night air. She pulled her jacket tight around her waist. It had been weeks since she experienced an evening like this. Being in Florida had tricked her into thinking the whole world was warm.

She made the short walk over to Nathan's dorm and rang the bell to get buzzed into the building. She caught a glimpse of him from the glass door as he came barreling down the stairs. Her heart skipped a beat. He was wearing navy track pants. A small Hawks logo was sewn on the pocket with the number twelve underneath, and he had on a tight white T-shirt that barely contained his muscles. His hair was pushed back, and his curls twirled up alongside his ears. She realized then that it didn't matter if he was wearing athletic clothes, his uniform, a suit, or a casual sweater. He was gorgeous, no matter what.

A huge grin came across his face as he spotted her. Their eyes met, and her legs became unsteady underneath her.

Before he got to the door, she mumbled under her breath, "Keep it together, Abigail, and be cool."

He opened the door, and the heat from the building touched her face.

"Hi!" she said.

"It is not possible," he said with a grin.

"What?"

She squeezed past him as he held open the door. She waited and then turned to him.

"That you got better-looking!" he said, quickly touching her face. "Nice tan."

"You're one to talk," she said in a flirty tone as she touched his arm. "Work out over the break?" She playfully gave his arm a squeeze.

"Maybe a little bit." He laughed. "Come on in."

They walked through the second set of doors and to the stairs. She followed behind him, watching him as he moved in front of her. She didn't want to disrupt her thoughts with words, so she stayed silent until they reached his floor. His hallway was still virtually empty. It was only five in the evening, and tomorrow was registration day. By university standards, it was the official start to the semester, although classes wouldn't begin until Tuesday.

They reached his room, and the door was already ajar.

"Is he here?" she whispered.

Nathan just nodded his head. She walked in behind Nathan. Webber was lying on his bed. A small light attached to his bunk was on, and he was reading a book. He became startled as he saw her walk in, and he quickly put the book down as he swung his legs over the bed.

"Hey, Abigail! What a surprise."

"Hello, Webber. Have a nice holiday?"

"Yeah, I did. And you?"

"Very nice," she said.

"You're tan. Florida was nice, I take it."

"Yeah, beautiful. Hard to come back to this."

"Hey!" Nathan said in protest.

"You know what I mean," she said sweetly.

Webber regarded Nathan, then Abigail, and then back to Nathan. He noticed something different but just couldn't put his finger on it.

"So, what's up?" Webber asked with his eyebrows bent.

"Uh, nothing really," Nathan said.

Abigail could feel her body get warmer as the room got quiet.

"Oh, sorry. Let me take your coat," Nathan said to her.

Thank God. She was starting to sweat.

"Thanks." She slipped it off.

He took it and laid it on his chair. She could feel Webber's eyes on her.

"Sit down, Abby," Nathan said.

"Thanks," she said, taking a seat on the edge of his bed.

He sat next to her, and they both stared at Webber.

There was an uncomfortable silence until Nathan spoke, "So, Spidey, remember that night in the library?"

"Yeah..." he said, drawing out the word.

"Well, Abby and I, you know, we're…" He put his hand on Abby's leg.

Webber, like a cat to a laser pointer, zoned in on his hand touching her.

"We're seeing each other now, and just…" He glanced at her with a massive grin.

"Yeah, we just wanted to tell you first 'cause you're our friend," Abigail said quietly.

Finally, Webber spoke, "Hey, that's awesome."

The way he'd said it though made Abigail feel sad. She surmised that maybe, in some small way, this announcement was breaking his heart just a bit even though it was completely unintentional.

"You guys seem great together. It's cool."

"Yeah, thanks, buddy," Nathan said. "Appreciate it. We just wanted you to hear it from us, so cool."

"Totally," he scoffed.

Abigail forced a smile. But her eyes said, *I'm sorry if I've somehow hurt you.*

Seeing that, Webber gave a slight nod in her direction.

"So, you guys want to maybe go get something to eat or hang in?" Webber asked, attempting to change the subject.

"Oh," Abigail said, "what about pizza? You guys in the mood for pizza?"

"Sure. I could eat pizza, I guess," Webber said.

"Great!" she said quickly before he could change his mind. She stood up and walked over to the phone. "How about meatball pizza?"

"Yeah, that's actually my favorite," Webber said even though his voice still sounded melancholy.

"I'm in!" Nathan said.

Abigail ordered a large meatball pizza and a two-liter of Diet Coke. "No, I'll pick it up," she said before hanging up.

"Pick up?" Nathan questioned.

"Yeah, thought I could use a walk before the pizza. You'll go with me, right?" she said to Webber.

Catching on, Nathan said, "Yeah, do you mind? I gotta call Coach before six anyway."

"Sure thing. I'll walk down with you."

"We'll be back." Abigail headed toward the door.

Webber got up and slipped on his black Chuck Taylors and gray wool peacoat from L.L.Bean that he'd gotten for Christmas. Then, he followed Abigail to the hallway. They walked in silence, and once they were outside, she stopped.

"Hey," she said.

"Yeah?" He stopped in his tracks.

"You want to talk about something? Like, what we just told you?" she said quietly.

"Not really."

"Okay…" she said, clearly disappointed.

"Ugh," he said with a grumpy tone.

"What was that?" she asked.

"Nothing."

"Webber." She stared at him.

"Nothing."

"*Webber*?" Her voice was strained.

"It's just…I mean, typical, I guess."

"Typical. What's typical?"

"This, you guys. Just emblematic."

"I'm not sure I'm following you."

"The handsome jock gets the pretty girl every time; that's all."

"It's not like that."

"Really?"

"Yeah."

"If you say so."

"Is that what you think of me, of him?" she said despite her attempt to mask her growing irritation.

"No," he said almost too quickly. He wasn't convincing.

"Then, what is it exactly? What is bothering you?"

"I don't know, Abigail. Can't you just let it go?"

"No, I can't, Webber. Not after what you just said."

Frustrated, he picked up some snow, balled it in his hands, and threw it across the street.

She laughed.

"What's so funny?"

"Who's the jock now?" she said with a smirk.

Slowly, Webber's scowl turned up, and he began to laugh. It was the kind of laugh that you wanted to be sad, only it would take over you until you were laughing uncontrollably hard. Abigail joined in since his laugh was so contagious. It was quirky and high-pitched. After about a minute, their laughter began to break.

"Why am I always apologizing to you?" he asked.

"You're not, not at all."

"Yes, I am, and I'm sorry, Abigail. It just caught me off guard, and I guess I always figured it would happen because I knew he liked you and…" He trailed off.

"You did?"

"Of course. Abigail, you don't leave much not to like."

"Much?"

"Yeah, you have your flaws."

"Hey! So do you, Mr. Apology." She laughed, gently tapping him on the arm.

"I'm aware."

Standing right in front of him, she took his hand. "We are friends, good friends, right?"

"Of course."

"So, be my friend, our friend. Hey, I know you brainy types."

"*Us* brainy types," he corrected.

"Us. I know you don't want to like Nathan, but you do, and honestly, he thinks the world of you. He's a great guy. You know it, and I know it. So, don't tell me this is typical, okay? We both know it's different." She let go of his hand.

"I know," he said, his voice somber. "It's just…he had to scoop up the hottest chick in Biology," he said awkwardly. "I mean, come on, what happened to all his groupies?"

"Oh, Webber!" She laughed. "Who knows?" She poked his chest. "You know what? Pizza's on you. You owe me!"

"Fair. We'd better go if we want it hot."

As Abigail began to walk down the street next to Webber, she couldn't help but glance up at him. She noticed that his face had transformed. He no longer seemed upset. He seemed to have accepted what he knew he had no control over. Ultimately, there was no use in feeling bad for him. She was elated, and so was Nathan. Webber was their friend. Friends were happy for one another, no matter how much it might sting at first.

Webber walked into the pizza place and paid for the pizza and soda. He smiled kindly at her as he pushed open the door and handed her the two-liter. They walked in silence for only a moment before Abigail knew she needed to end the conversation on a higher note.

Without breaking stride, she said, "You're one of my closest friends here. You recognize that, right?"

"Yep, I do." He put his arm around her shoulders.

When they walked back into the room, Nathan was sitting at his desk. He turned and saw instantly that something had changed.

Webber came in and tossed the pizza box on his desk. "Let's dig in. I'm starving!"

Abigail gave Nathan a nod.

"Okay, great. Let's eat," Nathan said.

They ate the pizza. In fact, they finished every piece between the three of them.

"You guys were right. Meatball pizza is the best!" Nathan leaned back on the base of the bed, his long legs spread out across the floor. He appeared satisfied, only he knew it had nothing to do with pizza.

"It's the best," Abigail agreed.

Nathan drew his arms over his head, stretching out his torso.

She was dying for just one moment alone with him. She had thought about him almost every second of every day they were apart, and seeing him now after their whirlwind day together before Christmas gave her such a rush of emotions.

Nathan regarded the empty pizza box on the floor and sighed, thinking of how he could get Abigail alone without offending Webber. He glanced at her out of the corner of his eye. Her breasts pushed against the form-fitting white V-neck waffle shirt. Her denim jeans hung low on her hips, and he could see her thong peeking out. He noticed the tan lines from her bikini. Just thinking of her in a sexy bikini made him feel excited.

"So…" he said.

Abigail stood up. "So, I should probably get going. I'm pretty tired from the flight."

Nathan scrambled up off the floor. "Okay. I'll walk you back."

Webber stood as well. "Hey, call me, and let me know what Bio class you get into. You are going to try getting into Professor Hamilton's class, right?"

"Absolutely. Try to get into the one at nine. That's the one I'm shooting for."

"Will do. Good to see you, Abigail." His expression was sincere and sweet. He leaned toward her and gave her a hug.

In that moment, she was reminded that, despite her new relationship with Nathan, she had made a friend at school, a really good friend.

Nathan and Abigail walked out the door and down the hall. As they approached the bottom floor, Nathan grabbed her hand and pulled her toward the side door. Without saying a word, he yanked open the door to the laundry room. It was dark and quiet, and not a machine was in use.

"What are we doing?" she asked innocently.

He pushed the door closed behind them and locked it. "I got you a little something for Christmas." He reached into his pocket and pulled out a small box.

Her eyes got wide as he approached her, holding the box.

"Oh, Nathan, but I didn't have—I didn't get anything for you," she said.

"Well, I don't give gifts to get gifts," he said with a wink. "I saw this and immediately thought of you." He handed her the box.

Her hands trembled as she opened it. Inside was a beautiful silver necklace with a moon charm dangling on the chain.

"Oh my God, it's beautiful!" she exclaimed as she took it out.

"It's exactly like your birthmark," he said.

"How special. Thank you, Nathan."

"You are more than welcome, Abby. Here, let me put it on you."

He took it from her as she turned and held up her hair. He put the necklace around her neck and secured the clasp. As she turned back around, he backed her up against the wall.

She swallowed hard. "Nathan." His name barely escaped her lips.

"Abby," he said, eyeing her intently.

Her heart beat obnoxiously in her chest as his steel-gray eyes burrowed into hers. She could have sworn he'd licked his lips. It gave her a rush all over.

"Is it crazy how much I thought about you?" he asked in a low, husky voice.

Barely able to speak, she whispered, "You, too. All the time."

"Good," he said. "All I've thought about was our last night together. I've wanted so badly to kiss you again."

"Please don't wait a moment longer." She got up on her tippy-toes.

He leaned in closer and bent his head down. He pressed one arm on the wall behind her, and the other, he gently placed on her cheek, resting his fingertips behind her neck. He drew her face toward his and kissed her. It was the most sensual kiss she had ever experienced. It was so deliberate and soft. There was a longing she experienced when their lips met.

She slipped one arm around his waist and slightly pressed her other arm on the front of his chest. Their bodies were forced together. She could feel his heart pounding. He kissed her again and again, but they were soft, as though he were kissing her for each moment he'd thought of her.

Finally, he rested his forehead on hers.

"Are you too good to be true, Abby?" he said with bated breath.

"Are you?"

He laughed slightly. "I guess that was a silly question, huh?"

"No, not at all." She ran her fingertips across his chest. She could feel his muscles ripple underneath.

He pulled her in close and hugged her tight. She gave him a squeeze back as she rested her head on his chest. She intentionally let out a long sigh. They stayed there, unmoving in their embrace, neither wanting to be the first one to break free.

Finally, he broke the silence, "You're still coming with me next weekend to the awards banquet, right?"

She buried her face deeper into his chest, breathing in deep. "Yes, of course."

He smelled exactly as you would think a hot, sexy quarterback would smell like—football leather mixed with a woodsy cologne and that alluring smell of Irish Spring soap. She slowly let her breath out.

"I even bought a new dress."

"Oh, really?" he said playfully. "Something sexy, I hope."

She giggled. "Maybe. You'll just have to wait and see."

He released her and took a step back. Eyeing her up and down, he said, "You could wear a paper bag and still look good."

"I'll do better than a paper bag for you."

Suddenly, they heard the door handle move on the laundry room door, and then there was a hard tug.

Then, a voice said, "Weird. It's locked."

Abigail and Nathan waited in silence for the person to walk away before they quietly unlocked the door and snuck outside. They burst into laughter as they reached the sidewalk.

"You're always sneaking me into places," she said, laughing.

"I know." He draped his arm around her shoulders. "I'll tell you one thing."

"What's that?"

"I'll never forget the English building. That will be forever etched in my brain."

"Me, too." She rested her head on the side of his chest as they walked together back to her dorm.

When they got to the door, he finally removed his arm. "Guess I'll see you tomorrow, right?"

"Yeah, of course. I can meet you for lunch?"

"I'd love that. Say two? So it won't be as busy."

"Great idea." She reached up and planted a big kiss on his lips. "Good night, Nathan."

"See you tomorrow." He winked and then motioned for her to go inside. He waited until she was in the second set of doors and on her way to the stairs before he turned to leave.

Nathan walked back to his dorm, taking his time, thinking about Abigail. He smiled the whole way back, just imagining the next time he could be alone with her. When he reached his building, he opened the heavy glass door to his dorm and walked inside. He went into the lounge to grab a Gatorade before heading back up to his room. The TV was on, and as he was passing the pool tables, he stopped. Quickly, he turned to leave.

"Wait, wait, don't. Just don't, okay?" Tank said dryly.

"What, Tank?" Nathan said coldly.

Tank didn't say anything as he took his feet off the couch in front of him.

"What?" Nathan said again.

"Nothing. Jesus!" he said, annoyed.

Nathan stood and crossed his arms over his chest.

"Sorry. I just mean, you don't have to leave on my account; that's all," Tank said under his breath as he shifted back on the couch.

"Well, what do you expect me to do, man?"

"Nothing." Tank ran his hand through his greasy hair. Frustrated, he quipped, "Where the hell have you been anyway?"

"Excuse me?" Nathan said, puffing his chest a bit. Even though Tank had about two inches and fifty pounds on him, he had no intention to automatically play mouse to an elephant.

"I tried to find you before the holiday break…" He struggled for the words.

"I know. Marcus told me, but I'm not sure what we have to talk about."

"Yeah, well, I did try and find you, but no big deal," he said defensively.

Unbeknownst to Tank, Nathan had been fully informed by Coach that he had personally requested that Tank leave early, go home to his family, and get some rest. It was Coach's way of acknowledging that Tank had some issues he needed to iron out. Nathan never asked questions about what sort of problems he was having. Nathan was too afraid to get wrapped up in his world. Tank acted so irrational at times that Nathan just needed to keep his distance and leave the decisions up to his coaches. It wasn't his call after all. Besides, at the time, Nathan had been eagerly anticipating the Christmas break to go home and take a break from football, too—well, maybe not football so much as just a break from Tank and all his drama.

"Well, whatever. I tried to find you. Coach said…" Tank again struggled to find the words or make a clear sentence.

Nathan's patience was waning. "Coach said what?" he pressed.

"Nothing," Tank said again, agitated. Then, in a louder tone, he pushed out the words, "Coach said I needed to find you to say I'm sorry, okay? Sorry for the day in the locker room. Happy?" he barked.

"Yeah, really happy," Nathan said sarcastically.

He wasn't trying to make things harder on Tank. That wasn't in Nathan's nature, but this was no apology. If after all those days off and Tank was still acting like this, well, he was pushing Nathan into a corner. Nathan had never been pressed so hard by another teammate before, and after talking to his dad over the break, he agreed that he might have to say something to his coaches if Tank continued to accost him. He prayed it wouldn't come to that.

"You know what?" Tank said through gritted teeth. "I'm trying, okay?"

"Yeah?" Nathan said with a hint of challenge in his voice.

"Yeah." His eyes narrowed.

"Yeah, well, try harder, big guy."

With that, Tank's face began to turn red hot. He stood up and staggered toward Nathan. As he got closer, Nathan could smell sweat and booze.

"Dude, you stink. Get out of here before the dorm monitor sees you. Seriously, you'll freaking blow your ride here. You want that?" he warned.

On day one, Coach had cautioned the entire team to stay on the good side of the dorm monitors—or DMs, as the students liked to call them. If you got kicked out of the dorms for any violation, you would automatically be off the team—university rules.

"Oh, yeah? You're the one who's going to blow it," he said, pointing his finger at Nathan.

Ignoring his nonsense, Nathan said again, "Tank, listen to me. If they catch you, you're dead. Understand me? Coach has no tolerance for this shit."

Again, Tank pointed his finger at Nathan, but this time, he poked Nathan once in the chest.

Nathan's anger began to build. "Tank, you don't—"

Without warning, their heated conversation was interrupted. "Everything okay in here, fellas?" Simon asked firmly.

Simon was the skinny dorm monitor with the tight crew cut from the seventh floor. Everyone knew Simon was the one you did not want to mess with. He was a stickler for the rules, and frankly, he didn't care who you were. He had no interest in whether you were an athlete or not. In fact, he'd love to kick an "entitled jock"—his words—out of the dorm.

Simon started to walk toward them.

Nathan knew he'd smell the booze on Tank, so he had to think fast. "Who? Us?" He laughed as he threw his arm around Tank's shoulder and playfully tousled his greasy hair. Immediately, Nathan regretted touching his unclean hair, and it took all of this high school acting skills not to wince in disgust.

Tank squirmed under his grip.

"We're just talking football. You know us," he said, knowing full well the mention of football would want to make Simon run in the other direction.

As long as they were behaving, Simon wanted no part in their conversation about "stupid football"—his words.

Simon stood in the doorway just a moment too long and glared at them before finally saying with a hint of repugnance in his voice, "Yeah, right. Okay." Then, he turned and walked out into the main lobby.

"Let go of me," Tank barked.

"My pleasure, trust me. Dude, do us a favor." He wiped his hand on his sweatpants. "Go take a shower."

"Screw you." He stumbled back.

"Screw me? Hey, next time, I'll let Crew-Cut Simon decide whether or not you should take a shower. How does that sound?"

"Whatever."

"Exactly." Nathan walked over to the vending machine, feeling he was getting nowhere.

"I don't owe you shit."

Nathan waved his hand in revulsion, and with his back to Tank, he said, "I wouldn't expect anything more."

He pretended to take his time in choosing which drink to buy, but in reality, he just wanted Tank to leave. He had had enough of him for the night, and thankfully, when he turned back around with his Gatorade in hand, Tank was nowhere in sight.

The rest is up to him. Nathan twisted the cap on the bottle. *If he gets caught drunk in the dorm, he'll have no one to blame but himself.*

Twenty-One

JANUARY 4, 1996

Tank stumbled out into the cold night, wearing only his T-shirt and sweatpants. He neither cared nor had any intention of going up to his room to get his coat. He knew where he was going, and he was determined to get there.

He staggered up the walkway to Jessica's dorm, slipping on a patch of ice. He attempted to steady himself on the wall next to the door and finally caught himself on the edge of the wall. But then he fell to the ground, scraping his entire forearm. He winced in pain.

He got up and went over to the phone box on the dormitory wall. He dialed Jessica's extension number on the keypad and waited as the phone rang.

"Hello?" Her voice was sweet and soft.

"Don't hang up, please," he slurred. "It's me. I'm locked out, and I don't have a coat. I'm—"

"You're not wearing a coat?" she barked.

"I had nowhere else to go," he said. He wasn't lying. He had nowhere else to go—well, more like, no one to talk to. He was alone and desperate to feel something or someone. He could not tell which one.

The silence was maddening.

Finally, she spoke, "I'm coming down."

He waited, leaning up against the wall, shivering.

Jessica walked down the stairs. He tried hard to focus on her as she approached the double doors. She pushed the first set open and then quickly pushed the other set to the outside, holding the door open with her foot. She was much prettier than he remembered from the last time he had seen her during the week before break.

They had been hooking up on and off for months now ever since the party at the Ridge. She'd been his good-luck charm all night while he dominated in beer pong. He had grown fond of her because, despite his original thought that she was just another groupie, he'd quickly realized there was much more to her. She seemed to desire more than a hook-up. She challenged Tank with her wit, and he liked that about her, too.

Unfortunately for her, he was emotionally unavailable to her. What he needed was a physical connection. He had to feel something other than anger or sadness. Those emotions seemed to be his two favorites these days.

He mustered a smile. "Hey there."

"Hey," she said as she turned.

He followed her through the doors and up the stairs. She didn't say a word to him as he walked into her room. She lived in a single, which explained why she had bags of clean laundry from home strewed all over the room. She moved some items off her bed and onto her desk.

He took a seat on the edge of her bed. He was gigantic compared to the size of the furniture. It was easy to forget he had just turned nineteen. His head was heavy as he rested it in his hands. He closed his eyes. He could hear her moving about the room, virtually ignoring him.

Then, she stood still and gasped. "Tank! Your arm."

Startled, he picked his head up and inspected his forearm. It was covered in blood. "Oh, must have been when I slipped." He tried to wipe the blood on his sweatpants. "No biggie."

"No, don't," she said, her voice soft again. "Here," she said, reaching for a towel. "Use this." She bent in front of him and wrapped the towel around his arm. She noticed he had goose bumps, so she grabbed her comforter and draped it around him in spite of his protests.

He began to shiver as the warmth of the blanket fought with the coolness of his skin.

She sat on the bed next to him. He briefly glanced at her from the side and noticed again how naturally pretty she was. Her curly, dark hair spun like ribbons down her back. Her long eyelashes touched her cheeks when she blinked her eyes, and her lips were pouty and cherry red.

He had not spoken to Jessica in over a week, but after his lousy holiday break, he wanted to try again. "How have you been?"

"Good. You?"

"Good. Seeing anyone?"

With a brief hesitation, she said, "No. You?"

"No. That's why I came over."

"I don't know, Tank. New year, new me." She waited as she listened to him breathe.

The last time they had been together, he'd left suddenly, and he never reached out to her to explain why he had bolted.

"If you didn't want to see me, why did you answer the door?" he asked, his tone much softer than even he'd expected.

"You said you were locked out," she said, giving him a suspicious stare.

"Yeah, I know," he said. "But still, you could have left me in the cold."

"I wouldn't do that, no matter how much I detested the person."

"Detested?" he scoffed. "So, now, you're saying you detest me?" he asked, leaning in closer to her.

She leaned away from him.

He figured, at some point, she'd get sick of him popping in and out of her life. Before Christmas break, he couldn't have cared less, but considering what a terrible time he'd had at home, he was hoping that she wouldn't pick today as the day to finally get sick of his lack of commitment.

"Tank, you seem like you've had a rough day."

The expression on her face told him everything he needed to know. She appeared a little disgusted. He stood up and saw his reflection in her mirror. His hair was unkempt and greasy, and for someone with blond hair like his, this was even more noticeable. His eyes were hollow and dark. He barely recognized himself anymore. In just a year's time, he had changed so much. Now, he was dirty, heavier, and perpetually drunk.

He took off the comforter and dropped it on her bed. He could see the blood that had stained his pants and arm better now. He feverishly rubbed his eyes as he began to sober up.

She stood behind him and handed him another clean towel.

"Come," she said with sadness. "I'll be the lookout while you shower." Without asking, she walked toward her door, opened it, and waited for him. She grabbed her shower caddy and followed him toward the bathroom.

He didn't speak a word as he walked into the women's room and went straight to the shower. He turned on the shower, letting it run to scalding hot. He took out her shampoo and washed his body and hair all at once. He scrubbed the rough stubble on his face and then let the hot water rinse his skin clean.

After turning the water off, he pulled back the curtain. He wrapped the towel around his waist, grabbed his clothes, and pushed open the door. She stood there, against the wall, waiting for him. She didn't appear the least bit embarrassed that he was nearly naked. She had seen him before in far less, but this was different. Instead of seeming interested, she viewed him with pity, and he wanted to crawl into a hole and die.

He followed her back down to her room like a lost puppy, head down and all. The scrape on his arm was clean and not nearly as bad as the blood had indicated, but he needed a bandage nonetheless. As if she knew what he was thinking, she went into her desk drawer and took out a huge Band-Aid and gauze.

"Sit here," she said, pointing to the desk.

"All right." As he did, the towel stretched to the limits around his large body.

She quietly dressed his scrape. He ran his free hand through his wet blond hair, nervously eyeing her. She seemed changed, as though she was at ease with the situation regardless of their limited time together over the past few months.

He surveyed her as her fingertips moved effortlessly across his skin. She was different than she had been in the past. It was almost like, for the first time, she understood the type of guy he was—a noncommittal, one-night stand, entitled athlete. It was as if she just expected that Tank wouldn't want a serious relationship. At some point in their courtship, she'd just figured he was the type of guy who would take full advantage of being on the football team. It appeared to him, by how confidently she was acting now, that she had made peace with it, that she knew she had no choice. These assumptions made Tank feel even worse, but he didn't dare ask her, for fear he was one hundred percent accurate.

"I think that should do it, Tank," she said matter-of-factly.

"Thanks, Jess." He inspected the bandage.

She didn't move. He waited before reaching up and putting his arms around her waist. He wasn't sure if she would slap him across the face or be okay with it. He took a chance. He pulled her a bit closer. Even with him sitting and her standing, he was still taller than her. He swallowed hard and tried to get a read from her. It was impossible.

"What?"

"Nothing," she said abruptly. She stepped back and went over to her dresser. She took out an XXL T-shirt and tossed it in his general direction. "At least this doesn't have blood on it," she whispered.

"Thanks." He got up and went closer toward her, his chest still damp from the shower.

Notwithstanding her attempt to keep neutral, her face flushed as he stood in front of her, his massive body towering over hers. She swallowed hard. His vulnerability was starting to freak her out. They stared at one another for what felt like an eternity. He was different, she was changed, and neither one knew how to understand the other. It was maddening.

Then, as if this moment wasn't weird enough, Tank leaned over to her and took her again around the waist, pulling her closer to his body. She made no attempt to resist, and then he said the last thing she had expected.

"I lied. I was never locked out. I had to see you. I need a friend right now, and I think you're all I have."

He could hear her breath catch, and he was too afraid to look at her, too afraid that she might actually just feel sorry for him. Then, her hand caressed his chest. She traced a bead of water as it attempted to move over his muscles. He shivered at her touch, and then he was finally able to gaze into her eyes. He saw what he so desperately wanted yet knew he could never articulate. He wanted her badly, and she wanted him.

She ran her tongue over her cherry-colored lips, and as she did, a sudden craving came over him, one he had never experienced before. He found her at a point in his life when he needed someone. Yet even more, he desired to feel something other than his emotions, something only two bodies could satisfy together. She was just the physical distraction he yearned for during an otherwise despairing year.

So, instead of asking, he started to pull her T-shirt over her body, taking great care as he did. In the past, it had been aggressive and quick with them, usually in a drunken stupor after a late night of partying, but not this time. He wanted it to be different. He needed it to be different. As her shirt fell to the floor, he leaned down and gently kissed her soft lips.

As their mouths found one another, her hands began to explore his body. She ran the tips of her fingers down his massive arms and back until she found the knot in his towel and released it. The towel landed on the floor. She peered down at his body and knew he was ready for her. With eager fingers, he unbuttoned and then pulled her jeans, delicately sliding them down her slim hips, and she stepped out of them. With muscles twitching, he easily picked up her tiny frame and drew her face toward his. As he observed her flushed cheeks and pouty lips, he couldn't help but give her a sly smile before kissing her again.

As their lips parted, she said, "I'll be more than your friend, if you'll let me."

He wrapped his arms tighter around her body. He walked over to the bed and laid her down. He seductively crawled on top of her, running his hand in between her legs. He took one glimpse at her body as it rose to meet his hand and knew she was ready for him.

"Let's start today," he said.

Twenty-Two

JANUARY 16, 1996

The first two weeks of the semester had gone by quickly.

Abigail and Nathan spent almost all their free time together. They tried desperately to steal any moments they could but made a concerted effort to also spend time with their friends.

Just last week, Nathan had surprised Abigail by inviting all their friends to her favorite Chinese restaurant for her nineteenth birthday. Abigail had been on cloud nine as all their friends mingled together during her impromptu birthday party. She had known their two worlds were meant to collide.

Unfortunately, things for Nathan weren't as simple. Nathan was often torn between being an important athlete on campus and Abigail's boyfriend. He was often asked to parties and such, so many times that he felt obligated to at least stop by and say hello. The last thing he wanted to be accused of was not recognizing the importance of his scholarship and his commitment to the school. But in reality, all he ever wanted to do was be with her. She consumed his thoughts more than anyone had before. He felt alive and happy, all thanks to her.

For at least a few days, Abigail had tried to avoid Bree but wasn't too surprised when Bree approached her. Bree, with gritted teeth, had conceded to Abigail and told her what a good catch she'd snagged—insinuating, of course, that it must have been Abigail who had pursued him. Abigail had chosen not to set her right. She knew, in the end, Bree was just feeling hurt that Nathan wasn't interested in her after all.

It was the Friday before the banquet, and just knowing what a long night tomorrow would be, Abigail and Nathan had decided to stay in and have some time alone. Most of their friends had left for a fraternity party on the other side of campus.

Nathan knocked on her door. She eagerly opened it. He was holding a meatball pizza and a VHS tape of *Bull Durham*. He was grinning from ear to ear.

"Hey, ready for the ultimate date night?" he asked, stepping into her room. He put the pizza on her desk and handed her the tape.

"Ultimate, huh?"

He pulled his jacket off, revealing a tight Hawks T-shirt and baggy jeans. She sighed to herself, thinking she must be the luckiest girl in the world. She was falling fast and hard.

"Pizza, Abby?" he asked.

"Yes, please."

He brought the box over to her bed, and they sat up against the cement wall with the box between the two of them. After his third slice, he was sated and welcomed her to come snuggle, placing the nearly empty pizza box on the floor. He pulled her into him, and she obliged, moving near him.

"Mmm," he groaned. "This feels nice."

"It does," she responded as he began to run his hand down her silky hair.

There was a beautiful silence between the two of them, neither wanting to move nor speak. It was the perfect moment, and she wished it would last forever.

Finally, he spoke, "Abby, if you never moved again, I'd spend the rest of my days at school, right here." He chuckled briefly.

"Nathan," she said quietly, "I'd be just fine with that."

He squeezed her shoulders, drawing her in closer.

"You excited for the banquet tomorrow?"

"Excited? Yes, I think I am. It's a lot of pressure, but I'm happy to be going, nominated and all."

"You sure your dad is still okay with me going?" she asked.

"Of course."

She sensed his hesitation. Then, she asked, "You miss your mom, huh?" Her eyes searched his.

One night after a party, Nathan had told Abigail the devastatingly wretched and heartbreaking story of his mother's passing. She knew how much it had affected and shaped his life. However glad she was that he could share such a tragedy with her, on many occasions, she wished he had not. By not sharing, it would in some way mean it'd never happened, and that was what she wished for—that it'd never happened.

"Yes." He hesitated. "I know she would have been proud of me, of this nomination, and the year I've had. It does make me miss her more."

"Is it okay that I asked?" she said sadly.

"Yes, I appreciate you even more because you did."

"I'm here for you," she said. She stretched up her face toward his, gently kissing him on the cheek.

"Thank you." He leaned in and deeply kissed her.

Her body melted into his as their lips parted.

"Now, if we have any intention of watching one of my favorite movies, we'd better do it before I rip off your clothes," he said with a devilish stare.

Oh my, this movie had better be worth it.

Abigail had nervously anticipated this night for over a week. But here it was, the night of the Atlantic Coast Conference Awards Banquet, and she, Abigail Luna Price, would be escorted by Nathan Ryan, the most-talked-about freshman quarterback in the conference. Abigail was so nervous for him. From what she had been hearing all week and what had been written in the papers, this was a big deal for the school. All their friends were planning to gather in Bree's room as a surprise to wish Nathan good luck.

Abigail painstakingly spent the next two hours blow-drying her hair and desperately trying to apply makeup despite her shaking hands.

She turned and said to Laura, "How much more time do I have?"

"Half an hour."

"Ugh, I look terrible. I can't go."

"You are stunning." Finally, Laura said, "It's time. We're all meeting in Bree's room. You ready?"

Abigail took a deep breath, held it a moment, and then slowly turned to face the full-length mirror hanging next to her closet. She squeezed her eyes shut and then opened them. She viewed her face and then made her way down to her feet.

Laura gushed, "Oh my God, you look"—she broke off for effect—"beautiful, Abigail."

Feeling her friend's sincerity, Abigail turned to her. "I couldn't have done it without you."

Turning back to the mirror, she smoothed down the tight little black dress her mother had bought for her in Florida. It hugged all her curves and dipped low in the front to accentuate her cleavage. Her tan had faded a little bit, but she was still sun-kissed. She decided to leave her long hair down with large beach waves cascading down her back. Her makeup was flawless.

Within moments, she heard a loud burst of applause and rowdy cheers.

"Nathan must be here," Laura said gingerly, as she knew the mere mention of his name would send Abigail into a fit.

Abigail swallowed hard and quickly grabbed her black clutch from her dresser. She tossed in her keys, her lipstick, and a small compact mirror. She tucked it under her arm and finally turned to Laura. "You'd better push me out, or I'll hide in here all night!"

"Smile, okay? You're going to have an awesome night!"

"I know. Thanks, Laura," Abigail said nervously.

She followed Laura toward the door. They walked down the hall to Bree's room. There were so many people from their dorm gathered there that they had spilled out into the hallway and beyond. The music was blaring. Abigail could feel all eyes on her.

Whispers of, "That's Nathan's girlfriend," came from acquaintances from other dorms.

Then, as she made her way closer to the room, she noticed people she at least recognized, and they were all wishing Nathan good luck from the Hawks with sincere smiles.

She had never experienced anything like this before.

Laura pushed their way into the doorway of Bree's room as she tightly clutched Abigail's hand. Laura could see Nathan inside as he towered over all those surrounding him. He was high-fiving and getting good-luck hugs from all his friends. It was nice of Bree to plan this surprise send-off for Nathan even if she did have another motive. Abigail knew Bree wouldn't just give up on him just because he'd turned her down.

"He's in here." Laura turned to Abigail.

Abigail let out a deep breath and closed her eyes for a moment. Laura squeezed her hand and guided her into the room.

"Abigail!" Melissa yelled.

Nathan froze at the sound of her name and turned to see the crowd parting as Laura led her through Bree's room. He nearly gasped along with the others as she approached him. She was stunning, and even the word *stunning* truly failed to do her justice.

"Hi."

The crowd got quiet. She could feel her skin flush.

Seeing her embarrassment and knowing how hard it must be for her to have all eyes on her, he bent down close to her and whispered in her ear, "I have never seen a girl look as unbelievable as you do tonight." He stood back up and left her alone, if only to get the spotlight off of her. He knew it was killing her. He turned back to his friends.

"Abigail, you are hot!"

"Thank you, Melissa," she whispered.

"You look nice," Bree said as she pressed out a smile.

"Thanks, Bree. So nice of you to do this."

"I know," she cooed, enjoying some of the spotlight herself.

"Here." Laura pushed a cup in front of Abigail.

"What is it?"

"Liquid courage. You need it!" She laughed.

Without asking another question, Abigail tipped the cup back and drank the contents. It burned as it worked its way down her throat. Then, Laura handed her a mint.

"Thanks, Laura. What would I do without you?"

"Nothing. Now, go have some fun."

Nathan motioned with his head for Abigail to move toward the door as he held up his hand and pointed to his watch. When Abigail moved through the crowd toward the door, she spotted Webber and Logan near the desks. She waved.

Webber very sweetly put his hand over his heart and mouthed the word, *Wow*.

She blushingly turned away. *That was almost as sweet as what Nathan had said.*

She made her way to the end of the hallway and turned to watch as Nathan approached her, high-fiving and shaking hands as all their friends shouted, "MVP! MVP! MVP!"

Despite his attempts to hush the crowd, they continued to cheer for him. A rush came over her. He was not only handsome in his navy Brooks Brothers suit with the orange-and-blue-striped tie he had bought during the break, but with his hair pushed back and his steel-gray eyes, his appearance was respectable and classy. It was no wonder he had drawn all these people in.

As he took her hand, he grinned at her. He had this way of gazing at her that made her feel like a thirteen-year-old girl with her first school crush.

"Ready to go?" he asked as he pushed the button for the elevator.

"Yeah," she softly squeaked out.

They stepped onto the elevator.

"Don't be nervous, okay?"

The doors closed, and he pushed L for the lobby.

"Is it that obvious?" she said, not meeting his eyes.

"One, you're not looking at me. And two, if anyone should be nervous, it should be me."

"What? Really? Why?" she said, surprised.

"Well, I'm the one who should be nervous that some guy is going to grab who I'm positive will be the hottest girl at this thing."

"Nathan," she gasped, "stop it."

"I'm serious, Abby. You are gorgeous."

With a red face, she quickly blurted out, "You are, too, Nathan. I mean, you are so handsome."

"Well then," he said as the doors slowly opened, "I guess I already won tonight."

She could smell his cologne and body wash as he pulled her out of the elevator. He was intoxicating to her.

They drove an hour to the banquet at the White Eagle Conference Center near Hamilton, New York. The conference organizers were expecting over six hundred guests at the event. Nathan drove down the long driveway to the parking lot near the side of the center. He parked and reached behind him to grab his sport coat. Abigail waited for him, as he had requested. He got out and quickly walked around to open her door. He took her hand, and she swung her legs over and stood up.

They walked hand in hand into the main lobby, which was decorated with sports memorabilia, vintage football jerseys, and Big East Conference signs hanging over each of the large entrances to the banquet room. Two older women were sitting at a registration table near the first entrance. Abigail and Nathan approached.

"Name and school, please?" a heavyset woman said.

"Nathan Ryan and my guest, Abby Price. Onondaga State University."

"Great, Mr. Ryan. Here are your table cards. Please find your way in. The cocktail hour is from six to seven, and after the first course has been served, the awards ceremony will begin at seven thirty." She handed the cards to Nathan.

"Thank you," he said politely.

"Yes, thank you," Abigail said quietly.

They made their way into the cocktail room. It was in full swing, and there had to be at least four hundred people already chatting, drinking, and eating.

Nathan noticed a high-top table near the side and motioned toward it. "Why don't you stay here, and I'll go get us a couple of drinks?" he said.

"Oh, sure. That's fine," she said sweetly.

"Good. Don't go anywhere. I'll be right back."

He turned and walked toward the bar. She never took her eyes off him.

Tank pulled into the lot and put his truck in park. He climbed out, and with shaking hands, he buttoned his wrinkled suit jacket. He tried smoothing it down, but it was no use.

"You ready to go?" he asked Jessica.

She nodded and opened her own door. She got out and hurried up behind him. He never even turned to see if she was there.

They entered the building and walked up to the women at the table.

"Name and school, please?" a woman with long, dark hair asked.

Nervously, he ran his hand through his hair. "Tank, err, Thomas McPherson, Onondaga State University."

"And?" the woman said, eyeing Jessica.

"Oh, uh, Jessica…" He blanked on her last name.

"Nichols," she said flatly.

"Sorry," he mumbled.

"Great. Mr. McPherson, Ms. Nichols, here are your table cards. Please find your way in. The cocktail hour is from six to seven, and after the first course has been served, the awards ceremony will begin at seven thirty." She handed the cards to Tank.

"Thank you, ma'am." He took the cards from her.

He took a deep breath as he walked into the crowded cocktail reception. Immediately, he regretted coming. There were too many people here, and he hated small talk. He wasn't good at it. He desperately needed a drink to calm his nerves. He was at least glad he had someone with him.

"Why don't you find us a table?" she asked.

"Yeah," was all he could muster as he scanned the room, searching for an empty table.

"I'll be right back." She maneuvered her way toward the ladies' room.

He started to walk along the back wall, in and out of groups of older men talking about their glory days. He couldn't help feeling depressed as he caught snippets of their conversations, and he could only hope that it would never be like that for him. He was about to turn around and go back in the direction Jessica had gone, but no sooner had he started to turn than he saw *her*, standing alone at a high-top table. He froze. A chill ran up his body, and without realizing what was happening, he started to walk straight toward her.

He bumped into a man and barely said, "Excuse me."

His eyes were locked and focused on her.

She caught a glimpse of him as he approached the table. Startled, she took a step back as his eyes bore into her. He stood there without saying a word as he ran his eyes up and down her, taking in each and every detail of her face, her body, and her mannerisms.

Abigail's eyes widened as she waited for him to speak. He did not.

"Hello," she said politely.

He gasped inside. On the outside, he was still frozen.

A moment passed, and finally, he spoke, "Who are you?" He viewed her as though she weren't real.

"I'm sorry?" she said, trying to remain polite.

She quickly scanned the crowd to see if Nathan was coming back. Unfortunately, she could see him all the way across the room, surrounded by five older men with white hair and dark jackets. He was holding two drinks, and it was apparent that the ice in them was melting.

Please catch my eye, Nathan! she screamed in her head.

"I know you. Who are you?" Tank said again with a dark tone.

"I don't think we've ever met," she said, carefully choosing her words. "I mean, I don't recog—"

He cut her off, "What is your name?"

"What is your name?" she said with a hint of agitation in her voice.

"Tank," he said. "Yours?"

"Abigail," she said softly. "See? We don't know each other."

She wanted to leave and go over to Nathan, but he appeared to be talking to some important people.

"Who's this?" Jessica said in a bubbly voice.

Tank barely turned to see her.

Feeling even more on alert but thankful to at least see another girl, Abigail said quietly, "Abigail."

"Hi, I'm Jessica."

"Hi," she said, wishing more than anything she could run away.

Thankfully, she could see out of the corner of her eye that Nathan was approaching, and he did not appear pleased.

"Hey, guys," he said flatly with a touch of displeasure. "I see you've finally met Abby."

"Abby?" Tank said with a raised voice. "You said your name was Abigail."

Nathan cut in, "It is, big guy." Then, eyeing Abigail, he said, "I guess I'm the only one who calls you Abby." He laughed.

She kept her eyes wide. He took notice.

"Hey, Jessica," Nathan said with little interest.

"You all know each other?" Abigail asked with gritted teeth.

"Yeah, Tank is on the team, and I met Jessica...well," he said with a smirk, "a while back at a party."

"Ah," Abigail said, stepping closer to Nathan.

"Yes, so you guys are both up for Rookie of the Year. That is amazing. Guess you both had excellent seasons," Jessica said.

"Some better than others," Tank quipped.

Tank had not taken his eyes off her, and Abigail was starting to feel uncomfortable.

"What's that supposed to mean?" Nathan asked.

Tank just leered at him.

"Can we go get something to eat?" she said slightly under her breath.

"Of course." Nathan put their drinks down.

"Please tell me you two are not..." Tank grumbled.

Jessica glared at him with obvious disappointment.

"Dating? Yeah, Tank," Nathan said.

Tank glared at Abigail with an expression of anger and hurt. It frightened her.

"So, *you're* the one from the article?" Tank finally said, almost second-guessing himself.

Feeling relieved, she said, "Yeah, that's me."

"Yep, you've finally met the mystery girl." Nathan laughed.

Abigail gave him a quizzical stare.

"No, there is something else, something I can't quite place," Tank said softly.

"Sorry," she finally said, "I can't help you. Can we go grab something?" she said, reaching for Nathan's hand.

"Yeah, sure. Hey, guys, we'll see you at the dinner."

"Bye," Jessica said.

Tank remained silent.

As they walked away, Abigail said, "He was giving me the creeps. He kept saying he knew me."

"Oh, from the article. Like I said, he wanted to know who you were, and I sort of played him a bit and said you wanted to remain anonymous. I'm sure it just ate away at him. He's been a little tough to deal with. The team has been just sort of ignoring his strange behavior. Really nothing to worry about."

"Okay," she said with hesitation, "if you say so."

"It's fine. The guy's just a bit messed up, and quite frankly, he has this thing about me. Don't think he likes me too much."

"No?"

"Nah. Can't quite figure out why, but I'm not going to solve the mystery tonight either."

The dinner bell rang quietly throughout the cocktail reception, and a man in a suit with white gloves announced that everyone should begin moving into the main banquet hall to find their tables. Dinner would be served in ten minutes.

Nathan and Abigail searched for table seven. It was near the front of the room, in the middle. Coach Stanfield was sitting at the table with his wife, and they were also seated next to Coach Bromley and his wife. Introductions were made, and Nathan and Abigail sat down next to them. No sooner had they taken their seats than Nathan saw Tank and Jessica approaching the table. The only two seats left were directly across from Abigail and Nathan.

Abigail struck up a conversation with Coach Bromley's wife as they enjoyed the first course of Caesar salad.

As the dinner progressed and the opening remarks began, Abigail could feel Tank staring at her. Trying desperately not to let it ruin Nathan's evening, she did everything in her power to ignore Tank's persistent glares. Thankfully, Nathan was chatting with the coaches and players from other teams as they passed by the table so that he had little time to take notice. In fact, no one else seemed to acknowledge it to the point where Abigail began questioning her own assessment of the situation.

Finally, it was award time, and Abigail could focus her attention back toward Nathan. The program listed twelve awards to be handed out this evening. It was the same group of awards as at most sports banquets— Coach of the Year, MVP, Rookie of the Year, and so on.

For the most part, the speeches were kept short and sweet. As they worked their way down the program, she observed Nathan's demeanor changing. He seemed to be fidgeting more. He barely ate his dinner and sipped nervously on his ice water as the MC began announcing the players who had been nominated for Rookie of the Year.

"Nathan Ryan, quarterback, Onondaga State University," the gentleman at the podium said.

Nathan's face flushed.

A few people hollered at his name, but for the most part, people kept still as all the names were read.

"Thomas McPherson, tight end, Onondaga State University."

Tank grumbled something as his name was called, Abigail noted. Jessica reached over to touch his arm, but he seemed not to welcome her gesture.

There was silence as the representative from the Big East scanned the crowd before taking the envelope off the podium in front of him. He seemed to open it slowly, as though he alone would build enough momentum to drop the ultimate bomb on everyone in the audience. He knew the torture he was putting the players and their families and friends through as he read the winner to himself. Then, finally, he looked up at the crowd and seemed to turn his attention toward the center of the room.

With a deep breath, he leaned down toward the microphone and said, "The award goes to Nathan Ryan, Onondaga State University!"

Applause erupted in the banquet hall.

Abigail had an overwhelming sense of happiness at the sound of his name as it echoed through the banquet room. She wanted to gasp and scream, but she remained calm and composed.

Nathan hung his head in disbelief as the entire room stood up in applause. It was a huge accomplishment. He knew it, his coaches knew it, and everyone in the room knew what an incredible year he had had.

After he stood up, he leaned over and planted a kiss on Abigail's cheek.

She squeezed his arm and whispered in his ear, "I'm so happy for you, Nathan."

He turned to each of his coaches and hugged them. Then, he made his way around the table. When he got toward Tank, Tank reluctantly shook Nathan's hand, attempting not to be obvious at his disapproval that Nathan had been chosen over him, as his coaches eyed him.

"Lucky break, huh, Two?" Tank said with a smile, knowing full well Nathan was the only one that could hear him.

Not wanting Tank to ruin his moment, Nathan just shrugged and said back, "That, and hard work." He released Tank's hand and made his way to the stage.

The applause quieted as he got closer to the microphone.

He pulled out a card from inside his coat pocket, placed it on the podium, and put his other hand on the trophy. He smiled. "Thank you so much," he said, his voice echoing through the now silent banquet hall. "First, I'd like to thank the Big East for this wonderful banquet. I'd also like to say what an honor it is to even be nominated along with the other players here tonight. It has been a great year for so many of you, and I truly feel grateful to be recognized." He waited through the applause.

"Thank you to Onondaga State University for allowing me to not only represent your institution as a student athlete, but also for the years of tradition and excellence that has surrounded the school and its athletic programs. There is nowhere else I'd rather play. To my coaches, thank you for believing in me and supporting me. I can't thank you enough for the opportunity.

"To my teammates." He stopped.

There was a brief sense of sadness as he began to recognize his team. The year had not gone exactly as he had envisioned it would, and most of that was due to the only other person from his team who was here tonight.

He continued, "Here's hoping for three more great years together."

He searched his table and caught Tank's eyes. There was no emotion in them, and he appeared absent. Nathan nodded toward him, if for nothing else, to give the illusion to others that his teammate supported him.

"Lastly, I'd like to thank my parents for all their love and support. My dad has been there for me through many tough times and always put me first despite anything he was going through, and I wouldn't be here today…without him."

He collected himself before saying, "Mom, I know you're watching over me. I hope I've made you proud." He stopped again and then said in a quieter voice, "I even think you might have sent a special person my way, so thank you, Mom."

He gazed over at Abigail. She had tears in her eyes, and she got a rush when he acknowledged her. He seemed so proud and appreciative, and it was only the third time she'd heard him speak of his mother.

The room was silent as he scanned the crowd. Then, he picked up his trophy, gazed up toward the sky, and raised it slightly in honor of his mother. There wasn't one wife in the whole place with a dry eye. Maybe even a few of the coaches themselves were affected.

Nathan took his card and trophy and turned and walked off the stage as the room erupted with applause. He quickly hurried down the stairs. Lights flashed as he got his picture taken with representatives from the Big East in the mock studio they had set up for the media next to the stage.

Abigail waited with anticipation for him to return to her side. She wanted so badly to tell him what a wonderful and beautiful speech he'd just given. Her chest was bursting with pride, and even though she'd never known his mom, she unequivocally knew his mother would have been proud.

Tank, on the other hand, sat there, sulking, with his arms folded over his large chest. Strangely though, he seemed to be more disappointed by the fact that Nathan had won, as opposed to himself losing. He had spent a majority of Nathan's speech observing Abigail watching Nathan.

She'd tried to ignore him, but she just couldn't. Even more so, she wasn't sure if Jessica just didn't care or hadn't noticed or if she was just used to his peculiar behavior to put any stock into it today. Jessica had sat there through most of the awards banquet, picking at her nail polish or gawking at the other players. Maybe they both had wandering eyes. Abigail did all she could not to make eye contact with them, and that in itself was painfully obvious.

It seemed like hours before Nathan returned to the table, but in reality, it was fifteen minutes at most. When he approached, Abigail stood and threw her arms around him. She was even surprised by her reaction, but it just felt right. As they finally let go, he wiped a small tear from his eye.

"Your mother is proud of you, Nathan. I just know it," she said sweetly.

He regarded her with soft eyes and said, "Thank you, Abby. I appreciate that."

"Congratulations!"

She couldn't say for sure, but from what she could see out of the corner of her eye, it seemed that Tank was still glaring at her. She couldn't wait to leave the banquet.

The Big East representatives made their final closing remarks as dessert was being served. It had been a long night already, and Abigail and Nathan still had to drive the hour or so home.

"We'll leave as soon as we can," Nathan whispered to Abigail. "Promise."

"Sounds good," she said.

A final loud round of applause ensued as the video depicting what would be the remaining stars for the upcoming season was shown on the big screen on the stage. She actually liked seeing Nathan in action. He was such a good player.

"Bye, Coach Bromley," Nathan said, reaching out to shake his hand.

"Proud of you, Nathan. Great year. Really great year."

"Yes, all year, my husband said that you'd be a star, and he was right," his wife remarked.

"Well, thank you. Appreciate it."

"Nice meeting you, Abigail," Coach said.

"Thank you, Coach," Abigail said softly.

Abigail went to grab her coat, but Nathan, as kind as he was, took it for her and draped it over his arm. He took her hand, and with a quick wink at her, he started to lead them through the crowd. She could see the main doors ahead, only they seemed to be miles away at the rate they were going, shuffling through the crowd that was all trying to leave at once. Still, she tried to be patient, as this was Nathan's night, one she was sure he would remember for a long time. As she was politely introduced to a few alumni along the way, Abigail noticed Tank and Jessica were right behind them, making the same patterns in and out of the crowd.

As they approached the doors, Nathan opened Abigail's coat to help her put it on. He pulled her hair to one side in an attempt to help, and in doing so, he accidentally pulled down on the strap of her dress, exposing her shoulder. She flushed until she felt a slight shove and what she assumed was Nathan grasping her shoulder. She turned quickly to see Nathan grabbing Tank's arm.

"What are you doing?" Nathan asked in a hushed but angry voice.

Ignoring him, Tank said, "What is that on your shoulder?"

She put her jacket on in a hurry. "What?" she attempted to ask.

Nathan took her by the shoulders and moved her toward the door. Tank followed them with a clueless Jessica trailing behind.

As they hurried out the main doors, he repeated with desperation in his voice, "What is that on your shoulder?"

"Tank!" Jessica yelled as he hurried in front of her.

Feeling fearful as Nathan rushed her toward the car, she peered over her shoulder to see Tank still heading in their direction. Nathan unlocked her door and gently forced her inside before handing her his trophy. Then, he turned with his chest puffed as Tank approached the car. Abigail could clearly hear their conversation through the closed door. It was not friendly. She reached up and locked the door.

"Dude, you are making Abby uncomfortable. Knock it off." He was backed into a corner to defend his girlfriend. He could not allow the aggression he was currently feeling grow within him and take over. He would risk appearing like a total jerk.

"Whatever. Listen, you think you're so much better than everyone else. Well, guess what? You're not!" Tank yelled.

"What in the hell are you talking about?" Nathan said through gritted teeth. This was getting way out of control between the two of them, and the scariest part for Nathan was that he still had no solid evidence as to why Tank disliked him so.

"I want to know what that is on her shoulder!" Tank's eyes bore through the windshield.

Abigail tried not to lock eyes with him. Thankfully, it was too dark to see his expression.

"I need you to turn the hell around and get out of here!" Nathan started to walk toward Tank in an attempt to back him away from the car.

Soon, Jessica approached, and Coach Stanfield was with her.

"What the hell is going on here?" he yelled. Then, he noticed other players and coaches heading toward their cars in the parking lot, so he stepped closer to Tank and Nathan. Firmly, he said, "Never mind. Nathan, get in your car and take Abby home."

Nathan attempted to speak, but Coach just raised his hand and motioned toward the car door. Nathan dropped his head, feeling ashamed more than anything that he'd found himself in this situation but, worse, because it was in front of Abby.

"You, don't move," Coach barked at Tank. "And, Jessica, is it? Take his keys, and he'll meet you in the car," he said. His words were harsh despite his attempt to try to speak nicely to her.

Coach Stanfield waited for Jessica to take the keys from Tank, and then he approached Tank. "I swear to God, if you don't knock it off and quit embarrassing our program, Coach Bromley is going to find out about this on Monday. Let me tell you, after the incident in the locker room last month, you leaving the semester early"—he took a sniff for effect—"your general lack of hygiene, and don't think I can't smell booze on you. Do you think I'm stupid?"

"No," Tank said under his breath.

"Your time is almost up, McPherson. Do you want that scholarship pulled?"

"No," he said again.

"Then, you'd better wise up—and fast." In a more reserved tone, he said, "Now, take your friend here home, and shit, try not to scare her any more than you already have. And please tell her to drive *you* home." He shook his head and walked away.

Tank waited and then glared down at the Onondaga State Football pin attached to his jacket. In one swift movement, he pulled it off, ripping his jacket in the process. With tremendous force, he threw the pin into the woods. Tank let out a groan as he turned on his heel and walked toward his truck.

Jessica was already sitting in the driver's seat. She seemed nervous and confused. She quickly buckled her seat belt as Tank hopped in.

"Let's get the hell out of here," he barked.

Jessica put the car in drive and drove the entire hour home in silence. It wasn't until she entered the main gate to campus and pulled into the parking lot that he finally turned to her.

"I can't be alone," he said.

"I'll try to help you," she said hesitantly.

"I don't want your help. I just don't want to be alone."

"Same thing," she said flatly.

It didn't take long before Abigail turned to Nathan with noticeable concern. "Nathan, what was that all about? And don't tell me to ignore him," she said with a hint of anger in her voice.

"I know; I know. You're right. I have no idea, but believe me, I plan to get to the bottom of it. I'm so sorry, Abby. I can't say that enough."

"I know, Nathan. It is not your fault. I'm upset, too, because I feel like this…us…he ruined your night."

"Oh, no way. I'm not going to let that guy ruin my night. No freaking way!"

"I know, but if I wasn't here, none of this—"

"Abby! Don't you think my night would be ruined by you saying that? I am so glad that you're here. I wouldn't change that for anything."

"That's kind of you to say, but—" She could feel the sting of tears in her eyes.

"But nothing. Don't make me pull over this car, Abby, 'cause I will, and I'll show you just how much I appreciate you," he said playfully.

She hesitated, wishing she could smile, but she had this lingering feeling that something was just not right. "Nathan, it's just so creepy, the way he was staring at me. You don't know how he was acting before you got back to the cocktail table. It was so *weird.*"

"He's *weird,* and like I said, he has issues, but that doesn't excuse it. Maybe he likes you, Abby. Ever consider that?"

"Nathan, it's not like that. He had a date. I don't know," she said, feeling frustrated that Nathan didn't seem to get the strangeness of the interaction with Tank. It had nothing to do with liking a person. It was different.

Nathan turned briefly toward her. "We'll work it out, whatever this is. Now, please don't be worried about him. I hate to see you upset over a misunderstanding."

"Okay. But I don't think I misunderstood anything back there, Nathan. Do you think I just made it up?"

"No, no. Sorry, I didn't mean it like that. What I meant is, the guy is just not in a good place, and I think he lashes out a lot. Trust me; he's done it to me a few times now. I guess I'm doing a terrible job of trying to say that I'll handle it on Monday, promise."

"Okay," she said softly. She gazed out the window and tried to calm her mind. She took a deep breath and then added, "It was beautiful, what you said about your mom and—"

He cut in, "And you. I meant that."

She turned to him. "I sensed it." She reached over and put her hand on his leg.

"Good."

When they returned to the dorm around eleven thirty, the party on Abigail's floor was still in full swing. The DMs usually didn't allow parties on the floors, but it just so happened that their DM, Brittney, was a huge football fan. She was kind enough to not only turn a blind eye, but to also join in.

"They're here!" Brittney yelled.

Everyone turned as Nathan and Abigail walked in.

Someone yelled, "Well?"

With a red face, Nathan held up his trophy, and the entire floor erupted in cheers.

"Ah, man, congratulations!" Webber made his way toward Nathan. He shook Nathan's hand. "I know how hard you worked for this. Well deserved!" he yelled over the music.

"Yeah, we're so happy for you!" Melissa said.

Bree squeezed her way through and handed Nathan a cup. She turned to the crowd. "Excuse me!" Bree yelled. "Can I have your attention?"

The hallway got quiet, and someone turned down the music in Bree's room.

"Thank you," she said as she flipped her hair to the side.

All eyes were on her, and she loved every minute of it.

She raised her glass. "To Nathan!"

Everyone yelled, "To Nathan!"

Seeing that Bree had conveniently forgotten to give a drink to Abigail, Laura snuggled up next to her and gave her drink to her roommate. "Seems like you could use this," Laura said with a questioning expression.

"Thanks," Abigail said flatly as she took the cup.

"What's up?" Laura asked.

"Nothing," Abigail said unconvincingly.

"Oh no, you don't." Laura gently grabbed her friend by the arm. "Nathan, congratulations. Uh, Abigail and I are just going to our room for a bit—to take off these shoes and stuff." She motioned toward Abigail's high heels.

"Okay, sure. Don't be too long."

Before they left Bree's room, Laura quickly bolted to the left. "Wait here. I'll be right back." She grabbed two new drinks and returned. "Okay, now, we can go!"

They walked into their room, which had been kept open as part of the floor party policy created by Bree. So as not to call attention, she kept the door halfway opened, and then they walked over to their beds. Abigail sat down, and Laura sat across from her. Handing Abigail another drink, Laura waited patiently for her to spill the beans. She waited and waited. Then, she sipped her drink and waited some more.

When Laura couldn't take it anymore, she said, "So, things with Nathan are okay, right? What's the issue?"

Abigail put the cup to her lips, and with three huge gulps, she drank most of the contents, swallowing hard. Then, she briefly shook her head. "It's fine—I mean, great. It's great, Laura. I was—I am so happy for him, but…" She closed her eyes as the events of the evening flashed before her—the stares, the yelling, the grabbing, the embarrassment of it all. She squeezed her eyes tight, not wanting to open them and face Laura.

"But what?"

Finally, she opened them. Laura seemed concerned and confused.

Abigail peered around their room to make sure they were alone. "I want to tell you, but I'm not sure if it's me or what?"

"Abigail, you know you can tell me anything. No judgment here." Laura rested her arms on her legs.

Abigail took another sip of her drink. She wasn't a drinker per se, but every once in a while, she'd allow herself to have one or two, and this was one of those times. "There was this guy. Maybe you know him? They call him Tank, I guess." She turned her head, trying to fight back her tears. "I don't know, Laura. It was so bizarre. He kept staring at me, telling me he knew me and…"

Laura got up, came over to Abigail's bed, and sat next to her. She put her hand on Abigail's leg, trying to reassure her that everything was okay even though she had no idea why her friend was upset.

"Tank, huh? Yeah, I think maybe Bree knows this girl he used to hook up with. Um…Jessica?"

"Yeah! Yeah, she was there!"

Seeing Abigail getting more anxious as she began telling the story, Laura poured the remainder of her drink into Abigail's empty cup, hoping maybe the alcohol would relax her a bit.

"Go on," Laura said as Abigail took another sip.

Abigail's hands were shaking. "I met her, but when she wasn't around, Tank kind of kept glaring at me, and at the end of the night…he sort of tried to grab my shoulder. Then, Nathan had to step in—"

"Wait, what? Tank grabbed you?"

"Shh, keep it down. Yeah, it was so creepy, and to be honest, I was a bit freaked out, but I didn't want to make Nathan more upset. Then, Tank followed us to our car and tried to talk to me. She came by—Jessica, I mean—and he was, like, ignoring her and yelling at Nathan about me—"

"Like, he likes you or something?"

"No. That's just it. It was nothing like that." She took another sip. "It was like he had seen a ghost or something."

"What? Oh, Abigail, this is too much. What a weirdo!"

"Poor Nathan. They were yelling in the parking lot—well, more Tank than Nathan—but then their coach came over and made us leave. As we pulled away, we could see him barking at Tank, and the girl was just sitting in the truck. It was just too much. I'm worried there will be repercussions with the team on Monday, and I'll be partially to blame. Plus, I feel like I've ruined Nathan's night even though he won't admit it."

"Well, for what it's worth, it sure doesn't seem like you did, okay? He seems so happy, Abigail."

"I know. I'm trying to forget it all ever happened. But…" She stared off, feeling at a loss for words.

"Well, for now, you should. Let's go celebrate." Laura stood up and extended her hand to Abigail before gently pulling her up from the bed. She hesitated for a moment, making sure her friend didn't want to talk anymore, before she went over to Abigail's closet and got out her flip-flops. She placed them in front of Abigail's feet.

Forcing a smile, Abigail kicked off her shoes and slipped on her flip-flops, and her aching feet welcomed the cushiony beach shoes.

Laura reached up and wiped a bit of makeup off Abigail's cheek. "Boy, for someone as upset as you, you're still stunning."

"Thanks, Laura," she said as she leaned in for a hug.

Laura squeezed her tight and whispered, "Of course, anytime. And next time you see that creep, you tell him I said he's a real jerk!"

"Let's hope I never see him again." She released their embrace.

"Come on." Laura gently took her friend's hand.

Abigail followed Laura to their door. They were about to enter the hallway when they ran into Webber right outside their door.

He seemed surprised and stammered, "Oh, I was just coming to see you guys."

"We're going back to the party. Come with us," Laura said cheerfully, trying to keep any hint of their conversation a secret.

He regarded Abigail intently. "You okay?"

"Yes, of course. Why?" she said, seeing the obvious concern on his face.

Did Nathan say something to him already about what had happened?

"Nothing. Have a good time?"

"Yeah, it was nice."

"Okay. Just asking. No big deal."

Laura pulled on Abigail's arm. "Come on, you two. Oh, by the way, I'm staying in Jen's room tonight. Casey is out of town." She winked at Abigail. "Catch my drift?"

"I'm catching it," she said with a giggle as the alcohol started to swirl in her brain.

"Good. Now, let's find the guys."

They ducked into Bree's room, and much to no one's surprise, Bree was cozied up next to Nathan, flirting and laughing as she sipped her drink.

"Can I hold your trophy?" she asked playfully.

Not catching her innuendo, he quickly said, "Sure, if you want." He handed it to her.

Feeling bold, Abigail walked right up to him, pulled his tie in a way that forced him closer to her, and planted a kiss on his lips.

He blushed and said, "What was that for?"

"Just wanted to say congratulations again!" she said, slightly winking at Bree.

Bree stood there, holding a plastic trophy, while Abigail had the real thing.

"Thanks!" He smiled. "Another drink?"

"Sure. Why not?"

Nathan walked over to the makeshift bar that was usually Bree's desk and poured two drinks.

"Nicely played, Abigail," Bree hushed under her breath.

"You, too."

They drank and listened to music until about one in the morning when the DM finally came around and said that it was time to start closing the party down.

"Where's Laura?" Nathan asked.

"She's staying in Jen's room tonight."

"Really?" he said, trying to hide his obvious excitement.

"Yes." She gulped.

It had been hard for them to find time alone, neither wanting to kick out their roommates on a regular basis. And in the case of Webber, they knew he didn't have anyplace else to go.

"Well, what are we doing here then?" he asked as he took her arm. He scooped up his trophy off the dresser. "Thanks, Bree!" he yelled.

He headed down the hallway, pulling Abigail along by the hand. Abigail just giggled as she heard Bree mutter something about the party not being over. Nathan and Abigail couldn't have cared less.

Nathan walked into Abigail's room and quickly shut the door and locked it. He put the trophy on her desk and centered it in the middle. "A token of me."

He took off his coat and laid it on the desk chair. He started to unbutton the top button on his shirt as Abigail leaned against the wall. She waited as he pulled down on his tie to loosen it. Then, with both hands, he grabbed it and began to remove it. It was then she heard that sound—the sound a tie made against a collar, the rubbing together of silk and cotton. She always loved hearing that sound in the movies and on TV. If nothing else, it said there was a man in the room, and he was getting undressed. How could she not like that sound?

He placed his tie on top of his coat. She surveyed his every move. He seemed not to notice, which she liked even more.

Then, he asked, "You checking me out?" He playfully unbuttoned a few more buttons on his dress shirt.

She nodded as the effects of the alcohol rushed over her.

With a swift and effortless motion, he went over to the window and pulled down the shade. "Your turn."

"You'll have to help me." She turned her back and held up her hair.

He walked over and gradually unzipped her dress. He gently pulled it down her shoulders and kissed her neck. She turned toward Nathan and reached up to finish unbuttoning his dress shirt. She pulled his shirt out of his pants and slowly dragged it down his shoulders, deliberately gliding her fingertips over his muscular skin.

His body was something to gaze at, a real masterpiece. His waist was thin, but he wasn't skinny at all. His muscles were perfectly stacked from his chest down to the top of his pants, one after another after another. The muscles right over his hips were set in flawless arches. He had luscious skin, perfect broad shoulders, and long and lean arms. She couldn't find one thing about him that she would change.

He towered over her as his shirt dropped on the floor. He ran his fingers over her shoulder as he pushed her hair back. He noticed her blush as he pulled down her dress, revealing her lace bra and panties. He let the dress fall to the floor. She stood there, as beautiful as ever, and a surge of excitement came over him.

He slightly backed her up against the wall. Her five-foot-four frame seemed to crumple as he wrapped his arm around her waist. His breaths began to deepen.

He had waited patiently to be alone with her again. He needed to be alone with her. He was so drawn to her that he could hardly sleep at night. Thinking about her—imagining when and where he could see her again, kiss her again, and touch her again—was all he could do to get through the day. His heart ached when she wasn't around.

She unhooked his belt along with the top button on his pants and pulled them down to the floor. Never letting her go, he stepped out of them, and in one swift motion, he picked her up and carried her over to the bed.

He laid her down and let his body lean over her as he gazed into her eyes. "Oh, Abby," he said with a sexy grin, "you've got me hooked. You recognize that, don't you?"

She couldn't wait a moment longer. "Kiss me, Nathan."

He teasingly gave her a sweet kiss on the lips and then laughed.

"Oh, you're playing with me, are you?" she said with a pout.

He liked that she began to squirm as he stared at her and said, "Maybe. Ask me again."

Her breathing began to get heavier as the anticipation of kissing him, really kissing him, started to build.

"Kiss me, Nathan…please," she said in a breathless whimper.

He leaned over and kissed her neck, her collarbone, and then slowly moved across to the other side. Then, he kissed back up her neck to her ear, nibbling a little, as her breaths got deeper and deeper. He removed her bra straps and gently unhooked her bra. She took it off and threw it on the floor.

My God, her breasts are magnificent.

He could tell by how hard her nipples were that he was turning her on. He could feel her body moving underneath him as he kept his body only slightly pressed on hers. He pulled on her hair, exposing the front of her neck.

She moaned and begged, "Nathan, please."

Finally, he wrapped his arms around her body and pulled her over on top of him, her hair falling down on his chest. He grinned at her.

"You're terrible," she breathed.

"Kiss me, Abby." This time, he couldn't wait any longer, so he pulled her head toward his.

She ran her hands all through his messy curls as they kissed.

God, I missed feeling him like this.

They didn't get nearly enough time alone.

He spun her again and pressed his body on hers. He moved his hands from her hips and slowly ran them up her legs, gently caressing her over her panties. She made a sharp gasp as he began running the tips of his fingers in between her legs.

Oh God. I can't wait any longer.

He kissed the top of her breast.

She moaned, "I want you so badly."

Something inside her told her she was ready.

He stopped only for a brief moment to glance up at her, but her eyes were closed. He knew she was enjoying his touch.

"Are you sure, Abby?" He returned to moving his fingers.

"Yes," she said as she opened her eyes. One look at him, and she knew this was their moment. "Yes, I swear, I'm so ready."

"I want you, too, Abby. You know I do," he said before they kissed.

She melted in his arms, and as she did, she couldn't help but think that he was well worth the wait. She was finally ready to commit herself to Nathan, and she knew this moment would tie them together forever.

Twenty-Three

JANUARY 24, 1996

Tank tossed and turned all night, thinking about his last day at home over the Christmas break.

"Merry Christmas, buddy," he said as he laid the poinsettia his mom had given him on Jonathan's headstone.

"Sure do miss you," he said, wiping away a tear.

"School—hell, life just isn't the same without you. I think about you every day." He took a deep breath. "I saw your mom, dad, and Will a lot over the break. We spent Christmas Eve together. My mom had them over for dinner," he choked out, "like we used to."

The tears started flowing faster. He sank to his knees in the snow. He began to sob. He couldn't stop despite how hard he'd tried to force back the tears. He didn't regret going to the cemetery. He never did even though it made him sad. He just hated that he missed Jonathan so much.

"I still think about the last time we talked, and I don't wish it away, but it worries me. Somehow, it just haunts me..." He trailed off as he picked up some snow in his gloved hand and threw it across the plot.

"I'm struggling. I know it's not your fault, but I just am not handling this well." He laughed a bit to himself as he took the flask out from inside his coat pocket. He took a swig. He hated whiskey, but it was all his dad had in the liquor cabinet.

"This is the first time I've admitted that." He swallowed hard. He felt the snow beneath his knees start to melt through his jeans. He stood up.

He wiped a tear away as he wondered to himself if Jonathan knew he was here. He got closer to the stone and wiped some of the snow off the top. He tapped it twice and said, "Love ya."

Last night after the banquet, he'd wanted so badly to tell Jessica all this to explain his erratic behavior, but he just couldn't get himself to tell her. She still had no idea who Jonathan was. He wanted to tell her that he could not decide what was worse—being home or going back to school. He was trapped in his own misery and knew he had no one to talk with.

Could she be the one to save me?

As he had driven back to campus after Christmas break, he had decided that he would try Jessica one more time, only to be with her yet again last night and tell her nothing.

He tossed and turned all night long until he finally fell asleep around five in the morning.

Tank woke up in a sweat.

He gasped for air as he sat up in bed. He'd had the same dream again. It haunted him night after night.

"Jesus," Jessica quipped, "you nearly gave me a heart attack." She rubbed her eyes and tried to pull the covers back over her.

"Yeah," he said groggily. "Uh, don't be mad, but I forgot I have to do something this morning, so…" He trailed off. He was embarrassed that, for a moment, he'd thought he was alone.

"Oh, really?" she said sarcastically as she sat up, glancing at the clock. "I get it. You don't want to be here."

His head pounded from all the alcohol he'd drunk last night. "I'll explain later, I promise, okay?"

"Sure," she said, her voice dripping with disdain.

He scooted past her and pulled on his dress pants. He grabbed his shoes and socks and started to walk toward the door. He hesitated as he reached for the doorknob.

She glared at him, daring him to say something.

"Oh, my jacket." He picked up his coat off the floor.

It was obvious, if only to her, that he was in agony.

"Who's Jonathan?"

"What?"

"You kept saying Jonathan, and…I don't know…moon something or—who knows? Forget it. You were drunk," she scoffed.

His eyes widened as she said his friend's name, and within seconds, the memories of his last days with Jonathan came rushing back.

"What? Did I say something wrong?" she asked.

"No, it's just…I…"

She cut him off, "Listen, Tank, go take a shower and do what you need to do today, okay?"

"Yeah, I will. Hey," he said, "thanks for being cool."

"Sure," she said sadly.

After he closed the door, she reached over to her drawer, pulled out a bottle of Advil, took three, and washed them down with Gatorade. She winced as she swallowed. She put her head back onto the pillow and closed her eyes.

Tank, on the other hand, was not as lucky to just forget, to close his eyes and sleep off his pain. No, even as he walked mindlessly back across the quiet, dead campus, his memories played out before him like a broken record.

When Tank arrived at the hospital this afternoon, Jonathan was in a deep sleep. As usual, Tank didn't want to disturb his friend, so he just came in, opened his History textbook, and sat in a chair, waiting for Jonathan to wake up.

He began to stir.

"Wait till you see her," Jonathan whispered.

Seeing his eyes open, Tank asked, "Who, buddy?" Then, he inched closer to Jonathan's bed.

"Can I get some water?"

"Yeah, sure." Tank reached over and poured a glass of ice water from the pitcher on Jonathan's tray.

As Tank held the cup up to his mouth, Jonathan took a long sip from the straw.

"Ah, thanks."

"Sure, anytime. So, wait till I see who?"

"What?" Jonathan hesitated. "Oh, yes, the girl."

"What girl?" Tank asked.

"Her." He looked dazed and hollow. "The one," he said with certainty.

"What do you mean?"

"I keep seeing her..." He trailed off.

"Jonathan, you okay?" Tank said, knowing full well he wasn't.

Jonathan turned his head to face the wall. Tank could see his chest rise and fall.

"Dude, talk to me."

Jonathan turned with a tear in his eye. "I don't know what to say." He wiped away the single tear that had fallen. "But I keep seeing her, and she's at school. She's beautiful with navy eyes and long, wavy blonde hair. She has this mark on her—"

"Is this your dream?"

"I don't know. I don't know what it is. I mean, yeah, it is. It just feels so..."

"What?" Tank asked while putting his textbook on the table beside Jonathan's bed. Tank leaned in closer to Jonathan's bed. "Hey," he said in a whisper as he touched Jonathan's arm. "You can tell me. I'm your best friend, right?"

"Always," he whispered. He turned and stared out the window at the gray February day. He took another deep breath, and then he slowly turned back to Tank. "She said her name is Abby."

"Abby?"

"Yeah."

"She talks to you?"

"Yeah, sort of. I think she's the one."

Tank stopped dead in his tracks. It didn't matter that it was minus ten degrees out. He stood there, frozen in his mind, unable to move.

This can't be happening. He scanned the campus. Searching for what, he could not say. Then, he took a cold, deep breath and let it out.

"Abby?" he said out loud. "No way. It can't be. I can't freaking handle this."

He started to feel his body tingle all over. A mysterious sensation crawled over him, making him physically shudder.

What the hell is happening to me? Am I losing my mind, or did Jonathan actually see the future or the past or whatever the hell he was trying to tell me? Did I actually see a ghost? Is Abby some kind of heavenly being? No, of course not. Don't be ridiculous. She is real, and there is no way that Jonathan was talking about the same girl. It's impossible.

He spun around again, searching for a place to go to get away from himself, from the crazy thoughts he was feeling. He couldn't think about going back to his room, and he couldn't go down to the field house. All he knew was, he needed to get some air and grab a coffee or something to clear his head.

Abigail woke up to find a letter lying on the pillow next to her head. She'd slept so soundly that she never heard Nathan get up.

Last Goodbye

Abby,

I didn't have the heart to wake you. You looked so perfect.

Last night was perfect, too.

Sorry to run, but I know my father is dying to talk to me about the banquet last night. I hope you understand.

I'll call you later for lunch.

XO,

Nathan

She hugged the letter to her bare chest and took a deep breath in and then slowly let it out.

Last night. Yes, last night was something to remember indeed.

She slowly got up, taking her time, enjoying the new feeling she had.

She relived the awesome memories of last night as she pulled on a pair of jeans, a navy sweatshirt, and Columbia boots. She paid extra attention to her hair today, taking time in wrapping each strand around her round brush, almost as if she were in a trance. She put on her knit hat and gloves.

Not bad, she thought as she beheld herself in the mirror, pink cheeks and all.

She grabbed her bag and keys and walked out the door with a special zip in her step. She was no longer Abigail, the virgin, who had had a hard time with relationships. She was now Abigail, the girl who had finally found the perfect guy.

She wanted to spend some time alone, so instead of going to the cafeteria where she was sure Laura and the rest of the gang were, she decided she would walk downtown to Cool Beans instead. It was a small coffee shop, and thankfully, it wasn't the most popular in town, which was why Abigail frequented it on the days when she just wanted some quiet study time.

As she pulled open the door to the coffee shop, she was relieved, as she always was, to see it virtually empty. "The Freshmen" by The Verve Pipe was playing in the background. It was a sad song, but there was no chance of it affecting her today.

She approached the counter and ordered a bagel and a coffee. While waiting, she grabbed a seat at a small table near the window. She opened her textbook and then pulled out her Bruce Springsteen tape from her bag. She put the tape in her Walkman before she put on her headphones.

Adjusting the volume to low, she started to read chapter eighteen of her Biology textbook. She kept her head down as the music played softly.

"Wheat bagel with light cream cheese and a large coffee?" the girl behind the counter said moments later.

Abigail stood up and nearly froze. She would recognize that mass of a human being with shocking blond hair from anywhere. Standing directly in front of where her order had just been placed was none other than Tank. She blinked hard and steadied herself. Then, she questioned for a moment if she should just turn and walk right out, undetected.

"Wheat bagel, light cream cheese, and a large coffee?" the girl behind the counter said again, staring right at Abigail.

Tank glanced over his shoulder to see who the woman was so persistently staring at while holding the bagel and coffee.

"Oh no," he said under his breath. His shoulders dropped.

He noticed she wasn't moving either. Feeling terrible, he took the bagel and coffee and slowly walked over to her table. He put the bagel and coffee in front of her textbook and noticed the tape. He stopped and stared at the cover. Then, like a flash, he remembered her coming through the doors of the student union, singing the Bruce Springsteen song. Jonathan had told him that Abby listened to her music loud and sang like no one was around and that she loved Bruce Springsteen, just like he had.

Tank took a deep breath and shook his head. *Stop it! You're being crazy. This is crazy. She is not the same person.*

"What?" Abigail said with discontent. She didn't like the sound of her own voice. It was rude, unrecognizable.

Feeling it, he quipped back, "Nothing. Forget it."

He searched her face. It was the first time he was able to take her all in without interruption—her hair, her eyes, the way she fidgeted with her hands as she nervously tried to speak. He could tell this was difficult for her. She had probably never said an unkind word to anyone in her life.

"You know," she said before she even realized she was talking to him, "I'm getting real sick of you—"

She tore her headphones off her head and placed them on the table. He was disheveled, and he was obviously in the same clothes from last night.

Tank's anger began to rise. "You and that boyfri—"

She cut him off quickly, "Excuse me? You're the one who seems to have a problem with him and apparently *me* for some reason."

"You don't get it!" His voice rose. *You don't get it. My friend is dead, and I think he knew you.*

The woman behind the counter cleared her throat. They both turned, and she gave them the evil eye.

Abigail whispered, "No, I guess I don't." She went to grab her books.

Then, he said, "No, don't leave. I will."

He walked back over to the counter, grabbed his coffee, and started walking to the door. He turned, and with deep sarcasm, he said, "Let me guess. 'Thunder Road' is your favorite, huh?"

Wait, what? How the hell does he know that song is my favorite?

For a brief moment, she was stationary as he walked out the door. She had a strange emotion come over her, like she didn't want him to walk away, like she somehow had a connection to him, a very strange connection. She could not articulate the pull she felt toward the door. She dropped her book and ran outside after him.

"Hey!" she yelled.

He stopped dead in his tracks and then slowly turned. She caught up to him.

"How did you know that?" she asked.

"I know lots of things, *Abby*." He stressed her name, like it meant something. *I do. I know so much, and I'm scared to tell you. I know you'll think I'm crazy. What's worse is, you'll tell Nathan. Then, the whole team will know, and I'll never, ever hear the end of it.*

"My name is Abigail," she said firmly.

"It's also Abby, and Nathan wasn't the fir—"

"I'm not having this conversation anymore!" she said with a huff and started to storm away.

She was determined to leave him behind, so in a firm voice, he yelled, "Full moon tonight, Abby, but I guess you already know that!"

She didn't turn around right away. She sensed a chill run up her spine.

"*Full moon tonight, Abby,*" she repeated in her head.

Throughout her life, she had heard that countless times from her father and mother. Her birthmark was just a part of the reason the moon always seemed to pop up in conversations with her parents. They'd even named her Abigail Luna, and gave her the nickname Moon Pie, so naturally, as a kid, they always told her stories of the moon and how special it was, just like her. In fact, she had grown up loving any and all mysteries about the moon. She loved to learn about space, the earth, sun, and moon so much, and that was why she'd become so drawn toward and interested in the sciences.

"Why did you say that?" she said with an awful feeling in the pit of her stomach.

She turned when he didn't speak, but it was too late. He was gone, across the street and already halfway up the hill. She considered chasing after him, but all her books, wallet, everything was still inside the coffee shop.

She turned toward Cool Beans when she almost ran right into someone.

"Hey, you're Abby, right?"

She glanced over her shoulder, back toward Tank as he walked toward campus.

Marcus peered past her and squinted. He saw Tank before he disappeared behind a building.

"Yeah, sorry. Yes, I am."

"Yeah, yeah, Nathan's girl, right?"

"Yes," she repeated halfheartedly.

"He bothering you?" he asked sternly.

"Who? Nath—"

"No, Tank. Is he bothering you?" he asked again firmly.

"Well, no, I guess not, not exactly," she said. She stared at the ground and nervously smoothed out her sweater. "I'm…I'm sorry," she finally said. "You are?" she asked.

"Sorry, Marcus, captain of the football team."

"Oh, Marcus. Yes, yes, Nathan's told me a lot about you. Nice to meet you."

"You, too," he said with a sympathetic smile.

She faintly returned one.

Sensing her uneasiness, he said nicely, "Hey, I mean it, you need anything from us, just say the word. I live at the Ridge, okay?"

"Yeah, thanks. It's just…he…I don't know. He's kind of odd or sad or something, but I hardly know him so…" She trailed off. "Don't say anything to Nathan, okay?"

He appeared confused when he said, "Oh, sure. Again, just let me know if you need anything, all right?"

"Okay." She nodded and walked back into the coffee shop.

The girl behind the counter gave her a concerned face. She came over to Abigail, took her coffee off the table, and replaced it with a new one. "This one is hot," she said kindly.

"Thank you so much," Abigail said, feeling as though she wanted to spill her guts to the barista. But she didn't.

She finished her coffee and bagel and tried hard to put the last day or so behind her, but she found it harder and harder to concentrate. She wanted answers but didn't know what questions to ask.

Why did he say that about the full moon? Why had he grabbed my shoulder at the banquet? Why did he eye me so strangely? Then, she thought, *Maybe I do know what to ask him.*

She closed her book, grabbed her bag, and walked out the door. She turned quickly toward the window and waved slightly to the girl behind the counter.

Abigail walked into her room, and Laura was sitting at her desk.

"Hey!" she said cheerfully. "How was your night?"

"Fine. Did Nathan call?"

Seeing the look in her eye, Laura became more serious. "No, not that I'm aware of."

Abigail walked over to the phone, picked it up, and dialed his extension. It was dead. She hung up and tried again. Webber picked up on the second ring.

"Hey, Webber, it's me. Nathan there?" Her voice was hard.

"No, uh, Abigail, he tried calling you, but it was busy, over and over..." He faded off.

She sensed hesitation in his voice. "Webber?"

"Uh, no need to worry, but he had to go home to see his father. It's his uncle Dave. He had a heart attack."

"Oh no. What? Oh God, that's terrible."

"He said he'd call you when he could talk. I think he was going right to the hospital. You okay? You sound kind of...off," he said.

"Yeah, um, can I ask you something?" she said. "Does a guy named Tank live in your dorm? He plays football with Nathan."

"Yeah," he said with reluctance. "Why?"

"What room?"

"I don't know, Abigail. He's not on our floor. Why are you asking? He doesn't seem like a good guy—"

Abigail cut in, "Hey, keep this between us, okay? I don't want to worry Nathan."

"Abigail, I don't feel right about...well, I guess I won't say anything."

"Thanks," she said. "I'll talk to you soon, and if for some reason you talk to Nathan again, tell him I'm so sorry. Our phone must have been off the hook or something."

"Okay. Bye, Abigail."

"Bye, Webber."

Abigail hung up and walked back over toward her desk.

"Everything all right?" Laura asked.

"Oh, yeah. Well, not really. Nathan's uncle was visiting his dad, and now, he is in the hospital. Nathan's real close to him, so he had to go home. They think he had a heart attack or something. So sad. God, I hope he is okay."

"Oh, Abigail, I'm so sorry. Tell Nathan we're thinking of him."

"Of course," she remarked, trying not to seem in a hurry. "Hey, I kind of had another strange run-in with that guy Tank today...at the coffee shop."

"Oh, really? Are you okay?" Laura said with wide eyes.

"Yeah. I think so. It's probably nothing. Although it's kind of hard to put my finger on it. He acts sad one minute, and then he gets kind of mad for no reason. Also, he says all these cryptic things."

"Yeah, well, like you said from the banquet, he's odd. And he tried to grab you. Don't you think the best thing you could do at this point is just steer clear of him?"

She knew Laura was right, but something was pulling her toward him. He was becoming this mystery she had to solve.

If the tables were turned, I would absolutely tell Laura to keep away from him. Crap, if I'm going to find anything out, even just to see if there is something behind all this, I'll have to keep it from Laura, just for a little bit. Ugh, I hate keeping things from her. I feel so torn right now.

"Of course, obviously. But, hey, not to change the subject, but I'm going to go check my mail in the union. I'll meet you later for dinner. If Nathan calls, tell him I'll call him back, okay?"

"Sounds good," she said.

Abigail grabbed her keys and quickly opened the door before Laura could say a word. She hurried down the hall, toward the stairs. Once she was out of her building, she scurried across campus. She began to focus on a man up ahead. She saw what appeared to be Tank swaying as he approached his truck. He climbed in.

No way. He's drunk? It's only noon. He can't be!

Abigail yelled, "Tank, wait!"

Tank started to drive away but slammed on the brakes as he saw her. She approached the truck.

"I need to talk to you," she said with resentment.

"Leave me alone, Abby," he replied.

"I wish I could, but I feel like you are trying to tell me something, and I want to know why you're doing this to me."

"To you?" he yelled. "Can't you see what you're doing to me?"

"What are you talking about?" she barked back. She wasn't getting anywhere with him. Maybe she needed a new approach. "I'm sorry. I just don't understand," she said in a quieter voice.

Tank put his arm on the window. Abigail reached up and touched it. He quivered and pulled away.

Embarrassed that her approach was unwelcome, she said, "I'm sorry, but please?"

Tank let out a deep breath. Before he even spoke, he already regretted his words. "Does the name Jonathan Higgins ring any bells to you?"

"No. Wait…who?"

"Never mind. Just forget it, Abby." With that, he slammed his foot on the gas.

She reeled back as he nearly ran over her foot in an attempt to get away before she could say another word. She was left standing there, even more confused than she had been fifteen minutes ago.

"Jonathan Higgins," she whispered to herself. "Who is that?"

Twenty-Four

JANUARY 24, 1996

Abigail hurried across campus to the library. She walked in the door, showed her ID, and then went straight to the fourth floor.

"Where do we keep the yearbooks from our athletic programs?" she asked the woman behind the desk.

"Back corner, to the left."

Abigail hurried back and pulled the 1995 football media book off the shelf. It was the same one she had seen in Nathan's room. Quickly, she turned toward the roster page. She scanned the page until she found Tank's picture and information.

THOMAS MCPHERSON, FAIRMONT, NEW YORK

"Fairmont," she said out loud. She returned the book and went back to the desk.

"How can I search for someone in Fairmont, New York, say, from last year?" she asked. Then, she quickly said, "It's for a paper."

"Microfiche probably," the woman said. "You can try the local paper or just do a search."

"Sure, the paper."

She knew Tank played football, so there was probably an article in the local paper about him as a player, going to Onondaga State, or something. She needed to find out more about him.

The woman searched a database only she could see. She jotted down a few numbers and letters and then said, "Follow me."

Abigail walked behind her to a large file cabinet in the center of the room where the microfiche was stored in open-top envelopes that were placed in drawers by a coded alphanumeric system. She searched through the drawers and pulled out several envelopes that she handed to Abigail.

Abigail went over to the microfiche machine and put the first film in the machine. *The Fairmont News* was displayed on the first page. She noted the date—January 2, 1995. She scanned through to the Sports section, but nothing stood out. Then, she went on to the next section and then the next and then the next. Finally, she saw his name. It was a brief note, something about Tank choosing Onondaga State, blah, blah, blah. It was nothing of interest to Abigail.

She scoured the microfiche for over an hour, going through each paper headline by headline. By the time she got to the end of February, she was about ready to give up, but since the woman had so graciously pulled out all the microfiche for her, she felt obligated to carry on.

At March, she took a deep breath, feeling almost silly to be sitting here for so long, going through page after page of *The Fairmont News*.

What am I trying to find exactly? At this point, I have no idea.

She scanned the front page, the Help Wanted section, and the Entertainment section until she finally got to the Sports section.

COMMUNITY MOURNS THE LOSS OF FOOTBALL STAR JONATHAN HIGGINS.

She read it again.

"Jonathan Higgins," she said aloud to herself. *Jonathan Higgins. Wait, what?*

She quickly scanned the entire article, searching for anything that would make sense. She saw a picture of Jonathan, and she stared directly into the black-and-white photo, longing for something to ring a bell, but all she felt was more confused.

Why is this so important to me?

Then, she noticed the photo of what appeared to be Jonathan and his teammates. The picture was grainy and hard to make out. She zoomed in, and right there in the center was someone who resembled Tank. Quickly, she searched below at all the names, and in the middle, it said, *Thomas "Tank" McPherson.*

Feeling angry and somewhat scared, although she was not sure why, she put twenty cents into the machine and made a copy of the article.

She waited patiently as it printed out. She had no idea what she was going to do with the article, but she neatly folded it up and stuffed it in her pocket.

She left the library and went back to her dorm. Dusk was settling in, and in that moment, she realized how long she had been gone. Abigail hurried back to her room and opened the door. It was dark in the room. She took off her coat but not before sticking the article in her jeans pocket.

She felt apprehensive for a moment that maybe Laura had gone to the student union to find her. She switched on the light, and written on the whiteboard was a note from Laura.

Nathan called. He's okay. He said to call him tonight, 10 p.m. Went for an early dinner. Meet us there.

She instantly turned around, closed the door, and headed down to the cafeteria. The entire five-minute walk there, she tried to come up with a million excuses as to why she had been gone for so long. It wasn't that she didn't want to tell Laura. She was just leery of telling all the girls at dinner. According to the article, a boy had passed away, and it just didn't sit well with Abigail to talk about something like that, knowing so little about it.

She entered the cafeteria and quickly grabbed a sandwich, a garden salad, and a glass of milk. She headed to the section where all the girls usually sat. Just as she got close, she spotted them. They were all standing up and putting their trays on the belts.

She approached Laura. "Hey, so sorry. I'll explain later. This has been such a crazy day," she said.

"No worries. You okay? Get my message about Nathan?" Laura asked.

"Yeah, thanks. Anyway, I stopped by the library. I had to find—" She stopped as Bree approached. "But, hey, I can talk to you when I get back to the room. I'm just going to grab a seat. I'm not all that hungry," she said in the most upbeat voice she could muster.

"Talk to Nathan?" Bree asked.

"No, not yet. I'm going to call him when I get back."

"Tell him I'm thinking of him. I know how close he is to Uncle Dave."

How does she know about Uncle Dave and how close they are?

She brushed the thoughts out of her head and quickly answered, "Of course I will. I'll see you guys later."

"Sure you don't want me to stay with you?" Laura asked.

"No. Honestly, I'm going to eat quickly, and I'll be back, but thanks!"

"See ya," Bree said.

"Bye. See you guys in a bit." Abigail turned and headed back toward a table. She grabbed a student newspaper and sat down to read it as she ate.

She started to eat her turkey sandwich, but all she could think about was the article folded up in her pocket, as if it were burning a hole right through her jeans. She pulled the article out of her pocket, smoothed it on the student paper, and started reading it.

The article was sad, and she found herself engrossed in the story of this boy, but there was nothing in it that struck a chord with her, so she read it again and again until her eyes burned. Still, nothing. She sat back in her chair, picking slowly at her salad, as she stared at the article.

"Jonathan Higgins, Thomas McPherson...do I know them?" she said quietly.

She started to feel tired from all of the day's activities. She was anxious to go back to her room to call Nathan.

She peered out the window in front of her and could see that the snow had just begun to fall. It was beautiful, and it reminded her of that first night with Nathan as they'd watched the snow fall. She missed him.

"I see you've done your homework," Tank said in an unhealthy, deep tone.

Abigail nearly jumped out of her skin at the sound of his voice. She whipped around. "You scared me!" she said with a scowl.

"Where did you get the article?"

She tried to cover it.

"No use. I already saw it," he said. "Library?"

Her voice barely squeaked out, "Yeah."

"Can I sit?" he asked.

"What do you want, Tank?" she said.

"I don't know, Abby."

"Well, you have to know."

"Can I sit, please? People are starting to stare."

She glanced around, and as if on cue, the cafeteria began to fill up with the dinner crowd. She nodded toward the chair across from her. He pulled out the seat and sat down.

"I see you showered?" she said impolitely.

"Yeah, well, I suppose I had to, didn't I?" He glared at her. He couldn't believe he was sitting across from her. Part of him wanted to run away, far away, and never come back, but the other half of him was drawn to her, and he was too scared to tell her why.

"You're looking at me weird again," she said in an abrupt tone. She pushed away her tray.

"Just don't leave, okay?" he said under his breath.

"Why should I stay?" she asked.

"I don't know. I just don't want..." He trailed off as a group of students came and sat at the table right next to them. He glanced over at the table, and one of the students said hello to Tank. He nodded and then drew his eyes back down to the floor.

"Well?" she asked.

He glared at her, as if to say, *Please keep your voice down.*

As it was, she was already whispering.

"Can I talk to you in private, please?" he said through gritted teeth.

"I don't think so, Tank," she said back.

"Please," he pleaded. His eyes seemed to soften for the first time since she'd met him. "I think you need to hear what I have to say." With that, he stood up and pushed in his chair. As he began to pass her, he stopped. "My truck is out front. I'll wait only ten minutes, and then that's it. I'll never bother you again."

He walked off before she could say a word.

She tried not to pay any attention to the table next to her. She could feel their eyes on her. She waited a moment or two before she took the article, neatly folded it back up, and tucked it back safely in her pocket. She thought long and hard about what she wanted to do. Something was telling her to stay, just let him leave and forget about all of this nonsense, but unfortunately, an even stronger part of her was telling her that she needed to hear what he had to say.

She pushed back her chair and picked up her tray. With a sudden sense of urgency, she placed her tray on the belt and hurried to the side of the cafeteria where she exited out the door. His truck was idling in front. The snow had started to fall, and there was a beautiful white blanket covering the campus again.

She went around the back of his truck and to the passenger side. She took a deep breath before pulling on the handle. The door was unlocked. She climbed in. He didn't say a word to her as she closed the door. There was silence. He started to pull out onto the street.

"Where are we going?" she asked.

"I don't know, Abby. I didn't exactly plan this." His windshield wipers scraped across the window.

Her heart began to beat wildly.

"Well, it's not exactly a nice night for a drive," she said with a deep hint of sarcasm. She peered over at him and noticed a shiny object in between his legs. "What's that?" she asked, pointing.

"Nothing," he said flatly. "It's just a flask. It's fine."

"Have you been drinking?"

"No, I haven't," he said with a slight laugh.

It irritated Abigail. "Maybe this was a bad idea."

"Too late. Shit, I'm sorry." He paused and then added with a softer tone, "It's just a drink, I promise."

"Just tell me what you wanted to tell me, so I can go home," she said, trying hard to see the road in front of her.

"I will. I will."

They were on the edge of campus now and heading toward some back roads.

"Let me just pull over here, so I can tell you. Is that okay?"

"Fine, but make it quick. It's coming down."

He pulled over to a gravelly section on the side of the road. It was set back just enough to keep them out of the way of the passing cars on the road.

"Okay, I'll try…" He trailed off. He put the truck in park and turned off the headlights.

She swallowed hard. She was starting to regret her decision to get in the truck with him. She hardly knew him, and her last two interactions with him had been a bit hostile. With the snow coming down like it was now, she was trapped in his truck. At least before, she could have just walked away from him.

"Well?"

"Hey," he snapped.

Her eyes widened as this huge man barked at her. She was frightened, and he immediately noticed and backed down.

"I'm…I'm so sorry. Can you just let me gather my thoughts, so I will hopefully never have to say this again? I might need a little time to do this."

She leaned back toward her door, her eyes wide. She was a bit fearful of this three-hundred-pound guy staring out into the distance. She didn't know him at all. In fact, all she knew of him was that he had a bad reputation and an even worse attitude. Oh, and on occasion, he'd grab women he didn't really know at football banquets.

She slowly spoke in a reassuring voice, "Oh, okay, Tank."

"Thank you," he said.

Good. Keep the beast calm.

He took a deep breath and then another. Then, he spoke, "My best friend was—I mean, *is* Jonathan Higgins." His voice trailed off for a moment.

She could see him swallow hard. He took a swig of his flask.

"The boy from the article?" she asked.

"Yes. He died from a brain tumor almost a year ago."

"I know. I read the article."

He turned to her, as if to say something unkind but he stopped.

"I'm sorry. Go on."

"We were best friends since we were six years old. We were always together. His family and my family—we would get together for holidays, all kinds of stuff. We were better than friends. We were brothers." He sniffed and took another swig from his flask.

This person—no, this boy is baffling me and beginning to defy everything I thought he was. He is hurting. Maybe that is why he acted the way he did?

"I'm sorry about your friend," she said in a hushed voice.

"Thank you," he said softly. "I would do anything—*anything*—to get him back. It's not fair…" He struggled to get each sentence out.

She wasn't trying to seem unsympathetic, but she could not for the life of her understand what this had to do with her. So, she asked as sweetly as she could because, if for nothing else, she didn't want to be rude to him, "But, Tank, what does this have to do with me?"

"I know. I'm sorry." He shifted in his seat to face her. "Please don't leave when I tell you this, okay?"

Feeling her heart beat faster, she slightly turned in his direction, so they were now facing one another. He reached down for the flask and took a deep pull. She gave him a slight frown.

He ignored her. "You want some?" he asked. "You might need it."

"Tank, please!" she said.

"Okay, okay." He took a breath in and then slowly let it out. "I used to visit Jonathan in the hospital. I would sit by his bed for days, sometimes nights. Just the two of us. But he was in and out of consciousness for most of his last weeks. His poor parents were drained, so I did everything I could to be near him." His voice was somber and lonely. "One day, when I came in the room, I thought he was sleeping, but then he started to talk."

"What do you mean, started to talk?"

"Like, he was talking to someone."

"Oh," she said, her voice confused.

"I didn't think much of it until the next time I visited him. The same thing happened and then again and…finally, he told me he had been talking to someone." There was intensity building behind his eyes. He waited to see if she was absorbing all of this information.

She eyed him, her brows bent, waiting for him to talk.

Then, he took a deep breath. "He said he was talking to *you*."

It took a moment for Abigail to realize what Tank had just said. Her eyes opened wide, and her mouth slightly dropped open. Then, she began to laugh. It was the kind of laugh that first started slow and then began to build, sometimes out of fear and sometimes out of disbelief. This was both.

"You're crazy. Don't be ridiculous," she said finally. "Are you punking me or something? Am I on *Candid Camera*?" Looking around the truck for effect, she let out a slight giggle. Then, it started to fade.

She noticed Tank was not laughing, nor was he smiling. In fact, he was dead serious.

"This is not a joke, Abby."

"I don't understand, Tank." Her mouth turned to a straight line.

"He described you, Abby. He said you would come to him and that you would talk to him. I thought it was crazy, too. I didn't believe him, but then that day in the union, I saw—no, I heard you singing as we walked in and you walked out. And your hair—*damn it!* I knew it was you. Something told me it was you. He was right. You exist!"

She started to get a weird feeling. The skin on her neck tingled, so she spoke deliberately, "Tank, I'm dating someone, and I thought you knew that. I'm sorry if I gave you the wrong impression."

"No!" he shouted. Then, he quickly changed his tune. "No, Abby, it's not like that, I promise. Just hear me out, okay?" He put his hand on her arm. His grip was firm.

She sensed his fingers tighten. She glared down at his hand and slowly pulled her arm away.

"Sorry, I didn't mean...I knew you wouldn't believe me. Maybe I am crazy."

"No, no. I just think you really miss your friend, Tank."

"Of course I do!" His voice rose again. "But this was real, I promise you. You have to believe me. Abby. When I saw you, it was like I saw a ghost. You are exactly as he described, and he said you were the one, the love of his life and that you were going to meet here at school."

"Tank"—her voice hushed—"he's not here at school. How could he have—"

"That's just it. He was set to go to school here. He was recruited and everything, almost ready to sign with me, and—"

"Wait, he was coming here? What do you mean, recruited?"

"Football, like me. Our whole lives, we had planned to play at Onondaga State, and it would have happened if..." His voice became hollow again, and he stared out into the night now clouded by a flurry of white snow.

There was silence in the car. Abigail's mind raced. She knew she had to find a way out of here. She knew Laura and Nathan were probably worried about her.

Nathan! Oh my God!

She still had not talked to him. She didn't want to upset Tank by telling him to take her home, but this conversation was going nowhere.

"Tank," she said, "I think somewhere, somehow, during all this, you misunderstood your friend or something. I don't know him and—"

"I *know* this, Abby, but how would he have known how to describe you then?" he asked sincerely.

"Well, it's not like I'm so uncommon or something. Blue eyes, blonde hair—easy, right?" She wanted to lead him off this ridiculous trail.

"No, I'm telling you. You have to believe me. It's true, and he even said your name. This has to be real, and I promised him...I made him a promise that..."

"That, what, Tank?" she asked cautiously.

"That I would protect you."

She could barely make out his words. "Protect me? Okay, this is getting to be too much. I have to go. Can you please drive me back home? I have heard—"

"No, not until you believe me."

"Excuse me? Believe you? Believe what?" Her voice now began to rise. It was her turn to let him know she wasn't standing for this.

"I promised him I would find you, and at the time, I didn't know what I was saying, but now that you're here, I have to—"

"Forget this!" she said. With that, she grabbed the handle and threw open the door. A bluster of cold wind and snow hit her right in the face. It was then she realized she had no coat on, no gloves, and no hat. She had left them when she went back to the dorm to get Laura for dinner. She didn't care. She scrambled out and began to run toward campus.

"Abby, wait! Don't!" he yelled. He tried to put the truck in reverse, but his tires began to spin in rapid circles. "Damn it!" he yelled as he punched the steering wheel. He quickly turned off the ignition and opened the door. In a full sprint, he began chasing Abigail.

"Abby, wait! Please!" he yelled.

She turned. "Oh my God," she yelled. "He's chasing after me. He is crazy!"

She turned to run faster but slipped on the slick ground and fell on the pavement. The pebbles cut her flesh on her hands, scraping away her skin. Blood began to tarnish the white snow. She scrambled to her feet. He was getting closer.

"Abby, please listen!" His voice was not angry but pleading for her to stop.

She rounded the corner and saw that the Ridge was close by. She took off fast. Her clothes and hair were soaked, and her hands were bleeding.

She ran up the stairs and knocked on the door. "Hello?" she said in a high voice.

She heard the door unlocking, and thankfully, Marcus opened it.

"Abigail? What the...are you okay?" He noticed her disheveled appearance and the blood on her pants and shirt.

"Yes, yes, I'm fine. I fell."

Then, suddenly, they both heard, "Abby, please, I just need to talk."

"Who is that?" Marcus said, peering past her. "Wait, is that Tank?" he asked in an unpleasant tone.

"Yes. It's fine. Can I just come in, please?" Her eyes were wide.

"Of course." Then, he yelled, "Tank! What the hell are you doing?"

Tank huffed up the stairs, his coat soaked from the falling snow. "Abby, I'm so sorry. I saw you fall. You—"

"Tank, I'm fine," she said coldly.

Marcus glanced back and forth between the two, his eyebrows bent deep in a disapproving arch. Tank seemed pathetic, almost like a lost dog waiting for someone, anyone, to care for him. Abigail looked like a girl who was being chased by a stray dog she just couldn't shake.

"What's going on here?" Marcus asked.

"Nothing. It's—" Abigail said.

"Nothing. I was just telling her something when my truck got stuck and—"

"Wait, why were you two in your truck? And where's Nathan?"

The sound of his name sent shivers down Abigail's body.

Nathan...

She wished more than anything that he were here. Her body began to shake.

"Jesus, come in." Marcus opened the door wider for her to step in, but as Tank approached the door, he quickly put his hand on Tank's chest. "Listen," he whispered, "I don't know what's going on, but so help me, if I let you in...you'd better not cause any trouble. Understand?"

"Yeah, I do."

He took a whiff of Tank's breath. "You've been drinking?"

"Not really."

"Jesus," was all he could say as he glared at Tank before allowing him to pass.

Tank immediately walked back toward the bathroom. Abigail was locked inside. He knocked on the door.

"Abby, please just let me talk to you," he said, his voice much softer.

Marcus stood in the hallway, arms crossed, closely scrutinizing Tank.

"Tank, I already told you. I think this is just a crazy dream or—"

He quickly cut her off, "Abby, please can we talk in private?" He glanced in Marcus's direction.

Marcus didn't move an inch.

Tank whispered, "I don't want everyone to hear what I'm talking about."

There was silence.

Tank slid down the wall and sat on the floor, knees bent, with his head resting in his hands.

"Hey"—Marcus approached Tank—"why don't you leave the poor girl alone, okay?"

Tank raised his head, and Marcus took a step back. Tank's face said it all. His expression was that of pure sadness and defeat.

"Jesus, what's with you two?" Marcus asked.

"Just forget it." He put his head back in his hands.

He waited in silence. She had to come out at some point.

He tried to go over each conversation he'd had with Jonathan, thinking painfully of the details—searching for something to jog his memory, something that would make her see—but it all seemed so silly now. He started to stand up, and he was about to tell her he was leaving when, all of a sudden, he thought of not a conversation he'd had with Jonathan, but the things he would say when he thought he was alone. Then, it came to Tank, like a flash across his memory bank.

"Moon Pie," he whispered. Then, he said it a bit louder as he stood up, "Moon Pie?"

He couldn't tell how long he'd been standing there before he heard the door unlock. Time was moving so slowly, but she finally cracked the door open. When she did, he saw her standing there with tears streaming down her face.

"What did you say?" she asked in a low voice.

"Moon Pie," he said like a frightened child.

"Where did you hear that?" she asked, hoping that Nathan had said it in passing.

In a broken voice, Tank barely breathed out his name, "Jonathan."

Marcus glanced back and forth at Abigail and Tank. Something had shifted, and he wasn't exactly sure what.

Abigail stepped out of the bathroom, and in a quiet voice, she said, "I'm listening."

Tank hung his head, trying hard not to cry.

Feeling an overwhelming sense to help them, Marcus piped up, "Hey, you guys can get some privacy in my room." He noticed neither of them moving. "It's cool. I won't let anyone—well, you can go in here," he stammered as he pushed open his bedroom door. "Abigail, I'll get you a blanket."

Abigail was the first to move. She walked into Marcus's room and sat down in an old brown recliner that was next to his desk. Tank followed in and took a seat in the desk chair. The room was covered in a thick silence.

Marcus returned with an Onondaga State football blanket, and for some reason, it gave Abigail a strange feeling as he handed it to her. Marcus presented a pained expression and then turned and closed the door.

Shivering, Abigail wrapped it around her wet clothes.

"You should take your sweater off. It's too wet, and you'll get sick," Tank said softly.

She just stared at him before she pulled off her sweater, leaving on her T-shirt. Then, she rewrapped the blanket around her body, and she sat back in the chair.

Finally, she said, "You heard that from him? Are you sure?"

"Yes, absolutely positive. I don't even know what it means."

Not wanting to give everything away, for fear this was just all a fluke, she asked, "What else did he tell you?"

"Well, lots of things, Abby. He told me that you liked Bruce Springsteen and that you would sing a lot to him. You didn't think you were a good singer, but you couldn't ever hear what others heard..."

Her eyes widened like navy saucers. Then, she said, "Because I always have my headphones on."

"Yeah." He nodded in agreement.

She pulled her legs up on the chair and wrapped her entire body with the blanket. It was as though she were trying to shield herself from the world.

"What does Moon Pie mean?" he asked.

"It's a nickname my father gave me."

"See, Abby? How could he have known that?" Tank asked, his face much softer than she had seen before.

"And you're certain you heard it from him?" she asked again.

"Yes, positive. I'm not trying to play with you. Believe me, this is really weird to me, too."

"I don't know, Tank. This just seems too peculiar. You're saying he described me? No one else you guys knew?"

"Yes, I swear it. First time you passed me at the union, I had a really strange feeling in my gut, but then the minute I saw you at the banquet, I knew. I knew that it was you. I was drawn to you. Your eyes and hair...it's your face. I knew I had seen it before." He motioned with his hand over his own face. He was searching for something that said she was grasping this. Unfortunately, he did not see what he'd hoped to see.

He took a deep breath. She waited for him.

Feeling defeated, he mumbled, "There is no other explanation, and the box—" There was a slight knock on the door. He froze suddenly.

"Hey, guys," Marcus said quietly.

"Yeah?" Tank said.

"Hey, I made you some coffee. It's for you, too." He glared at Tank.

"Thanks, Marcus. We're sorry to do this. That we are intruding," she said, taking the hot mug.

"Well, you're going to intrude all night."

"What?"

"Roads are closed, big guy. No way back to campus now."

"Oh no! Are you kidding?" Abigail got up and crossed over toward the window. She peeked through the blinds and could hardly see the bushes in the front of the old house. The snow was still falling heavily outside.

"Crap. I'm so sorry, Abby. This is entirely my fault."

She didn't say anything. She just stared out the window and wondered where Nathan was right now.

I miss him terribly. Is he doing okay? More importantly, is his uncle doing okay?

"Can I call my roommate?" she asked.

"Of course. Phone is in the kitchen."

Abigail walked out and went into the kitchen to call Laura. There was no answer, so she just left a message. "Laura, it's Abigail. I'm so sorry if I've made you worry. I'm fine. Stuck at the Ridge. Roads are closed, but I'll call you again in the morning. Sorry."

Marcus entered the kitchen. "Hey, everything okay?"

"Yeah, I'm sure. She wasn't home, so—"

"No, I was talking about you and Tank. Everything all right?"

Her skin heated as she began to realize that she would not be able to tell anyone what had happened, especially since she didn't understand it herself. She was embarrassed and tried to play it off. "Oh, yeah, fine. I'm just helping him with—well, it's fine, really."

"Listen, you don't have to tell me, but if you need me, I'll be in here, okay?"

"Thanks, Marcus," she said as studied this mere stranger, someone whom, as of twelve hours ago, she'd had no contact with at all. Now, here she was, wrapped in his blanket, drinking his coffee, taking refuge under his roof. She went to turn back toward the hallway.

"Sure thing."

Abigail entered Marcus's room. Tank was standing near the desk now and was bent over a piece of paper. Alarmed by her presence, he quickly stood up, grabbed the scrap of paper, and crumbled it in his hand.

She closed the door and took her seat again in the chair. She wrapped herself back up. "She wasn't there."

"Who?"

"My roommate."

"Oh, right." His expression was one of concern.

"What is it?" she asked.

"I don't know. I just feel so…" He trailed off again, staring into the distance.

"Tell me."

"I was just thinking about Jonathan. Over Thanksgiving, I asked his mom if she knew anyone named Abby or a friend or something, and she had no idea what I was talking about. So, I guess, for some reason, he only told me."

"You haven't really told me what he said to you—I mean, besides describing a blonde girl and the nickname. There are no other real connections. Maybe these were just coincidences? Like you said, his mother didn't know, so maybe it's something else."

"If that makes you feel better," he said sarcastically.

"What? None of this makes me feel better." She motioned to the room. "I'm—we're stuck here, so I'm just trying to keep the peace; that's all."

"Oh, so now, you're saying you don't believe me?" His voice sounded strained but not angry.

"Well, I guess I'm saying, maybe this is your way of dealing with a bad situation—you know, in an attempt to hold on."

"Hey, listen, I was doing just fine until I saw you, so…"

"Well, excuse me for living," she quipped. No sooner had she said those words than she realized the true impact of their coolness on Tank.

His face dropped.

"I didn't mean it like that. I…" she said, struggling to take her words back. "Gosh, I'm…oh shit, I'm really sorry."

"Abby, there is no other reason to explain this. I'm sorry. I believe he possibly saw his future."

"Future?"

"Yes, maybe he was able to see into the future."

"Oh, Tank. Don't you see what you are doing? You're creating these scenarios and trying to make them real."

"No, that is not what I'm doing." Now, his voice was beginning to rise. He fumbled with something in his hand. He walked over to her, and with a swift motion, he thrust a scrap piece of paper in her face. "Look at this. This is what he showed to me."

She couldn't focus at first, and then she saw what had been drawn on the small piece of paper. She blinked. She blinked hard.

"And that was why I wanted to see your shoulder."

"Ha! You did see it. That's how you know," she said with a smug tone.

"No! I didn't. I couldn't have. Your *boy* pulled me off, but I saw a slight mark, and I just had this gut feeling. After I saw you, I knew, if that was a moon on your shoulder, then it was true. You were the one he…"

He kept the paper in her face. She took it.

"It's correct, isn't it?" he barked.

Feeling the tickles go up her neck, she slowly stood. She could not explain why she thought it was necessary to show him, but something told her she had to. She turned, pulled her T-shirt off her shoulder, and exposed her flesh to him. It was exact. The size, detail, shape—all of it was exact. She sensed him raise his hand, and he gently ran the tip of his finger over her birthmark. Her skin flushed at his touch. She knew he needed to know it was real, that she was real. She waited for him to speak, and when he didn't, she pulled her shirt back up and turned to him.

His eyes were filled with tears. "Now, do you believe me?" He wiped his eyes.

"I believe something. I'm just not sure what I'm supposed to believe in, if that makes any sense. This just seems so unfathomable."

"Now, can you see why I feel so alone? Almost tortured by all this. Just when I'm about to forget for just a second so that I can breathe, there you are!" he cried.

"I know, and I'm sorry. I had no idea."

"How could you have?" He sat down on a chair, forcing his head into his oversize hands.

She took her seat in the recliner, rewrapping her body with the blanket.

She gazed at him. This enormous, rough football player had a story, a life beyond the way he appeared to others. It made her sad, almost disappointed in herself for judging him. But the way he'd acted didn't exactly give her any room to judge differently. She was struggling internally to find the right balance.

"You miss your friend, don't you?"

"Jonathan," he said. "Call him Jonathan, Abby."

She resisted saying his name, only she didn't know why. It was not like she knew him...right? *But I did know him. Somehow, we knew one another. Maybe?*

"Can I see a picture of him?" She slowly added, "Of Jonathan."

Tank leaned over and took his wallet out. He pulled out a photo of Jonathan and himself from high school. He was eager to show her. "This was the summer before our junior year, greatest year of our lives. We had the best football record in the state. We had a blast together."

Abigail stared at the picture. Her eyes were glued on Jonathan's face. She took in his features—his hair, his eyes, everything. He was tall and thin, much like Nathan. He had light-brown hair; it was almost the color of sand, and it was short and sticking up a bit in the front. His eyes were a deep blue-green. He had a beautiful smile. It was as if he were smiling right at her. She closed her eyes, trying desperately to make sense of all of this.

"Great picture," she said.

His face had changed. He appeared mildly happy.

"It makes you happy to talk about him, doesn't it?"

"Only sometimes. Other times, I get sad when I see a picture like this. Then, there are days it is just what I need to make it through my so-called life."

"Tell me about him, would you?"

"Okay. Where would you like me to start?"

"Well, what happened to him? I read the article, but what really happened?"

"Boy. Okay, getting right to the heart of it." For the first time, he sported a brief smile.

"Sorry. You tell me whatever—"

"I was just kidding. No, I should tell you about it. It's important."

"Okay." She settled in her chair with her cup of coffee.

Tank leaned back in the chair, closed his eyes for a brief moment, and let out a long sigh. Then, he began telling Abigail the sad, oddly humorous, and completely captivating story of the last few months of Jonathan Higgins's life.

"So, basically, he started going to Boston a lot, and I thought he was considering other schools, but..." Tank said.

"He wasn't?" Abigail chimed in.

"No, he was seeing specialists about his brain tumor. Yeah, I'll never forget the day he told me. It was like the room was spinning. People were talking, but I didn't hear a word of it. It was surreal."

"I can only imagine. I don't know what I'd do if this happened to my best friend, Rebecca. Just awful."

"Believe me, I get it. Life seemed normal for a few weeks until it was time to tell our classmates that he wouldn't be coming back to school. He started getting too weak to get up, and it was beginning to add stress to an already-stressful time. I was lucky the teachers gave me some slack, too. I was able to visit him on certain days, and toward the end, I spent almost all my evenings in the hospital."

"Was he in pain?" she asked, not really wanting to know if he was, for fear that he might have been.

"Not horribly. In the end, he seemed at peace. And I have you to thank for that, Abby."

"No, Tank. We have no way—"

He cut her off, "No, you don't. Don't go backward on me. You and I both know you did something to him. You can't be an angel because you're real, but maybe you are a living spirit or something. There must be something awfully special about you to have been with Jonathan..." He gazed down at the ground for a moment before adding, "I hope you don't mind me saying that."

"No, I just think that I'm just me—a nobody from a small town—and how I got here today, I'm not sure I'll ever understand."

"But you are, so maybe that should tell you something."

"I guess. Can I ask more about what he used to say?"

"Honestly, I'd just listen to him talk. Sometimes, he was awake or aware, and other times, he didn't know I was there. But he used to talk to you about music and animals. He was a huge dog lover—any animal in fact but he loved dogs. He had a boxer named Brewski."

"I have a dog, too," she said quietly.

Tank sighed.

"I'm actually studying to be a veterinarian."

Tank let out a laugh. "Of course you are. He said you loved animals."

He laughed again, but Abigail remained neutral, and he noticed.

"Something I said?" he asked.

"No, it's just…I think you need to realize, and please don't take this the wrong way, but I wasn't there, so I don't know what was said or how and when, so to hear things about myself from you or even more so from Jonathan is kind of tough to swallow. Do you see what I mean?"

"I thought you wanted to know?" he said, sounding wounded.

"No, Tank, I do, but this is just a lot to take in. Can you at least give me that?" She shifted in her chair. Her body was stiff and cold. She was getting tired. It had to be late by now.

"Yes, sorry. I know it's hard. In many ways, I guess I feel like I'm finally able to unburden my soul, but for you…well, you're taking on a whole new thing. So, I do get it, Abby."

"Thank you."

"He said you were kind of difficult, so…" Tank couldn't help but snicker.

"Ah, you jerk! You're kidding! You think this is funny?" She couldn't help but laugh, too. She picked up a pen off of Marcus's desk and threw it at Tank, hitting him square in the chest.

"Yes, but I'm kidding!"

They both began to laugh harder and harder. It was just what they needed.

"But, seriously, you can't tell anyone what I'm telling you. I know you don't owe me anything, but if the guys on the team knew…well, they'd never let it go. I haven't even told them about Jonathan even though Coach told me to talk to Marcus, but I just can't, you know? And Nathan…you can't say a word, promise? They won't get it."

"Your coach knows?"

"Yeah, of course, Abby. He recruited Jonathan."

"Oh, right. Sorry," she said.

"So, you promise me then?" His eyes were pleading her to protect his secret.

She thought about the secret he was asking her to keep from everyone but most importantly from Nathan. *How can I keep this from him? Tank's the one person on Nathan's team who he doesn't get along with, and now, I'm the only one who knows Tank's secret. I'm right in the middle of them. I don't know if I can do this.*

She could clearly see the desperation and sadness in Tank's expression. She knew she ultimately had no choice.

He found me and unburdened his aching soul, and in some strange way, he trusts me with this, more than anyone else.

Before Abigail could respond, Marcus knocked on the door and opened it.

"Tank, you can sleep on the couch. Abigail, you can take my room. I'll give you some extra blankets to use."

"Thanks. Appreciate it," she said.

"I'll be up in Troy's room if you need anything. He's away for the weekend. If you can't find me in the morning, I'll be out, trying to shovel the driveway. Promised the landlord I would. Feel free to watch TV in the living room."

"Thanks, Marcus," Tank said.

"Sure," he said flatly.

Abigail didn't feel like talking anymore. After Marcus left, in the hopes that she wouldn't get into another deep conversation with Tank, she quickly said, "I'm going to rest a little."

"Of course. I'll leave you for a bit," he said as he walked out the door.

She closed the door to Marcus's room and turned off the light. She left one of the shades slightly open, so she could watch the snow fall outside. As she lay there, all she could think about was Nathan, how she missed him, how she hoped he wouldn't be upset at her for not calling. She didn't have his number with her anyway, so she would have to call him first thing in the morning, as soon as she got back to her dorm.

She started to think about all that Tank had told her today, and for some reason, she kept thinking about Jonathan. She tried to shake the image of him from the picture, but she couldn't. Her heart began to race as she thought about him more and more despite her desperate attempt to get him out of her mind.

Did I really come to him? How is that even possible?

She heard a creak in the hallway, and she turned. She could see the shadow of feet standing in front of the door. She held her breath. She assumed it was Tank with the way he stayed there for minutes with no movement. When he finally walked away, she turned back to the other side of the room and watched the snow fall again. She didn't know when it finally happened, but at some point, she fell asleep.

Abigail heard a slight knock on the door. She grabbed her watch. It was eight thirty in the morning.

"Come in," she said, sitting up.

Tank opened the door. "It's me, Tank. Sorry to bother you. Didn't know if you'd come out for coffee, so I brought some."

He appeared as though he had not slept.

"Thanks. Appreciate it." She sat up in bed, pulled the blanket back around her shoulders, and took the cup of coffee. "You don't look so hot. You feeling okay?" she asked.

"Just, well, I drank a little last night. I couldn't sleep, so…"

"Tank, you should be more careful."

"I know; I know," he said, rubbing his face. He let out a huge sigh as he took a seat on the edge of the bed.

"I didn't sleep well either."

"Not surprised," he said with a slight laugh.

"It's your fault, you know," she said jokingly.

"I realize this."

They sat in silence for a bit, each slowly sipping their coffee, hoping it would take effect soon.

Tank stared at the ground, deep in thought. For such a big guy, he appeared so defeated and small this morning. His body was hunched over, his shoulders turned in.

She waited for him to say something, but he just seemed lost.

Finally, Abigail spoke, "So, you decided to come to Onondaga State?"

"Yeah," he said, snapping out of his funk a bit. "We both loved it here, and we wanted to go away to school to play together, so…" He trailed off. "It was hard. It's been a tough start for me in general here."

"Well, I can see why." She slightly rubbed her eye, still trying to wake up.

"I considered not coming, but my family and his family encouraged me to enroll, and then there was football and the scholarship and all that. I guess I'd have been pretty stupid to just give that up."

"I agree. Don't you think he'd have wanted you to come? You would have wanted him to come, right?"

"Of course." His voice got softer. "He said he used to see you here in his dreams. He told me he had a dream where he walked by you once on campus and said it was just love at first sight."

Her eyes widened as he said the word *love*.

"Really?" Her voice cracked a bit. "Wow."

"Yeah, wow. He sure was smitten by you. Sounded like you were meant to be." His voice faded.

Abigail turned toward the window as her face began to flush. She thought of Nathan, how she'd felt about him the first time she saw him and the first time they'd kissed. She knew what being smitten was all about. She hoped he would be back soon because she missed him terribly.

"Do you believe that?" she asked, not knowing why she was taking this conversation anywhere.

"I do. I believe you were meant to be. He was so sure of you, Abby."

Without realizing she was talking, she said quietly, "Only Nathan calls me Abby."

Tank glared at her, and his expression darkened. "I believe Jonathan called you that first."

"Wait, what?"

"Jonathan called you Abby, only Abby."

"Well…" She didn't know how to respond.

"Well, don't you see?" His expression was shadier now. "Jonathan was *your* meant-to-be, not Nathan. He's just a second."

"Whoa, wait a minute here, Tank." Now, it was Abigail's turn to deepen her expression. "You can't say that," she said sadly as she started to get up off the bed.

"Wait, wait. Don't go. Just hear me out."

"Hear what out?" Her voice rose a level.

"All I am saying is, Nathan is just a fluke. He's not the one for you. You must see that now. If Jonathan were here, it would have been him. I know it. He's a better guy."

Now completely off the bed, Abigail turned to him and put her coffee mug down on the desk with authority. With an angry voice, she said, "How dare you try to tell me—"

But she was interrupted as she heard a loud noise in the hallway and then the sound of footsteps.

With one swift motion, Nathan swung open the door. "What's going on in here?" he said, looking at Abigail and then at Tank. "Why are you yelling, Abby?"

Tank quickly stood off the edge of the bed. Abigail's heart raced as she saw Nathan standing in the doorway. He appeared exhausted, confused, and angry. She had never seen him like this, and it made her feel terrible.

"Nathan, hi!" She broke off. "It was nothing."

She could not believe he was standing in the room, questioning her. She was embarrassed. He should be at home with his dad, not here.

Nathan took in the scene of Tank near the bed and Abby wrapped in a blanket. In an angry, low voice, he said, "Did he touch you?" He was hurt that he even had to ask.

"No, Nathan. I swear," she said, equally hurt.

Tank started to laugh. "Here comes the hero, barging in to save the day."

Trying to ignore him, Nathan spoke to Abigail, "What's going on in here, Abby?"

"Nothing, really.…" Her words could not come fast enough because she had no idea what to tell him, if to tell him anything at all.

The whole story was unbelievable. He'd think she was crazy. He already thought Tank was. Besides, she didn't want to hurt Nathan's feelings.

"It's just that his truck got stuck in the snow, and the roads closed, so we had to walk—"

"Why were you in his truck?" Nathan asked.

"Well, we had to talk about the banquet…" Abigail could feel both of them staring at her, waiting for her to say something else, but she couldn't. She had a split-second decision to make. *Do I keep Tank's secret from Nathan, or do I tell Nathan everything and hurt this boy who has already suffered enough this past year?*

Her face flushed. She was in the worst possible place she could have imagined.

"Abby," Tank said in an angry voice.

"Tank, please, just don't," she said with apprehension.

"Tank, I suggest you leave," Nathan said, his face getting red.

"Ha! Why don't you leave?"

"Can't you see what you're doing to her? Get the hell out!" Nathan yelled.

Abigail jumped. It was so unlike him.

"You don't get her like I do," Tank said with a slight edge to his voice. "You never will."

"What the hell is he talking about, Abby?"

"Yeah, Abby." Tank glared at her.

"Please just leave me alone." She grabbed her sweater and started to walk toward the door, but Tank stood in the way.

Marcus came down the hall. "Hey, what's going on in here?"

He went to put his hand on Tank's shoulder to move him out of the way, but as he did, Tank swung his arm toward Marcus, knocking him back against the wall in the hallway. Marcus quickly got to his feet and lunged at Tank. The two began to scuffle back and forth, putting a hole in the wall in the process.

Feeling scared as the two of them exchange punches, she slipped past them and ran down the hall in an attempt to get out of the way. Nathan took off after her.

"Abby, wait!" Tank yelled.

She flew through the open front door, and with as much might as she could, she hurried down the stairs, not realizing the stairs were covered in ice. She hit the second to last step, and in one swift motion, her legs came out from under her. She landed hard on her head and leg. She let out a painful moan.

"Abby!" Nathan yelled as he saw her fall. He ran down the steps two at a time and crouched down beside her. "Oh my God, Abby! Are you okay?"

She didn't want him to see her like this. "I'm fine," she said with a wince.

"Are you sure? You hit your head pretty hard."

"I'm fine," she repeated. She tried to move, but the throbbing in the back of her head and on her foot was too much, and she collapsed back down.

"Don't move, okay? I'm going to pick you up. Tell me if something hurts, okay?"

"Okay," she said in a soft voice.

He put one arm under her thighs while the other arm cradled her head. He slowly got up. He saw her face as it crinkled up in pain. He carried her over to his car and laid her in the back. He went to the driver's side and got in. He saw the blood on his sleeve as he put his hands on the steering wheel. He could hear her quietly sobbing in the back of the car.

"Abby, I'm taking you to the hospital, okay? Your head is bleeding, so I have to take you."

She reached her hand to the back of her head and could feel the warm wetness against her hair. She brought her fingers back and saw the dark red blood that now coated her hand. Before passing out, she whispered, "I'm so sorry."

Nathan quickly carried Abigail into the emergency room. He ran up to the counter as a nurse hurried over to him.

"What happened?" the portly, dark-haired nurse asked.

"She fell down some stairs and hit her head badly. I'm not sure if she passed out because of the blood or the fall." His voice was quivering.

The nurse ran to the back, grabbed a gurney, and wheeled it around. Another nurse came over with a neck brace.

"Gently lay her down," the nurse said after securing the neck brace around Abigail's neck.

Abigail started to come to, and with a low voice, she said, "Where am I?"

"Sweetheart, can you tell me your name?" the taller, fair-haired nurse asked.

"Moon Pie," she whispered.

With a concerned face, the nurse turned to Nathan.

He quickly said, "Her name is Abby, um, Abigail Price."

"Okay, Abigail, you are in the hospital. Can you tell us what happened?"

She quietly spoke, "I fell."

"We're going to take you in for some X-rays." The nurse then turned to Nathan and said, "What is your name, son?"

"Nathan."

"Nathan. You her boyfriend?"

"Yes, yes, I am," he said for the first time with a bit of a heavy heart.

"Great. We'll come find you in the waiting room when we know more."

Nathan stood still as the gurney disappeared out of sight. With his head hung, he had an overwhelming sense of sadness as he turned and headed toward the waiting area.

The first hour and a half just dragged by. Every time the sliding doors of the waiting area opened, he'd anxiously glance up, hoping to see Abigail walking in of her own accord. No such luck.

Finally, the shorter, dark-haired nurse came in. "Nathan?"

"Yes." He eagerly stood up.

She came over to him and motioned for him to sit. He took a seat in a dark brown chair facing the nurses station. "Nathan, Abigail gave me permission to speak with you. She is going to be fine. However, she let us know that she has a history with seizures, so we need to keep her overnight to monitor her. She hit her head pretty badly. She has some stitches and a slight concussion."

Seizures? She has a history of seizures? How did I not know this?

The nurse added, "She also hurt her foot. She has a contusion on her left ankle, so we put her in an air cast. But that should heal within the next few weeks or so. Any questions so far?"

He swallowed hard. "Can I see her, please?"

"Yes, but she does need her rest, okay?"

"Of course." He stood up and followed the nurse to Abigail's room.

Before going in, she said, "We will be admitting her within the next hour, and then we'll move her upstairs."

"All right."

She pushed open the door, and Nathan walked in. He felt a lump in his throat as he regarded her, lying there. Her head was wrapped in white gauze. Long blonde strands of hair were coming out the bottom, and some of the strands were dark and crusted with blood. Nathan's eyes welled up with tears as he quietly approached the bed. She was pale. He took a chair and slowly moved it next to her bed. She lay there as still as a cat bathing in sunlight, only she did not seem as content or happy. He didn't have the heart to disturb her, so he sat back, closed his eyes, and waited for her to wake up.

An hour went by before he opened his eyes. He was exhausted and drained from the morning. He sat up in the chair. He slowly reached up and put a hand on her arm. She was cool to the touch. He went out to the nurses' station and asked for another blanket. The nurse gave him a warm one. He went back into the room. He laid the warm blanket over Abigail's body.

He leaned over her and gently touched her face. "Abby," he whispered.

She slowly began to move. He sat back down in his chair and rested his head on her arm.

"Nathan," she whispered back.

He glanced up. She had tears in her eyes.

"Please don't cry." He held her hand.

"I am so sorry. You should be with your dad and uncle."

"Abby, please don't worry about that now. I just need you to get better."

She tried to shake her head, but she was too sore to move. She winced as she attempted to sit up.

"Let me move the bed. You stay put." He grabbed the remote and moved the back of the bed forward.

"What happened?" she asked.

"You fell on the ice. Hit your head. Do you want me to call your parents?"

"No, I will later. They'll just freak if you tell them."

"But, Abby, the nurse said you have a history of seizures. Maybe you should call them."

"No, it's nothing. I'll call them later."

"The nurse said they are going to admit you today, so they can observe you overnight."

"Great," she said dryly.

"Your ankle is hurt, too."

"Can I see?"

Nathan got up and pulled back the bottom of the blanket, exposing her foot in the air cast.

"Just perfect." With a sigh, she said, "I'm so sorry."

"Abby, let's not talk about it here. You need to rest and get better." His tone was firm.

She glowered out the window. *How did I get here? I had been so happy just a week ago, and now, I feel like this—torn between two people, keeping secrets, and getting hurt in the process.*

"Okay," she said, still unable to lock eyes with him. "Can I ask how your uncle is doing?"

"He is going to be fine. He is at my house, recovering."

"You came back so soon. I thought you'd stay longer," she said.

His face was tied up with concern. "I had planned to stay longer," he said quietly.

"What do you mean?" she asked, sensing something wasn't right.

"Nothing, Abby. We'll talk later." He started rubbing his temples. His clothes were wrinkled, and he had blood on his jacket. He took it off and laid it on the chair. His tall and lean body appeared tired and stressed.

"Whatever you want to do," she said in a soft voice. She wasn't in a position to argue with him. She owed him that much since he'd left to come and get her at the Ridge.

He came close to her. He sat on the side of her bed, facing her. Her heart raced. He reached up and touched her cheek. His hand was so warm and tender on her face. His handsome face showed the rough stubble of the last few days. He looked rugged, and despite his weary eyes, her heart still skipped a beat when he locked eyes with her.

"I missed you," he said.

"I missed you more."

He leaned forward and put his fingertips on her chin. He softly kissed her on the lips. It was a wonderful kiss.

"I was hoping to have done that sooner."

Nathan finally left the hospital around seven in the evening. He had been there all day. He was exhausted and in desperate need of some food and a shower. He promised Abigail that he'd be back first thing in the morning. His first class wasn't until eleven thirty, so he would come and get her before then.

With tremendous hesitation, Abigail called her parents. She knew what their reaction would be and was prepared for the barrage of questions. She'd carefully rehearsed each answer, and she was able to keep them from coming to school. Her parents told her they would call the university and let the Registrar's Office know that she would not be in class for a few days.

Lastly, Abigail called Laura. It wasn't an easy conversation. Laura had been worried when she heard she was in the hospital...well, that just put the icing right on the already-burned cake. Laura seemed annoyed at first, in that caring kind of way, but once she heard about the accident, it sent her into a tizzy of questions, followed by lectures.

Abigail was exhausted after she got off the phone. The nurse gave her some pain medication for her foot, and it sent her right into a deep, deep slumber, a much-needed night of sleep.

Twenty-Five

JANUARY 26, 1996

Nathan came back in the morning. He appeared rested but not one hundred percent. He still had not shaved, but Abigail didn't mind. His handsomeness showed as he walked into the room in his tight blue sweater, dark brown corduroys, and brown boots, his hair still slick from the shower. She was inadequate next to him. Her hair was greasy and matted. At least she had a fresh bandage around her head. She had to wear hospital pants home since she could not get the air cast over her jeans, and the doctor did not want her to take it off just yet.

He drove her back to the dorm. He parked the car in front and helped her get out. He steadied her as she tried to use her crutches in the snow. She cursed as they slipped out from under her.

He laughed. "I've never heard you use such an obscene word, Abby."

Face red, she said, "Please forgive me for these next few days, okay?"

"Ah, admitting defeat already?" His voice dripped with sarcasm.

"You know, if I could get a snowball, I would, and I'd throw it right at you!"

"Careful, Abby. I have tremendous precision when it comes to throwing, particularly a snowball," he said with a sly smile.

She couldn't help giggling as she hobbled her way to her room. Thankfully, most of the girls on the floor were in class, so she was able to get to her room without a scene. She opened the door and found a note from Laura.

> *I'll be back around 2:30 p.m. I'll bring you some food. Miss you and hope you are doing better. P.S. You have a few messages on the machine.*

Abigail hobbled to the other side of the room. She took her jeans and tossed them on the bed but not before removing the article she had printed and stuffing it in her top drawer.

"You tired?" Nathan asked sweetly.

"Yes, exhausted." She laid her crutches against the dresser as she tried to remove her sweater.

He came across the room and pulled it up for her, trying hard not to disturb the bandage on her head. Once the sweater was off, he gawked at her, and she thought she just might melt into the floor. Unfortunately, she caught a glimpse of herself in the mirror, and she was horrified. Her hair was bloody and matted, her face was pale, and her eyes were puffy. She appeared frail, as though she had not eaten in weeks. She frowned at herself.

"You still are beautiful to me." He put his arms around her waist.

"I look awful."

"Abby, you're gorgeous," he said so sincerely that it almost made it worse. "Now, what can I do for you before I go to class?"

"I desperately need a shower. Would you mind helping me?"

He gave her a devilish stare. "I can do that, of course."

He reached down and gradually rolled up her T-shirt. With a careful touch, he pulled it over her head. He tugged on the string on her hospital pants, and they loosely fell to the floor. He slid her panties down as well. He bent down in front of her, and as she lifted her bad leg, he pulled the pant leg and panties off. Then, he stood and picked her up to allow the other pant leg to fall off. He set her back down.

She wasn't sure if, in her condition, Nathan undressing her should be so erotic, but she felt a tingle all over as she stood there, practically naked, while he took all her clothes off, one piece at a time. She could feel her heart beating loud when he reached behind her, and with one swift motion, he unhooked her bra. She swallowed hard. She wanted to grab him and kiss him all over, but he walked back toward her door, grabbed her robe, and held it up for her to put each arm in. He then came around the front and secured it around her waist. Her body moved toward his as he let go of the tie. She was speechless.

Finally, he asked, "Enjoy that?"

Embarrassed that he'd noticed, her face flushed. "What? Uh, no—I mean, thank you."

"Next time, it's *my* turn."

She couldn't move.

He winked at her. "Come on, Abby. The shower is waiting."

"Uh-huh," she mumbled, her eyelids heavy with sedation.

She moved at a snail's pace down the hallway. He stayed right by her, supporting her with his arm as he balanced her shower caddy in the other hand. She winced a little with each step. Her foot and head pounded.

"If this is anything like how you feel after a game...ugh, I'm not sure why you do it," she said.

"Yeah, and I don't get hit half as much as the rest of the guys. But I guess it pays the bills for now, right? Either that or I do it for all the girls." He smirked as she dropped her shoulders. "Kidding," he said.

"Right, of course," she said, mustering a smile.

They arrived in the common area between the two hallways.

He helped her to the door, but knowing they were not alone, he stopped at the entrance and said kindly, "I'll wait here in case you need me, okay?"

"Okay," she said before making her way into the bathroom. She went into the first stall and turned on the water. She then leaned her crutches on the wall next to her. She reached into her robe pocket and put on the bath cap the nurse had given her. She was not allowed to get her stitches wet for twenty-four hours.

She tried not to take a long shower because she knew Nathan had to get to class, so she washed her body and face as quickly as she could. She turned off the water, gently toweled off, and put her robe back on. She hobbled out and went over to the door. Nathan was standing right where she'd left him.

"Ready?" he asked nicely.

"Yes. Thanks for waiting."

They walked back to her room and went inside. She went over to her dresser and took out a pair of panties, sweatpants, and a tank top. He helped her pull the tank top on and get her panties and sweatpants over her cast.

"I'm sorry I have to run, but I can't be late for class."

"I know. Thanks so much for helping me." She blushed as he smoothed down her tank top.

"Of course. I'll come back after my classes. One forty-five sound good?"

"Only if you have time," she said, feeling embarrassed that she needed to be taken care of and even more embarrassed as to the reasons.

He quickly kissed her on the lips then said, "I'm making time, Abby." Then, he said, "We need to talk."

Before she could protest, not that she would, he turned and walked out the door. Yes, they did need to talk. She owed him that. Seeing herself again in the mirror reminded her of the terrible series of events that had taken place. She was a mess, and she needed to quickly get her life back on track.

She grabbed the bottle of medicine the hospital had given her for the pain out of her bag and took two. She hobbled over to her bed and lay down. She pulled the covers up over her body but left her injured leg exposed to allow it to be untouched. Even the weight of the blankets made her foot ache. She could feel the medicine start to work. Her eyes became heavy, and she slowly drifted off to sleep.

She had no idea how long she had been asleep when she heard a knock on her door. Groggy from the medicine and with a dry throat, she yelled, "Who is it?"

"Tank."

"Oh, come in."

She tried to sit up but was still feeling the effects from the medicine. Finally, he came into focus.

He walked over to her. "Oh my God, Abby!" Tank said with a concerned and painful voice. "What happened to you?" He knelt next to her bed.

She gasped when she saw him and immediately said, "What the hell happened to you?"

His face was swollen on one side, his eye was barely open, and his bottom lip was cut and bruised. He looked terrible—no, worse than terrible. His blond waves almost touched his shoulders. She had never noticed how long his hair was. He had a baseball cap pulled down in an attempt to hide his face. It was not working.

"Oh, Abby, are you okay?" he said, ignoring her question.

In a hoarse voice, she slowly said, "Yes, I'm fine, Tank."

"But what happened?"

"I slipped on the ice. I guess I hit my head pretty bad, got some stitches, and"—she pointed to her foot—"hurt my ankle, too."

"Oh my God, I am so sorry. This is my fault. I feel terrible," he started rambling nervously. "I called you a few times and left messages, but when I didn't hear from you, I got worried, so I came over as soon as I could. I just feel so bad about what happened and—"

"Tank, Tank, please slow down." She raised her hand to her head.

He stopped quickly and just stared at her. "Sorry," he said quietly. He sat down on her bed.

She observed this sad, pathetic boy before her. He seemed scared, confused, and distraught. For some reason, Abigail began to feel sorry for him. Maybe it was the medicine that made her feel so courageous, but without reservation, she reached up and pulled off his hat. He let her. His hair fell past his face. She gently ran her hand over his puffy cheek and then moved her fingers down. She traced the tips of her fingers over his swollen lip. He winced only slightly at her touch but did not pull away. In fact, he did not move. He started to close his eyes, and from the corner of his good eye, a tear fell.

"This is all my fault. You were at the Ridge because of me. Look at you, Tank. Your face. Did you see a doctor?"

He opened his eyes—at least what he could of the left eye. "No, I'll be fine."

"Open the fridge over there. The hospital gave me an ice pack. It's in the freezer." He started to protest, but she quickly cut him off, "I'm not asking, Tank. Please go get it. You need to put it on that eye."

He stood up and walked over to the fridge. She noticed he was slightly limping as well. He grabbed the ice pack along with a bottle of water and a chair from one of the desks. He pulled the chair close to her bed, handed her the water, and sat down before placing the ice pack on his eye.

"Thank you," she said, taking the water.

"It's the least I can do. I swore I'd protect you, but look at what I've done. I'm so sorry, Abby."

"It's okay, Tank, but I think you and I need to talk."

She scooted her body up, and he helped prop her pillow on the bed frame, so she could sit up. He touched her hair and saw the blood.

"Abby, is it bad?" he said with concern.

Coming from a football player, it did give her pause.

"Well, it's not great, but I'll be fine. The doctor wants me on bed rest for a few days, and then I'll be back at classes."

"Oh, good."

"How is Marcus?"

"I'm not proud of the fight with Marcus or anything of this, if that's what you think, not even for a second, but he won't take my calls."

"I didn't think you'd be proud of your behavior, Tank," she said, sounding motherly. Her own tone caught her off guard.

She fumbled with his baseball hat on her lap. He held the pack on his eye, still trying to focus on her.

"Tank, I don't want to fight with you anymore. Look at us." She slightly laughed.

He tried to crack a smile, only his swollen face wouldn't allow it. "Me neither. I really don't."

"Okay, good. Then, please understand where I'm coming from."

"Only if you'll promise to understand where I'm coming from," he said with great concern. When she didn't say anything, he continued, "Don't you see, Abby? This is like a miracle. What are the chances of something like this happening in our lifetime? If you didn't know it was true, would you ever believe it if someone had told you this story?"

He had a good point. She would never believe this if someone had told it to her. In fact, she might even think they were crazy.

"So, think about it. Open your mind to the possibility that has come to us. For me, I owe it to Jonathan, my best friend, to at least try to let you know about him, about all the things he told me about you, about you and him. Can't you at least agree with that?"

Maybe it was the medicine, or maybe it was her concussion. She had no idea, but for some reason, Tank was starting to sound not like a crazy person, but a person with a new mission in his life. He was actually starting to sound sane to her.

"Yes," she said.

He removed the pack from his eye and inched closer to her. "Thank you, Abby." Then, he put the ice pack back on his eye.

"So, what next?" she asked.

"I'm not sure."

There was silence in the room. She could feel the connection between them grow. She was the keeper of his secret, and in turn, she was risking her relationships with Nathan, Laura, Webber, and all her friends just to help Tank out. It was a chancy proposition but one she was somewhat committed to already.

Just a few days ago, she would have been horrified to be alone with Tank, but now, she was almost comfortable with him. All this time, he had just been misunderstood. She felt a bit wicked that she had assumed he was just another jerk. In some ways, she needed to make it up to him somehow.

"So, tell me more about Jonathan and his family," she said.

"His parents are great. They are good friends with my parents, and he has a brother, William—eh, Will. He's like my little brother. He's a lot like Jonathan—so smart and athletic. He's just a good kid, and they were close. We were all close. He plans to visit here next month. I get the feeling he wants to follow in his brother's footsteps."

Abigail could see the joy it brought Tank to talk about Jonathan. She nodded, listening intently, as Tank went on to tell her all about Jonathan as a child—from the time he'd gotten his braces stuck in Tank's sweater as they wrestled in the basement to when he'd rescued his dog at a shelter in town to when he'd run for student council president in seventh grade and won. Tank went on and on about Jonathan's life for over an hour.

Abigail rarely interrupted because, for the first time since she had met Tank, he actually seemed happy.

"He never had any girlfriends in school. We were so focused on our grades and football because we had plans, ya know. So, imagine my surprise when he started talking about you. It wasn't like he was this girl-crazy guy. Honestly, he was thoughtful and kind, and all the kids in school liked him. He was friends with everyone, not just the athletes and popular people. Once, he personally invited the whole class to homecoming just so no one would be left out. He was really special, Abby. I know that sounds corny, but he was. He almost preferred the geeks and brainy kids because he always said they would be better friends in the long run. In many ways, he was right. I envied him. It was so easy for him to have friends."

"He sounds like a special person," she said quietly. It reminded Abigail of someone else she knew as well. She stared ahead, thinking about Nathan, and then it hit her. "What time is it?"

"Uh, one forty. You must be starving."

Her heart skipped a beat. Nathan would be here any minute. "Uh, you'd better get going. If Nathan sees you here, he's gonna—I didn't tell him, but at least let me explain a little to him, so—"

"What? Who cares?" he said, turning back into the old Tank.

"Tank, please don't."

His face softened. "Okay, okay, I'll leave, but I'll see you later?"

"Yes, yes, of course."

"We have lots more to talk about."

"Hey," she said as he started to get up, "take care of yourself, will you?" She handed him his hat.

He gently pushed back his hair and put it on before pulling it down to shield his eyes. Then, he smiled. "That goes the same for you, Crash! I don't know who is in worse shape—me or you?"

She giggled a bit and made a funny face at him. He laughed and then pointed to his eye. They both were in pretty pathetic condition.

"I'll see you soon." He walked out the door.

It seemed like less than a minute before her door opened, and Nathan walked in. His face was somber, his expression unfamiliar to her.

"Hi!" she said, trying to sound cheery.

"Hey," he said.

"How was class?"

"Just fine. Got out a bit early. How are you feeling? Get any rest?" he asked.

She was squirming under his stare, but she tried to hold steady. "Yes, I did. Felt good."

"Good, good." He came into the room and rested his hand on the chair.

The chair! Oh no, he knows that chair wasn't there before.

She tried to think quickly as he gently tapped his fingers on the back of the chair. She noticed he wasn't sitting down either. He kept his gaze on her. Now, she began to fidget in her bed.

There was silence.

"Your head still hurt?" he asked.

Okay, now, he was just making small talk, and it was making her feel worse.

"No, I took some medicine, so I guess it is okay."

"Good." His eyes locked on hers.

"What, Nathan? Please tell me what you are thinking. Please," she pleaded.

He dropped his backpack on the floor and said in a cool tone, "Okay if I sit on this seat?"

Okay, so he knew something. She just wasn't quite sure what he knew.

"Of course." She could feel her heart start to beat faster.

He slowly sat down, not taking his eyes off her. His stare sent shivers up her spine.

"Abby," he said slowly.

"Yes?"

"I'm trying to give you an opportunity here. Are you going to take it?" he asked.

"Uh, um," she stammered. *Opportunity for what?*

"Abby…" he said again. "I saw him."

Crap.

"Tank?" he said again.

Double crap. "Oh, yeah—"

"Look," he interrupted sharply but surprisingly not in a rude way, "I said we needed to talk, but I think it is *you* who needs to talk, Abby. So, I'm trying to give you a chance to tell me what you think I need to know, okay?"

What a fool she had been. She should have tried harder to tell him the truth the other day in the hospital, today even. She owed him that much.

"Nathan, I'm so sorry."

"Why, Abby? What are you sorry for? Tell me." He seemed less mad and more concerned.

"Nathan, I feel terrible about what happened, that you were involved and—"

"Abby, you're not getting to the point."

She could tell his patience was wearing.

"I know; I know. I just don't want you to be angry with me."

"I'm not," he said flatly.

"Nathan?"

"Abby, what is going on? Are you two…" He raised his eyebrows.

"What? No! Oh God, no. Nathan, it's not like that, I swear!" Her voice squeaked as it rose about three octaves.

"Then, what is it, Abby?" Now, it was his turn to raise his voice. "I get a call that you are with Tank. I go to the Ridge, and there the two of you are, sleeping at the house even. I didn't hear from you, and then you're running out, away from him, from me. I don't know what to think. You land in the hospital, and then today, he's here, in your room. What gives?"

"Today?" she said, her mind racing.

"Abby, please don't insult me. You don't think I saw him leave your dorm? The chair is here. Put two and two together, and it's not hard. Were you going to tell me he was here? Am I going to have to ask you to tell me everything? Because, you know what, Abby? That says something in itself." His face had reddened as he got more and more heated with his words.

He was dead-on. Right now, she had nothing to hide—just a bunch of silly, crazy conversations about a guy who was supposedly the love of her life, who was now deceased, who just happened to be the best friend of Nathan's archenemy. Yeah, sure, that would be easy to explain. Nathan wouldn't think she was crazy at all. Wait, of course, he would because it *was* crazy. The whole thing sounded absurd.

Her head swirled with confusion.

When she didn't speak, he started to get up. He reached to grab his bag.

"Wait, Nathan. Please don't go."

He stopped moving.

"Please just don't go."

He slowly started to sit back down.

"Nathan, I can't say enough how sorry I am, and the reason I keep saying that is because of your uncle Dave. That is where you should be right now, not here with me. So, I'm not sure who called you, but they shouldn't have." He started to protest, but she held up her hand. "Please just let me finish. I never meant to involve you because there is nothing to involve you in, okay? There is nothing—and I mean, nothing—going on between Tank and me. Nathan, he is a friend, and that's all."

"Since when?" he cut in.

"I don't know. Since I thought maybe he *needed* one." Her eyes were soft and showed deep concern.

Nathan let her continue.

"He came by here today because he felt terrible about what had happened. He didn't know I had been in the hospital. He tried to call me, but obviously, I wasn't home, so he came by, and that's all. I hadn't known he was going to pop in, and I never told him to. Heck, I haven't even checked my messages, so please just don't be upset with me, okay? It kills me to think you are."

"But why, Abby, if he was your friend, would you run out of the Ridge like that? You seemed horrified that I was there, not pleased at all, and you even tried to run from me. Then, he and Marcus fought, and"—he motioned to her body—"this happened!"

"I know; I know. I panicked. When two big guys start throwing punches and putting holes in walls…well, I just reacted and started to run. Believe me, I feel pretty stupid that I ran like that. But I sure did pay the price for it, now didn't I?" She glanced down at the comforter pulled up over her body.

He was right, and only she truly knew why she hadn't wanted him there. It wasn't because she didn't like him—of course not. It was because she had been confused about Tank and...well, Jonathan.

Nathan leaned over in the chair and got closer to the edge of her bed, closer to her face. "Abby, can you tell me why you got in the truck with him?"

Crap.

"I was eating in the cafeteria alone because I missed the girls, and he saw me. He apologized for the banquet, for what happened when I was walking out, and he offered me a ride. It'd started to snow, so I sort of just took the ride to my dorm. He seemed really sorry." She waited for Nathan's reaction.

He didn't give one.

"Ask Marcus about how I ended up at the Ridge. I'd met Marcus at the coffee shop earlier, so I sort of knew him, too, and he said if I ever needed anything, I could go to the Ridge. When the truck got stuck, that was what we did."

She was banking on the fact that he wouldn't ask Marcus because, if he did, she'd certainly have a mess on her hands. Marcus's story would be much different; that she was sure of. So, she was praying that Nathan would just believe her and drop this whole situation and forget about it.

"But how did you end up at the Ridge?"

"We took the long way around because the roads were bad, and it was hard, getting back up the hill."

She searched his face, hoping he was feeling a little bit better about the circumstances. She liked Nathan so much and did not want to jeopardize her relationship with him, but she also owed Tank just a little bit more time. He'd told her a huge secret, and she couldn't just spill it the first chance she got. If nothing else, she felt terrible about all of this, but until she could figure this out, she would have to keep up the story.

"Nathan," she said, observing his concerned face, "I want you to know how much I care about you, how much I thought about you when you were gone." These weren't lies or stories. These were real feelings.

Nathan was handsome, rugged, sweet, and incredibly worried about her. She had disappointed him, and it was killing her.

"Do you believe me?"

He got up and kicked off his shoes. He went to the end of her bed and slowly crawled in next to her. He lay on his side and spooned alongside her fragile, pale body. Abigail winced slightly as he settled in.

"Abby," he said, slanting closer to her, "I do believe you, and I want you to know I feel the same about you. That is what makes this so hard."

"What's so hard?" she said, a pained tone in her voice.

"Please understand that I'm feeling apprehensive about all of this."

She swallowed hard. *Is this his way of telling me just how much he cares, or does this just have to do with Tank?*

She turned her head. "Okay," she whispered.

"I don't trust him, Abby, not one bit."

He gave her such a serious expression. It made her question what exactly she was doing, what she was trying to accomplish, with all of this and what, if anything, she should be worried about as far as Tank's motives were concerned. She wished in many ways that she could tell Nathan exactly what she was going through, to gauge his reaction—or anyone's reaction, for that matter. Then again, she feared he might just think she was foolish to believe a guy like Tank. After all, they hated each other.

"Please don't worry about me, Nathan." Her voice became softer. She didn't want to talk anymore. She wanted to kiss him. She searched his eyes. "Nathan, I'm sorry. Please, can we just put this behind us? I'm a smart girl. I can handle myself."

I am a smart girl. Just confused right now. You have to at least give me an opportunity to take care of myself and be friends with whom I want to. I know you're not the type of guy to tell someone who to be friends with. If anything, that is why I like you so much. Because of what happened yesterday, I know that you'll keep an even stronger eye on Tank. You won't let him hurt me. I know this, Nathan. So, please trust me.

"Okay, Abby. Okay."

Her eyes ran up and down his face. She was patiently waiting for something to tell her that these horrible two days were finally over.

"Are you feeling okay?" he asked, his voice sounding more familiar.

"Yes, I'm doing okay."

"Good," he said, his voice getting heavier.

He got closer to her. She could now feel his breath near her face. Her heart beat faster.

"Good," she said in a breathy voice.

"So, you said you missed me?" he asked so close to her face but not quite close enough. He let his breath linger on her lips.

"Yes, I did." She was barely able to speak.

"Great." He could feel the tension from the last few days building.

He gazed down at her delicate yet tough body. He just wanted to pounce on her, but because of her condition, he had to move with care, and that almost made it more enjoyable.

He leaned down and noticed her lips part as her breathing remained heavy. He pressed his lips on hers and let his tongue move its way into her mouth. She welcomed it. He could feel her start to come alive as she pressed her body onto his. She ran her hand around his waist, resting her fingers on his perfect backside. She pinched his ass, and his head snapped up at her. He granted her a wicked grin.

He took his hand, touched her neck, just under her chin, and then traced his hand down her middle, between the valley of her breasts, teasing her by taking his time. He moved his hand under her top, onto her soft, flat belly. He could hear her moan as he started to drag his hand up her shirt, gently cupping her breast. He squeezed it, and her back arched in response to his touch.

She began pulling his shirt up his body, over his stomach. He took her cue and supported himself on his arm. With a swift motion, he pulled his shirt over his head. His body was firm, and she tried incredibly hard not to lick her lips as he leaned on top of her. He began kissing her again, only this time he was just as eager. He wanted her so badly, but he tried to be gentle, making sure not to hurt her. He started to pull her tank top up. Exposing her stomach, he began kissing her body all over.

Then, in a breathy voice, he asked, "Should I lock your door?"

"Yes," she moaned.

Nathan quickly got up and walked over to the door. He went to secure the lock when he heard voices outside. He could feel the handle turn. Laura popped open the door and started to walk in when she noticed Nathan standing there in nothing but his pants.

Flustered, she said, "Oh my, I'm so sorry." Her face began to turn bright red.

"Are we interrupting something?" a coy voice said from within the doorway.

Great, Bree.

Bree pushed her way in, and with devilish eyes, she sized Nathan up and down. She walked into the room, and with a judgmental tone, she said, "I see you are feeling better, Abigail." She snickered slightly.

Nathan walked over toward the bed and grabbed his shirt. He pulled it over his head and then bashfully ran his hand through his hair.

"I'm fine, just fine," Abigail announced.

Once Nathan had his shirt on, Laura quickly hurried over toward Abigail's bed and leaned down, giving her friend a hug. "I was so worried about you!" Before she let go of the embrace, she whispered in Abigail's ear, "Sorry for the interruption."

Abigail blushed at the thought and whispered, "It's okay. Bree got a good glimpse at him."

Laura laughed at her friend's sarcastic observation and knew she was going to be okay. She stood up. "Thanks for taking care of her, Nathan," she said sincerely.

"Of course. No need to thank me."

"I brought you a turkey sandwich," Laura said.

"Thank you so much," Abigail said.

"You gave everyone a real scare."

"Yeah, we were so worried about you." Bree's voice, however cold it sounded, was in fact hinted with a slight bit of sincerity.

"Thanks. I'm fine really. Just slipped on some ice."

"Well, you'll be fine, but the doctor did say you need plenty of rest, remember?" Nathan scolded and then winked at her.

"Yes, I remember."

"Well, I'm going to go and get some work done, okay?" He gave Abigail a kiss.

"Of course." Then, she softly added, "Thank you for everything."

He gave her another kiss before he started to walk out. "Ladies, take care of her."

"Of course, Nathan. We'll take good care of her," Bree cooed.

"Thanks, Nathan. See you later."

With that, he opened the door and walked out.

No sooner had he left than Bree announced, "I have some work to do as well. I'll see you guys later. If you need anything, Abigail, just ask!" She scurried out the door before Abigail could say a word.

"She means well. Really. She's just…" Laura said.

"I know; I know. I guess I'm not one hundred percent sure what I did to her, but she's—"

"Oh, please. She's like that with everyone. Besides, she is oozing with jealousy. She can't stand the fact that you got Nathan. It kills her."

"Oh, Laura," she said with concern.

"What, Abigail? What is it?"

"I-I almost screwed the whole thing up!"

Laura sat in the chair and leaned toward Abigail. She put her hand on Abigail's. "Abigail, what are you talking about? Screwed what up?"

Abigail was confused, torn, and uneasy about the events that had happened over the last few days. She had no way of knowing how Laura would react to all of it. But even then, Abigail had no idea where to begin. _Is there even a story to tell?_

"Nathan and me…" she said with a whimper.

"Abigail, you two were just, um…how do I say this? From our perspective, you two seemed like you were getting along just fine." She was trying to make her see that everything was okay, that it was all in her mind.

When Abigail's expression remained neutral, Laura sat back. "Hey, it's been an interesting couple of days. I think you need to give yourself a break, okay? Have you eaten?"

"No."

"Then, please eat this, and we can talk or not talk. I'll just stay here with you, okay?"

Her face was so sincere and kind that it was already starting to make Abigail feel better. The idea of not talking about it was even more appealing than Laura could ever know.

"I am pretty hungry."

"Good," she said as she unwrapped the sandwich. "I even brought you this!" She pulled out a container from the bag. "Ice cream!"

"Laura, you are the best."

"I know," she said with a smirk.

They talked periodically while Abigail devoured her meal.

Abigail talked mainly about how she'd just slipped on the stairs because of the scuffle, how understanding Nathan had been for bringing her to the hospital, and how the doctor wanted to keep her overnight merely because of her prior history with seizures.

Laura didn't ask a lot of questions, which was refreshing, until she said, "So, how did you end up with that guy, Tank?"

Abigail could feel her face flush. "Funny story actually."

Laura seemed perplexed.

"I was leaving the cafeteria, and he was out front in his truck. Well, he saw me and just sort of rolled down his window. He said he was sorry for the banquet and stuff. It was snowing, and I was getting wet, so he asked me to get in. I decided to take the ride." She was talking fast.

Laura just tilted her head. "Oh, weird. Thought you believed he was creepy?"

"He's fine really. Maybe just misunderstood? Or something like that."

"Misunderstood? How so?"

Feeling the pressure to come up with something, anything, Abigail reached up to her head, as if she were in a pain. "So hard to say really. You know guys and their emotions. I think he just doesn't handle his well in certain situations. Can you get my medicine from the dresser? My head is starting to ache."

Laura got up. "Of course." She handed Abigail the pills. "Hey, so I'm going to study and let you rest."

"Oh, thanks so much. Yeah, I think I'll try to take another nap or just chill. Can you bring the phone over here? I should probably check in with my mom and dad."

Laura pulled the phone from off the dresser and put it on the chair beside Abigail's bed. "If you need anything else, just holler, okay? I'll have my headphones on."

"Okay, thanks, Laura." She didn't know what she'd have done if she didn't have a roommate as great as Laura.

It started getting dark outside.

Abigail assumed about an hour or so had passed since she called her parents to check in. She was feeling better but definitely not one hundred percent. The doctors had told her it would be a day or two before she started to feel like herself again—at least as far as the concussion went. Good news was that it was a mild concussion, so her recovery would be quicker than expected.

She was just about to get up and make her way to the bathroom when the phone rang. Not wanting to disturb Laura, Abigail quickly picked it up. "Hello?"

"Hey, it's me," Tank said.

"Hey," she hushed.

"Just wanted to check in to see how you were doing. I know we got cut off earlier, so..."

Did we get cut off?

"I'm fine. Doing better."

"Why are you whispering?" he asked.

"My roommate is studying."

In reality, she feared Laura would think it was odd that, all of the sudden, Tank had begun calling her.

"Well, I was wondering when I could see you. Err, I mean, I have something I think you'll want to see."

Feeling confused by his request and questioning to herself if she should be seeing him at all, she said under her breath, "I'm sort of out of commission for a few days here, but can I call you when I get out?"

"Oh, yeah, of course. I'll check in with you anyway."

"Okay," she said.

"Hey, let me know if you need anything. I mean it. Anything, okay?"

"Thanks. Appreciate it."

"Just doing my job," he said with a slight laugh. "Hey, just don't say anything to anyone."

"Secret's safe," she said.

"Thanks."

She glanced over at Laura.

Laura searched Abigail's face, trying to gauge her friend before asking, "You need any help?" She pulled the headphones off.

"No, no, I'm fine. Please keep studying."

Abigail watched in the reflection of the window as her friend put her headphones back on. *Forgive me for lying, Laura. Someday, I'll tell you all about this, promise. Hopefully, you'll understand why I had to keep his secret.*

Twenty-Six

FEBRUARY 12, 1996

On Friday, Abigail left her Biology class as quickly as she could on crutches. She was hoping to avoid chatting with Webber, if for no other reason than she'd promised Tank that she would meet him after almost a week of not seeing him. He had been telling her all week that he had something to show her.

"Abigail!" Webber yelled.

She leaned on her crutches and turned slightly. "Hey, Webber. Sorry, I'm in a bit of a hurry."

"Oh, of course. Just wanted to say hello," he said, sounding almost sad.

She had been so preoccupied over the last few weeks that she had barely spent any time with him. They'd spent a few hours together studying, but that was about it.

"I'm sorry," she said. "That was so rude of me to say that. How are you?"

"It's fine. Besides, I'm doing well, not much to report on my end. More importantly, how's the foot?"

"So much better. Only another week on the crutches, and I'll be feeling as good as new," she said.

"Great news. You must be ready to get rid of them."

"I won't miss them; that's for sure." She glanced down at her watch, trying not to seem obvious.

He noticed. "Where are you off to in such a hurry?" he said jokingly.

Crap. She couldn't tell him. "I told Laura I'd meet her for coffee."

He gave her these eyes that said, *I'd like to join.*

Quickly, Abigail added, "Yeah, I think she's having boy troubles."

"Oh!" Webber's face flushed. "Hope she's okay."

"I'm sure she will be," she lied.

"Okay, I'll see you later."

"Bye."

Whew, that was close.

She knew if she'd told Webber she was going to meet Tank that he would try to tell her not to go, and he might tell Nathan. Until she found out what Tank needed to show her, she had to keep this little rendezvous a secret for now.

She quickly hobbled her way across campus, doing her best to avoid the main paths and walkways. She went behind the arts building and across the street toward a partially empty faculty parking lot. She could see Tank's truck idling in a spot near the back. She couldn't help but feel uneasy as she approached the vehicle. He had his head back, and his eyes were closed. She gently knocked on the passenger window. He did not startle as he opened his eyes. He leaned over and unlocked the passenger door. She tossed her crutches into the bed of the truck while balancing on her good leg. In one swift motion, she pulled open the door, hopped into the seat, and pulled the door shut.

"Hey," he said, his face lighting up.

"Hey," she said back.

"Thanks for meeting me."

"It's okay."

"How are you feeling?" His face showed concern.

"Much better. Thanks. And you?"

"Good." He shifted into reverse.

"Where are we going?" she asked.

"I found this cool spot." He waited, looking both ways. Then, he pulled out of the parking lot. "I'll show you."

"Tank, I don't—"

He quickly cut her off, "Just relax, Abby. You're—we're not doing anything wrong."

Maybe he is right. We're not doing anything wrong. But why does it feel that way? And why do I have to lie to all my friends? Is it because no one seems to really like Tank or understand him? Then again, sometimes, in order to keep one person's secret, you have to lie to another. Talk about a tangled web.

"I guess not. It just feels like—"

"Abby, chill. I'll have you back before anyone misses you, promise."

Huh, she thought to herself.

She was hoping someone was missing her right now. She hoped Nathan was missing her. She knew that she missed him, wished she were with him and not here in Tank's truck.

"Okay." She stared out the window as they drove down Main Street, the campus slowly fading away in the background.

They traveled west for about ten minutes before Tank turned down a dirt road. The street sign read Le Sort Road. Interestingly enough, Abigail knew that meant *fate* in French. She thought about that for a moment as the foliage passed her by. They sat virtually in silence as his truck bounced up and down along the poorly settled road. Then, as they went farther along, trees covered each side of the road like a thick carpet, so thick that she could barely see in between them.

"We're almost there," he finally said.

She gripped the door handle as her body bounced around.

As if by magic, the road ended, and the trees seemed to part as Tank slowly rolled his truck to a stop. What lay in front of them was almost indescribable. A blanket of snow covered the ground, untouched and beautiful. The trees appeared as though they had been pushed back to create a clearing off to one side, and an old stone wall had been built in a semicircle around them. It appeared as though man and nature had collided. The sun barely peeked through the thick branches of the trees above. On the other side of the opening was a small wood cabin with a tiny front porch. Abigail could only imagine how long the cabin had been there and who, if anyone, lived in it.

"What is this place?" she asked under her breath.

"Amazing, right?" He gazed forward. "Come on. I'll get your sticks."

He grabbed the box sitting next to him on the bench, opened the door, and hopped out. He went behind the truck and took her crutches out of the back. She opened her door and swung her legs around before gently lowering her good leg onto the snowy ground below. She took each crutch and placed them under her arms. She moved away from the door, so he could close it. She couldn't take her eyes off the scenery in front of her. It was too breathtaking. It seemed familiar to her, yet she had no idea why. The view gave her a chill up her spine as she took in her surroundings.

"Careful, okay?" He started walking toward the wall near the cabin.

"Tank, are we allowed to be here?" she asked.

He turned to her. "Sure. Why not? No one lives here. Abby, trust me."

Tank got to the wall and waited for Abigail to catch up. She stood next to Tank as he peered beyond the trees. She could see through the thick pine trees covered with snow, and if she squinted just right, she could barely make out a field ahead.

"You see that?" he said, pointing.

"Yeah. You mean, that field?"

"Yes."

"Remember that, okay? Remember what it looks like today."

Her eyes danced over the scenery, taking it all in.

Abigail took a deep breath and let it out. She decided she would wait for him to tell her why they were here. She had noticed the box on the seat.

She saw he was holding it now. She kept her eyes glued ahead and waited patiently.

Finally, he said, "Come over here." He motioned toward the cabin.

Like a puppet on a string, she followed close behind, never questioning.

Tank took a seat on the steps of the old cabin. They creaked as the weight of his body rested on the timeworn wood. He slid over a bit to allow her room next to him. She took her crutches out from under her arms and placed them on the ground by the post of the porch. She gently hopped on one foot and sat down. He rested the box on his lap. It was a black Adidas sneaker box. The cover was tattered, and the sides were bent a bit. It was obvious it had been sealed with duct tape at some point.

She viewed the clearing from this angle and couldn't believe that it was even more beautiful. She knew now why whoever had built this cabin put it here and not where Tank's truck was. From this angle, the wall and the field were more visible. She imagined for a moment what this place must be like in the fall or spring. It must be gorgeous.

"Abby," he began, "when Jonathan was in the hospital..."

Okay, he's diving right into this again.

"He gave me this box. He told me that I would know the right time to open it. I knew when I met you—no, when you and I talked at the banquet, that something was different. Something had changed."

As he spoke, her eyes shifted down toward the box. Her heart began to race, and her body flushed despite the cold February air.

"Okay?" she said quietly.

"After I saw you lying there in your bed, head wrapped up, leg in a cast, it dawned on me that it was time for me to really let you in. I trust you now. But I wasn't always certain that I would be able to. Things have been—no, I have been spiraling out of control, and I need to get my life back on track."

"Okay?" she quietly said again.

Tank opened the box. By the way he lifted the lid with such trepidation, she was convinced a live creature of some kind was going to jump out. She actually leaned back a bit as his arms moved up and removed the tattered top. When nothing came out, she moved back forward as he removed with great care a three-by-five leather notebook. It had pages sticking out but was secured around the width by a thick rubber band.

"Abby," he said, his voice nervous, "what I'm about to show you might freak you out, but please just take it slow. I know I did. It's a lot to digest, okay?" His face showed great concern.

For the first time since getting in the truck with him, she was frightened.

"Tank, you're scaring me," she said, her eyes wide.

"No, no, I don't mean to. I mean, it is *awesome*. Just...well, here."

He handed her the book, but she could not move her hands. It was as though some kind of force was preventing her from lifting her fingers and taking hold of the book.

"Here," he said again. "Don't be afraid, okay?"

He motioned toward her with the book. Feeling a twitch in her limbs, she reached up and took the book. She held it on her lap for what felt like an eternity.

"Go ahead. Open it," he encouraged.

She wouldn't say he was smiling, but he did appear happy.

She gently took the rubber band off the book and laid it on her lap. She took a deep breath and opened the leather cover of the book. She gasped quietly as she saw her own face staring back at her. The sketch was unmistakable. It was her. From her eyes to her hair to her nose and eyebrows, it was her.

Her hands began to tremble.

"Go on," he said with a gentle voice.

She turned the page, and there she was again. There was no mistaking that it was her. She turned another page and saw a picture of her and her dog, Skyler.

This is impossible. She turned yet another page.

There, Jonathan was kissing her on the cheek, and the expression on her face was electric. Then, the following pages were filled with notes, written like the ones you'd imagine a peculiar person might scribble. There were feverish ramblings of words and phrases, like *I love you, love of my life,* and *never forget.* There were dates and times scrawled about and so on. She started to flip through the book, her eyes welling with tears. She passed a drawing but swiftly returned to it.

"The field," she whispered.

"Amazing, huh?" Tank said under his breath.

In the picture, she could see the tip of the stone wall, and just past it appeared to be the field, only drawn as what you would imagine it might be like in the spring with beautiful wildflowers and tall, lush trees. In the distance, two people were walking hand in hand.

She couldn't review the book anymore. She closed it and began to cry.

Tank put his arm around her and squeezed. "Abby?" He draped his hand over her bicep.

She couldn't answer.

"Abby, are you okay? Look at me."

She tried to push him off of her, but he held on to her arm.

"No, I'm not okay, Tank," she said with anger in her voice. "Did you do this?" she asked, staring at him.

"What? No. Are you crazy? Why would I?"

She cut him off, "Why? I don't know why, but you'd better tell me!" Her voice was loud.

His eyes grew big.

"Abby, that would be the cruelest joke ever. I'm not like that, honest. He was my best friend. Why would I ever do this to you, to him? What could possibly be my motive? Imagine my reaction when I saw the book, those drawings. I didn't even know he could draw. From what I saw in art class, he was no Van Gogh; trust me.

"Besides, I found this place first. I have been coming here since the beginning of school. I was desperate to find a quiet place to get away from everyone, everything. The book affected me, too, but he wanted me to have it, me and no one else!" His blood rushed to his face. He wasn't angry. No, in fact, if anything, he was more like a scared little kid.

"But what does all this mean?" she said, sounding hopeless.

"I don't know, but I was hoping we could find out together."

"Find what out?"

"I'm not sure exactly, but it is something. You have to at least agree with that."

"I don't know, Tank. I just don't know what to think about anything." She wiped her tears away with the sleeve of her coat.

"You obviously loved each other. You can't ignore that."

"Love...love?" she said. "I don't even know him."

"But, Abby, he was trying to tell us that you did."

She couldn't figure out why those words stung so deeply, but they did. Maybe because, at that very second, as the words were coming out of his mouth, she actually began to question what was real. It scared her. It scared her to death.

"Tank," she said softly, "why are you doing this?"

"Why? Because I made him a promise. That's why."

"But, Tank," she said, trying to choose her words wisely, "how could you have known what you were promising?"

"Well, I guess I didn't...but now that I see you and this"—he motioned to the book on her lap—"and all the other things, I have to keep my promise. I just have to." He drew in a deep breath. "He wanted me to protect you. He wanted me to make sure you knew about him, that your life was meant to be with him."

Her heart sank as she sat there and listened to him. She wanted so badly to get out of this mess but was suddenly drawn to this whole idea of a past love. She questioned for the first time what in her life was truly factual. She wondered if anything was and, for that matter, if she believed in fate.

Fate.

Nathan.

Nathan had no idea she was going through this. He would be devastated that she had been sneaking around behind his back.

But doing what? What am I doing exactly?

She had never told Nathan, but she loved him. She just knew she did. She'd never felt that way around anyone, not even James. Nathan deserved better than she was able to give him right now, and unfortunately, that was the one thing she knew to be real. Maybe he would have been better off if they had never met.

Wait, what am I thinking? she yelled in her head. *Stop it!*

Her body began to shiver. It was getting colder, as the sun had begun to set.

"Tank, I need to go. Please take me home."

"Of course. But keep the book and go through it, will you?"

She found herself nodding her head. In her mind though, she was yelling, *No!*

The ride back in Tank's truck was quiet. Abigail was emotionally and physically drained from the past few hours. As Tank got closer to campus, Abigail glanced at her watch.

"Can you please drop me off in the back of the building?" she asked.

"Okay, if that's what you want."

"Yeah, I think it's best for right now."

Tank drove down the side street behind a few of the administration buildings and toward the dorms. He knew that she didn't want to be seen getting out of his truck. It partly made him upset, but the other part of him was trying to understand.

He pulled up and turned off his headlights.

"Thanks," she said kindly. She went to reach for the door handle when Tank's massive hand landed on her arm.

"Abby?" he said in a much softer tone than she was used to.

"Yes?" she said.

"If you ever need to talk…I hope you'll come to me."

She noticed he did not remove his hand from her arm. She let out a long sigh. She glanced over at him. His face said it all. He was concerned, sad, and confused, just as she was. He was the only one who knew what she knew, the only one who had lost a friend last year. Somehow, the loss of that friend had thrown them together whether they liked it or not. Maybe that was why she knew she could not betray his trust. She could not tell anyone about their secret. In a way, they both had no choice in the matter. Jonathan had led them here, and neither one of them could answer why.

Finally, she spoke, "Just so you know, I'm not mad at you."

He let out a deep sigh. "Okay, I hope not. Really, I'm not trying to hurt you, honest."

"I know, Tank. I just feel like my head is spinning and—"

"Tell me about it. Trust me; I get it, Abby—or at least, I'm trying to." He took his hand off her arm. "I know this is strange. I get that. Just stick with me, won't you? Just until we figure this out?" he asked.

She sincerely wanted to tell him she would stick with him through it all, no matter what, but right now, she just couldn't do that, not until she at least had the chance to flip through the book again. She did, however, give him a slight smile as a sign to show that, if nothing else, she was willing to try.

"So, I'll call you, all right?" She pulled on the handle and started to open the door.

"Okay. Oh, hey, Jonathan's brother is coming to town to visit in a few weeks. I'd like you to meet him."

"I'd like that," she said.

The smile that grew across Tank's lips told her she'd said exactly what he'd hoped for. She grabbed the box with the notebook inside and hopped out of the truck.

With her crutches under her arms, she made her way to the dimly lit door of her dorm. Once she was inside, she turned as Tank drove away.

What have I gotten myself involved in?

Abigail got off on her floor and started down the hall. As she unlocked her door, she could hear music playing, and Laura and Bree were chatting. She walked in with the box tucked tightly between her arm and the crutch. The two of them were sprawled on the carpet between the beds, devouring all the latest fashion magazines. Her heart sank a little as she saw them laughing and smiling, not a care in the world.

"Hey!" Laura said.

Come on, Abigail, put on a happy face. "Hey!" she said, forcing her happiness.

"Where have you been? Shopping?" Bree asked.

"Oh, yeah—well, sort off," she said. *Crap. Please don't ask to see what is inside the box.* Thinking on her feet, she said, "My mom sent me some old sneaks I needed."

"Oh, nice." Bree turned her nose up.

"So, we were getting ready to go to dinner. Want to come?"

"Yes," she said. She desperately needed to get her mind off of what had just happened.

"Great. Let us know when you're ready." Laura smiled.

Abigail went over to her closet and put the box on the top shelf. She gently draped a sweater over it, so the box wasn't visible. She caught a glimpse of herself in the mirror. She appeared tired and washed out.

Laura got up and came over to her, placing a hand on her shoulder. "Are you okay, Abigail?"

"Yeah, I'm just tired; that's all."

"Okay. Let me know if I can help with anything."

Abigail sensed by her remark that Laura wasn't buying her tired speech, and in many ways, she couldn't blame her. Abigail hadn't exactly been selling it well.

"Ready to go?" Bree piped up.

They both nodded in unison. Abigail leaned back on her crutches and made her way out the door.

The cafeteria was in its usual busy frenzy for a Friday evening. All the students were trying to eat before they made their plans for the night. The girls liked to eat early, so they could spend the next few hours hanging out and getting ready while most of the guys liked to quickly shower and head to someone's house for a few beers before a party. It was the same routine weekend after weekend, yet you never got bored.

"The cafeteria is a funny place," Bree declared as she put her tray down. "It's so easy to spot exactly where certain groups sit. They always flock to the same location. The potheads always sit near the frozen ice cream machines. Go figure." She rolled her beautiful brown eyes. "The sorority girls sit near the fraternity boys, and they seem to take up the most tables. Not interested in joining them, *thanks.*" She flipped her hair to the side and then continued, "The hippie kids sit in the back corner, usually near the potheads. There are our beloved athletes. As you all know, they sit in the back room. Then, the best for last, there are the regular students, like me, who sort of fill in the rest of the tables."

"Huh. I see you've put a lot of thought into it," Maddie said with a slight chuckle.

Bree squinted her eyes at her and then quickly said, "Yeah, of course. Maybe we should make up our own group. You know, the best-looking girls of OSU."

"Really?" Laura said with a laugh.

"Yeah, but I'll be the judge of who gets in."

Abigail couldn't help but snicker, if for no other reason than Bree would always say exactly what she was thinking, good or bad. There was something to be said for being honest, however brutal it might be at times.

Nathan opened the door to his room and walked in. He put his books on his desk with a thud.

Webber was sitting in his chair, his nose buried deep in a book. "Oh, hey. Coach called," he said with a quizzical glance. "Said he needs to see you at five and not to be late."

Huh. Wonder what this is all about. "Okay, thanks."

"Everything all right?" Webber asked.

"Yeah. Why?"

"I don't know. Just checking." He pushed his glasses further up on his nose.

Nathan glanced at the clock on the wall. It was four forty-five. "Well, I'd better go, I guess." He picked up his keys and opened the door. "I'll see you in the cafeteria."

"Yeah, sounds good. And, Nathan, if you need to talk about anything, just let me know, okay?"

"Thanks, Spidey. You're a good bud," he said before closing their door.

He thought about when Webber had called him to check in on his uncle Dave. When Nathan had asked if Webber had seen Abby, he'd hesitated before saying that she'd called and asked questions about Tank. What Abigail hadn't known was that Webber had been in the cafeteria that night as well and had seen the two of them talking. The conversation had been strange and private, and it obviously hadn't been idle chitchat between two old friends. So, once Abigail had left the cafeteria, Webber had walked out, and that was when he'd noticed her getting into Tank's waiting truck. If nothing else, Webber had been concerned for not only her safety, but also for both of his friends. He'd wanted to make sure Nathan was aware of her questions about Tank, considering what Webber knew of the night of the football banquet.

Nathan walked down to the field house and opened the door to the locker room. Coach's door was closed, but Nathan could see the light was on.

Coach Stanfield popped his head out of his office and said, "Nathan, he'll be with you in a moment." His voice sounded cold and unwelcoming.

It gave Nathan a chill.

Moments later, the door yanked open, and Marcus and Jason came walking out. Startled to see them, Nathan took a step back.

"Congrats, Rook." Marcus shook Nathan's hand. "Didn't get a chance to congratulate you the other day."

"Yeah, congrats, buddy. Way to lead the team," Jason said sincerely.

"Appreciate it. Couldn't have done it without you guys."

"We know you couldn't have done it without us." Marcus winked.

"Hey, man, so sorry about all the crap the other day. I talked to Abby, and I think everything should be cool now. Hopefully, things with Tank will improve."

Marcus's expression turned serious again. "Yeah, we shouldn't have any more problems." He tapped Nathan on the arm.

His face was still battered from what Nathan assumed was his scuffle with Tank. The bruise around his eye was now yellow and light purple.

Marcus continued, "You doing okay? How is Abigail? I'm sorry about the stairs. I scraped them and put salt out, but, man, I just feel terrible about all that."

"Oh, not your fault. She feels awful about what happened to you. But, yeah, she is doing better. She'll be fine."

"Good."

"Yeah, tell her we hope she gets better soon," Jason added.

"Thanks, Jay." Nathan's face turned red. He again turned to his captain. "Sorry you had to get involved."

"Don't sweat it. I just hope it all gets sorted out and—"

He was cut off by Coach's scratchy, low voice, "Nathan!"

"Hey, gotta go. I'll see you guys in the café." He walked into Coach's office.

"Close the door, Nathan, and take a seat."

Nathan didn't speak. He just did what he had been told. Coach's eyes seemed dark, and his face was strained. It was cold in his office. Nathan shuddered as he observed Coach, waiting eagerly for him to speak.

"Nathan, I've been made aware of a situation," he started off.

"Okay, Coach." Nathan's nerves began to rise.

"I wanted you to get the news from me first and only me," he said, his eyes darting back and forth at a rapid pace.

Oh no, this does not sound good.

Coach stated in an exhausted, deep voice, "I am suspending McPherson from the team, effective this evening."

A lump formed in Nathan's throat. He tried to swallow, but he couldn't push it down. "What? Why?"

"It wasn't an easy decision, but right now, I—the staff feels it is best for this team."

"But, Coach, I don't under—"

Coach cut him off, "Son, sometimes, you have to make the hard decisions, but right now, we feel this is best for all involved." His voice was firm, indicating there was no room for discussion. "We think—we know he has some personal things he needs to focus on, and he just can't go around, getting into fights with his captain. There is a level of respect I want my players to have for one another, and I feel like, at this point, a hard message needs to be sent. And I'll determine in time whether or not he has received that message. Do you understand what I'm saying?"

"Okay, Coach. Thank you for telling me." He went to stand up. He felt terrible, but quite honestly, he wasn't sure why.

"One more thing," he said as Nathan placed his hand on the doorknob. "I try not to get involved in this sort of thing, but do us all a favor and look out for your girlfriend around him. This might set him off a bit. Understood?"

Nathan could not believe the words that had just come out of Coach's mouth.

What the hell does that mean? How does Coach even know about Abby and Tank, and why is he concerned? Shit. Marcus. It had to be Marcus. No one else knows about what happened.

He wanted to ask Coach so many of these questions, but he was frozen in his tracks by the remark Coach had made.

Instead, Nathan just mumbled, "Okay, I will, and thanks, Coach, for telling me personally."

He pulled the door open, and with a swift motion, he walked out.

Forget feeling sorry about Tank. What does this have to do with Abby? Is she in some kind of trouble with Tank?

Nathan's mind raced as he hurried toward the cafeteria.

As usual, Marcus, Jason, and a group of football players were sitting at a few tables in the back.

"Hey," Marcus whispered to Nathan as he put his tray down, "don't say a word about what Coach said, okay? He called me and told me he couldn't get ahold of Tank, so he won't find out until Monday." His voice was stern, and his eyes darted back and forth between Nathan and Jason.

"I won't say a word. Believe me…I don't want him to hear it from me. That much I know." There was sadness in Nathan's voice.

"Me neither," Jason whispered.

They sat back and could see Tank coming toward them with a tray of food. Nathan wanted to ask Marcus if he knew what Coach meant when he'd mentioned Abby, but he didn't have time.

"Be cool," Marcus warned.

Tank approached, and his demeanor seemed different. "Uh, hey, guys. What's up?" he said to all of them but avoided making eye contact with Marcus.

They had not spoken since the fight. The tension was palpable.

Tank put down his tray on the other table, sensing he wasn't welcome at Marcus's table.

"Nothing. You?" Jason finally answered Tank.

Nathan peered over at Tank, and all he could think about was what Coach had said about Abby. He was dying to know what Coach meant. Nathan toyed with the idea of asking Tank, but part of him assumed it had to do with the fight he'd had with Marcus. Well, at least, he hoped that was all it had to do with.

"Same old, same old," Tank said. He took a bite of spaghetti.

Nathan peeked at him out of the corner of his eye. Tank wouldn't look over, and Nathan couldn't help but wonder why.

Is he avoiding making eye contact because of Marcus or Abby or what?

Abigail, Laura, Maddie, and Bree were eating their dinner when they noticed the other girls from their floor approaching.

Melissa, Jen, Casey, and a few other floor mates came up to their table.

"Abigail!" Melissa screeched as she put her tray down. She gently hugged her friend around the shoulders. She had not seen Abigail since the accident, and she'd missed her friend dearly.

"Melissa! I feel like I haven't seen you in ages."

"Abigail, I heard about what happened. I called you as soon as I got back but got your machine."

"I know. Thank you. I was hoping to see you today, but the day ran away from me," she said.

Melissa sat down across from her. "So, how are you feeling?"

"Oh, fine. I just slipped on some ice. Took a hard spill; that's all."

"Yeah, I heard there was a fight or something, and it involved you. Is that true?" she asked innocently.

Abigail's face turned red as the table got quiet. They all seemed to be waiting for her response.

She gave an uncomfortable laugh and replied, "Oh, no, nothing like that. They were fighting about…well, I don't know really. Guess they don't care for each other much, but anyway, enough about my silly fall. How was your internship? Did you love New York City?"

Thankfully, no one seemed to notice her sudden change of topic. They were all equally excited to hear about Melissa's internship in New York.

Each year, the university would award one freshman in the English department a two-week internship at a publishing firm in New York City, and Melissa had been chosen. It was a huge honor. She had been featured in the school paper before she left, and the school editor had already told her they planned to run another follow-up article in *The Weekly Blue* next week.

"It was amazing," she gushed. "The people were so nice, and I actually got to do some work, not just make copies and fetch coffee. They asked me if I wanted to come back for the summer!"

"Oh, Melissa, that is so exciting!"

"How was the shopping?" Bree asked.

Melissa stopped. "Not sure, Bree. I didn't have time to shop."

"Oh, huh. I would have made time. It is unreal." She put her fork back into her salad.

Melissa rolled her eyes, and Abigail couldn't help but snicker.

Feeling the center of attention shift away from her, Bree piped up, "Anyway, girls, I have a big announcement!" She reached into her pocket and pulled out a stack of black tickets. "These are tickets," she announced, holding them up for all to see, "for the annual Black Hearts Party at Sigma tonight! And we are all going!" She beamed.

The annual Black Hearts Party was always the weekend of Valentine's Day. Since Valentine's Day was Sunday, they were going to host the party on Friday, so they wouldn't compete with all the other Valentine's Day parties on Saturday. Everyone had to wear black to get in, and tickets were sometimes tough to come by. Sigma had started the tradition years and years ago as a way to poke fun at the customary Valentine's Day parties the other fraternities were having. The Black Hearts Party became known as the anti-love party.

"Wow, awesome! Thanks, Bree," Laura said.

"Girls' night out sounds good!" Jen said.

At first, the thought of going to a party tonight just made Abigail feel tired. She had already had a long day. But the more she thought about it, the more she wondered if maybe a girls' night out, away from all the men in her life, would do her some good. She could get her mind off everything that was going on. It would also keep her from sitting in her room alone with that book.

"Sounds great. Thanks for the tickets," Abigail said.

As she did, she could see Laura's reaction. It was one of disbelief, and it gave Abigail just the motivation she needed to have some fun with the girls tonight. Laura gave her a slight nudge under the table. Abigail glanced over at her, and Laura just nodded. Her friend knew that she needed a night out, too.

The girls chatted over dinner for the next half hour or so. Abigail was starting to feel better already. She needed to be away from all the other things she had going on right now. It wasn't that she didn't want to be with

Nathan—of course, she did—but she didn't want to think about Tank and the secret she was keeping. It was starting to make her feel guilty for sneaking around with Tank and talking about Jonathan. Worse, after seeing herself and Jonathan in the book, the visual had made it more real. It was no fault of Nathan's. He was just an innocent in all of this.

The girls decided—or were more so told by Bree—that they would all meet in her room, dressed all in black, at eight thirty. Jen, Casey, and Melissa headed back to their rooms to start to get ready. Laura and Bree went and put their trays on the belt. Abigail followed close behind, leaning on her crutches.

"Hey, there's Abigail." Jason noticed her near the return line.

Nathan noted Tank's reaction to her name. He appeared to shudder at the sound of her name being whispered among the group.

"Where?" Nathan said. He noticed Tank kept his eyes on her. Finally, Nathan turned and waved for her to come over.

Abigail saw Nathan waving from across the room. He was so striking, sitting there with that beautiful smile on his face that she tried hard not to let her emotions get the best of her. She was happy to see him, and a warm sensation rushed over her.

"Laura, Nathan is in the back room. He wants me to go over there."

"No problem," she said.

"Great!" Bree chimed in.

It wasn't exactly what Abigail had had in mind, but maybe with the two of them there, it would be more of a distraction. She made her way over to the table with the girls close behind.

"Hey, Abby. How are you?" Nathan asked as she approached the table.

His voice was sweet, and it made her blush.

"Good. You?" Before he could respond, she said, "You guys know Laura and Bree?"

The players sort of nodded and grumbled in acknowledgment of the girls.

"Hey, ladies." Jason winked at them.

Bree was in her element. She could not have had a bigger smile on her face.

"Abigail!" Marcus said loudly.

She felt embarrassed at the sight of him.

"Feeling better, I hear."

"Yes, thank you, Marcus," she said, her face as red as an apple.

Tank never took his eyes off Abigail as she stood next to Nathan. She glanced over only once and made eye contact with Tank. He tipped his head, and she gave him a slight nod back. It was awkward, no mistaking that, especially around Marcus. It was the first time all of them had been in the same room since a few weeks ago. Abigail was incredibly uncomfortable but tried not to show it.

"Anytime. You know that," he said under his breath.

Attempting to seem casual, she asked, "What are you guys doing tonight? Any plans?"

"Not really," Marcus said. "But you ladies know about the big Cupid's Party tomorrow night, right?"

"Of course!" Bree said. "We'll be there. Tonight, we're all going to the Black Hearts Party."

Marcus laughed. "Well, well, you ladies sure are going to make your rounds this weekend. Good for you, but watch out, men of OSU, the hotties are on the prowl this Valentine's weekend."

Abruptly, Tank stood up, and without saying a word, he left the table. He walked over to the belt, returned his tray, and quickly walked out the back door. It took all of Abigail's might not to go after him just to tell him she was sorry she'd treated him like he didn't matter, but she had no choice in front of all his teammates. But she knew if she did go after him, it would cause more trouble than it was worth right now. She knew Tank was having a difficult time with all of this, and maybe he just needed some space.

She noticed Nathan observing her. She stopped watching Tank as he left and questioned to herself if she was being too obvious. She felt badly, too, because she had not had a chance to talk to Nathan all day, and now, she had plans with the girls. Maybe he'd had something in mind for them. But she knew, at this point, she had to go. She *wanted* to go.

"Ready to go?" Jason asked Marcus as he stood up.

"Yeah, cool." Marcus stood up.

Feeling an opportunity as she noted Laura and Bree start to walk away with Jason, she turned to Nathan and said, "Would you mind if I talked to Marcus for a second?"

Marcus stopped in his tracks and waited for Nathan to respond.

"Of course not," Nathan said.

"Thanks. I'll meet you outside?"

"Sure." He got up from the table, walked to the garbage, and put his tray on top of the bin. He glanced back before walking out the door.

She could see the concern on Marcus's face.

Don't embarrass yourself, Abigail.

Finally, she said, "Thank you."

"No worries," he answered back.

"Your eye looks better. I mean, I'm assuming it does."

She took in his face. The bruises were fading, but still, it reminded her of that day. That day alone had put her on a whole new path, one she could not have anticipated.

"Yeah, well, you should see the other guy." He laughed.

Abigail slightly chuckled. Even though it was true, that other guy was Tank, her friend, and he was going through a hard time that no one could ever understand. It made her uncomfortable to laugh.

"Hey, I don't want to keep you, but I just wanted to say that I can't thank you enough for your understanding the other night. I know I put you...I put everyone in a tough situation. I know you didn't ask for that, and I'm sorry."

He searched her face. His lips parted, but then he hesitated as though he had something important to say but couldn't. Finally, he spoke, "Whatever it is, Abigail, I hope you figure it out. Nathan's a great guy. I'm not here to preach to you, but just be careful. This thing you're doing with Tank...well, he's not who you think he is."

Feeling slightly offended by his remarks, she quipped back, "Maybe he's not who *you* think he is."

She thought about how Tank hadn't told anyone about the passing of his best friend, so it bothered her that his own teammates misunderstood him.

Marcus's eyes widened.

"I'm sorry. I didn't mean to, um...well, I just wanted to say thank you. I can't say that enough, and I'm sorry."

"Okay, Abigail." His voice was flat. "I think they're waiting for us." He started to walk toward the door.

She followed behind. That hadn't gone quite as well as she had planned, but at least she had gotten to say what she wanted to say. There was nothing Abigail could say to Marcus that would get him to change his opinion of Tank. In many ways, she couldn't blame him for that. They had gotten into a bad fight a short time ago.

Marcus held open the door for her, and she walked out into the cold night. Nathan and Jason were standing at the bottom of the walkway. Abigail had a twinge of guilt in her heart as she caught eyes with Nathan.

"See you guys tomorrow," Marcus said.

"Later," Jason added as they walked toward campus.

She was nervous, standing there, alone with Nathan. It wasn't a bad nervous, but her heart raced a bit. He reached over and grabbed her hand. She almost leaped out of her skin at the feel of his hand in hers.

"So"—Nathan took her out of her thoughts—"how was your day?" He leaned in close to her.

"It was good. I mean, fine, no big deal. And you?"

"Happy it's Friday."

"Yeah, glad it's Friday."

"You okay, Abby?" he asked.

"Oh, me? Yeah, fine. Just a long day, but I'm great," she lied.

"So, going out with the girls tonight, huh?"

"Yeah, Bree just told us she got us tickets. You know Bree. She doesn't ask; she tells."

"Ha!" He laughed.

Standing there with only the glow of the streetlights on his face, he appeared like a vision; only she knew he didn't know it, which made her like him even more.

As if catching her in her own thoughts of him, he said, "What? Do I look funny or something?"

"What? No. I was just—"

"Staring at me?" he asked with a smile.

"Sorry, I didn't mean to. I just haven't seen you today and…"

"You missed me. I know." He smirked as he draped his arms around her neck and gave her a squeeze. "Missed you, too, Abby."

His arms felt so good around her despite the crutches tucked under her arms. She turned her head to one side, resting it on his chest, and closed her eyes. She took in a deep breath.

"Don't let me go," she whispered.

Her saying that meant more to her than he could have possibly known in that moment.

He rested his chin on the top of her head and squeezed her again. She couldn't tell how long they stood there until he finally said, "I have to let you go."

She let out a disagreeable sigh.

"So I can do this." He pulled her back, leaned down, and gave her a long, electrically charged kiss.

She swore, her legs would have given out had she not been leaning on the crutches. Even as he drew back, she had to force her eyes open.

"Hey, when you get back from the party, give me a ring." He gave her his infamous, sexy smile.

"Okay," she mumbled. "But I won't if it's too late."

"It's never too late for you, Abby. Besides, Webber went home for the weekend. You knew that, right?"

She swallowed hard and bit her bottom lip. "No, I didn't know that."

"You guys should talk more." He chuckled.

If only he knew how right he was. I have hardly spoken to Webber these past few weeks. I feel terrible about that because I haven't been a very good friend.

"Did he go home for any particular reason?"

"Not really. Guess he just wanted to."

"Oh, good for him. Decent excuse to get all his laundry done."

"Exactly."

"Got any plans tonight?"

"Nothing much. Maybe watch some TV *and* wait for you to call me."

She glanced up at him. "Well, I'd better get going. I know the girls will be waiting for me. I'll talk to you later."

"Have fun tonight—but not too much fun without me." He gave her a quick kiss on the forehead.

"Bye."

She never moved as he walked down the street toward his dorm. She was paralyzed by him.

Damn Black Hearts Party. I'd much rather be alone with Nathan Ryan than be with a bunch of anti-love students at an anti-Valentine's Day party, she grumbled to herself as she reluctantly crutched her way back to her dorm.

Along the way, she decided that she would get rid of her damn crutches tonight. She had faithfully been on them and had had enough. If she was going to this party, she was going to make the best of it, and that meant, no crutches.

Twenty-Seven

FEBRUARY 12, 1996
BLACK HEARTS PARTY

When the elevator opened up on Abigail's floor, she could hear the blow-dryers and music playing as she made her way down the hall. *It's definitely a party night.*

All the girls were getting ready, doing their usual routines. She glanced at the clock as she entered her room. It was almost seven. If she was going to shower and get ready, she'd better do it now. She grabbed her caddy, and with no crutches, she walked gingerly down the hallway to the bathroom. She passed Laura on her way out.

"No crutches?" she asked.

"Nope, can't do it anymore. Tonight is the night for freedom!" She laughed.

Abigail showered fast and shaved her legs. She was in and out in no time. Her ankle seemed better, still swollen but the bruise had faded quite a lot. She dried off, making sure not to put too much pressure on her foot. She hobbled back down the hall and to her room. It only hurt slightly, not enough to get her back on the crutches.

She opened the door. Laura was already dressed in all black. She wore a tight, long-sleeved black shirt, black jeans, and black boots.

"Wow, hot stuff!"

"It's all black!" She laughed, giving Abigail a spin.

"I have no idea if I have anything black. I know I have some black pants, but…" She started to open her drawers and rummage through her clothes. "I have this old T-shirt." She pulled out one of her workout tees. It was faded and had the letters *Glens Falls High School* on the front.

"I'm not sure that's going to cut it. And if I think that, try getting it past Bree." Laura laughed.

She was right. Bree would never give Abigail the ticket if she showed up dressed in an old gym T-shirt.

"I have this you can wear."

Abigail's face scrunched up a bit as Laura handed her a black shirt.

Laura quickly added, "Just try it on before you make a face, okay?"

Abigail found her black pants and slipped them on. Then, she put on a black lace bra and the shirt over her head. She could feel how tight it was as she pulled it down.

"Uh, Laura, I'm not sure about this," she said, turning to her friend.

When she saw Laura's reaction, she knew her answer.

"Oh, you are *so* going to wear that!" Laura sounded just like Bree, and it was nauseating.

"What? No, I can't!" She pointed to the front.

The shirt was a tight black lace turtleneck, but what made the shirt so sexy was the strategically placed hole that was cut out just above her breasts, so you could see the top of her cleavage.

"Seriously, Abigail, you're hot. Just wear it. And who cares? Besides, you have no other choices, remember?"

"You did this on purpose."

Laura went back to applying her makeup in the mirror.

"I'll get you back. Just remember that," Abigail huffed. She put on her makeup, going a bit heavier on the eyes, and then blow-dried her hair straight.

At first glance, she resembled a little of her usual self, but the more she regarded her sultry look, the more she actually liked it.

And why not look a little sexy? Everyone else there will be dressed just like me...I hope.

Once they were ready, they went down to Bree's room. She always kept her door open for people to come in and out as they wanted. She was, if nothing else, exclusively inclusive.

"Whoa, check you out!" Bree said, her eyes ablaze.

"Sexy, right?" Laura added.

"Absolutely!" That was honestly the first time Bree had ever complimented Abigail and really meant it.

Although Abigail never needed her approval, it did feel nice. "Thank you, Bree."

"Now, if I may just add one little touch?" Bree reached over her dresser and opened a large train case that sat on top.

Abigail could see it was filled with makeup, lotions, and brushes. Frankly, it looked like she had held up the makeup counter at Macy's. She dug through it, searching feverishly, and then she pulled out a tube of lipstick.

"Here, try this." Bree opened the tube. "Allow me."

She leaned forward toward Abigail's lips. Abigail had no choice in the matter as Bree quickly went to work.

When she was done, Bree said, "Perfect."

Abigail turned to face the mirror. She didn't want to admit it, but it was flawless. Her lips were the color of dark pink roses. It was something she had never done before.

"Like it?" Bree asked.

"Yeah, I do. I like it."

"Good. Keep it." She handed Abigail the tube.

"What? No, I—"

"Just take it. I have, like, a million others," she said with a huff.

Abigail took the tube and stuffed it in her pocket.

"Great. We all set then?" Bree announced. "Let's go break some hearts!" She laughed as she turned out the light near her dresser.

Abigail slipped on her coat and followed the others down the hall.

Melissa cozied up next to Abigail. "I'll walk with you. You're brave to be without your crutches."

"I had to. I couldn't take them anymore." She was walking slowly, no doubt, but the air cast on her foot made it much less painful to walk than she had imagined it would. *So far, so good.*

Thankfully, they all took the elevator down.

They stepped out into the cold night air. It had to be below thirty degrees at this point. It was chilly, but they only had a short walk to the party.

The Sigma house was located on the edge of campus. The girls decided to take the side road to get there because it was better lit than the trails that cut through the back of campus. They could hear the music as they got closer to the house. There was a line out front. It had to be about thirty people deep.

Quickly, Bree hurried to the line and got in it before a few other groups behind them could. She had little patience for lines. She'd announced that to some of them during their first week at school when they had to wait in line to get their textbooks.

Not caring about the line per se, Abigail and Melissa brought up the rear of the group but were cut off from the rest as they gingerly walked up to the house.

"Come up here," Bree demanded to them.

Reluctantly, Melissa and Abigail moved out of line and got back in with their friends.

"Cutting the line, I see," a deep voice bellowed behind Abigail.

She turned, startled and embarrassed. "What? No, I'm sorry. We're with them. She has our tickets."

"I'm only joking," he said.

Abigail squinted in the darkness to try to make out his face and quickly realized it was no one she knew. He was of average build but muscular. He had dark, short hair that was spiked up in the front.

"Oh, sorry. I just know it's rude to cut, so—"

"So, you did it anyway." He laughed.

"It would appear so." She giggled.

There was brief silence as the line slowly moved forward, and as they did, the music got louder.

"First time at the Black Hearts Party?" the guy behind her asked.

"Yes. You?"

"Nope, came last year. It's a fun tradition."

She glanced past him. It appeared he was alone.

"My friends are inside already." He laughed. "I'm not *that* pathetic."

"No, I—God, I'm really sorry. I cut in line and then offended you. I—"

"Come on," Melissa said.

Abigail sensed a slight pull on her arm as Melissa tugged her coat.

"I already gave him your ticket."

Abigail turned and saw that the door was being held open by one of the freshman pledges dressed as Cupid. It was terribly humiliating just to witness it. She walked in with Melissa on her arm, and she could not have been prepared for what was in front of them.

The room was dimly lit. The ceiling was draped in thick black fabric from one side to the other. Hanging in between were cutout black hearts. There were vases of dried roses in every corner and on the bar located in front of them. Pledges were dressed as either Cupid with a fake arrow stuck through their heart with blood dripping down or some kind of a doctor or something dressed in scrubs with fake blood all over the front of them. It was more like Halloween than anything else. All the Sigma brothers had black T-shirts on with bold red letters across the front that said, *Love Stinks*. Everyone else was dressed all in black. It was cool and a lot to take in.

"This is amazing!" Melissa yelled in Abigail's ear.

"It's like Halloween meets Valentine's Day! This is crazy!" she yelled back.

Abigail found the room where everyone was stashing their coats. They all left theirs on the pile in the room and then made their way back to the bar.

"Let's get a drink."

"Sure." She followed Melissa through the crowd.

Abigail noticed the sign over the bar that said *Love potion. Drink at your own risk*. Bree noticed it, too, and laughed as she ordered one for each of them.

By the time they each finished their first drink, the party was packed wall to wall. The drink, which was served in a red Solo cup, tasted a lot like Kool-Aid.

Melissa and Abigail went up to the bar for a second drink. Laura and Bree had found a few cute guys to talk to by the back corner. Abigail recognized one of the guys from her Calculus class. He had always seemed nice enough in class.

"Seems like Laura found a guy to talk to, huh?" Melissa yelled in her ear.

"Yeah, I'm happy for her. Sometimes, I feel she gets stuck in Bree's shadow and sort of fades into the background. I mean, it's through no fault of her own, but…" She took a sip of her drink.

"No, I hear you. Bree has that effect over people." Melissa rolled her eyes.

"I know, but it's hard not to like her," Abigail said with a grin. She started to feel the effects of the alcohol, and it made her giddy. "So, things with you and Logan, huh?"

She smiled wide, and as she did, she could see the grin come over Melissa's face.

"Abigail, he is just awesome and kind! We have a lot of fun."

"That's great. He does seem like such a nice guy."

"Yes, and so smart!"

"That's wonderful, Melissa. You seem happy."

"I am. He called me every day while I was at the internship. He's supportive and just easy to talk to."

Abigail loved watching her friend gush. She was truly happy for Melissa. Uncomplicated love—that was what every girl dreamed about having.

"Hey, let's go walk around a bit?"

"Yeah, let's do that." Abigail followed closely behind as Melissa made her way to the basement.

There was a whole finished basement with couches, a pool table, a bar, DJ, and dance floor. It was crowded, but they eventually made it to the couches. They stood and surveyed the dance floor that was packed with students.

"Wanna dance?" Melissa asked hesitantly.

"Oh, I don't know about that. Maybe after one more drink, I will."

"Fair enough." Melissa gulped her drink down. "I'll go get us more!" She laughed, taking Abigail's cup.

Abigail sat down on one of the couches, feeling self-conscious as she glanced down at her exposed flesh. She had to admit, the shirt did look good on her. It was much more risqué than her usual style, but she was not alone. Most of the girls tonight were scantily clad.

She sensed the rise and fall of the couch cushion. Assuming it was Melissa, she said, "Some shirt I got roped into wearing." She turned and stopped talking because it was not Melissa. "Oh, I thought—"

"Thought I was someone else, I take it. Nice shirt, I might add." He glanced at her with his eyes wide.

"You're the guy—"

"That you insulted out front? Yep, that's me."

"I'm so sorry. Like I said, I didn't mean it that way."

"I know. Just giving you a hard time. I'm Dan."

"Hi, Dan. Abigail."

"So, Abigail, where are your friends?" he asked with a coy smile.

"Funny. My *friend* is getting me a drink."

"Ah, mine, too," he said with a chuckle. He waited for a few people to go by before he spoke again, "So, Abigail, what's your major?"

"Biology. Yours?"

"Undecided. I have another semester before I have to choose. I was actually leaning toward biology, believe it or not."

"Really? Cool. What classes have you taken so far?"

"Oh, I'm drawing a blank. What's that guy's name in Bio one-oh-one and two-oh-one?"

"Rhodes?"

"Yeah, yeah. Rhodes. Great professor."

"Yeah, he is. I really like him."

"What's up with the air cast? You hurt your foot?"

"Yeah. It's silly. I fell on some ice. So stupid."

"Jeez, well, you ought to be more careful." His grin was peculiar.

She wasn't quite sure what to say to that.

There was silence until he said, "Cool. Anyway, so, what do you think of this party. Crazy, huh?"

"Yeah. I didn't know what to expect, but it certainly wasn't this!" She laughed, glancing around the room.

"I know. I tried to convince my girlfriend to come, but she thinks it's just a bunch of people sitting around, feeling sorry for themselves. I told her it's nothing like that."

"I know. I think my boyfriend was surprised I was coming, too!"

They both laughed as they viewed all the students drinking, laughing, dancing, or making out. It was anything but a feel-sorry-for-yourself kind of night.

"They're the ones missing out, I guess."

"Yeah, guess so."

Immediately, Abigail started to think about Nathan. *I wonder what he is doing right now. Is he in his room? Is he sleeping, awake, or watching TV?* She missed him and couldn't wait to see him tomorrow for the Cupid's Party. This would be their first Valentine's Day together. She found herself staring off, thinking of him.

"So, anyway," Dan said, interrupting her daydream, "I see my friend over there. I should go grab him. Nice meeting you, Abigail." And with that, he got up and disappeared into the crowd.

"Here you go!"

Abigail turned to see Melissa standing there, holding her drink.

"Sorry it took so long."

"No worries. I was talking to, uh—never mind. Have a seat," she said, pointing to the cushion previously occupied by Dan.

"Actually, come back here. I saw Laura and the others by the bar."

"Oh, great." As Abigail stood up, she could feel her body sway a bit. The alcohol was starting to make her feel loose, different, and carefree. She meandered through the crowd and to the back corner where all the girls were now holding court with the guys they had met earlier.

"Laura!" Abigail said enthusiastically.

"Hey! We've been looking for you!"

"Oh, sorry. We just sort of wandered down here."

Laura pulled her a bit to the side. "See the kid next to Melissa—with the writing on his shirt?"

Abigail leaned slightly past Laura, trying not to be obvious. She shook her head.

Laura continued, "He is so cute and nice. He's a Sigma. His name is Justin, and they are having an after-party that we can stay for. He is so cool."

"That's great, Laura," she said, more referring to the guy than the after-party. She took another sip of her drink.

"You having fun?" she asked Abigail.

"Yeah, definitely. This is great."

"Good, good. Me, too!" Laura gave her a wink and then went back next to Justin.

Abigail noticed he slid his arm around her waist and whispered something in her ear. Laura just laughed.

Abigail finished her drink.

"You ready to dance yet?" Melissa asked.

"Uh, one more drink, and then I will…promise."

"Okay, but you promised."

"Promise."

She grabbed Melissa's cup and went back to the bar. She came back within five minutes and handed Melissa her cup.

"Bottoms up!" Melissa laughed.

Abigail tried to gulp it without spilling it. "Melissa, I can't!" She laughed.

"Come on, Abigail. Where is your crazy side?"

"Crazy side? But I don't—"

"Exactly. Time to loosen up. Now, drink!" She laughed, and she finished her punch.

Quickly, Abigail drank what she could before Melissa grabbed her arm and pulled her toward the dance floor. Luckily, it was so crowded, and they were able to blend right in, barely noticeable in the sea of black-dressed moving bodies. They danced through one song, then another, then another, and another. Abigail could feel her foot beginning to throb ever so slightly, but she didn't care. She was having too much fun.

They danced together for what seemed like hours before Melissa needed to use the restroom.

"I'll come with you," Abigail said.

They waited in line for the restroom for about ten minutes.

"You know that guy?" Melissa asked.

Abigail saw Dan smiling at her. She waved slightly.

"Sort of. I met him earlier. Nice guy!"

Finally, they were able to go in. They moved quickly as they had witnessed the nasty banging on the door by the other girls if people didn't get out in record time. Abigail surveyed herself in the mirror. Her face was flushed from all the dancing, and the perfect amount of glistening sweat rested on her forehead.

"One more drink?" Melissa asked.

"All right, but don't make me gulp it, okay? Or I won't dance with you anymore!"

"Deal!"

They grabbed another drink each, and then moved toward the dance floor. As she passed, she waved to Laura. They stood as spectators for a bit as they sipped their drinks. Abigail was thirsty from all the dancing, and the drink tasted surprisingly refreshing.

Then, without warning, Melissa yanked on Abigail's arm. "This is my favorite song!"

She pulled Abigail to the center of the floor, and she nearly spilled her drink. "No Diggity" by Blackstreet blared through the speakers. It was not exactly Abigail's idea of a favorite song, but seeing the look on Melissa's face as she moved to the music said it all. She was having a blast.

Other students started to gather around Melissa and dance along with her, as if she had commanded the floor all her life. Abigail found herself watching more at this point than she was dancing. Melissa was putting on quite a show.

She can really dance. Abigail started to back away.

Abigail slowly worked her way to the outskirts of the floor. She could feel her foot pounding as her air cast got tighter. It had not been the best idea to dance so much on it the first few hours off the crutches, but there was no use in beating herself up over her bad decision now. She needed to sit down, she decided. She glanced over at the couches, but they were taken.

She went back over and found Laura snuggled up next to Justin.

She motioned for Laura to lean in, so she wouldn't have to yell over the music. "Hey, my foot is killing me. I'm going to head upstairs and see if I can find a place to sit for a bit." Abigail said.

"Okay. Want me to go with you?"

"No, no. I'm fine. I probably should have been a bit smarter about this and not danced so much."

"Yeah, silly. Way to dive right back in."

"I know; I know. Stupid of me. But, hey, if I can't find a place to chill, I might just head back to the dorm."

"Not alone?"

"Our dorm is right there—like, five minutes away. I know you guys want to stay for the after-party. Honestly, I'll be fine."

"You sure?"

"Yes, have fun. I might be back down. I just need to sit."

Abigail walked gingerly toward the stairs, hoping that there would be plenty of places for her to sit upstairs. She just needed to rest.

She first went to the front room; she noticed it was even darker now than before. The rooms were faintly lit by candles only. She glanced around and quickly realized there was a reason for the dim lighting. Couples were lounging all over the couches and chairs, kissing and fondling one another. This made her feel terribly uncomfortable, so she left and went toward the back room.

She forced her way through crowds of students, bumping and banging her way in an attempt to make it toward the back room. But, suddenly, she felt uneasy or confused even. Her mind was tipsy, and her foot was throbbing. As she stood there, seeing all the people making out, it dawned on her.

What am I doing here? If I leave now, I can get home and call Nathan. Maybe he is still up, and I can see him.

A rush of excitement came over her.

Better yet, I'll surprise him.

Then, on an impulse decision, one clouded by alcohol and love, she went to the back room, rummaged around for her coat, and put it on. Like a flash, she moved through the crowd, passing all the heavy breathers at the front room, and made it to the door without seeing anyone. She knew she should tell someone, but she figured at least Laura knew that she had wanted to leave. With a slight twinge of pain in her foot, she pulled open the door and stepped out into the cold February night.

She took a deep breath. The air almost burned as it filled her lungs. It was much colder than before. Her body shivered, and she pulled her coat tightly around her frame. She took a step forward, trying not to push off on her bad foot. She was in agony.

"Abigail?" a deep voice said.

Startled, she turned to see who it was. She squinted toward the side where the voice had come from. Then, a guy emerged from the shadows that hugged the house near the front door.

"You scared me, Dan," she barked.

"Oh, I'm sorry. I didn't mean to," he said. "You leaving?"

"Yeah, I'm going to my boyfriend's." Her head started to whirl.

"Yeah, I'm leaving, too. Where you headed?"

"Boyd Hall."

"That's where my girlfriend lives. I'll walk you," he said nicely. He started walking toward the side of the house.

"Oh, great. Thanks," she said, slightly changing her tune.

"Yeah, Coach doesn't want us staying out late."

"Coach?" she asked, her interest perking up a bit. "You play a sport here?"

"Yeah, football."

"No kidding!" She laughed as she followed close behind him.

He chuckled and said, "Why is that funny?"

"It's just…well, my boyfriend is Nathan."

He gave her a quizzical expression. "Nathan?"

She cocked her head to the side, clearly confused.

"Oh, right. Yeah, duh, Nathan. Of course, Nathan Ryan." He chuckled strangely, and then there was an awkward pause before he said, "Oh, so *you're* Abigail. He talks about you all the time."

"Does he?" she cooed.

"Yeah, sure. Of course, all the time." He hesitated for a moment and motioned to the side. "Hey, let's cut through here. It's much faster." He led her toward the wooded path.

"Oh, sure. Thanks."

"Ladies first." He motioned for her to go in front of him.

The path was deep with untouched snow. Not thinking clearly that this would be harder with her foot, she ventured forward into the woods.

"It clears up a bit ahead." He was reassuring. "I could tell from earlier that you were limping. Is it bad?"

"Well, it does hurt quite a bit tonight. I'm off the crutches." Then, she nearly stumbled on the ice. "Darn it."

She was hoping he did not know about the situation with Marcus and Tank. She was embarrassed and was praying he wouldn't ask her any more questions about her foot. They reached a clearer part of the path. She could see the lights of the campus buildings in the distance.

There was silence.

"So, your girlfriend lives in Boyd?" Abigail stated, hoping he might talk a bit more about himself.

"Uh, yeah," he said halfheartedly.

Abigail could faintly hear other students leaving the party. She could hear the sounds of their feet on the hard snow. She kept her head down as she tried to concentrate on the path ahead. The trees were thick on both sides, and her foot throbbed more and more as she stepped on the heavy snow.

"How long have you been dating…what did you say her name was?"

She felt him draw near.

A chill ran down her spine as he said in a low voice, "I *didn't* say her name."

The darkness clouded her vision enough that all she could do was try and concentrate on walking on the uncharted path.

"Well, what is her name?"

"None of your business," he barked.

Her voice quivered. "Does she live in Boyd?" *Something doesn't feel right.*

"We're not going to Boyd," he said.

Oh no. What the hell is going on?

She stopped quickly. She started to turn toward him. But before she could face him, he violently threw his arm around her chest. He yanked her back, forcing her body to crash against his. She went to scream when he clasped his other hand over her nose and mouth, making it difficult to breathe.

"Shut up." His voice was rough.

Her eyes widened at the unfamiliar tone.

"Understand?"

She could only whimper at his request.

"If I let you go and you scream, you don't want to know what I'll do to you."

Scared, she shook her head. Then, he released his hand and quickly spun her around. She gasped for air. His eyes were dark. This was not the same person she had met just hours before.

He's a monster!

His lips were in a hard line as his eyes squinted. There was no emotion on his face at all.

She started to react, and she opened her mouth to shout, but before she could, he knocked her back and pushed her up against a tree. She stumbled as the pain in her foot shot up her leg. Her mind raced, yet she was unable to respond to what was happening to her. He pressed up against her with great strength, nearly knocking the wind out of her. He yanked open her coat, ripping the lace on her shirt as he did. Then, he grabbed her hands and forced them behind her, against the tree. He kissed her, hard and aggressively. She wanted to scream or struggle, but ultimately, she was paralyzed with fear.

Then, unexpectedly, she heard footsteps on the snow getting closer with tremendous speed. Like a truck barreling down the path, someone hit Dan with such might that both of them were knocked to the ground. Dan flew almost ten feet or so in the air before falling firmly on the icy footpath below. He cried out in pain as Abigail saw his arm fold underneath him, bending in a way that was not intended.

Barely able to catch her breath and filled with terror, she tried hard to scramble to her feet but with no success. She observed, as if in slow motion, this enormous man charging at her. He was dressed all in black with the hood from his sweatshirt shielding his identity. He got closer and quickly bent down. As if with superhero strength, in one swift motion, he scooped her up.

Her breathing was rapid and frightened as she tried to get free from him.

"No, no, please don't hurt me!" she cried out.

"It's okay, Abby. You're safe."

She stopped. "Tank?" she breathed. "Tank, what are you—"

Before she knew what hit her, she began to moan in pain. He pulled her close to his body as he jogged his way up the path and out of the woods, leaving Dan yelping in agony. They got to the edge of campus, and Tank slowed to a walk. His breathing was heavy from adrenaline.

"What were you doing there? I never saw you," she whimpered as she gazed up at him. She didn't know what to expect, but she was not prepared to see that his expression was cold and disapproving.

"What were *you* doing?" he said, finally glaring down at her.

Her eyes filled with tears. He had come out of nowhere, and she had no idea what he had seen or witnessed. She studied his face, trying desperately to read him. He seemed distant. Then, for a brief moment, she thought of what would have happened had he not been there.

"I was going home." She could barely get the words out. She was so angry that she'd put herself in that situation.

"With *him?*" His voice was heated.

She knew it was out of concern.

"No. Of course not. He said he was a football player." Her eyes got wider.

Did Tank not see his face? Does he regret hitting Dan? she wondered.

But then she saw the alarmed expression Tank gave her.

"What? What is it?" she asked, feeling his body tense.

"I'm taking you to Nathan's," he responded quickly.

"How did you know where I was?"

"I told you I would protect you, Abby," he said coolly. He jogged up the walkway toward Boyd Hall.

"Thank you," she whispered. With that, she rested her head on his chest and closed her eyes, tears streaming down her face.

"It's okay, Abby. I promise." His voice was soft and quiet, just like the Tank *she* knew.

Tank carried her down the hall to Nathan's room. Unable to knock, he yelled slightly, "Nathan, open up. It's Tank. Come on, man, open up."

Abigail and Tank could hear Nathan grumble as he approached the door.

"What, dude?" He pulled the door open, obviously irritated at the thought of his unwelcome visitor.

Without warning, Tank moved toward him.

"Oh my God, what happened?" Nathan barked.

"Dude, let me in, will you?"

Nathan stepped back as Tank made his way into the room. He went over to Nathan's bed and gently laid Abigail down.

"What the hell? Tell me—" he yelled.

Tank put his hand up. "Hold on, hold on. Everything is okay. Just slow down, okay?"

Taking a deep breath, Nathan walked over to Abigail and knelt beside her. Her body was curled up in a fetal position. She was shivering.

"Abby, are you okay?" He noticed she was barely able to shake her head. He grabbed a blanket off the chair and covered her.

"She might be in a bit of shock."

"Shock?"

"Yeah, can I talk to you in private?" Tank said flatly.

"What? No, tell me—"

Tank cut him off, "Nathan, I *need* to talk to you in private." He motioned again for Nathan to come with him.

Reluctantly, Nathan followed. Tank stepped toward the other side of the wall, near the desks.

"Dude, we got a problem," Tank said, barely able to catch his breath. "I'm so freaked out, Nathan. This is no joke."

"Come on, tell me!" he hissed under his breath.

"Shh, listen. I saw her and some guy go into the back trails near Sigma," he began.

"What?"

"Shh, man. No, it wasn't anything like that," he said, knowing where one's imagination could take a person, similar to where it had taken Tank's when he was watching Abigail.

"What were you doing there?"

"Uh, I was at the party," he lied, pointing to his black clothes for effect. "Anyway, remember the other day when Coach told us there were a few reports on campus and other schools about some guy going around, telling girls he played a sport? I think he said lacrosse or something, and then there were reports of assault?"

Nathan's eyes were wide. "No…" He shook his head. "No, Tank, please tell me it…"

"I'm sorry, man. I got there as soon as I could."

"I'll kill him. I will." Nathan's voice was controlled but angry.

Tank had seen Nathan mad before, but this was something else. This was beyond angry. This was on the verge of rage.

"Let's stay calm, okay? Trust me; I wanted to kill the guy, too. Good news is, I hit him hard. I think I broke his arm."

"What? Where is he then? Come on, let's go." Nathan went for the door.

Tank grabbed him on the arm. "No. Hey, we have got to be smart about this, okay?"

"Since when are you reasonable about—" he started to say but was interrupted by Abigail.

"Don't go, *please*," she begged.

They both whirled around to see Abigail was pale, shivering, and barely able to stand. Nathan quickly moved to put his arm around her just as Tank did the same. For a brief moment, they locked eyes, and then Tank let her go.

"Abby, please sit. Please."

Nathan sat down next to her on the bed. Tank pulled up a chair from the desk and sat near her.

"Oh, Abby," Tank said softly.

Nathan noticed for the first time the way he spoke to her.

314

She wiped the tears from her eyes, her makeup now on her hands. "I feel so foolish. I met him in line, and he seemed harmless." She glanced at Nathan, trying to gauge his reaction.

He was stone-faced.

"Then, he came up to me again and said he wanted to be a biology major, so"—she sniffled—"we talked about school. Then, hours later, I left the party on my own."

"What? Why?" Nathan asked. "Why would you leave alone, Abby?"

"I wanted to see you," she replied.

Nathan pulled her close. "Abby, no, I didn't mean to blame you. I'm sure someone would have left with you. Oh, I'm so sorry."

"Abby, you know better though," Tank said firmly.

She examined his face. His expression was back to being uninviting.

"I know. But once I got outside, there he was. He said he was going to see his girlfriend, and I told him about you." She glanced at Nathan with sad eyes. "Then, he said he was a football player, that he knew you and that I was the Abigail who you talked about and all that. He seemed so nice..." She stopped and then whispered, "Harmless. I never would have thought a guy on your team would...you know."

"Did he tell you his name?" Nathan asked softly through gritted teeth. He feared more than anything that he might actually be one of his teammates. Then, he would really want to kill the guy.

"Yes, he did. He said his name was Dan."

"Dan?" Tank and Nathan repeated at the same time.

There was no Dan on their team, not even as an alternate, not even on the staff.

Nathan dropped his head and shook it.

Tank reached for the phone. "I'm calling the police. If this guy is as hurt as I think he is, he'll need medical attention, so maybe we'll get lucky." He dialed the extension for the campus police and spoke briefly with the dispatcher. "Hey, they are calling the state police to come here instead. They want to talk to all of us, okay?"

"Yeah, okay," Nathan said. "You okay to do this, Abby?"

"No, I'm not, but I have no choice now, do I?" There was marked sadness in her voice.

"Hopefully, they'll get him if you do," Tank added as he took his black sweatshirt off. He got up and walked over to Nathan's fridge. He pulled out a drink for each of them. "Got any aspirin?" Tank asked.

"Yeah, top drawer." Nathan pointed to the dresser.

Tank took some out and threw a few in his mouth as he rubbed his shoulder.

"You hurt?" Abigail asked.

"I'll be fine. Don't worry about me."

"What about you? What hurts?"

"My head," she said, touching the front of her head. "My arm is sore and, well, my foot."

"Where are your crutches?" Nathan asked.

"In my room."

"Oh, Abby. Let me see your foot," he scolded.

She lifted her leg, and he gently took off her wet shoe. Her toes were swollen, and so was her ankle.

Seeing the swollen foot, Tank handed her some aspirin as well. "You could use these, too."

"Thank you," she said. Something about his presence was making her feel comforted yet worse at the same time. She knew he was hurt because of her, and she tried to stop herself from thinking that it could have been worse, much worse for both of them.

"Take off your coat. It's wet, too." Nathan started to pull the coat off her shoulders.

She winced as he pulled it off her arm. He tried not to react as he saw her torn shirt; instead, he pulled the shirt across her, covering her exposed flesh.

"I'll be fine." Tears started to form again. "I'm fine," she said again softly as she bent her head down. Her head was spinning from all the alcohol, and her body felt like it belonged to someone else. She could never remember a time when she'd ached as badly as right now.

Nathan pulled her in close, making sure not to hurt her more.

Tank paced back and forth as they waited in silence for the police to arrive. As if on cue, there was knocking at the door.

Tank yanked the door open, inviting the police in. Two tall, relatively fit men entered the room. The one in street clothes identified himself as the chief of police, John Frankel. The other officer was dressed in a police uniform, and he handed Nathan a card as he introduced himself as Officer Murphy, lead patrolman. Brief introductions were made, but they quickly got down to the business at hand.

"Can I please see your student IDs?" Frankel asked. He looked up at Nathan and recognized him immediately. "Hey there, Nathan."

"Hello, sir." Nathan quickly turned to the bed to focus on Abigail. "This is my girlfriend, Abby."

"Hello, young lady," he greeted her with sympathetic eyes.

Handing back Tank's ID, the younger officer said, "Thank you, McPherson."

Tank firmly nodded his head and said, "Thanks."

"So, can you each tell me how you are all involved in what took place tonight?" Officer Murphy asked.

Naturally, most of the focus was on Tank and Abigail. Nathan remained silent a majority of the time, listening intently to the details. He was hearing it all for the first time.

"Miss Price," Chief Frankel said after about fifteen minutes of going over the early part of her evening, "you then left the party alone, correct?"

"Yes." She was ashamed and angry with herself for being so careless.

"When did you see the suspect?"

"A second after I left. I didn't hear anyone, but he called my name, so I turned around."

"So, he immediately knew who you were. Okay, what happened next?"

"He said he would walk me back, that we were both going to the same dorm."

"Okay, how did he know what dorm you were going to?"

"He asked me, and I told him," she said.

"Then, what?" he asked as he feverishly jotted notes down.

"He said we should take the path because it was faster, so I did."

"What path is this?"

"The one next to Sigma, behind Montgomery Hall, I guess."

"Could you find the path again if we needed you to?"

"Yes." Although the mere thought of it made her shudder.

"Did he touch you?"

"Yes." Her voice trembled. Out of the corner of her eye, she noted Nathan's eyes on her, and they were deeply concerned.

"How so?"

"He grabbed me from behind, um…" she stammered. "Then, he put his hand over my nose and mouth and forced me up against him."

She heard Nathan quietly gasp.

"Was he attempting to suffocate you?"

Eyes wide at the idea of it, she said, "No. He was just telling me not to scream, but I had a hard time breathing." Her eyes welled up with tears again.

"Okay. Then, what?"

"Then, he pushed me up against a tree and pulled my arms behind my back and…" She hesitated, wishing more than anything that Nathan and Tank were not here to hear this. "Then, he forced himself…he kissed me." Her voice was barely audible.

She could see as Nathan put his head down and clenched his fists. It broke her heart.

He eventually released one tightened hand and rested it on her knee. "I'm so sorry, Abby," he whispered.

"So," the officer said to Tank, "you were also at the party?"

"Yes." He firmly nodded his head.

"Okay. Who did you go with?"

"Myself."

"You went to the party alone?"

"Yes."

"Okay, and you just happened to leave after Miss Price did, and you witnessed the events she described?"

"Yes," he lied.

"Do you two know one another?" he asked.

"Yes," they both said at the same time.

"And you, Nathan. Where were you?"

"Here in my room."

"All night?"

"Yes, all night."

Chief Frankel stared at Tank, waiting a moment, while the other officer finished his notes. "Did you strike the suspect?"

"Yes, I did, sir." His chest puffed with pride. "I ran up to them both as he held her against the tree, and I struck him…them."

"Them?"

"Yes. Unfortunately, sir, he had her arms. I was not aware, so it knocked her over as well." He glanced at Abigail as he spoke, "It was not my intention to hit them both."

"Did the suspect fight back?"

"No, I hit him pretty hard. I believe I might have seriously injured him—his arm at least. From my point of view, it seemed like it could have been broken."

"Broken?"

"Yes, broken."

"I bet you could hit a guy hard," Officer Murphy said.

"Been doing it since I was ten years old." There was an unmistakable glimmer in his eye. *I hit that bastard hard.*

Chief Frankel cleared his throat and spoke to Officer Murphy, "Call dispatch and have them put a call into the university hospital and the campus infirmary. See if we can get fortunate tonight." He then turned to Abigail. "Miss, are you sure you do not want any medical attention? Your arm is okay? What happened to your foot?" he asked suspiciously.

"I slipped a few weeks ago."

She could see Tank's shoulders slump.

"Yeah, Abby, are you sure? It would make us all—" Nathan said.

"No, I just need to put this behind me for right now, please." Her voice was pleading, almost pathetic.

"Okay." Nathan gently grabbed her cold hand. "If we need to go in the morning, we will, right?"

"Yes," she said, eyeing the officer. "Promise."

"We will call you tomorrow, okay?"

"Yes, okay," she said. "Thank you."

Nathan walked the officers out into the hallway. Tank quickly went over to Abigail and sat down next to her. He put one arm around her shoulders, and she rested her head on the inside of his chest as she closed her eyes. He placed his head on top of hers and just held her. Neither said a word.

Nathan came back in. He was sure they had not heard him open the door because neither of them moved. "Tank, can I see you for a second?"

Tank picked up his head and took his arm off her shoulders. She kept her eyes closed as she slowly lay back on the bed.

"In the hall."

"Sure." He grabbed his sweatshirt on his way toward the door. He quietly closed the door.

"What's up?" he whispered.

"Hey, I can't thank you enough for what you did for Abby tonight. I think what she really needs right now is some rest."

Tank's heart sank. He knew Nathan was right, but what he was even more certain of was that he was the third wheel here tonight. He would have to leave even though every bone in his body believed that it was he who should stay. He wanted to stay. He was the one who had protected her. He was the one who had saved her, and he was the one who wanted to watch her sleep to make sure no one would ever harm her again.

"Of course. She needs her rest," he said.

"I owe you." Nathan patted Tank on the arm.

"Tell her I'll check in with her tomorrow, okay?"

By then, Nathan had already gone in the room, leaving Tank standing alone in the hallway. He pressed his head against the hard cement wall and let out a frustrated sigh.

"Sleep, Abby," he whispered.

Twenty-Eight

FEBRUARY 13, 1996
CUPID'S PARTY

Abigail woke up in the morning with a pounding headache, a throbbing foot, and a sore arm. She was in rough shape. Her hair was in a wild form, and as she rubbed her eyes, she could feel the flakes of mascara move across her cheeks. She was a mess.

The bed creaked as she sat up. Her body ached horribly. She gazed over at Webber's empty bed. She was happy that he had gone home for the weekend. She didn't want him to see her this way.

"You're awake," Nathan said softly as he came from the other room.

He had already showered and gotten dressed, looking like a million bucks. It did nothing but made her feel worse. She tried to cover her face.

"Don't, Abby," he said, pulling her hand down. "Here." He handed her a washcloth. "It's warm. It will make you feel better."

He is so considerate. She leaned back against the metal frame of his bed and draped the hot washcloth on her face. It felt better than good. It felt great.

"I got you some breakfast, too. You need to eat, okay?"

"I feel awful." Her voice was hoarse.

"I can only imagine."

He brought over a coffee, water, and bagel with butter. He pulled a chair next to the bed, using it as a tray for her breakfast. She could see the bright sunlight through the washcloth.

"What time is it?" she asked.

"A little after eleven. I talked to Laura."

"You did? Thank you. What did she say?"

"Well, thankfully, she had assumed you were here anyway, so she wasn't worried last night, but..." He trailed off.

"But?" she said, taking the washcloth off her face.

"She's worried now."

Abigail's face said it all. She knew he had told Laura what had happened, and she couldn't blame him for that.

"I had to tell her, Abby, just in case he tries it with someone else. You understand."

"I know. I'm actually relieved that *you* told her and not me."

He came over, sat down on the bed, and turned toward her. "Good. I want them all to be careful. I feel terrible. Coach had mentioned something to us, but when he talked about lacrosse and other schools...I don't know. We—I mean, I guess I just figured it wouldn't happen here. I feel like this is such a safe place to be."

"I know. Me, too. Foolishly, I thought I was safe. It's scary to think how wrong I was." She touched his arm.

He put his hand on top of hers and gave it a squeeze. "Laura wanted me to remind you that she would be down in the math lab today, something about tutoring high school students."

"Oh, yeah. Forgot about that."

There was a brief silence as Abigail reached over and took the cap off the water bottle. She could tell Nathan had something on his mind.

"So, good thing Tank was there, huh?"

"Yeah, I don't know what would have..." Her voice trailed off.

"Try not to think about it, okay?" he said. "You're safe. Did you see Tank at the party?"

"Uh, no, actually. I didn't...I was with the girls, dancing, and I don't know. It was crowded."

"Just wondering. A good coincidence that he left when you did, I guess."

"Yeah, just my luck, I suppose." Her voice was emotionless, and she began to stare into the distance.

"Abby, are you okay?" His voice was sad, concerned.

"Yes, Nathan, I am. I'm fine, I promise you. Lesson learned last night; that's for sure."

"Okay, but you'd tell me if you weren't, right?"

"Yes, I would. You have my word." She pushed a smile across her face. She had to convince him she was okay, or no one would ever let this go.

She took a bite of her bagel and slowly sipped on her coffee. She was trying to show him that she was doing fine, eating and all.

"So, you excited for the party tonight?" she asked.

"*What?* No, Abby, we shouldn't go," he said, regarding her with a furrowed brow.

"Nathan, I'm good. Besides, what are we going to do? Sit here and feel sorry for me? I want to go, be with our friends, and show everyone I'm okay. Don't you believe me?"

"I don't know, Abby. Can we just think about it?"

"Okay. However, I'd hate to leave you behind—and on Valentine's Day, no less."

"Valentine's Day is tomorrow."

"Not according to school, it's not. It's tonight." She sported a real smile this time.

"You're impossible, you know that?"

"I can be."

"Promise you'll do nothing but rest today."

"Yes, Doctor." She gave him a sly grin.

"Oh, well, if I'm the doctor, then you are definitely using your crutches tonight and not a word about it." He playfully pinched her leg.

"Hey!" she yelped. "Fine, I'll use them." Actually, she had every intention of using them tonight. Her foot was hurting, and if she ever wanted to get off of the crutches for good, she'd better take it slow tonight.

"Good, because when I went out this morning to get your breakfast, I went to see Laura and got you these." He got up and walked to the other side of the room. He came back around a moment later, holding her crutches.

Abigail burst into laughter. It was the type of hilarity that was bordering on uncontrollable. It was a buildup of all the past week's insanity, coming to a head with unmistakable amusement.

"What?" he said.

"You..." she said, barely able to speak. "You're just so..."

He stood in the middle of the room, leaning on her crutches. She could not stop smiling.

"Such a good boyfriend?" His words nearly stopped her in her tracks. *Boyfriend. Good boyfriend.*

As her expression quickly faded, she said sincerely, "Yes. Yes, you are. I mean it."

"Good." He crutched his way over to the bed, leaned down, and gave her a loving kiss. "Wish we could have done more of that last night."

"Me, too." She took another bite of her bagel.

Abigail finished the rest of her breakfast and coffee, all while trying desperately to convince Nathan that he did not have to walk her back to her dorm in the middle of the day. She could make it there on her own. She eventually stood and put on her jacket, covering the rip in her shirt. A shiver went down her spine, but she pushed her feeling down deep.

"I'll come by later at eight, okay?" Nathan said.

"Okay."

He leaned in and gave her another kiss. Then, he whispered in her ear, "More to come later."

Her face reddened as she clumsily made her way out the door.

Abigail was relieved to have the room by herself. The last thing she wanted to do was rehash the whole night. In fact, what she intended to do was gather all her friends at once before the party and tell them what had happened last night, so they got the whole story from her. Better yet, she'd show them that she was fine. She'd admit that she'd made a mistake by leaving the party alone. Hopefully, the police would catch the guy soon. She called Melissa, Jen, Casey, and Bree and left messages for them to meet in her room at five before they went to the cafeteria for dinner.

She took a long, hot shower. Once back in her room, she put on a clean pair of sweatpants and her favorite long-sleeved shirt. She piled her hair on top of her head and secured it with a rubber band. She sat down at her desk and took out her journal.

Dear Nathan,

I can't even explain to you the events that have taken place over the past two days, but I'll try.

I am even more convinced than I was earlier that, for some reason, Tank and I were supposed to meet. Sounds crazy, right? I thought so, too, until he showed me the book.

His friend, Jonathan, passed away last year, for reasons neither of us can explain, I came to him in his dreams. I have proof. But even this proof doesn't make me rest any easier. In fact, it frightens me so.

I'm scared, Nathan. I'm scared there is something out there beyond my control, pulling me in one direction when my heart wants to go in the other.

I know this isn't making sense, but in a lot of ways, it makes sense to me...and to Tank. I know you don't like him, but like him or not, we are connected, and there is nothing I can do to disconnect us.

And, no, he wasn't at the party. He was following me, but it's not what you think.

Xoxo,

Abby

She went over to the closet and took out the old shoebox. Then, she went over to her bed, got under the covers, pulled them up to her chest, and propped her head up on her pillow. She took out Jonathan's book. She liked the idea that they, from what little she knew, had journaling in common. Both wrote down all their thoughts, and it was a comforting coincidence. She took a deep breath and then opened it.

The pictures scattered throughout the book were, on some levels, amazing. One page after another and another were of her. They were all of her. She tried to take herself out of the moment and just see the images for what they were. She tried to decipher what he had been trying to tell her. But the more she viewed the book, the more she saw the drawings and ramblings of a dying boy in love. Her heart sank. The sadness of not knowing him was getting to her. He'd apparently known her, but she, as far as she could tell, did not have the distinct pleasure of knowing him, and it was slowly eating away at her.

If what Tank had said was true, that she'd kind of kept Jonathan happy as his life was nearing an end, then she wanted so badly to try and understand how that was possible.

Would my life have been different today if I had known him?

She reviewed each page, reading the dates and times of events and visions. He had written when she came to him, and his descriptions were real, honest, and raw. There were unclear messages, not like dialogue but things she might have spoken to him. Little was said about him or what he had been going through and how he had coped.

But it unmistakably appeared as though they had been in love. With the image of him kissing her on the cheek, the expression on her face, she could not deny that it seemed to be love.

She noted nothing had been entered past February 28, 1995. His last entry in the book had lyrics quoted from a Jeff Buckley song titled "Last Goodbye."

Abigail had that feeling—like a jolt of electricity had just gone through her core, and now, she was left with the hard, hollow beat of her heart within her chest.

I can't help but feel this way as I read his last entry in his book. I know that song by heart. It has always resonated with me and long before I ever knew Jonathan Higgins existed.

Her emotions welled in her chest as she tried to calm her overworking mind. She knew the only way to do that was to sleep. Or at least try to.

She tucked the book away back in the box and pushed the box underneath her bed. She reached over to her disc player, put her headphones on, and pressed play. Jeff Buckley's *Grace* album was already in her Discman. It was never far from her.

She couldn't tell how many times she'd listened to that song before she fell asleep, but it was the first time *she* dreamed of Jonathan Higgins.

Laura nudged Abigail, trying not to startle her. She gently pulled back the headphones and whispered, "Abigail, wake up."

Abigail slowly moved her body. She did not want to wake up but could hear Laura's voice telling her to do just that. She opened her eyes, trying to focus on the face peering over her.

"Laura?"

"Yeah. Hey, sleepyhead, you okay?"

"Yeah, I fell asleep. What time is it?"

"Late. It's almost five o'clock."

"What?"

"Yeah. Hey, I just got back, and these were sitting outside the door." Laura held up two vases filled with dark pink roses. "They're both for you."

"What?" Confused, she sat up. "Wait, it's almost five? I told all the girls to come here at five, so I could talk to them." She rubbed the sleep out of her eyes.

"You've got time." Laura held up the flowers. "I'll just put these on the desk for now."

"Thanks."

As Laura walked over to the desks, there was a knock at the door. Trying hard not to drop the flowers, she quickly put one on each desk. She opened the door, and Melissa, Casey, and Jen were all standing there with eager expressions on their faces.

"Hey, guys. Come in!"

"Everything okay? What's going on? I heard—" Melissa asked.

"She's waiting for us in here."

Abigail could hear Bree entering the room as she grumbled under her breath, "This'd better be important."

"Hey, Bree." ·

Bree gave a sweet but fake smile to Laura.

Melissa rushed over to Abigail. "Where did you go last night?"

"I know. I'm so sorry. So stupid of me. But I wanted to talk to you guys because the word will be getting around campus about what happened, I imagine. But, more importantly, I care about you. We should all be more careful because I know I wasn't."

"What are you talking about? What happened to you?" Melissa said.

Abigail swung her legs over the side of the bed. Her foot throbbed as the blood started rushing toward her toes. She grabbed her air cast and slipped it back on.

"Well?" Bree asked impatiently.

Abigail glanced at her, and she could see the frustrated expression on Bree's face.

"I won't keep you guys, but I wanted to let you know that I did something extremely stupid last night." She stopped and looked at each one of them. "I left the party alone, and I almost paid the price for it."

"Abigail, what are you saying?" Melissa said with deep concern.

"Do you guys remember that guy who was talking to me in line and then later that night?"

They nodded their heads, their eyes wide with worry.

"Well, the police—"

"Police?" Jen quipped.

"Yes, the police. They think he waited for me outside the party. He told me he knew Nathan, that he was also a football player, and that he had a girlfriend in the same dorm as Nathan. He told me he'd walk me back over. Well"—she took a deep breath—"he tried to attack me on the path behind Montgomery Hall, and if it wasn't for"—she stopped, not sure why she was hesitating to speak his name—"well, Tank, actually, then I don't know what would have happened." Tears began to find their way into her tired eyes.

"Oh, Abigail!" Melissa gushed. She sat next to her friend on the bed and put her arm around Abigail.

Bree crossed her arms over her chest, as though she disapproved of the story.

Abigail spoke directly to Bree, "I tell you this not for the story, but so you don't make the same stupid mistake I did. I trusted him. I thought he knew Nathan, and I guess, according to police, he has done this before."

"We are just glad you're okay," Laura said. "No one here thinks this is any kind of story to ever be telling. I can assure you of that!"

Laura peered in Bree's direction. Bree slowly uncrossed her arms.

"Thanks. I don't want you guys to worry but to just be safe and to tell your other friends the same. They think he got hurt in the fight—"

"The fight?" Casey asked.

"Yeah, Tank hit him pretty hard and thinks he probably will have to get some medical attention. They will hopefully get him then."

"I hope they nail the guy!" Jen said.

"We all do. I'm glad he's hurt," Bree said with disdain. "He deserves it." She crossed her arms again and turned her head toward the window. She was making it clear to everyone in the room that she was not willing to discuss this further.

"I know," Abigail said, glancing in Bree's direction.

Abigail observed Bree's eyes soften as she lowered her head. It wasn't often that it happened, so when it did, Abigail took notice.

Bree stared down at her feet, her cheeks flaming red. Something about the way she was acting made Abigail pay heed to her. Abigail wanted to approach her, so she reached her arms forward in an attempt to grab her crutches. When she did, her arm became exposed from her shirt, and she noticed the large bruise on the inside of her arm.

"Oh my God, you're hurt!" Laura pounced in for a better inspection.

Shyly, Abigail pulled her sleeve back down and stood, wincing as she rested on her foot. "I'm fine. It's just from the tree, I think. I can't really remember, but it's fine." She peered at Laura, as if to nicely say, *Back off.* "I won't keep you guys. I'm sure you're going to the cafeteria before the party, so I'll see you later."

They hesitated, not wanting to leave, but feeling that maybe they should.

"Okay, we'll see you later." Melissa gently hugged her friend. Then, she whispered in Abigail's ear, "Please take care of yourself. I'm worried." And with that, she turned and walked toward the door.

"I'll bring you back the usual," Laura said sadly.

It only made Abigail feel worse. Her attempt here was to reassure everyone that she was all right, but how could she do that when she wasn't convinced of it herself?

"Thank you," she whispered as she tried to fight back her tears.

Bree hesitated, still leaning on the wall. Abigail went to speak, but as though Bree sensed it, she quickly pushed herself off the wall and spun on her heel. Within seconds, she was gone.

However, Abigail was glad they left. It had been an emotional few days, to say the least. In fact, she hadn't intentionally meant to kick them out, but the thought of rehashing the entire story through a series of questions just wasn't sitting well with her right now. She wanted nothing more than to put this behind her and move on.

She just hoped the cops would catch the guy soon, so she would feel safe again. The police had warned her that if they did, she would be asked to identify him and press charges, should it come to that. At that point, she knew she'd have to tell her parents, and she was not thrilled about that. It had been hard enough, telling Nathan and the police, but the thought of worrying her parents made her heart palpitate.

She pulled up her other sleeve and stared at the identical bruise on that arm as well. It must have been from when he'd held her arms behind her back. She squeezed her eyes shut, wishing the bruises away, wishing that these reminders of last night would just disappear by the time she opened her eyes but they did not. She pushed her sleeve down and grabbed her crutches.

She walked over to her desk and stared at the two vases of pink roses.

Oh, the roses.

Both cards were addressed to her but in completely different handwriting. The school had had a charity drive in the student union last week, so students could send flowers on campus for Valentine's Day, and Abigail knew that the flowers had come from the charity drive.

But two of them?

She opened the first card.

> *Dear Abby,*
>
> *Here is to many more Valentine's Days together.*
>
> *—Nathan*

The card made her swoon, so much so that she almost couldn't get herself to open the next card, but naturally, she had to.

She tore the envelope open on the second card.

> *Abby,*
>
> *Jonathan would have wanted you to have these.*
>
> *—Tank*

She stared at the card for a few minutes, and then as if not by her own doing, she slowly bent down and placed the card in the garbage can, facedown.

The girls arrived back at the dorm just as Abigail began to blow-dry her hair.

Once Laura got back from her shower, she switched on the CD player and put in her *(What's the Story) Morning Glory?* CD by Oasis.

"Who are the flowers from?" Laura asked as she slipped on her jeans.

"Nathan," Abigail lied.

"Lucky girl."

"Yes, I am, and he's coming at eight to pick us up."

"I'd better get moving then." She pulled on her tight red V-neck sweater.

Abigail inspected herself in the mirror. Thankfully, she didn't appear as tired as her body felt. The deep pink shirt she had on gave her a bit of color that she so desperately needed. She applied the pink lipstick Bree had given her and even dabbed a bit on her cheeks. She went lighter on her eye makeup; it was just more like her. She sprayed on her perfume and took one last glance before sitting back on her bed and putting her leg up one more time. It was a welcome relief to be off of it. She closed her eyes. The hum of the blow-dryer and the faint, captivating whine of Liam Gallagher felt soothing as she slowly drifted away.

"Abigail. Abigail," Laura whispered, gently placing her hand on Abigail's arm. "You fell asleep again. It's almost eight o'clock."

Abigail began to stir. She moved her body from side to side. There was a part of Abigail that told her to just stay asleep, rest, and call it a night, but then she remembered it was the Valentine's Day party, and she wanted to go out and have some fun.

"I'm awake," she said with a hoarse voice. "I was just resting."

"Well, rest time is over then." Laura snickered as she pulled back her covers.

Abigail opened her eyes. "You look fantastic, Laura."

She twirled around. "Why, thank you. So do you!"

Abigail swung her legs over the bed and grabbed her crutches. She went over to her dresser and inspected her image one more time, smoothing down her hair and touching up her makeup a bit.

"You sure you're up for this tonight?"

"Yeah, I've spent more time in this room than not, and…well, I'd just like to go have a little fun."

"Of course. I understand."

There was a knock on the door.

"I'll get it." Laura made two strides toward the door and pulled open the handle.

"Hey, Laura. What's up?" Nathan granted her his winning smile.

"Not much."

"Ah, I see you both got flowers!" He observed the two vases, one on Abigail's desk and the other on Laura's.

"Well—" Laura began to say.

Abigail cut her off, "Yes, we *both* did. Thank you so much for mine. They are beautiful." She made her way over to Nathan and reached up to give him a thank-you kiss on the cheek. She could see Laura studying her, a deep question across her face, but she tried to ignore it for now.

"You're welcome. And you look great. You both do." He turned toward Laura. "Who's the lucky guy?" he asked.

Laura peered at Abigail. Abigail's eyes widened. It was understood.

"Huh." Laura laughed. "More like admirer," she said, hoping to brush Nathan off.

"Ah, well, maybe you'll see him tonight." He laughed as Abigail exhaled.

Whew, that was close.

When they arrived at the Cupid's Party, one of the guys recognized Nathan and pulled him and the whole group out of the long line. Nathan, at times, would be treated differently than the other students. It just sort of went hand in hand with him being an athlete at the university.

Abigail nervously surveyed her surroundings as they walked out of line and toward the side. The same off-campus house hosted the Cupid's Party every year. It was a huge, old white four-story colonial home that sat back off the road and down a brief dirt driveway. It had a wraparound porch that extended all the way around the house to a large fenced-in backyard. Had there not been college students occupying the house for the better part of fifteen years, it would have probably been considered a beautiful home. Unfortunately, now it was run-down and in desperate need of a paint job and some overall love.

"Hey, Nathan. I'm Mark. Welcome to Cupid's Party. If you need anything, just let us know." Mark opened the side door and allowed the group of them to enter that way.

It was locked from the outside with a padlock, ensuring that other students wouldn't try to sneak in that way without a ticket.

"Thanks, Mark," Nathan said, shaking his hand.

The music came wafting out as they stepped inside the side door that led them to the kitchen.

"Anytime, Nathan. Anytime. Enjoy the party, guys."

"Pays to come with you, doesn't it?" Bree cooed. "I hate lines."

Nathan just shrugged his shoulders. Turning to Abigail, he asked, "You doing okay? Let me know if you need to sit or anything,"

"Of course. Please stop worrying about me. I'll be fine."

"I can't help it. You know that," he said with a wink.

She blushed and started to follow Laura and Bree through the door toward the living room.

The house wasn't as decorated as the Black Hearts Party, but there was the usual display of cutout hearts stuck to the walls and hanging from the ceiling. There were white and red Christmas lights strung from doorway to doorway. The lights made it festive. Abigail even found herself smiling at the lights. Most of the furniture had either been removed or pushed against the walls, leaving plenty of space to move easily from room to room.

To the left was a set of French doors. The doors were covered with white cloth panels that led to a glassed-in sunroom in the back of the house. It was lit with tall, tapered candles, adding to the ambiance.

The bar was in the front room, probably once the formal dining room. Now, there was just a large wood bar that stretched from one side of the back wall all the way to the other. The bar had a small wood flap on two hinges near the end to allow a person to go behind it.

With Nathan taking the lead, they made their way through the crowd to the bar. He was bombarded with high fives and greetings as he politely tried to get closer to the bar. Abigail did her best to remain close but decided to hang back. There was no sense in her trying to crutch her way through. She let the others know where they could find her.

As students passed her by as she leaned up against the wall, the strangest feeling hit her.

Is he here? Is Dan stalking his next victim? Did Tank really hurt him so badly that he would need medical attention? Why haven't the police called me yet?

Her mind raced, and her heart rate doubled as she surveyed the activity surrounding her. *Maybe Nathan was right about not coming out tonight. Maybe I should have stayed home.*

Nathan made his way out of the crowd in front of the bar and over toward her, balancing two drinks. He caught one look at her, and his smile suddenly faded.

He handed her the drink. "Thinking about last night, aren't you?"

"No, no. I'll be fine."

"*Abby…*"

"Well, maybe just a little. I was wondering if he might be here; that's all."

"Oh, Abby. I'm so sorry, but I can almost guarantee that he is not here. No way would he show his face around here. And believe me, if Tank hit him the way I think he did…well, I just know there is no way he'd be here."

He put his arm around her and gave her a gentle squeeze. She peered up at him. She had to convince him that she was okay regardless of whether or not she believed it herself.

"Now, you said you wanted to come, and I reluctantly agreed, so"—he smiled wide—"let's have some fun, okay? Get your mind off things."

"Yes, sounds great." She needed to get her mind off of last night. "And thanks for being so understanding about me wanting to come. It's not like I didn't hear your concerns and all. But sitting in a room, thinking about it…I just feared that would be way worse."

"I know. Trust me; I do get it." He smirked and then said, "Now, I have no idea what is in this Love Potion, so proceed with caution."

He raised the cup to his lips and gulped the bright red concoction. Abigail did the same.

It actually didn't taste bad. If anything, all she could taste was the Kool-Aid. She scanned the room. Everyone seemed so happy—or at least, the students seemed like they were having a good time.

She was quickly brought back to reality as Jason and Marcus approached them from across the crowded room.

"Hey!" Jason yelled over the music.

Marcus raised his glass toward Nathan with a grin, but it quickly faded as his eyes set on Abigail.

He leaned in close to her. "I just wanted to say that I heard about what happened, and if there is anything you need from me, you just say the word, okay?" His voice was flat—not cold, but flat.

"Boy, bad news travels fast. But thank you," she said.

"You're welcome." His expression darkened. "But if you don't mind, we need to steal Nathan for a bit. We need to talk to him." His eyes flashed at her, letting her know he was serious.

She glanced over at Nathan and quickly excused herself. "Hey, I'm going to find Melissa. I'll be back."

Before Nathan could object, Marcus had his back toward her and shielded Nathan from protesting. As if defeated, Abigail slowly crutched away from the crowd and toward the glassed-in room. Thankfully, there was not a single person in the room as she pushed open the French doors and stepped down into the sunroom. She walked over to the back glass wall and stared out into the dark sky. Moments later, she sensed a slight breeze as the doors opened and closed again, letting in the music from the other room as quickly as the air came and went.

"I was hoping I'd get to see you," Tank said.

She wheeled around as her heart pounded in her chest. "You startled me," she said.

"Sorry, I didn't mean to."

"How long have you been here?" Abigail asked.

"About an hour. I came with Jessica. She...well, she wanted me to bring her, and so I came."

Her expression softened. "Oh, that's great, Tank."

"I guess." He took a few steps toward her. He reached his hand out and gently took hers. "Abby, are you okay?"

She didn't pull her hand away. She gazed at him, and with tears in her eyes, she said, "I am because of you."

"I told you, I made a promise. And I'll always keep that promise." His voice was low, sad almost.

"But how did you know?" she asked.

He took one step closer to her. It was then she saw the bruise across his cheek and neck.

She gasped. "Oh my God, you're hurt!"

"I'm fine really. I've taken worse bumps than this before." He chuckled. "What about you? You seem okay, but I hit you..." He couldn't complete the sentence as the memory of him hitting Dan along with her rushed back into his head.

He squeezed her hand. She winced.

"I'm so sorry. I didn't mean—" he said.

"No, it's just...well, my arms, they hurt..." She trailed off. She couldn't bear to see the expression on his face, so she turned her head.

He held up her hand and moved her arm, so it was facing up toward him. He gently pulled up her sleeve on her sweater and exposed the bruise. She kept her head motionless as she didn't want to see his reaction.

The room was agonizingly silent.

Then, he slowly pulled her sleeve back down, but he still held on to her hand.

"I hurt you," he whispered under his breath. "My God, I never meant to—"

She finally was able to look at him. "Do you have any idea what you did for me?" Her voice had a slight edge. "If it wasn't for you..." Her voice cracked. "If it wasn't for *you*..." she stressed.

He hung his head toward the ground.

"Tank," she pleaded. She waited for him to pick his head up. When he did, she said, "I've taken worse bumps and bruises than these before," she said, trying to get him to smile.

The corner of his mouth curved up a little.

"I'm so sorry, Abby," he said, looking intently into her eyes.

"No need to be. You saved me." Trying to change the subject a little, she said, "I am a bit concerned though that I haven't heard a word from the police all day. Have you heard anything?" she asked.

"Yes, I did." He hesitated, still holding her hand. "Chief Frankel mentioned he would call you in the morning, but a guy checked into a hospital about forty miles from here with a broken arm and collarbone. Said he was in a bike accident, but he fits the description you gave, so right now, they are investigating him further."

"Oh, so did they arrest him?" she asked, her voice shaking.

"No, they don't want to scare him off. They called to ask me if I could remember what side I'd hit him on and how, like what arm he landed on, so they are checking out a few things before they make any moves. But you're safe, Abby. I promise you."

Tank's eyes were filled with concern as he said, "I'll never let anyone hurt you, Abby, ever again. That guy is lucky that I only broke..." He hesitated, feeling the rage reenter his body.

"Tank, you can't put yourself in a position like that, not for me...not for anyone."

"Don't be ridiculous, Abby," he quipped.

"I'm not. I'm being realistic. What would happen to you if the police decided to press charges? Think about what could happen to school, football, and your career. All because of...what?" She dropped his hand as her emotions started to take over. She took a step back. "Because you made your friend a promise to protect a girl he'd never met?"

Now, it was Tank's turn to take a step back. He inhaled sharply, feeling her words sting. "Why won't you say his name?"

"Why? Because I don't know...I don't know..." She trailed off.

"*Jonathan*," he emphasized, "wanted me to look after you, and that is what I intend to do. You can fight me all you want on this, but you will not...you cannot change my mind." His words were firm.

She faced the glass windows again. She slightly dropped her head, observing her tired, aching body, and she finally whispered, "I can't ask you to protect me, knowing that you could lose everything or even worse..."

He came closer. "Or even worse?" he asked.

"Yes. What if something happened to you? Huh? Did you ever think about that?"

He put his hands on her shoulders. "Abby, nothing will happen to me; trust me."

"How do you—"

"Abby, look at me." He spun her shoulders around, so she was now facing him. He stared hard into her eyes. "Abby, why am I doing this?" he asked quietly.

She hesitated and then took a deep breath in. "Because Jonathan wanted you to."

The sound of his name made Tank's mouth turn slightly up at the corners.

"Yes, because Jonathan asked me to. He brought us together, so I could be there for you when he couldn't be, whenever you need someone, and that is what I'll do."

"I know, but—" she attempted to protest.

Tank interrupted, "He is watching out for me and you. I truly believe that, so nothing is going to happen to me, okay?"

She glanced up at his face and noticed he smiled slightly. It was becoming increasingly hard to stay angry at Tank. She didn't want to be mad at him. In fact, she was beginning to care for him. Her objection was out of concern for him, if nothing else.

Her eyes softened.

"There you go." He slightly laughed. "That's the Abby I want to see."

"By the way." Her tone sounded like a mother scolding her child, "you should not have sent me those flowers." She playfully punched him in the arm. "You almost got me in big trouble."

"Well"—he smirked—"I meant what I wrote, and speaking of trouble, I'd better get going. Jessica is probably freaking out. I'll call you."

He was about to walk out when she said, "Tank?"

"Yeah?"

She reached over and threw her arms around his massive body, trying not to lose the crutches out from under her arms. He made a slight groan as she squeezed him.

"Thank you. Thank you so much." She could feel his body relax as he reached around her and hugged her back.

"You're welcome, Abby."

They heard the music come into the room.

"Oh, there you are."

Abigail dropped her arms, and Tank followed. They stepped apart.

"Nathan is looking for you," Laura said.

"Oh, yeah, we were just talking. Where is he?" Her face flushed.

"Hey, Laura," Tank said.

"Hey, Tank. He's by the bar with the rest of us."

"Oh, okay."

"Jessica is there, too."

"Oh shit. All right, after you two." He motioned toward the door.

They made their way through the crowd toward the back room. Abigail could see Nathan's expression change as he saw her and Tank walk in together. Marcus and Jason were standing next to him, and their expressions mimicked Nathan's. Abigail observed Tank. He hung his head as he approached the group, which was uncharacteristic for him.

Abigail put on a smile for everyone. She made her way next to Nathan. "Hey."

He slightly leaned down toward her. "We were wondering where you went."

Her face filled with heat. "I was in the back room. Just saying thank you to Tank, for helping me."

Nathan intently searched her face. She lowered her eyes. He glanced over in Tank's direction. It was apparent by how Jessica's arms were flailing about that she was arguing with Tank.

"Well, it seems like it might have caused him issues, too," Nathan remarked.

The tone of his voice was unrecognizable. In fact, it made her skin prickle. She glanced up at him, his eyes never leaving her face.

"What are you saying, Nathan?" she said.

"I don't know, Abby. What am I saying?"

As if by sheer dumb luck, Melissa came bounding over. "Hey! There you are. We were wondering where you ran off to!" she exclaimed.

Abigail stammered, "Sorry, I—"

Before she could finish her sentence, Nathan cut in, "I'm going to grab a drink. I'll let you two catch up."

Nathan's smile was forced, she could tell. He made his way to the bar with Jason. She knew Marcus was watching her, and it made her feel a bit uneasy, like he somehow knew all about this tangled web she was caught in.

Tank slowly made his way over to his captain. Marcus gave him a noticeably blank expression. It bordered on cruel.

She attempted to focus back on Melissa. "Hey, are you having fun?"

"Yeah, totally. But are you? You seem…I don't know…distracted or something. You feeling okay?"

"Yeah, of course. I'm fine. Just a lot on my mind, I guess. Let's not talk about me anymore, okay?" Her voice was strained, and her expression was pleading.

Melissa's face wrinkled up a bit and then finally relaxed. "Okay, whatever you say," she said, grabbing Abigail's arm. "So, did I tell you that Logan booked us a night at a bed-and-breakfast in Vermont next weekend? Isn't he so sweet?" she gushed.

"Oh, Melissa, I'm so happy for you. That will be awesome!" Abigail was genuinely happy for her friend, and it was a welcome feeling at that. She tried hard to focus on her friend's story, but all she could think about was Nathan and what a mess she had made out of these last few weeks.

She was brought back down to earth when Melissa said, "If you need to get away, I'm happy to give you my room key for the weekend. We'll both be gone, so the room can be all yours."

"Oh, Melissa, thanks. That sounds nice. I think I'll take you up on that, but just don't tell anyone, okay? I mean, for now. Just in case I really do want some peace and quiet."

Melissa winked and said, "Your secret is safe with me."

Secret. Another secret. She had so many these days that she was having a hard time keeping them all straight.

The party was in full swing, and most of the girls that Abigail had come with were out on the dance floor, enjoying themselves. Abigail, however, had somehow become the quintessential wallflower, standing up against the ill-painted walls, leaning on her crutches. She'd been sipping her Love Potion, but from what she could tell by how little Nathan had spoken to her tonight, the potion was *not* working. At all. Period. He wasn't completely avoiding her. She could see him across the room, talking with some of the players, but not unlike the football banquet, it would take him forever just to get across the room with so many people stopping to talk to him. So, in some way, she couldn't really blame him.

When she scanned the room, she would catch Tank watching her. He'd nod from time to time, but for the most part, he kept his distance.

Jessica kept close to him, peering over her shoulder at Abigail. She was clearly saying, *Back off. He's mine.*

If she only knew that she didn't need to feel that way...

With two fresh drinks in his hand, Nathan approached her. "What's a beautiful girl like you doing, standing here alone?" He flashed those pearly white teeth of his. "Here," he said, handing her a drink. "Looks like you need a refill."

"Yeah, only I'm not so sure this potion works." She took a sip.

There was silence. It was killing her. She knew he was upset, but he wouldn't say why. To be honest, she didn't want to get into it with everyone around.

She grinned slightly as Laura and Bree danced. She envied their simple lives. She wished she were out there with them instead of leaning on her crutches with an aching body as Tank surveyed her every move from across the room. Add insult to injury, she knew she was slowly pushing away this incredible guy standing next to her.

Her days and nights were becoming exhausting. Life was becoming arduous, but it was hard to sympathize with herself when she knew she had made her life more difficult by lying to everyone.

She sensed Nathan lean in close to her. His breath tickled her ear.

"Listen," he whispered, "you've been through a lot these past few weeks, and I'm sorry."

"It's not your fault," she said, avoiding eye contact. She took another gulp—not a sip, but a real gulp. *Come on, potion, work!*

"Abby," he cooed, "if you don't look at me, I'm going to leave."

She shot her head up, only to realize he was laughing.

"Ha! Got you now, didn't I?"

"Nathan, that is not fair to say to me," she protested.

"Neither is you not making eye contact with me, now is it?"

"Ugh," was all she could say.

He was right. She took another gulp.

He peeked at his watch. "It's almost midnight. Let me take you home, okay?"

"What? Why?"

"Because, Abby, enough is enough. We came, we saw, and now, I think you and I need to leave."

She knew he was right, but it was just so defeating.

"Okay," she said, "but I need to let—"

He cut her off, "I already told Marcus and Jay to let the girls know and to make sure they all got home safe. They'll be in good hands, promise."

"Well, all right then. I guess we can go." She took one last look at the girls dancing, and her heart sank.

They were so happy and carefree, and right now, she felt the opposite. She scanned the room and briefly caught Tank's eye. She headed toward the front door of the house. He smiled slightly at her, and she did the same.

Nathan and Abigail walked down the side road toward campus in virtual silence. It was bitterly cold. She tried with all her might not to slip on the icy road. She was hell-bent on not injuring herself again.

Her dorm was first, and she started to head in that direction. She sensed Nathan stopping.

"What?" she said.

"Nothing. I just thought you would be coming home with me tonight." His voice was firm.

"Oh, I just assumed that when you said you would take me home—"

"Yeah…with me."

"Oh, okay."

"Well"—he took a step closer to her—"do you want to come home with me, Abby?"

Her heart raced. He towered over her as he peered down at her, waiting for her to respond.

"Yes."

He came closer. "Yes, what?" he asked, his tone deep.

She could hear his breath quicken.

"Yes, Nathan, I want to come home with you."

His expression did not change.

Is he testing me or something?

"Then, come on, baby. It's cold."

Baby? He's never called me baby.

Inside his dorm, they took the elevator up to his floor and walked down the hall to his room. She could tell by the deafening silence that most of the guys on the floor were out somewhere, maybe even at the Cupid's Party.

He unlocked his door and allowed her to go in first. After she did, she leaned her crutches on the wall near his desk. It was so good not to have those under her arms anymore. He switched on the small desk lamp, barely illuminating the room. She sat in the desk chair and gently pulled off her shoes. Her foot throbbed as the pressure from her shoe released the blood to her foot.

"Feel okay?" he asked.

"Yeah, just sore from being on my foot all night."

"You should ice your foot, Abby," he said, his tone a bit scolding. "Come." He reached out his hands toward hers.

She took his hands, and he pulled her up. She followed him across the room toward his bed, gingerly hopping on one foot.

"Let me get you some more comfortable clothes." He walked over to his dresser and pulled out a T-shirt.

He came back toward her. He reached down to her waist and drew her sweater up. As if mesmerized by him undressing her, she raised her arms and allowed him to pull it up over her head. Her hair fell like spun silk past her shoulders. He then reached to the button on her jeans, and in one swift movement, he unbuttoned and unzipped them at once. She wriggled her hips as he slid the jeans down her legs, and then she stepped out of the jeans. Her heart fluttered. He took the T-shirt and pulled it over her head. He regarded her arms. He ran his fingers over the bruises.

She didn't say a word as he slowly sat her down on the edge of the bed, as if she were made of precious china. He leaned her back against the metal frame. He took a blanket and propped up her foot. He went over to the mini fridge and took out two ice packs.

"The benefit of dating an athlete is that we always have plenty of ice." His expression was tame, as though he'd said the word *dating* without much thought.

It was a bit unsettling to her. Dating seemed so noncommittal.

She surveyed his handiwork while he carefully wrapped her foot with a bandage, securing the ice.

"Thank you."

He glanced up at her, his hands still wrapping her foot. "You're welcome, Abby."

"You've been so patient with me…" she began. "I don't know what—"

"Not now, okay, Abby? Right now, I just need you to focus on feeling better, okay?"

Feeling shunned by his unwillingness to talk almost shocked her into silence.

She whispered, "Okay, Nathan."

Do I even have a right to feel dismissed by him? After all, I have consistently rebuffed his attempts to get the truth out of me even though I really do want to tell him everything. I just simply cannot right now.

"Just relax and ice your foot." He covered her body with a blanket. "I'm going to take a shower. I'll be back shortly."

"Oh, okay, sure. I'll be here." She laughed, only he didn't seem to catch on.

He grabbed his shower caddy and towel. He turned on the radio near his desk on low and went over toward the door. He didn't acknowledge her. She wasn't sure why, but she wanted him to before he walked out.

It seemed like a long time, but in reality, it was only about ten minutes before she heard the doorknob turn, and the door creaked open again. Her jaw nearly dropped wide open as he walked into the room. He was like something out of *GQ*, wearing only a towel tucked around his waist. His body was still wet, his hair was slicked back, and the shadow of stubble on his face made him appear older and even more handsome, if that were at all possible.

"Hey," he said in a gruff voice.

"Hey." She was barely able to meet his eyes. She was so focused on his beautiful body.

"Foot feeling okay?" He took the towel off his waist and ran it over his chest and arms. He was completely naked, and he didn't seem to mind one bit. When she didn't answer him, he asked, "Abby? Your foot feeling okay?"

"Yes. It's cold, so…" she stammered.

"Of course it's cold. It's ice." His voice dripped with sarcasm. He turned toward his dresser, exposing his naked backside to her.

There was a lump in her throat. He took out a pair of boxer briefs from his top drawer and slipped them on. She could not take her eyes off him. He playfully ignored her.

He moved around the room with ease—going from his dresser to his mini fridge to get water, back to his desk to change the radio, back to his dresser to put on deodorant, back to his closet to hang up his towel, and then finally back into the middle of the room, never once speaking to her. She lay there, motionless, just drooling over him. She wanted him to come over to her so badly, but she could not get the words to cross her lips. Her body started to melt into his bed. She was exhausted but desperately wanted to have him close.

"May I?" He motioned to her foot.

She nodded. She could not concentrate on her foot when he was standing there in front of her like that. His hair was a bit longer than when they'd first met, so a few curls were flipped up at the sides. It was so sexy. Her heart accelerated as he bent over and touched the top of her foot.

"Does that hurt?" he asked.

She winced a bit.

"Okay, I think I have my answer." He took his hand away. He went over to his dresser, dispensed a few ibuprofens into his hand, and gave them to her. "Take these. They'll help with the pain while you sleep."

As if on autopilot, she took the pills and swallowed them with the water he had given her.

He moved away, back toward his desk, and turned off the radio and the light. The room was so dark and quiet. She had an uneasy feeling, like they were starting to drift apart.

She could see his shadow move across the room toward her. She swallowed the lump in her throat as he approached. He bent down toward her and pulled the blanket up over her body again. He then moved closer, toward her face.

In a gentle voice, he whispered, "Happy Valentine's Day, Abby."

With that, he kissed her on the lips, touching the side of her face. Before she could even move, he was standing back up and making his way toward Webber's bed, who happened to have gone for the weekend. She heard the creak of Webber's bed as he climbed in.

Her heart felt as though it had been filled with cement. It was so heavy. She had been pushing him away, and she was devastated at the thought.

As she lay there, wide awake, she cursed herself for getting mixed up in all this crazy stuff with Tank and promised she would make this right, no matter what it took. She waited to hear the sounds of Nathan's deep breathing before she would even consider closing her eyes to sleep. Little did she know, he was faking it.

He, too, was lying there, eyes wide, staring at the cement wall, cursing himself for falling for a girl who was so obviously in love with someone else.

Twenty-Nine

FEBRUARY 14, 1996

Abigail awoke sometime after nine thirty. She already knew before she opened her eyes that Nathan was gone. She slowly sat up and unwrapped her foot from the now-room-temperature ice pack and hopped over to the dresser.

> *Abby, I didn't want to disturb you. Getting a workout in, and then I'm off to finish my History project with my group. I'll call you later.*
>
> *P.S. Make sure you rest today and stay off that foot, okay?*

She crumbled up the note and threw it in the trash. It wasn't because she was upset. Well, okay, maybe she was a little upset. He could have woken her up. Obviously, he had known something was not quite right, and she would have liked the opportunity to talk to him, but he hadn't given it to her.

But what exactly would I have said? I promised Tank I wouldn't tell his secret. In many ways, it has become my secret. I'll just have to wait until later, until I can truly grasp all of this before I can share my dilemma with Nathan—or anyone for that matter.

She feared the waiting would drive her insane.

And it did. She waited and waited for hours in her room, pretending to study, but he never called. She contemplated calling him, but he'd said he'd call her.

Maybe he needs some space, she thought as she stared out her window. *Maybe if I don't press him too hard, then we can just pretend like nothing is wrong. Yeah, that's it. I'll just ignore my problems, and they will all go away. It's the perfect plan.* She knew this was the furthest thing from the perfect plan; in fact, it was awful, but she didn't know what else to do.

She even went to the cafeteria, hoping to see him, but he wasn't there. She sulked as she made her way back to her room with Laura and the girls.

Laura went in the room first. Abigail came in after, leaning her crutches on the wall. She grabbed her textbook off her dresser and hopped over to her bed. She put her foot up on a pillow and sank back on the bed. All this did was remind her of last night with Nathan. She let out a deep sigh.

Laura stood in the middle of the room, her eyes fixated on Abigail.

"What is it?" she asked.

"Not sure, Abigail. Do you want to tell me?" she asked. Her tone was strange, not accusatory by any means. It had more concern in it than anything else.

"What do you mean?"

"I don't know. Do you want to start by telling me who the flowers were from?"

She hesitated. "They're from Nathan."

Sensing her lie, Laura sat down on Abigail's bed. "I hope it goes without saying that I am *your* friend, and my loyalty lies with you, so if you need anything, maybe even just someone to talk to, I hope that person will be me."

Speechless, Abigail lowered her eyes toward the ground. Despite what Laura had said, she still felt amazingly alone.

"I've-I've just had a lot going on; that's all," she whispered.

"I can only imagine, Abigail, with your accident and then the attack. It's a lot, and I'm here for you, if you'll let me be."

Her eyes welled up with tears. "Thank you. You're doing it right now."

Laura leaned over and hugged her, trying not to squeeze too tightly.

"Good." She leaned toward the dresser and took a few tissues from the box. "Here," she said.

"Thank you."

"Well, I haven't done anything, but I was thinking of heading down to the common room to watch a little TV. *Friends* is on. Care to join me? You can put your feet up down there, too."

"Thank you, but I think I'd better rest, keep my foot up, and try to get through my Kinesiology homework," she said as she fumbled with her textbook.

She glanced at the clock. It was eight and still no call from Nathan.

"No problem. I'll be back soon." Laura grabbed her keys and her backpack, and then she headed toward the door.

Abigail let out another deep sigh as she heard the door click shut.

She picked up the phone next to her bed and dialed Nathan's extension. It rang and rang, and finally, their answering machine picked up.

"Hey, it's Webber's and Nathan's room. Leave a message after the beep."

Beep.

"Hey, guys. It's me, Abigail. Uh, Nathan, could you call me when you get back?"

FEBRUARY 15, 1996

Abigail awoke to the sound of the blow-dryer. Startled by this sound so late, she quickly sat up in bed.

Laura turned hastily. "I'm so sorry. I didn't mean to alarm you."

"What? Wait, what time is it?"

"Seven thirty."

"What? No, I slept the whole night!"

"Yeah, I have my eight o'clock class on Mondays."

"Yeah, I know. I just didn't know I had fallen asleep; that's all. I'm just…"

"Slow down," she said with a sympathetic glance. "You won't be late."

"I know, but I'd better get in the shower." She noticed the phone—no light blinking, so no messages.

Laura was gone by the time Abigail got back from the shower. She took out her favorite jeans and a tight navy wool sweater. She dressed quickly, so she could take a little extra time drying her hair. She even put on a bit more makeup than usual.

It was a beautiful, bright February day, not quite as cold as it had been the past week, but chilly nonetheless. She zipped up her ski coat, and then she pulled open the front door of her dorm, barely able to balance on her crutches.

She made her way to the union to grab a bagel and water before class. She desperately wanted a coffee but had no way of carrying it with these crutches. That was just another reason to curse them. At least Mondays were lighter days for Abigail. She only had two classes and would be done by twelve thirty.

She had a hard time concentrating in her classes. All she could think about was Nathan. The minutes ticked by as she anxiously waited for twelve thirty, when she would head over to the cafeteria and meet up with her friends and Nathan, as she usually did.

Tick.

Finally. Thank God. She stood up and placed her crutches under her arms.

She walked out of the building and headed straight for the cafeteria. Her mind raced with different conversations and scenarios as to what she might say or what he might say, and before she knew it, she was handing her card to the woman and entering the cafeteria. She could see her usual table and all the girls sitting and chatting at a feverish rate.

Laura spotted her and got up. She walked straight toward her, as if on a mission. Abigail was barely able to balance her tray, and although she had gotten good at it, it was still quite a challenge.

The concern on Laura's face was startling. Abigail waited for her to speak as she approached.

"Abigail, there was a voice mail from Chief Frankel. He wants to talk with you as soon as possible."

Abigail's heart beat firm, her tray barely able to balance between her sweating palms.

Laura reached up and took her tray. "I'll wrap this up for you, if you want to go."

"Yes, please," was all she could say, her eyes as big as saucers.

"Do you want me to skip Calculus? I can come with you right now, if you want."

"No, it should be fine. He probably just wants to fill me in, right?"

"I'm sure that's all it is. It'll be fine. I know it." Laura patted Abigail on the back, trying to calm her nerves.

"Okay."

"Okay, I'll see you in a few hours, tops."

"Yeah, sounds good." Abigail quickly crutched her way toward the back room.

She was desperately hoping that Nathan would be sitting there—and Tank, too, for that matter. She wanted to let them both know that Chief Frankel had called.

As if her heart wasn't heavy enough, it sank even more as she walked in the back room to find the entire football table empty. She pushed open the exit to the cafeteria and headed back to her dorm.

Once inside, she sat down at her desk and pressed the button on the answering machine. There was a resounding voice that echoed out of the machine.

"Abigail Price, this is Chief Frankel. Could you please give me a call as soon as possible? Thank you."

She erased the message, and unfortunately, it was the only one. Quickly, she dialed his number.

He answered right away, "Frankel." His tone was gruff.

Abigail was too startled to talk.

He said, "Hello?"

"Yes, Chief Frankel, this is Abigail Price."

"Ah, Miss Price. Thank you for the prompt callback. I will cut right to it."

"Yes?" There was obvious hesitation in her voice.

"I'd like to ask you to come down to the station. We have a few photos we'd like you to look at, if you'd be so kind. Say, in thirty minutes?"

Her mind raced with more questions than she possibly could have imagined.

As if he could sense it, he quickly said, "I'm sure you have a lot of questions, and hopefully, we'll be able to answer them all for you once you arrive."

"Yes, of course, I'll be there." She gazed out her window.

"Would you like me to have someone come pick you up in a squad car?"

The thought of a squad car coming onto campus and picking her up was about as horrifying as the time she had fallen sick with pneumonia in high school, so her mom had come to pick her up with perm curlers glued to her head. Abigail had been embarrassed beyond belief.

Thankfully, and as if on cue, she saw Tank parking his truck in front of her dorm. He got out and headed to the front door.

"Uh, no, actually. I have a ride. Thank you."

"Okay, see you then." And with that, he hung up the phone.

The buzzer to her room rang.

She pressed the button. "Hello?"

"It's me, Tank." His voice was angry. "Let me up, will you?"

She could only assume he was angry at the fact that the police had caught the guy—at least, Abigail had assumed this from Chief Frankel—and that it was drumming up all kinds of emotions from Tank. She hit the buzzer, unlocking the front door.

She could have sworn that only twenty seconds had passed before there was a pounding on her door.

"Abby, it's me!" His voice was loud.

She hardly had time to get up from her desk to open the door when he pounded again.

"Tank, I'm coming…" She whipped open the door.

Just one glimpse at him told her more than she wanted to know. He was disheveled, unshaven, and had bloodshot eyes. From what she could observe, he was too drunk to be standing, let alone driving his truck. On instinct, she grabbed his arm and pulled him in, looking down the hallway to make sure no one had seen him.

"What the hell, Tank?" she scolded.

"What the hell, Abby? What the hell?" he stammered back.

She reached forward, as if to grab him, when he quickly jerked his arm back.

"I'll tell you, what the hell. Your boyfriend—yeah, number two—well, he got—no, he *made* Coach kick me off the team! I'm done! Out!"

As though the past few weeks had not been bad enough, she envisioned a metaphorically gigantic fist punching her right in the gut. It took the wind out of her.

Her mouth just dropped open. "What? *No*, it can't be."

"Yep! Bastards! All of them."

"Tank, there has to be some kind of a mistake." Her voice trembled. Tears welled in her eyes.

His expression softened.

He sank down in her desk chair, barely able to stand. "No, Abby, no mistake."

"But how do you know? Nathan would never do that. He knows how much you mean to…"

Tank narrowed his eyes. "Yeah, apparently, he *does* know how much, Abby, because you were one of the main reasons I got kicked off."

The gigantic fist came down again, landing another blow to her gut. "What? No. Why would you say that?"

"Because," he stammered, "Coach said my involvement with you was causing too many problems for Nathan and the team."

"What? That's ridiculous. That can't be right. Nathan would never…" Then, she thought about how he had behaved these past two days. *He was so cold and distant toward me the other night, and then he didn't call me like he'd told me he would. He always calls me when he says he will. Maybe he has been avoiding me because he knew this was going to happen. Why would he do this and not talk to me about it?*

Unfortunately, it all made sense, now.

"Yeah, well, he said it. The fight I had, the awards thing we were at, the guy who attacked you…Nathan can't handle that you and I—"

"The guy!" Abigail blurted out.

"What?" Tank hiccupped.

"Chief Frankel just called. I thought that was why you came here."

His eyes widened, and his pupils remained large. "What? Did they catch that son of a—"

"I don't know, but they want me down there in"—she peered over at the clock—"fifteen minutes. Crap. Tank, I have to—"

"I'm coming with you." He tried to stand.

"No, Tank, you can't go to a police station while you're drunk."

"I'm going with you." His words were slurred, and his body swayed.

Realizing time was of the essence, she finally agreed, "Fine, but I'm driving, and you're staying in the truck. Agreed?"

"Agreed," he said with reluctance.

"I mean it, Thomas. You'll be in major trouble if you get out."

"Thomas, huh? Well, since you called me Thomas, I have to obey." He crossed his arms.

She grabbed her jacket, a handful of mints from her drawer, and a bottle of water. She handed them to Tank, and then she pulled on her jacket.

"Chew these because you stink. Drink this and follow me. And don't talk to *anyone*. You hear me?" she scolded.

He mockingly nodded his head. She glared at him before opening the door and mumbled a quick prayer that no one would see them. She went down the side stairs to the outside path. They moved fast toward the front. She threw her crutches in the bed of the truck and hopped in the driver's seat. He got in the passenger side.

"Never sat here before," he finally said.

Angry at the mere thought of him driving, she snarled, "How dare you drive in your condition! I'm really pissed at you."

"I know," was all he could say. "Look, I'm having a bad day, Abby, and I don't need a lecture from you."

"Oh, yeah? Well, I've had a few bad weeks, Tank, so spare me the attitude."

She didn't know what had come over her, but the words had flown out of her mouth at an uncontrollable rate. She had never spoken to anyone in such a way. To be honest, it actually felt good. She'd needed to vent, and he'd just happened to be the nearest target.

There was silence in the car as she pulled onto the main road. She was still seething from his remarks.

As if he wanted to fuel the fire, he quietly added, "Jonathan once told me that you were awfully cute when you were angry."

She slammed on the brakes, jerking Tank in a forward motion. It had the exact opposite effect on him that she had intended. Instead of shutting him up, he began to laugh uncontrollably.

"You are incorrigible!" She glared at him.

Laughing even more, he slurred, "You're still cute."

"Would it be rude if I said that, right now, I hate you?"

He stopped laughing for a second. "Yes, it would."

"Good. I hate you right now."

"Good. I hate your boyfriend."

Ouch. Her heart sank.

They pulled into the police station. Abigail deliberately parked as far away as possible from the front door. She turned the key and took it out of the ignition, and then she shoved the keys in her coat pocket.

"What? You're not even going to leave me with the heat on?" he asked.

"No, I don't trust you right now not to do something stupid, and besides that, if someone comes to the truck, you would still be in trouble. Just being under the influence with the means to drive is an offense."

He turned and gazed out the front window as he shoved his hands deep into his coat pockets. "Fine," he said. Then, he whispered, "Hey…" His tone made her turn quickly. "I know this is going to be hard. Wish I could go in there and all, so I'm sorry, okay?" He reached over and gently patted her on the arm.

Stunned by his compassion, she slightly turned and gazed forward. She took a deep breath and slowly let it out. "Thanks. I needed that. I'll be right back."

As she walked toward the front door, she chuckled a bit to herself. She had no idea if what she'd just told him about the keys being in the ignition and all was even true. She had sort of just made it up on the fly, but it sounded legit enough. In the end, all that mattered was that he'd bought it, and he couldn't drive his truck.

Thirty

FEBRUARY 15, 1996

Abigail opened the door to the front entrance of the police station. As she walked in, it occurred to her that she had never been in a police station before. She hesitated before she made her way to the counter.

A young man, probably in his late twenties, in full uniform sat at the desk. He glanced up from his notebook, and with a serious tone, he said, "Ma'am, can I help you?"

She was nervous, and her voice cracked as she said, "Yes, I'm here to see Chief Frankel."

"Is he expecting you?"

"Yes, he called and asked me to come down."

No sooner had the young man behind the counter turned to get up than the other officer that had been in Nathan's room that night approached the counter.

"Miss Price, thank you so much for coming down." Officer Murphy reached for the gate to open it.

"Thank you, Officer Murphy." Her voice came out so quietly that it even surprised her.

"Please, come this way. Chief Frankel is waiting for you in his office."

Abigail followed the officer past a series of desks sitting face-to-face as administrative assistants sat, typing feverishly on their word processors. A few uniformed officers stood, huddled around a desk, getting their orders from their superior for the day. Officer Murphy led Abigail down a short hallway to an office that faced the main room of the station. The shades on the windows were drawn, which prevented Abigail from seeing who or what was behind the door.

Officer Murphy knocked twice before opening the door. Chief Frankel sat behind a large mahogany desk piled high with papers, newspapers, and empty coffee cups. He stood up immediately as Abigail made her way into the room.

"Miss Price. You look well," he said.

"Thank you," she said, feeling her face blush, not from embarrassment, but from feeling incredibly uneasy.

He walked over to the table situated in the corner of the room, and he motioned her to follow. She and Officer Murphy went over to the table and took the two remaining seats. She rested her crutches on the wall near her seat. She turned and scooted herself forward in an attempt to appear calm and ready for what they had to say, but inside, she was filled with anxiety.

"Miss Price," Chief Frankel began, "how are you holding up?"

"Oh, just fine."

"Did you seek medical attention?" he said, observing her crutches.

"Oh, no. That was from a previous accident. I fell on the ice, and, well, the situation the other night aggravated it," she stammered.

Sensing her hesitation, Officer Murphy spoke up, "Please relax, Miss Price. We are here to help you, okay?"

"Thank you. Of course." She appreciated the reassurance.

Chief Frankel shuffled a few papers in front of him and then quickly closed the folder. "So, Miss Price, I've asked you here today to try to identify a suspect that was recently admitted to a medical center in Rome, New York. We feel his injuries were similar to the ones we expect the perp would have sustained, according to the statement we took from Thomas McPherson. Before we begin, is there anything you'd like to add, regarding the evening in question?"

She swallowed hard. "No, sir."

He reached across the table and patted her shaking hand. Then, in a comforting voice, he said, "There is nothing to be afraid of here, okay, Miss Price? There is no pressure to pick someone out. If you are unsure for any reason, just say the word, and we will revisit this on another day. Please, I encourage you to keep in mind that the only right choice here is the one where you are one hundred percent sure. We have had a few other women come forward, so we will find this guy whether it is today or tomorrow, okay?"

His words were kind and did make her feel somewhat better.

She took a deep breath. "Yes, sir, I understand. Wait, a few other women have come forward?"

"Yes, but I'm not at liberty to discuss those cases."

"Oh, yes, of course. I understand." It was unsettling for her to hear that.

"Are you ready?"

"Yes," she said, trying to sound strong.

He nodded and then took the folder again. He opened it and laid out four pictures in front of her. Her heart raced as she scanned the photos. Then, as if by force, her eyes closed, and immediately, she was taken back to that night.

She took a deep breath and held it. The conversation that had played repeatedly in her mind these past few days started again.

"You're the guy—"

"That you insulted out front? Yep, that's me."

"I'm so sorry. Like I said, I didn't mean it that way."

"I know. Just giving you a hard time. I'm Dan."

"Hi, Dan. Abigail."

She opened her eyes, taking the pictures in again. She could feel the chief studying her every move. He sat motionless. Her heart raced as she deliberated over the photos, scrutinizing each one.

At the last photo, she reached over and slid it in front of her. She saw his eyes, his hair, and his build, and she said without hesitation, "That's him."

"Are you *positive?*" Chief Frankel's gaze was strong. It was clear he meant business. There was no room for error.

"Yes, Chief."

Chief Frankel motioned toward the door. It opened, and an officer in plain clothes came in with some papers. He leaned over the table, and the chief signed the sheet he had taken out for him. Then, Chief Frankel took the paper and had Officer Murphy sign it. Officer Murphy handed it to the officer, who took the sheet and walked out.

"Thank you, Miss Price. I know that was not easy."

She just acknowledged him by gently nodding her head.

Officer Murphy took the pictures, made a note in the book he had in front of him, and put the photos back in the folder.

"So," Chief Frankel said, "we do have this man under police watch since he still requires medical attention. Unfortunately, at this moment, that is all I can tell you. But, please, I want to reiterate that you are safe, okay?"

She again nodded her head in acknowledgment, but her expression told him otherwise.

"Miss Price, I know my words might not be reassuring to you now, but I will say this to you. I have a daughter about your age, and under these same circumstances, I would tell her exactly the same thing that I just told you. I hope, if nothing else, that will let you sleep a bit easier at night."

His expression had become softer. She believed him. It had been a while since her shoulders relaxed, and the beating of her heart slowed in the process.

"We will need to speak with you again as the case moves forward, and depending on what happens with the perp, we might need you to testify. I suggest, at some point soon, you contact a lawyer, okay? But, in the meantime, if you have any questions, please do not hesitate to call me."

Again, she just nodded her head.

Relieved, she started to stand. "Thank you." She put her crutches under her arms.

"You're welcome," he said. "Officer Murphy will see you out. I'll be in touch."

As she approached the chief's door, she turned slightly. She had a nagging feeling in her gut. It had been with her for days as she replayed that conversation a thousand times. She could not shake the feeling she had, so she asked, "Dan isn't his real name, is it?"

"No, Miss Price. No, it is not."

Thirty-One

FEBRUARY 15, 1996

Abigail pulled on the door handle and then tossed her crutches into the bed of the truck. Startled, Tank jumped in his seat. He had either fallen asleep or passed out, and she guessed it had to be the latter.

"Well?" he said, rubbing his eyes.

She hopped into the driver's seat, put the key in the ignition, and turned on the engine. It was freezing in the car. She rested both hands on the wheel and tilted her head toward her lap as she closed her eyes. Finally, she let out a huge sigh. "They got him. At least, I think they did. I guess he checked into a hospital, like, an hour from here or something, and he has a broken arm, so—"

"Woohoo!" Tank screamed.

Abigail twitched, noticeably irritated by his outburst. "Tank!"

"Woohoo!" he yelled again.

This time, he reached over and threw both arms around her. He pulled her close to him. He, like a baby bear, had no idea how strong he really was, and she was sure he was going to break her in half.

"Tank, you're hurting me," she said, her voice muffled by his enormous body smothering her face.

He squeezed her again, and he planted a huge kiss on her cheek. She turned several shades of red as she pushed herself off of him.

"Oh, I am sorry. I am just so happy," he said, noticing her discomfort.

"No, it's fine. I'm sorry. I am so relieved." She glanced at him. "And thank you, Tank. Thank you so much for being there that night. I hope you know how much I truly—"

He cut her off, "No need to thank me."

"I owe you. I do," she said.

"Owe me, huh?" He smiled wide. "You know how you can pay me back?"

She turned with a bent brow and glared at him.

"Abby Price, get your head out of the gutter. You can pay me by going out and celebrating with me. Please," he said, giving her puppy-dog eyes.

"Don't you think you've *celebrated* enough today?" she said.

"Huh, speaking of, you owe me twice today. I save you, and your boyfriend gets me kicked off the team? You owe me, Abby Price. Big time!"

Her jaw dropped at his bold yet unbelievably accurate statement.

"Come on, Moon Pie, just you and me for once."

"Hey!" she scoffed at the fact that he'd called her Moon Pie.

"What? You called me Thomas."

"Fair, I guess."

"Come on, drive." He tipped his head and stared at her with these huge silver puppy-dog eyes.

"Fine," she huffed. "Where to?"

"I know a place."

They drove about twenty minutes east of the police station.

Abigail had never ventured this way before. She pulled into a small lot and parked the truck. There were maybe ten or so other cars in the lot.

"Where are we?" she asked.

"Come on." He opened his door. He went around, grabbed her crutches, and met her at her door.

She followed him toward the back of the building to a beat-up metal door near a dumpster. The place was dimly lit. This place gave her the creeps.

Tank pulled open the door, and the soft glow of fluorescent lights filled the darkness. "Come on in."

She made her way in, passed the restrooms, and went toward the main room. Once inside, every patron sitting at the bar stopped what he or she was doing and turned to stare at them as they entered.

Abigail froze in her tracks. "Tank, I don't think—"

"Big guy!" someone yelled.

Tank raised his hand.

The bartender acknowledged him back. "Tank, how goes it?"

"Good, Jimmy, good." His smile was so real that it actually made Abigail smile.

"This here is Abby," he said.

Jimmy nodded. Abigail bashfully waved.

"Two beers," Tank said as he motioned Abigail toward a small table by the window.

Jimmy grabbed two bottles from the cooler and popped the caps off. He came around the bar and set them on the table. "You know the rules here, Tank."

Abigail's heart skipped a beat.

"I know, Jimmy. I know." He turned to Abby. The expression on his face was serious. "Jimmy, this is Moon Pie. Moon Pie, Jimmy."

She blushed.

Tank laughed. "Everyone here has a nickname."

Jimmy reached out his hand to shake hers.

She took his hand. "Well, that doesn't seem fair."

With a surprised expression, Jimmy said, "What's not fair?"

"Well, everyone calls *you* by your name."

Tank and Jimmy both laughed.

"What?" she said with a huff.

Jimmy pretended to glance over his shoulder in the hopes that no one would hear him. Then, he turned back toward Abigail. "My real name is Walter." He gave her a winning grin. "Welcome to the No Nickname."

She noticed he was missing a few teeth. He seemed goofy but harmless. He began to snicker. It made her laugh, and soon, they all began to laugh.

"I like this one, Tank." He motioned to Abigail and then walked away.

"I like *this* one, huh?" Abigail said. "Bring lots of people here, do you?"

His expression became serious. "Actually, no."

"Oh." She took a sip of her beer. It tasted good.

"But I just love dives like this. I mean, they couldn't come up with a better name for this dump than the No Nickname?"

She laughed, and then there was silence for a bit.

Finally, Tank broke the ice, "So, did you get a chance to read the book?"

Expecting that this conversation would come up at some point, she had been prepared. "Yes, I did."

"Well?"

"Well, I think this is crazy, but that's nothing new, Tank. What exactly do you want me to say?"

"I don't know. I guess that's part of the problem, but do you at least believe in the possibility that—"

"That what? That Jonathan once knew me and that we were—"

"In love."

"Yes. I suppose I believe in something. I'm just not sure what." She took a sip of her beer.

"Anything in the book resonate with you?" he asked, desperately searching for answers.

"Yeah. There is this song that I love, and he quoted it, but that could just be a coincidence after all."

"Huh. Unlikely at this point. I don't think there are coincidences. I believe we're dealing with facts."

"Facts!" She laughed.

"Don't laugh. This is not funny."

"I'm sorry. You're right. This is not funny. It's just so hard to think about. I am trying, Tank. I really am, but with all that has been going on…" She took another sip of her beer. Her eyes wandered around the small bar, and she started to wonder how a girl like her had ended up mixed up in all of this.

"I know. I'm sorry, but to be honest…I'm not sorry."

She shot him a look.

"I'm not sorry because I'm continuing on for my friend, and that's exactly what he wanted."

"Yes, but that's just it, Tank. What did he want? Did he want you to live vicariously through him and his memories? Did he want you to—"

"Just stop," he protested. "Just stop trying to tell me that I shouldn't do what he asked me to."

Feeling defeated, she gulped down the rest of her beer. She would never win on this subject, no matter what. In many ways, she was trapped in her own opinion because nothing she ever said to Tank would bring his friend back. The wounds were too new and deep for him to see this any different.

He motioned to Jimmy for two more beers. He brought them over and set them down.

"I didn't mean to get angry." Tank peered down as he ran his hands over the scratches on the table.

"Tank, as your friend, it would be nice if you didn't get so mad at me. I'm just trying to figure all this out, too, you know. I owe it to myself, to Nath—"

"Ha!"

Here we go again.

He pounded his fist on the table. A few regulars from the bar glanced over. Embarrassed, Abigail went to get up to leave, but quickly, Tank grabbed her arm.

"Just don't go, please."

She remained standing.

With desperation in his eyes, he begged, "Please, Abby."

She slowly sat down.

"I'm sorry."

"You say that a lot."

"I know. I'm a mess. Look at me. A total mess."

She rolled her eyes.

"What?" he asked.

"Well, I'm here, aren't I?" she said through slightly gritted teeth. This time, it was her turn to sound mad.

"I know. I know you are, and I forget that sometimes."

"But I have other things and people I have to worry about, too."

"Damn it. Why do you insist on bringing *him* up?"

"Thomas McPherson!" She glared at him. "I have to. All that's going on matters to me. *He* matters to me."

"Jesus Christ, Abby. Can't you see that he is not right for you? He doesn't deserve you. He's jealous. And he got your friend here," he leaned in closer to whisper, "kicked off the team. My livelihood and my scholarship are gone, done. I might be out of school next year."

"What? No!"

"Yeah. I can't pay for school. I'm on a full ride, and now, my dream is just slipping right away from me. Everything we—me and Jonathan—worked for our whole lives is gone because of *him*."

"I just don't believe he would do that." She took another sip. Her mind began to race, thinking of Nathan, who she thought he was, and maybe who he really *was*.

Do I know Nathan, or do I see only what I want to see?

"Believe it," he said flatly. "Believe it."

"Well, I'll have to talk to him, and if I need to talk to your coach—"

"You can't, Abby. It won't matter, and I don't need you fighting my battles for me. I'm not some sympathy case that I need anyone to…well, it won't matter. In fact, it will just make me look bad."

"Look bad, huh? You think it could get any worse?" she scoffed. "Huh. What happens when you tell your parents? What's going to be bad then? That you just let the coaches and the team win, let them kick you off? And over what? Me?"

"I can handle my parents."

"That's all you have to say? What about Jonathan's parents? What's it going to be like to tell them and his brother? You're ready to leave school in a few months? Is that what you're saying? I thought you were a fighter." This was her attempt to challenge him.

He stared at her in disbelief.

She knew in that moment that something had changed between them.

Is it the possibility of him not being around anymore that makes me want to fight, or is it that I know I can't do this alone?

In some ways, she might have given up so much already. If he were not here, she would be left unaccompanied to make up for all her lies and secrets.

Would anyone even believe me, or would they just know that Tank had left because of me and the rest was just some crazy, made-up story?

If nothing else, over these past few days, she had witnessed that she needed him.

She searched his face, hoping for a sign that he was still in there, that he had something left to give. She waited for him to respond, and when he didn't, she drove her point home. "Who is going to protect me if you're not around?"

He dropped his head. She could tell by his reaction that he'd wanted her to say that.

She reached across the table and touched his hand. "I won't give up if you won't give up," she said.

He raised his head. If she didn't know any better, she would have thought she saw a tear in his eye. She smiled softly, hoping he would do the same.

He took her hand and gave it a squeeze. "Boy, Jonathan sure missed out on you." He hollered over at the bar, "Two more, Jimmy."

It was quarter till twelve in the evening when Jimmy finally yelled over to them, "Hey, kids, closing up soon. I'll give you a ride. No way am I letting you drive."

"Thanks, Jimmy." Tank grinned.

"Yeah, thanks," Abigail slurred.

She was drunk, the drunkest she'd ever been, but the beers had kept coming, and so had the conversation. It was the most she had ever talked to a boy before. It was much easier than she had expected. Once they had been able to clear some of the cobwebs away, the two of them could talk about a lot.

Mostly, the conversation had come back to Jonathan, but in many ways, it was good. She was getting to know Jonathan more, and in knowing him more, she knew Tank even better.

She knew he needed to talk to someone. This connection between Abigail and Tank was something he needed more than she ever would. When a friend was hurting, you were there for them, no matter what. It wasn't as though Abigail had ever doubted Tank was hurting, but having spent the last few hours with him, she knew he was far from healing. She even questioned if he would ever really get over a loss like Jonathan's.

"You kids ready?" Jimmy switched off the light behind the bar.

Abigail went to stand and stumbled slightly, and then she grabbed her crutches and leaned on them. *So much better.*

On the ride home, Tank and Jimmy talked mostly about football as Abigail gazed out the window, feeling the heaviness of her eyelids. Jimmy pulled onto campus. Tank directed Jimmy toward the dorms.

Jimmy dropped Abigail off first.

"Good night, Jimmy, and thanks."

He just nodded.

"Night, Tank."

"Good night, Moon Pie." He chuckled.

She clumsily positioned her crutches under her arms and shut the car door.

Abigail stumbled to get her key in the front door. She finally opened it, staggered toward the elevator, hit the button, and leaned her body against the wall while she waited for the door to open. It seemed like it took forever to arrive.

She stepped in and hit the button for her floor. Once there, she made her way down the hall to her room, trying hard not to make a sound. Thankfully, the door was open, so she didn't have to fumble with her key again. The room was dark. She crutched her way over to her bed, took off her coat, and lay back on the bed. She closed her eyes.

In a hushed voice, Laura stated, "Nathan has been calling you all night."

Shit.

Thirty-Two

FEBRUARY 16, 1996

Abigail was barely able to open her eyes, but she knew it was light out. She cracked one eyelid and saw a bottle of water and three ibuprofens sitting on a chair next to her bed. It would be the first time in her life that Abigail skipped school. Ever. Period. Her head pounded with a fierce and ferocious beat.

"Nathan called four times last night." Laura pulled a sweatshirt over her head.

The bright sunshine streaming through the window made her head pound even more. She rolled over and turned her back to it.

Laura added, "I'll be honest…he did not sound happy."

Abigail let out a soft groan.

"Okay, well, I'm off to class. I'll see you later, okay?" There was a hint of sympathy in her voice.

"Okay," Abigail moaned. She heard the door close, and she let out a sigh of relief. She just wanted to be alone. She felt terrible—in more ways than one.

"Never again," she cursed.

As soon as she could muster the energy, she would call Nathan. Yesterday had really gotten away from her, and her intention was to call him, but she never got the chance.

But, in the meantime, she shut her eyes tight, knowing she was not ready to face the day.

She heard the doorknob jiggle, so she quickly turned her body to face the wall. She heard the door close loudly. She lay still. She was hoping maybe Laura had just forgotten something and would leave as fast as she'd entered. She held her breath.

"Wake up," Nathan barked. His voice was almost unrecognizable.

Her heart nearly leaped out of her chest. She moved back to her other side. She swung her legs over the edge of the bed and leaned against the cold concrete wall. Her eyes remained shut for a moment, and then she opened them.

He was pacing the room. Finally, he stopped in the middle with his hands on his hips and a disapproving glare in his eyes. For once, Nathan looked like crap, total and utter crap. Still, she was sure *she* was worse. He waited for her to speak.

Her mouth was so dry, and her voice was so strained, but she finally pushed out the words, "I can explain."

"I'm listening." His hands were still digging into his hips.

She was weak as she grabbed her head. The pounding increased with every second that passed. She peered up at him with only her eyes.

"Jesus, Abby. Are you all right?" he asked after getting a good glimpse of her.

"Yeah, I'm fine."

"You don't look fine," he said abruptly.

"Thanks," she quipped sarcastically.

His eyes got wide, and he swallowed hard.

"What's going on, Abby? Where were you all night?" When she didn't answer, he repeated, "Where were you, Abby? I've been worried sick."

"I was out and…" She rubbed her temples and closed her eyes.

"Just that? You were out?" He moved a little closer to her.

She peered up, as if to say, *Back off.*

He stopped dead in his tracks.

There was silence.

"Who were you out with?"

She grumbled. He waited. Nothing.

"Well, if you can't tell me, then I guess maybe that says something about whom you were out with."

Surprised at what he was insinuating, she said, "It's not like that."

"Then, why can't you tell me?"

"I don't know. Fine, I was out with Tank."

Her head pounded. The pain was unbearable. *Can't I just be alone for a little while to gather my thoughts and get rid of this awful headache, upset stomach, and aching body?*

This was her first hangover, and she knew that she never wanted another one ever again. What was worse was, she never in her wildest dreams would have thought that she wouldn't want Nathan Ryan around, but right now, she didn't want anyone around.

Nathan crossed his arms over his chest. She had never seen him this way before.

He almost, for the first time since she had known him, appeared unquestionably disappointed. "Of course it was Tank."

"Nathan, please. I just need a little more time. I'm just…God, my head is killing me, and I tried calling you, but…can we please just stop this for now?"

"Stop what? This conversation?" He didn't wait for her answer. "A conversation about why the two of you are always together?"

"It's not like that," she repeated through gritted teeth. She was a mere fraction of herself. Her tone was almost unnatural. She was angry, and she hardly knew why anymore.

Frustrated, he quipped, "I know you keep saying that, but why do I feel like you're not telling me something?"

"*Nathan*. It's…just…I don't know. He's my friend."

"Friend? Since when? That guy doesn't know how to—"

Feeling her anger rise as the memories of yesterday came flooding back to her, she lifted her head, and before she could stop herself, the words flew out, directed right at Nathan. "Yeah, and whatever issues you have with him—I mean, getting him kicked off the team, Nathan. Really? Just to try to keep me—"

He interrupted, "What?" His eyes grew wide. "I got him kicked off the team? Me?"

"Yeah, that just seems so…I don't know. It's not right."

Pain and anger swirled together in his eyes. "I guess you don't know me as well as I thought you did." He waited for her to say anything to the contrary, but there was nothing but silence.

"So, that's it then…I'll just see you around, Abigail." The hurt in his voice resonated throughout her room.

She peered up, but he had already turned and headed toward the door. She opened her mouth to speak, but nothing came out. She was numb, and before she knew it, he was gone.

"Abigail?" she whispered. *He never calls me that.*

Nathan closed the door. He had tears well in his eyes, but he fought them back. He rested for a moment against the concrete wall, hoping she might try to chase after him, anything to show him she still cared. There was nothing. He heard no movement from within her room. So, in a swift motion, he pushed off the wall and headed down the hall. As he passed by Bree's room, her door swung open. He cringed.

"Hi, Nathan!" she cooed.

"Hey, Bree." He couldn't hide the obvious gloom in his voice.

"What's the matter?"

"Nothing."

She started to walk with him, much to his disappointment. "Get into a fight with Abigail?" she pried.

"Something like that." Once the words had come out of his mouth, he regretted it.

"Oh, so sorry to hear that. If I can do anything to help, just say the word." She seemed to be enjoying his misery.

"I will." In an attempt to lose her, he took the stairs versus waiting for the elevator. He should not have been surprised when she followed him into the stairwell.

"Well, I hope you will. You know we are friends, so I can always find out what is up with her."

He rolled his eyes, knowing she was unable to see him. "Thanks, but that won't be necessary."

"I'm not sure if this has anything to do with it, but she does spend a lot of time with Tank. I know that much. That must really drive you crazy. I know it would drive me crazy." She was baiting him deeper into the conversation.

He pushed open the door to the dorm. "Why do you say that?"

"Everybody sees them together all the time."

"Really?" he said with obvious disdain.

"Yep, I even saw them at the police—" She stopped herself. "Sorry, Nathan, I have to go. Going to be late for class."

"Wait, Bree, the police?" he yelled after her.

A few students stopped and turned toward him. He had shouted *police* after all. He supposed that would grab anyone's attention.

But why did she say that?

Abigail reached over, picked up the receiver, and dialed Tank's extension. She waited as it rang.

He picked it up. His voice cracked. "Do you feel as crappy as I do?"

"Worse."

"Sorry about that."

"Me, too." She chuckled.

"Want me to come by in, say, half an hour with some large, greasy steak and cheese subs with extra pickles and mustard?"

"Mmm...that actually sounds perfect."

"Okay, great. See you soon."

"Tank?"

"Yeah?"

"Diet Coke, too."

"Of course." And with that, he hung up.

An hour later, Laura entered the room, and she could hear laughter. Surprised, she quickly peered around the door. She was flabbergasted to see Tank and Abigail on the floor, eating submarine sandwiches and smiling.

"Hey, Laura," Abigail said.

"Hey."

With little enthusiasm, Tank greeted Laura, "Hey."

"Hey, Tank. What are you guys doing?" she said, scrutinizing the mess on the floor.

"Nothing. Feeding our hangover." He held up what was left of his sandwich.

"Oh, *our* hangover?" She couldn't' hide the hint of irritation in her voice.

"Yeah, ours." He shot her a dark expression.

Laura shuddered and then directed her attention over at Abigail, thinking maybe she would say something, but instead, Abigail just took another bite of her sandwich.

"Talk to Nathan?"

"Yep."

Abigail was about to say he was disappointed in her, but Tank laughed and said to her, "And probably for the last time, huh?"

Abigail put her head down. The thought of that was devastating to her.

"What? What does that mean?" Laura again directed her question to Abigail and Abigail only.

"Just what it sounds like," Tank answered. He popped some chips in his mouth.

"Abigail, really? Are you okay?"

She still couldn't make eye contact with Laura. Instead, she mumbled, "Yeah, I'm fine. Can I talk to you about it later?"

Hurt by her response, Laura said, "Well, okay…I can see you two are busy eating, so I'm going to go to the cafeteria. I'll see you later."

Before Abigail could say another word, Laura went over to the closet, grabbed a few things along with her backpack, and headed toward the door. When she closed it, it made a loud thud.

"What's gotten into her?" Tank asked.

"I don't know. I think she's mad at me from last night."

"Well, she's not your mom, so…"

"I know, but she's a good friend and roommate. I feel bad."

"Oh, come on. You don't owe her anything. We just went out and had a good time. No harm in that."

"I guess you're right."

He slightly shoved her. "Of course I'm right."

She smirked.

"Now, eat up. You look like crap."

"Hey!" she protested. "So do you!"

"I know, but I always do."

"Says who?" Then, with a mischievous tone, she said, "I bet Jessica thinks you're attractive."

"All she cares about is dating a football player, and now that I'm not one…well, it wasn't meant to be, so to speak, with the two of us anyway."

"Don't say that. You never know. People can surprise you. It's possible."

"Isn't that the truth?"

The words resonated differently for Abigail. She thought about Nathan and how he had surprised her. She'd presumed he was different, but maybe Nathan was right. She didn't know him as well as she'd thought she did. It went both ways.

Sensing her darkness, Tank quickly changed the subject. "So, you still remember that Will is coming this weekend?"

She glanced up at him.

"You still want to meet him, right?"

"Yeah, of course." Although she was not convinced that this was a good idea just yet. *Am I ready to meet Jonathan's brother?*

"He's the best." Tank tried to lighten the conversation. "We just can't tell him about the book—not right away at least. Could be hard for him. He is just a kid."

"Whatever you think is best, I guess." She hesitated. "I suppose I'm just along for the ride."

Thirty-Three

FEBRUARY 16, 1996

"You okay?" Laura asked.

"Me? Yeah. Why?" Bree said.

"Oh, I don't know. You've been playing with the same piece of lettuce for, um, fifteen minutes."

"Yeah, well, you haven't said a word since you came in here. You look like your dog just died, all mopey and stuff," Bree barked back.

"Really? I'm mopey?"

"Yeah, you are," she said coldly as she finally peeked up from her uneaten salad.

"Well, I see. Sorry to bother you with my problems—for once."

"What's that supposed to mean?" Bree put down her fork.

"You know…" Laura started to say but quickly changed her mind. "Forget it, Bree. Just forget it. I'm going to be late for class."

With that, Laura abruptly got up and dropped her tray on the belt. She pushed the door open with even more might than she'd expected. Her storming out caused a bit of a scene, but she didn't care if she'd hurt Bree's feelings. She never seemed to care about anyone but herself.

Bree stared after Laura in disbelief. No one had ever spoken to her that way before, let alone walked away from her. She, of course, would speak to people that way. Sadly, she realized that as she sat there alone. It wasn't until she had gotten to college that she started to act the way she had.

She had grown up in the Hamptons, but considering who her friends were, she had always been measured as the nice one among them. But college was different, and so were her friends. She wasn't a Goody Two-shoes like Abigail, a follower like Laura, or an ordinary person like Melissa.

She was still Aubrey Van Tousen, daughter to one of the wealthiest entrepreneurs in New York City.

She sat there with a full pout on her face. She knew well enough that no one would dare approach her. This expression had worked her whole life, and today, she'd accept nothing less. She would be left alone. That, she knew well.

She slowly got up, acting as though she did not have a care in the world. She smoothed down her silk shirt and grabbed her leather jacket off the back of her chair. She swung her long, dark, wavy hair to one side and let it hang down as she put on her jacket. She twisted her mane as she walked out of the cafeteria with full confidence. She had to because, inside, she knew she was at her lowest.

Unfortunately for Bree, the campus was packed with students walking to and from classes. She was in no mood to see anyone, so she quickly ducked into the side door to the student union and waited until she heard fewer and fewer people walking by. She knew the afternoon classes would be starting at any moment. How did she know? Because she was about to skip hers.

When the coast was clear, she entered the west hallway of the student union, nearest to the coffee shop. She walked in and ordered a latte with skim milk. She waited near the back, pretending to browse through her notebook.

"Latte with skim milk?" the barista announced.

She walked over to the counter, took her cup, and put on her black Prada sunglasses. She walked out of the union and toward the one place she knew would be unoccupied and quiet at this time of the day.

She swiped her card at the desk and nodded briefly at the librarian who did little, if anything, to acknowledge her. Bree was just fine with that.

She walked up to the top floor and went into a private cubby area. She opened up her leather Burberry messenger bag and took out a pen and the paperwork. She placed her sunglasses on the table next to her latte.

She took a deep breath, stacked the papers directly in front of her, took the cap off her silver-plated pen, and started by writing her name at the top. She put in her address, phone number, and Social Security number. Then, she read the question on the top of the paper.

> *Please write a full description of the incident. Please note that this is a binding document.*

She put the pen down, took a sip of her latte, and sat back in the chair. It had been almost six months since the *incident*. She had spent these past few days dwelling on the events even more so because she knew what was coming. She knew she'd eventually have to tell, and in some ways, she hoped this would be the therapy she had so desperately been searching for. She was in pain, and she had no one to talk to. She was who she was, and most people like her didn't tell people things like this. She hadn't told her parents, for fear it would shame the family name. She hadn't told her so-called friends from home in fear of hearing *I told you so*. Even more, she wasn't about to tell virtual strangers here and become the typical freshman you read about in books or saw in movies. She wouldn't do that to herself either.

She picked up her pen, took a deep breath, and finally told her story.

On August 31, 1995, I met a girl named Missy outside the student union after I purchased some items in the store. She remarked about my bag, and we struck up a conversation. A guy approached us with a flier, saying there was a back-to-school party at a house at 142 North Adams Street. Missy and I decided to meet at 8 p.m. in front of the union and go over to the party together. She said she lived in Simmons Hall on the other side of campus, so the union seemed the best place to meet.

We walked to the party together with two other girls from her dorm, although I cannot remember either of their names. We got to the party around 8:30 p.m. and paid $5 at the door to get in.

We walked down the stairs to the basement. It was packed, and the music was loud. We soon made our way through the front room to the back where the bar was.

We spent the first hour or so talking to a group of people near the upstairs entrance. The music was blaring, and it was difficult to hear one another, so we decided to move upstairs to the main level. That was the last time I saw the two girls who had come with Missy from her dorm. I do not believe they came upstairs with us.

Missy and I sat on a couch in the living room with a group of kids we did not know. However, Missy recognized one guy from her hometown, and we ended up talking to him and a few of his friends for most of the night. Missy and the guy left to get us another drink from the bar in the basement.

A guy came in the room and sat down on the couch next to me. He was a bit bigger than average, had spiked, short hair, and was wearing an Onondaga State T-shirt. He struck up a conversation with me. We talked about sports, and he said he played lacrosse at school. He said he was a junior. He asked me what year I was, where I was from, and so forth. He said his girlfriend lived in the same dorm as mine and that she was a sophomore biology major.

I waited on the couch for Missy to return. After what seemed like half an hour or so, I excused myself and went into the basement to find her. I searched the basement and never found her. I was down there, looking for her, for about twenty minutes.

Since I knew no one else at the party, I decided to leave. I went up the basement stairs and opened the door. The two guys who had been taking money when we came in were standing near the door, smoking cigarettes. I walked past them and through the backyard toward the road. That was when I heard a male voice calling my name. It surprised me since I didn't know anyone at school yet.

She closed her eyes for a moment and put down the pen. Her eyes welled with tears as she tried to force the memories away. But it was no use.

"Hey, Hamptons! Bree, right?" he said, all friendly-like.
I turned and saw him jogging toward me. "Yeah?" I said.
"You leaving, too?" he asked.
"Yes, it would appear so," I said sarcastically.
"Well, I'm heading to my girlfriend's. I'll walk with you." He paused. "You know, you shouldn't be walking alone."

Great, the only guy I've met, and all he talks about is his girlfriend. Boring!

I rolled my eyes ever so slightly. He was acting macho, like I was some damsel in distress who couldn't walk the ten minutes home alone. I had done this a hundred times in far greater places than Syracuse, New York.

If he is some big-shot athlete, why is he not out with his team or his girlfriend? I mean, really, he's making sure I get home safe. Why does he even care?

"Ah"—he laughed a bit as we walked past a few parties—"I see you don't know the shortcuts yet." He said, "Come this way. We'll be home in a flash."

He motioned in the opposite direction we had come before. At least, that was what I thought. I hadn't been on campus or even off campus very much, and I knew little about how to get from point A to point B yet.

"If you say so," I said, utterly disinterested.

"I do," was all he said as he began walking in the other direction.

I considered not following him. I even stopped in the middle of the street, but he never turned or motioned toward me in the least, so I began to follow. We walked for a few minutes down the sidewalk. We even passed a few drunken field hockey players being hazed by the seniors. It did little to entertain me.

Last Goodbye

As we continued to walk, I seriously hoped I wouldn't ever meet this guy's girlfriend and become friends because that would mean I'd have to hang out with him more. I could not have been less interested at this point.

I followed him toward the path behind one of the buildings. I could see the glow of the streetlights from campus ahead.

"Ladies first," he said as he pulled back the brushes of a tree that shaded the path.

"Sure," I said halfheartedly.

I heard him chuckle a bit. It was then I realized that there was no path and that this was not a good situation. The skin prickled on my neck, and before I could turn, his arm grabbed me around my shoulders. He squeezed hard. I went to scream, but he covered my mouth and nose with his other hand.

I knew then that there would be no one to protect me, no one watching out for me. In fact, no one even knew where I was, except for him.

She sat for only a moment more before she picked her pen back up and pressed down hard on the paper as she wrote.

I'll tell the rest when it counts.

She scribbled her name on the bottom of the paper, folded it, and put it in the envelope Officer Murphy had given to her. On her way out of the library, she dropped it in the mail slot and was finally rid of August 31, 1995.

Thirty-Four

"Thanks for meeting me." Laura sat down across from Nathan. She wrapped her hands around the warm cup of coffee in front of her and then slowly raised it to her lips to take a sip. Her hands were shaking. Her nerves were on high alert.

"Of course. Sure." Nathan tried to sound happy, but it just wasn't in the cards for him today.

Laura stared at her cup of coffee. She took another sip.

"You okay, Laura?"

Inside, she smiled. Here was this guy, heartbroken, and he was asking her if she was okay.

"Are *you*, Nathan?"

"I've been better. Not going to lie." He shifted his eyes down toward the table.

"Well, I guess that's why I'm here."

"Okay…well, I appreciate your concern, but there is nothing you can do—obviously."

"Actually, maybe there is."

"What do you mean?"

Laura surveyed the room to make sure they were alone. She'd specifically chosen this coffee house and late at night with the expectation that they would be alone. Thankfully, she was right.

"Laura, you seem nervous. Everything okay? Are you okay? Is Abby okay?"

"Yes—well, no. I'm not sure. I was hoping you could help me. In turn, it might help you."

"What's going on, Laura?"

She took a deep breath. "What I'm about to tell you breaks all the unspoken rules and whatever of being a friend and even more so a roommate, so please hear me out before you.... just hear me out, okay?" Her voice quivered. "I really can't even believe I'm doing this."

"I promise. You have my word."

"Okay, here goes. Remember back to when Abigail got stuck at the Ridge overnight?"

"Yeah." Although he'd do anything to not think about that time.

"Well, she told everyone that she'd just run into Tank, but it wasn't true. Webber told me he could see them in the cafeteria. They were arguing about something. Which is really strange, but despite them arguing and their encounter at the banquet, she got in the truck with him anyway."

Nathan had had no idea that Webber had shared this with others. *Was Webber that concerned for Abby?*

The thought of others being as worried made Nathan pay even more attention to what Laura was saying.

"To be honest, from that night on, I started to notice a difference in her. Granted, she was in the hospital and all that...so for a time, I just chalked her erratic behavior up to her accident."

"She has—she did seem so strange when I went to the Ridge to see her. To make sure she was okay. I was concerned that Tank had been bothering her, like he had at the banquet. But I guess I never really let her tell me about it. It was just one thing after another...like the night she was attacked. Everything started to pile on."

"Exactly. Well, I know for a fact that Tank was not there at the Black Hearts Party, nor had he planned on being there."

Trying to appear as though he was following her story, he simply said, "How do you know?"

"So, I heard from Jessica that Tank had told her that he was going to be in his room, watching a movie or something, and that he just wanted to be alone. So, why would he then get dressed and go out to that party? Earlier that evening in the cafeteria, the girls and I had announced that we were all going, and that was in front of you guys, remember? Tank was there. Think about it. You, one, need a ticket to get in, and two, by the time Jessica spoke to him, it was only about half an hour or so before he was back in your room with Abigail."

Nathan's eyes were wide. "Laura, what are you saying?"

"I think he went there to watch out for her...to keep an eye on her, if you will. What other explanation could there be for him lying and then going straight to that party? Jessica was furious at him the next day. She told Bree all about it at the Cupid's Party."

Nathan was trying to follow along, but honestly, he could not grasp where Laura was going with all of this. "I guess, but the bottom line is, I'm glad he was there, whatever the reason."

"Of course! But I started to see how they were acting toward one another—the muffled calls, meeting up without telling me or anyone, and the secrets. Plus, there's the way he looks at her..." She searched for the right way to say exactly how she felt.

After all she had witnessed over these past few months, all the secrets she'd been keeping to herself, it was far more than she'd ever let on to anyone.

She took a deep breath and then finally said, "It's like...I don't know, Nathan...it's as though he *needs* to keep her."

"Needs to keep her?" he repeated. He thought for a moment about the words Laura had just spoken, and something—although he wasn't quite sure what—resonated with what she was saying.

Abigail and Tank's relationship was strange, to say the least. Their friendship had seemed to come out of nowhere, and he'd had this obsession with her from the moment he saw her picture in the paper. Then, add the run-ins, the fights, the night at the Ridge, his hatred for Nathan, and the way he watched her—it had always given Nathan a funny feeling.

"Laura, I appreciate you telling me all this, but in all honesty, I'm done. We are done. There is no going back. She made that clear to me the other day."

"But I'm not convinced this has to do with just Abigail and Tank."

"What?"

"Do you remember those flowers we told you were sent to me for Valentine's Day?"

"Yeah?"

"Those were from Tank to Abigail, but they were not exactly from him."

"What? I'm so confused." He sounded utterly deflated.

"Well, I knew she was acting funny about them, and then she devised that lie in front of you, so I immediately got suspicious."

"Okay."

"So, the next day, I noticed this in the trash, facedown." She pulled the card out of the front of her backpack, and with tremendous hesitation, she handed it to Nathan.

For as few words that were on the card, he held it in front of his eyes for a long time.

"Who's Jonathan?" he finally said with heaviness in his voice.

"I don't know exactly, but isn't that so strange? I have never once heard her say the name Jonathan, and then I see this?"

"Yes, completely strange. Why would Tank send her flowers from someone else, and why don't I know about this person? You don't think she was…I mean, is she dating someone else? That just doesn't seem like her." He sat back. He hated every bit of this conversation. *Just when I thought our issues were based off her lying about her friendship with Tank and that they believed I had been the reason Tank was kicked off the team, now, there might be someone else involved? Was our relationship doomed forever? Did I really lose her as quickly as I'd had her?*

Laura's eyes rose in excitement. "Exactly. And when, how? We see her all the time. This whole thing just doesn't wash, right?"

He slid the card back across the table. He needed to get the card away from him. He'd had a knot in his stomach for over a week, and this conversation wasn't making anything better. He had been feeling so depressed and lonely that he had even contemplated taking a week off to go home and see his dad. He wanted to ask his dad how he'd gotten so lucky in love and how Nathan had not.

He couldn't eat or sleep or concentrate on anything. Every day, he'd pray that he would run into Abigail on campus to catch her eye just for a brief moment, that she would walk up to him and explain how it had all gone so wrong for them. Instead, he hadn't seen her once—not by the fireplace in the union, not getting coffee, not in the cafeteria, not even with Tank. It was like she never existed, and it was the worst feeling in the world.

"Exactly. So, Laura, how is this conversation supposed to help me? To be honest, it is making me feel worse, and right now, I think I just need to start getting over her."

She waited for him to regard her before she said, "If I thought you really meant that, I wouldn't be here."

He was speechless.

She added, "I just think something is not right with her. Something is eating away at her. I can see it. I've *been* seeing it. Even during the good times, something is looming over her. And if I even try to ask her anything with Tank around…well, he just glares at me, like a bear protecting its cub. It's almost eerie."

"I know. I've seen it. He has lashed out at me over her a few times."

"Precisely! It's like he has a hold over her somehow."

"Did she ever tell you about the night of the football banquet? It was so weird. I could never figure out why. I always assumed he was just in love with her or something."

"She did tell me about that night, which made me even more suspicious. Well, maybe *suspicious* is not the right word, but I thought it was weird that they became friends."

"Me, too. And I kind of felt like a jerk for trying to get in the way of her being friends with people. But I don't trust him. You hear about all those stories when a person feels indebted to someone for saving them, so after he'd fought off her attacker, I tried to be sensitive of that."

Laura's smile indicated a hint of sadness.

"What?" he asked.

"I don't know. What you just said, I guess, makes me feel even worse for doing this."

"Doing what exactly?"

"Telling you all this and…"

"And…" he urged her to continue.

"And…for, well, this." She turned and unzipped her backpack that hung on the chair. "You told me you'd keep an open mind. You promised, remember?"

"Yeah. What is it?"

She turned back around and carefully put the book on the table, as though it would break if not handled with the utmost care. She slid it across the table toward him as she mumbled, "She might never forgive me for this."

Too intrigued for a moment to care about the relationship between Laura and Abigail, he reached for the book and brought it closer to him. He opened the book to the first page and gasped.

Abigail had the room to herself yet again. These days, it seemed like she and Laura were on different schedules. She wondered if that was on purpose. They were drifting apart, and she hated it. In fact, she was drifting apart from everyone, except Tank.

She sat down at her desk, pulled out her journal, took a deep breath, and put her pen to the paper.

> *I wish this dark cloud over my head would disperse. I feel terrible. It's been eight days since I last spoke with Nathan. He hasn't even called or anything. I never told him that the police arrested the guy who had attacked me. I guess I can just add that to the long list of things I never told him.*

> *I feel terrible about how it all ended. Why did I not try to stop him? I guess I'm just mad that he had something to do with Tank losing his scholarship. I mean, he had a full ride, and if he gets kicked off*

for disciplinary action, the school can take it all away. He has a hearing on it in April to see what is going to happen for next year.

Can't Nathan see that I'm just so angry about that? The fact that he hasn't even tried to call to tell me otherwise just reaffirms Tank and I are right. He did have something to do with it.

But that doesn't mean I don't think about him all day. It's killing me. I miss him. Tank doesn't understand that I love Nathan. I just do, and I guess that will just take time for me to get over. A long time.

I am going to meet Will this weekend. I'm nervous, and I have no idea why. That's not true. I know exactly why I'm nervous to meet him. I just don't want to talk about it.

"What is this?" Nathan turned another page.

"I'm not sure. I was hoping you might know something about it," Laura said.

"No. Why would I? She dated James, that guy from high school. I have no idea who this is. Hard to tell from a drawing, but obviously, they know one another." His voice was incredibly sad.

"Yeah, but how does Tank know him?"

"What do you mean?"

"I overheard them talking about seeing him this weekend but not to talk about the book when he is around. So, I'm assuming it's the person in the drawings that is coming."

"What? This weekend? Him?" He pointed to the open page. "Where?"

"Not sure. They didn't say, but he's coming, and to be honest, Abigail didn't sound all that thrilled. Then again, I could only make out bits and pieces of the conversation, but I got the impression that Tank gave this book to Abigail."

"We have to find out. I need to know if this is why we broke up." He sounded disgusted.

"Honestly, Nathan, I need to know that she is okay." She searched his face. "She doesn't seem like herself."

"I agree. She hasn't for a long time." He glanced back down at the book. He ran his hand over the page and then slowly turned it. Each page contained more and more details, and a bigger knot formed in his stomach.

He had the sudden urge to scream, yell, throw a tantrum…anything to get these feelings out of the pit of his stomach, but unfortunately for Nathan, that was not in his nature. He was not that type of guy, no matter how hard he wished in that moment that he were.

He flipped through the book until he got to the last page. "This is dated just last year, almost to the exact date as today. So, this book or journal or whatever you call it is relatively new." He paused, his face twisted in anguish. "Wait, there is no way that Tank and Abby knew each other last year, right?"

"No idea. This is so strange. Something is definitely going on with them."

"I agree, and thank you for telling me all this. She might not know it now, but you're a good friend."

"I hope so."

"You are. And maybe I need to be a better one to her as well."

"I think you are by just caring about her even if it is from a distance."

"Yeah, but from what I just gathered in this book, at a distance is where she wants me to stay. It's pretty clear that we just weren't meant to be." He was so sad and handed the book back to Laura. "Here, before she knows it's gone."

"I'm so sorry, Nathan." Laura was unable to make eye contact with him as he put on his coat.

"Don't be." He sighed. "She's lucky to be so loved. Isn't that what we all want for her?"

Thirty-Five

FEBRUARY 24, 1996

Abigail scrutinized over her outfit for way too long. She was trying not to be obvious to Laura that she cared, but Laura had hardly glanced up from her book in hours.

She had her headphones on, and the only thing she had said to Abigail in the last few hours was, "If you need me, just tap me on the shoulder. I'll have the music on while I study."

Abigail smoothed down her hair again and waited patiently for Tank to call even though she pretended to just be gathering her books for the library, which was where she'd told Laura she was going to meet her study group.

Finally, the phone rang. Laura didn't even flinch.

Out of sight, Abigail picked it up. "Hello?"

"Hey. It's Tank. You ready?"

"Yep. Where to?"

"We'll go back to Jimmy's place."

"Oh no, not another hangover." She nervously chuckled.

"Let's not repeat that. Besides, I want to drive back, not get stuck there all night. We might have to join Will at his hotel to show him the book."

"I know."

"Okay, so…"

"Okay…the No Nickname it is."

"I'll meet you out front in ten."

"See you then." She gently hung up the phone and peered around the corner.

Laura was humming some tune and taking notes on her notebook, oblivious.

Abigail walked in front of her and tapped her on the shoulder. Laura hit pause on her Discman.

"You heading to the library now?" Laura asked as she peeled one of her headphones off.

"Yep, cramming, so it might be a late one. But I'll see you later, okay?"

"Okay, cool. See you later."

Laura waited for the door to close and then about five minutes more before she crossed the room and went over to the window. She observed Abigail peer over her shoulder before she climbed into Tank's truck.

Laura grabbed the phone. "Hey."

"Hey. So, I'm guessing she's gone?"

"Yep, someplace named the No Nickname? Never heard of it."

"Me neither. Let me call the directory. I'll call you back." Nathan hung up and called the directory.

The address was listed, but the woman said it was one town over. He hung up.

"Hey, me again," he said after Laura picked up the phone. "It's a hike outside of town, so I'm going to see if I can find this place."

"Okay. Well, good luck, Nathan."

"I'll need it."

As Nathan drove to the bar, he went over and over every scenario possible in his head—what he'd say if Tank said this or if Abby said that, what he would do if a fight broke out. Tank could be awfully aggressive, but Nathan hoped that by being in a public place—a bar, no less—that it would be taken care of quickly.

What if this guy is really there? Who is he, and how do they all know one another? Do I want all my questions answered? Could this be the definitive end of me and Abby? In her eyes, is it already over? Is she over me?

He had not heard from her, and he was heartbroken over her accusations. The more miles that clicked off the odometer, the more he sensed he was driving closer to the end of him and Abby—for good.

Tank's face said it all as Abby got into the car. "Damn, Abby, aren't you a pretty little thing!"

Blood rushed to her cheeks as she closed the car door. "Tank, don't say that."

"Why not? It's true."

"I'm just nervous; that's all."

"No reason to be."

"Easy for you to say."

"A simple *thank you* would suffice."

"Thank you, Tank."

He pulled out onto Main Street. They were silent for most of the ride, which was typical for them. Abigail let out a deep sigh. She tried to shake her nerves as best as she could, but nothing was working.

"What time is he coming?"

"I said he should meet us there at eight."

She glanced at the clock on the dash. The dim numbers glowed *7:23*. *Good, because I need some time to sit and relax.*

Within minutes, Tank pulled into the sparse parking lot, which was typical for early evening. He saw Jimmy's car near the side, next to the dumpster. The faint light from the back-door sign lit up the rest of the parking lot. He parked next to a Toyota Camry with an Onondaga State Hawks football sticker on the back. He sneered at the sticker.

"You bring the book?" he asked with hesitation.

"Yes."

"Okay, well, let's not tell him right away. Don't want to freak him out or whatever." He pushed open his door.

He started to walk around to open Abby's door, but she had already begun to climb out. She put her messenger bag on her shoulder.

"I was just coming to help you, woman." He snickered.

"I'm sure you could."

"Want me to carry you?" He pretended to pick her up.

She squealed as she tried to move away. They both laughed. She peered up at him. For the first time in days, Tank seemed at ease, more relaxed than he had lately. She wanted to feed off that and try to make the best of the evening. She decided to keep an open mind and, if nothing else, take her attention off her life on campus to focus on her life here, tonight, with Tank and Will.

Tank pulled open the door and allowed her to go inside. She walked past the restrooms and neon lights and went into the bar. It was quiet. There were maybe eight locals or townies sitting at the bar and a few at some of the tables. A group of guys were playing darts near the back wall. There were no other women in the bar. She was the only one.

Jimmy yelled, "Big guy!" He waved and then waited for Abigail to acknowledge him before shouting, "Moon Pie! You're back. Good to see you."

"Nice to see you, too, Jimmy."

He reached underneath the bar and grabbed two cold beers. He popped the tops and set them on the bar.

Tank swiped them. "Good to see you, Jimmy."

"You, too, buddy."

Tank turned to Abigail. "Let's sit in the back."

Abigail headed toward the tables near the back wall. She set her bag on the empty chair and took off her coat. With relief, she sat down.

He put the beer in front of her and then sat down next to her.

"Don't they have anything better than Natty Light?" she asked.

"Since when are you a beer snob?" He laughed.

"Since I had taste buds, I assume." Her level of sarcasm was perfect.

"Ha! Natural Light happens to be a high-end cheap beer." He took another long sip. "Yum!" he boasted.

She took a sip. "At least it's cold." She noticed the clock behind the bar read 7:33. She let out a long sigh.

Surprisingly, he rested his hand on hers. "Don't be nervous, okay? He knows nothing yet, honest, so there's nothing to be worried about."

"Yeah, but just because he knows nothing doesn't mean that I don't."

"You're right. I just thought that might make you feel a little better, no?"

"I guess, yeah."

"Good. So, just relax for now. Drink your crappy beer, and we can talk about something else."

"Okay. Like what?"

"No idea. Don't girls always have something to talk about?"

"Seriously, Tank, did you really just say that?" She laughed.

"Yeah, I did." He was brimming with confidence.

"Okay, fine then. Let's talk girl stuff." Before he could protest, she probed, "So, what's up with you and Jessica? On or off?"

He quickly said, "Off."

"Why?"

"I don't know."

"When was the last time you spoke?"

She wasn't about to let him get away with one-worded answers. If he thought for one second that he was going to get her to shut up, he was dead wrong.

"At the Cupid's Party."

"What happened?"

"She was mad."

"Why?"

"Because she was."

"You must know why."

He took a long sip. "Of course I do," he said dryly.

"You going to make me work for this, aren't you?" She then quickly said, "Because she doesn't trust you?"

"What? No. Why would you say that?"

She smirked. "No idea."

"Try again."

"She doesn't think you pay attention to her."

"Something like that."

"Jealous?"

"Yep."

"Me?"

"Yep."

"Too easy," Abigail said.

"I knew you'd get it."

"She glares at me with daggers."

"I know."

"Don't let this ruin it," she said after a long silence. "It's not fair to you, Tank."

"We'll see."

"You try calling her?"

He didn't want to admit that he had tried calling her, numerous times in fact. But he had. "Yeah, couldn't help it. She hasn't returned my calls."

"Try again."

"Why are you so hell-bent on me trying?" He gave her a quizzical tip of his head.

She took a sip of her beer, trying to avoid the question.

"Huh? Why?"

"Don't know. Just 'cause."

"Not buying it. Why would you want to help her? She's always glaring at you."

"Yeah, well, she doesn't know why, so I feel bad, I guess. I don't know. You're different around her—that is, when I'm not around, I assume."

"How do you know?"

"I don't. I just know I'm the one causing the problems, so…"

"So, you think, by pushing us back together, you won't feel guilty about her not talking to me anymore?"

"What? No! Hey, that's not fair." She frowned.

He quickly said, "I'm only kidding."

But, really, he wasn't, and she knew it.

"I didn't mean it the way it sounded. I apologize," he said.

"That's the funny thing about words, Tank." There was a slight edge to her voice. "Once they're spoken, you can't take them back."

"Point taken, Abby. You're right. It's easier to think us not working out has to do with all of this, but in reality, I just never showed her I liked her."

She couldn't believe he was talking about this, let alone admitting he had feelings for Jessica. His face softened when he talked about Jessica for the first time since Abigail and Tank met.

"Well…call her again."

"Can we change the subject?"

"Sure." She regarded the beer in her hands and let out a sigh.

There was silence before she heard Tank say, "Hey, over here!"

From the corner of her eye, she saw Tank motion with his arm. Her heart began to race as she glanced up at Tank.

He whispered to her, "He's here."

It was like something out of a movie. The room, the voices, the movements all seemed to slow down. Will turned toward them and began to walk in the direction of their table. She swallowed hard. He undoubtedly was Jonathan's brother. It was unsettling how much he resembled Jonathan—at least from what she could tell from the drawings and pictures. Will was tall and slender with slightly messy, short brown hair. He had big brown eyes and walked with tremendous confidence for a seventeen-year-old kid walking into a bar. He had a killer smile, just like his brother's, yet she was barely able to crack a smile back. Her cheeks flushed crimson.

"You're staring," Tank said under his breath, snapping her out of her own thoughts.

"Sorry. This is freaky. They look exactly alike!" she said quietly through gritted teeth.

"Just be cool, will you? Relax." He gently patted her leg.

Tank stood and gave Will a big hug. "Hey, man! Looking good, Will."

"Hey, buddy. Great to see you."

"Always. How's your mom and dad?" Tank asked.

"Good. They said to say hello."

Feeling out of place, she sat perfectly still as they caught up.

Will turned to Abigail.

That prompted Tank to say, "Will, this is Abby."

A moment passed between them.

"Abby, nice to meet you."

"You, too, Will. I've heard good things." *I've heard good things,* she repeated in her head. *What am I? An eighty-year-old grandmother? Jeez.*

He politely pulled out a chair across from her and sat down.

"Ride okay?" Tank asked.

"Yeah, easy. Got here in no time."

"Team did well this year, huh?"

"It was a great year."

"Saw Coach last time I was home. Said he had some real good prospects coming up from junior varsity. Sounds like next year could be even better."

"We had some injuries that were a problem for us," Will said.

"He mentioned Danny's little brother there, what? Broke his leg?"

"Yeah, two places, no less. Not sure he'll even be ready for next year."

"Man, that sucks."

"What sport?" Abigail chimed in.

"Football," they both said in unison, only Tank's was said with more of a duh-you-idiot tone.

"Ah, of course." She felt stupid. She glanced down at her beer. It was empty.

"Beer?" Tank said to Will after he eyed Abigail's empty bottle.

"You sure it's okay?" Will asked nervously.

"We're cool here. No worries."

"Okay, sure. Same as her."

"Cool. Yeah, they only really have one kind, so…"

"But it's Tank's favorite," Abigail said with a smirk.

"Yours, too." Tank got up with the empty bottles. He made his way to the bar.

There was silence.

"So, how long have you known Tank?"

Good, an easy question to start. "Since…well…probably January, I'd say. You?" she asked, although she was pretty sure she knew the answer.

"My whole life. You like school?"

"Yeah, I do."

"What's your major?"

"Biology. I'm going to go into veterinarian medicine."

"Impressive." He smiled.

"Yeah, it's always been my goal."

"So, you'll have to go to graduate school, right?"

"Yes, four years."

"Wow, that's a lot of school."

"It sure is. And expensive, too!" She slightly laughed.

Tank came back over with three beers. He put them down on the table.

"Whatcha talking about?" He noticed their smiles.

"Just asking Abby about how you guys met and school."

Wait, what? How we met? Wait, does he think we're dating?

"Yeah, smarty-pants over here is going to be a doctor someday." He playfully punched her in the arm.

It hurt. She winced as she rubbed her arm. "You do realize your own strength, right?"

"Oh, Abby, please toughen up!"

"No, no, she's right. You nearly crushed my rib cage when you bear-hugged me earlier," he said, rubbing his side.

"See? Told you." She laughed. "You're…" She searched for the word. "You're…well, you're like a tank!" she said with a giggle.

Will laughed, too. "Exactly!"

He flexed one arm, and with the other arm, he slapped his own muscles. "Obviously."

"Jesus," Will said with wide eyes. "I see you've been drinking your milk. But you appear to be a little soft around the gut there, big guy."

"Ha!" Tank lifted up his T-shirt, clearly showing his washboard abs. "No way, dude. Rock solid."

Abigail couldn't help but peek. She had never seen Tank without a shirt. He was as big as she'd thought he would be. Her face flushed, so she looked away.

He noticed and pounced on the opportunity. "Drink it in, Abby!"

"Tank, stop. Not funny. Put your shirt down!"

"Look again, and I will."

Where is this confidence coming from? Is this how he is when he's in a good mood, or is he just acting like this because Will is here?

Calling his bluff, she looked again. This time, just to shut him up, she reached over and ran her hand down his abs. Shocked by her move, as if on instinct, he pulled his shirt down.

"I think Will is right. Feels soft."

With a horrified expression, he said, "Ha! Liar!"

She laughed.

"She got ya there!"

Feeling smug, she took a long sip of her beer as he glared at her in sheer disgust.

"Steel trap," he said, pointing to his head. "I'll remember that."

"Whatever gets you to work a little harder at the gym."

"You...ha! You think you're cute, don't you? You keep it up, and you'll be walking home."

"You wouldn't—"

"Oh, yes, I would. Right, Will? I can be a real hard-ass when I want to be."

"I'd have to agree, Abby. He sure can be."

"Oh, I know. I've seen it. But he can be a real pushover, too."

"Keep it up, Moon Pie—" Tank stopped himself, and it was noticeable.

"Moon what?" Will asked, leaning forward.

"Oh, nothing," Abby said quickly. "Just a silly nickname." She swiftly brushed off his question.

"We'll tell you later," Tank said.

Abigail glared at him and mouthed, *What?*

She thought they had agreed they weren't going to. To be honest, she had no idea what the game plan was. All she knew was that little slipup brought her back to reality. She had been enjoying herself quite nicely until she was so abruptly reminded of why she was here.

"Oh, sure," Will said.

Tank apparently thought the opposite. "So," he said, "my mom told me they were having a service for Jonathan on the anniversary."

Abigail could hear the air escape Will's lungs.

With a tired voice, Will said, "Yeah. Hard to believe, right?"

"I know, buddy. I know." Tank reached over and gently patted Will on the arm.

Feeling as though she should say something, she added, "Yeah, Tank told me. Sorry about your brother." The words stung as they left her lips.

"Thank you, Abby. March 1st will be a tough day."

Her eyes got wide. *March 1st? March 1st? March 1st! No, it can't be.*

"March first?" she questioned slowly, thinking about the last entry in the book. *February twenty-eighth.* She squinted at Tank and then back at Will.

"Yeah," Will said, not noticing her shock.

There was silence for a moment.

Her mind raced with unpleasant thoughts she could not shake. She knew Tank was glaring at her, but she didn't care. She had to know. It was imperative that she knew the entire story. It was to her advantage that Will didn't know her well enough to know that she was acting strange.

She kept her eye on him as her brain finally sent the message to her mouth. "What time?"

Tank gasped.

"Time?" Will said, confused.

"Yes, time." Her tone was cool. Her head swirled, and before she could stop herself, she said, "Time of death."

"Abby!" Tank quipped.

Abigail jumped a bit, but despite Tank's protest, she did not turn toward him. Will's eyes were wide, and he appeared utterly confused. She kept steady, waiting for him to answer.

Finally seeing that she needed to know, Will referred to Tank and said softly, "He knows. He was there."

She slowly turned her head to him. He knew by her expression that she was not playing around. She recognized the face he was giving her, making sure she knew what she was asking.

I do. I know exactly what I'm asking you, so please tell me.

His eyes searched her face, and when she didn't budge, he spoke, "Seven forty-eight p.m."

If she thought the hit Tank had given her on the arm hurt, it was nothing compared to the gut-wrenching pain that just landed in her stomach. She nearly passed out as all the color drained from her face.

"Abby, say something," Tank said under his breath. "You're acting weird."

She kept her eyes locked on his. *Something isn't right, but what is it?*

"Abby, please."

Snapping out of it for a brief moment, she said, "He's going to find out anyway, so…"

"Find out what?" Will was extremely confused at this point.

"*Abby*," Tank said again.

"What's going on here, guys?" Will asked.

A few moments of silence passed before Tank said, "Will, what I think Abby is trying to say here is…" His voice trailed off as he peered past Will and toward the main door. His eyes were wide like silver dollars as he deliberately whispered, "Holy shit."

Thirty-Six

Nathan pulled into the parking lot. His heart sank as he spotted Tank's truck in the first row. He wasn't sure what he'd expected to feel when he got here, but he hadn't been prepared to feel sad. He sat in his car for about fifteen minutes, thinking that maybe he shouldn't go in. He should turn around, forget all of this, and move on. But he couldn't. His arm reached for the car door and pulled the handle despite the words that chanted over and over in his head to just go home.

He walked around to the front. He stood frozen in his tracks as he saw them in the window. Abigail was here. So was Tank, and so was Jonathan. At least, it appeared to be the kid from the book. Nathan regarded them for a few moments only because he was unable to move, but then the fear of them catching him leering in the window struck his core. He pulled open the heavy wood door of the bar and entered.

What an interesting place. He walked down the hall and toward the main room.

The walls were lined with picture frames that had old newspaper cutouts of Onondaga State football articles dating back years and years. There were old jerseys hanging on the walls, next to dusty banners and old autographed footballs on a shelf. If nothing else, he assumed he might be welcomed in a place like this. He walked toward the bar and hadn't been prepared to be greeted quite so quickly, but alas, this place was virtually empty, and he was confident in thinking that no one had thought Nathan Ryan would be making an appearance tonight.

"Well, well, guess who just walked into my bar!" Jimmy announced.

The townies at the bar all turned at the same time to see who Jimmy was talking to. He was greeted with a barrage of handshakes, pats on the back, and offers to buy him numerous drinks, more than he could possibly consume in one evening. Nonetheless, he was much more comfortable than he had anticipated. He still had not glanced over his shoulder to see if they noticed he was here, but something told him they knew.

"Nice to see you kid. Name's Jimmy. Welcome to my dump." He laughed.

"Thanks, Jimmy. Appreciate it."

"Great year, kid. Great year."

"Thanks. You go to the games?" he asked even though he couldn't shake his nerves.

"When I can get out of here, you bet."

"Good. Next year, I'll drop by some tickets."

"Appreciate it, kid," he said with a slight grin. "You here to see your buddy Tank?"

"Yeah. Can I get three beers?"

He popped the caps off three Natty Lights and placed them on the bar. "They're on me."

"Thanks, Jimmy." Nathan tossed a five-dollar bill on the bar for a tip since the beers were on the house.

He grabbed the bottles in his hands and turned slowly toward the back of the room. All eyes were on him as he made his way, zigzagging through the tables. He kept his eyes on Abigail, knowing she wasn't able to meet his. Tank was, to put it kindly, sneering at Nathan as he approached the table.

Nathan set down the beers, and almost immediately, Will stood up.

"Wow, Nathan Ryan. Nice to meet you. What a season. Impressive." Will extended his hand to Nathan, much to Tank's disapproval.

"Thanks." Nathan took his hand. He shook it with force.

"Please sit." Will moved over a seat.

"Uh, thanks…" He waited for Will to introduce himself.

"Sure. Oh, sorry. Will Higgins," Will said.

Nathan stared at him. He resembled the kid in the book that Laura had shown him.

But maybe a little different. Who the hell knows? They were drawings after all. Why else would this kid be here?

"Oh, sorry. Thought you were Jona—"

Abigail reached over and grabbed Tank's massive forearm as his body began to lunge forward, like a cheetah ready to pounce. She pressed on his arm as she abruptly stood up, knocking her chair over. The entire bar went silent with all eyes on them. Her face flushed red.

She turned, and with pitiful eyes, she said to Tank, "Please don't, not here. Please." She was begging.

He slowly leaned back in his chair and crossed his arms over his chest.

She turned to Nathan. "Can I please talk to you outside?" Her voice was firm.

She started to walk toward the back door. Nathan, seeing the commotion he'd apparently caused, hesitated only for a moment before he turned on his heel and followed her.

Tank slowly leaned over and picked up her chair.

"Dude, what was that all about?" Will asked.

"Sorry you had to see that."

"No, I thought you and Abby..." He pointed to Tank.

"What? How do I explain this? She used to date him."

"Nathan? No kidding. But what's up with you two? Teammates and you don't say a word to each other? Something going on here?"

Tank started rubbing his temples. His stress level began to climb as each moment of silence passed.

Will waited patiently. "Hey, if it's none of my business, then just say so."

The last thing Tank wanted to do was hurt Will more than he had already been hurt.

"Buddy, they used to date, and well, Nathan and I don't get along too well and..."

"I get it. You, him, her—triangle? Can't say I blame either of you," he said with raised eyebrows and a slight grin.

"What? No, it's complicated. I mean—oh, hell. I guess I'll just start at the beginning."

Will's eyes were wide with anticipation. Tank seemed nervous, out of place, and anxious to speak.

Will thought, *This has to be good.*

Abigail stormed out in front of him. Two people from the bar were smoking under the neon light beside the door. Abigail hesitated. She waited for Nathan to catch up, but instead, he walked right past her and straight toward his car. He leaned on the back door and folded his arms.

There was silence as she approached him.

"You look good, Abby," he said right as she said, "Why are you here?"

"Ha!" He laughed uncomfortably. "Okay, so I see we are going that route. Fair enough."

"Sorry. I didn't mean to..."

You look good, too.

Seeing him again was breaking her heart, but she couldn't find the words to tell him. If she could only convey that just moments before he'd arrived, she had learned that Jonathan had died at the same moment she had her seizure last year. And that was not just a coincidence. But Nathan didn't know about any of this. He wouldn't believe her. He'd think she was crazy, that she was making up more excuses as to why she was always with Tank. She could already see the disappointment in Nathan's eyes as he stood there with his arms folded. This was all too much for her to handle right now. He shouldn't be here.

"No, it's fine. Reasonable question," he said, his arms still folded.

"Okay, so…"

"So…Jesus, Abby, I had to see if you were okay."

"Me?"

"Yeah, I'm worried about you. Your friends are worried about you. You do remember your friends, don't you? Spidey—when was the last time you talked to him?"

"What's that supposed to mean?"

"I don't know. Why don't you tell me?"

"I have no idea." Her tone was unwelcoming.

"No idea. Okay." He shook his head slightly. "Well, I didn't come here to cause any problems. I just wanted to see, to know for sure, once and for all, why we didn't work out."

Didn't work out…once and for all.

His words stung. She just stared at him.

Where is he going with this?

"I get it, Abby. Joke's on me, right?"

"What?" she said, shifting her feet back and forth.

"You, Tank—I get it. I get that you guys used to know each other. For reasons I can't explain, you didn't feel you had to tell me. He felt…" He tried to push down his emotions. "Jesus, my own teammate, Abby. He didn't feel the need to tell me that you guys were friends years ago."

She was as confused as ever. "What are you talking about?"

"This, you, him, that guy. What's his name? Will, Jonathan? Whatever. I'm the one who got played, and I just came here to see for myself. I needed to tell you—"

She cut him off, "What? How did—how do you know?"

"Know what exactly, Abby? Because you sure don't tell me anything anymore."

"About him?" Tears welled in her eyes. "Jonathan…" She trailed off in a whisper.

Seeing her pain, he started to back off, and with a soft but firm voice, he delivered the blow of a lifetime, "I saw the book, Abby."

Instantly, she was taken back to the day at the field with James, right before her seizure. The same feelings were happening. Her body began to break down, and her legs were getting weak. She started to experience something similar, and it was scaring her to death. She stepped back and balanced herself on the car next to his.

"The book," she said almost to herself. "But how?"

He didn't answer, and then it dawned on her.

How did he know I was here? How would he have gotten into my room and taken the book? How did he know all of this?

Then, like a ton of bricks had just been placed on her chest, it hit her, and it hit her hard.

Laura.

Abigail held on to the door handle.

"No," she said in disbelief, shaking her head. "No…she wouldn't."

"Yes," he said. "Because she cares about you, Abby. You can't blame her. She's worried sick about you."

"No. She wouldn't betray me," she whispered. A tear rolled down her left cheek, and she quickly wiped it away.

He tried to step closer to her, but she put up her hand.

"I'm here because I care about you, Abby. Your friends care about you."

She wanted so badly to say the same, but she was too hurt, too stunned to speak. She returned her eyes back down toward the ground.

"But you know what? I don't *need* you, Abby."

She whipped her head up to look at him, stunned again.

"I don't," he professed. "I never needed you, but I *wanted* you, Abby." He forced back his tears. "And maybe right now, they…" he said, pointing toward the bar. "They—for some reason you're not willing to tell me—*need* you, and I guess I'm here to tell you that you should be where you are needed."

Her mouth dropped open.

"But I can only hope, Abby, that someday, you'll look back and realize there is a difference."

She screamed in her head, *Tell him! Tell him!*

But nothing, not a peep, came out.

She was so torn. She had kept Tank's secret for months, and after all that, Nathan had found out on his own.

But what exactly does he know?

He waited, giving her plenty of time to speak, and then finally, he pulled open the car door and draped his arm over the top as he turned to her. "It's okay. I understand. You can't tell me anything. I guess I just came here to tell you that I'm…well, I'm going to try to move on."

The tears began to fall.

He went to get into the car. Then, he turned. "By the way, I told Coach I wouldn't play next year unless Tank was back on the team. It was never my decision, Abby. It wasn't my call. I thought *you* would have known that." He turned and faced forward, gazing out into the night as a few snowflakes began to fall. "Never understood why the guy didn't like me, but now, I do, so…I tried to make it right."

And with that, he got in the car, pulling the door tight. He put the key in the ignition, and with one swift turn of the key, all Abigail could hear was the deafening roar of his car as it filled the silence between them. She reached her hand out, but it was too late. He was gone, out of her life, and she was powerless to stop him.

As she slid down the side of the car with her hand still reached out in front of her, she landed with a crash on the cold, damp ground.

Nathan thought he had hit rock bottom the day he walked out of Abby's room—no, correction, the day she *let* him walk out of her room, but he was wrong. He felt worse now. Seeing her again was torture. Seeing her with them put him in agony.

He could only watch for a second in his rearview mirror before the sight of her became too much. Seeing her sink to the ground was like a knife stabbing him in the heart. But he couldn't help her. She didn't want his help. He'd asked, she'd refused, and now, he was leaving—alone. He had hoped she would have told him everything.

I expected very little, so why am I so disappointed?

Maybe it was because, for the first time in his life, he had fallen in love, and it didn't last nearly as long as he wanted it to.

The entire ride back, he replayed the conversation over and over.

Finally, as he drove down the winding road back toward campus, it hit him, and he said aloud, "Jonathan Higgins."

Abigail didn't know how much time had passed when Tank and Will came running up to her. Their voices were muffled, but she just sat there, motionless. She was—or had become within these past few months—a fraction of the person she remembered being. Sure, life always had its ups and downs, but sadly, the last time she'd felt up was when she was with

Nathan. He was always the same person. He never wavered, not once. She loved that about him, but she was slowly starting to realize why someone like him could no longer love someone like her. She needed to figure out her place in this mess before she could even hope that he would forgive her. He deserved better, and she knew it. It hurt like hell.

"Abby! Abby, are you okay?"

Tank bent over her, his massive body shielding Will's view of her. She was grateful of that. He tried to pull her up onto her feet, but no voluntary movements were coming. Just like the time before, he scooped her up, and with brisk steps, he brought her over to his truck.

She leaned her head on his chest, and with a slight whimper, she said, "I've ruined everything."

Tank let out a deep sigh as he allowed Will to open the passenger door to his truck. Tank placed her in the car and then shut the door. She couldn't hear what they were saying, but their words sounded aggressive and unpleasant. The conversation continued, so she slowly turned her body in toward the driver's side and tucked her legs up into a ball as she closed her eyes.

Finally, Tank came around and got in the truck. He placed her bag in between them and started the car. It was cold and it was snowing heavier now. Normally, she loved to watch the snow as it seemed to draw itself toward the headlights, but right now, she felt nothing and kept her eyes shut tight.

He let out another deep sigh before putting the gear into drive and made his way out of the parking lot. There was silence.

After just a few moments, Tank broke the quiet. "Abby, are you okay?" His voice was soft, tender almost.

It made her feel worse. Everyone was worried about her. She didn't know how to answer such a simple question because it was so complicated. But she was starting to realize that if all these people were worried about her, then there must be a reason, and she needed to start to figure it out.

So, she admitted what she had known all along, "No, I'm not."

She opened her bloodshot eyes and gazed at him. His expression grew somber. He turned back toward the road. The snow was coming down in thick, heavy flakes, leaving a beautiful coat on the road. She could see the headlights behind them as they glared into the back window of the truck. She was sure that Will was close behind.

It seemed like an eternity before Tank finally spoke, "I know."

"Just don't take me home, okay?" She closed her eyes again.

"Okay."

Thirty-Seven

FEBRUARY 25, 1995

Laura was surprised to hear a faint knock on her door this late in the evening. It was just past midnight. She pulled her wool sweater tightly around her body and slowly got up. She walked toward the door. She waited until she heard another faint knock.

"I know you're in there," Bree said quietly. "It's me. Can you…"

It wasn't what she started to say that made Laura want to open the door, but rather the strain in Bree's voice that made her unlock and open it. She knew who it was, however unrecognizable Bree's voice seemed at the time.

"Bree, hey. Is everything—" Laura was barely able to get the words out.

Bree pushed her way in the door and burst into tears. These were not the fake pay-attention-to-me tears that Laura had seen so many times before. These were real, and it was alarming.

Laura wasn't even able to get a word out when, all of a sudden, Bree turned and threw her arms around Laura, essentially becoming a heap of a person. This was, by all accounts, the exact opposite of what one would expect of Bree.

"Oh," Laura gasped as her arms swung around Bree's body.

Bree felt weak but heavy, like a wet towel. Laura sensed Bree's body sobbing, and all Laura could do was hold her still. She would wait for Bree to be done, ready to pull away, as Laura was sure this was a rare occasion at best.

They stood together until Laura finally reached up and stroked Bree's long, silk-like hair. It was incredibly soft and smelled of lilac and rose water. In that moment, Laura's anger with Bree from their argument in the cafeteria dissipated to a point where she no longer was mad at her friend. If nothing else, she felt sorry for Bree, the quintessential girl who always appeared to others like she had it all. Deep down, Laura knew better.

"Oh, Laura, I'm so sorry…" Bree started to say.

Laura gently shushed her, letting her know there was no need to apologize.

Finally, Bree pulled away. Her makeup was a mess, which was another rare moment. Her eyes were tired, as though she had not slept in days.

"No, you don't understand." She wiped away her tears.

"Okay. Is everything all right?" Laura asked.

"I don't know. I feel like I've lost who I am. Like…" She searched for the right words, but none came. With hunched shoulders, she went over to Laura's bed and lay back on her pillow.

Laura gently lowered herself next to Bree, paying close attention to her movements. She sensed a breakthrough coming, and she did not want to disturb the progression.

Laura reached over to the table lamp and switched it on. She accidentally touched Bree's leg, and Bree shuddered.

"Bree," she said softly, "I am your friend."

Laura's voice was sweet and kind. Bree peeked up through her long eyelashes and began to cry again.

"Thank you," she whispered. "I'm sorry I haven't been a—"

Laura quickly cut her off, "Would I be here if I thought for one second that you weren't my friend?"

"I guess not," Bree whispered.

"No, of course not. Now, what's going on, Bree? You can tell me anything." Laura observed Bree's eyes fill with concern. She knew what Bree was about to tell her was not good.

"My first night at school, I went to a party," she began.

Laura sat and listened, trying hard not to react to the horrifying story unfolding in front of her. She kept her eyes locked on Bree's while Bree talked about her first night at college, how the events that had happened changed who she once had been, and how the more she'd felt different and affected by that night, the more rigid she'd become.

After about an hour of crying, Bree finally seemed to dry up. "See? That's why I wanted some big and strong guy to sweep me off my feet—to protect me, to make me feel like I'm not just some stupid freshman girl."

"Oh, Bree. You have to know that you are so much more than that."

"Yeah, well, when you see someone who has it all and they don't even know it, it makes you wonder."

"Are you talking about Abigail?"

Bree hesitated and then slowly shook her head. Admitting that someone else had what she wanted, that someone else had the life she had hoped for, was much more than a girl like Bree would ever be willing to confess—that was, until now.

"Bree, if you think she has it all, you're wrong. No one does."

"Really? Well, from where I'm standing, it sure seems like she has it all." Bree was undoubtedly sad. "I mean, she has Tank rescuing her and Nathan pining over her, and she seems like she couldn't care less."

"That is not true," Laura said softly.

"Really?"

"Yes, you'll just have to trust me on this one for now."

There was silence. Only the ticking of the clock on the wall could be heard. Laura waited for Bree to speak as she could see Bree's mind racing as her eyes darted back and forth across the room.

"I think they caught our attacker."

"What?"

"Yes, I saw Abigail and Tank at the police station."

"Oh my God, what did Abigail say?"

"Nothing. I waited for them to leave before I went into the station."

"But you were there?"

"Yes." Tears began to well in her eyes again.

"Oh."

"After hearing what happened to Abigail, I decided I should have spoken up. Being afraid of what others might think is exactly what I hated most in all the friends I ever had while growing up. Maybe I cared so much that I…I don't know…"

"Hey, look at me, will you?"

Bree slowly lifted her head, and a tear moved down her cheek.

"You are not the reason this happened. *He* is the reason this happened."

"I guess."

Laura reached up and gently touched her hand, squeezing it slightly. Bree did not pull away. In fact, she leaned in closer to Laura and rested her head on her shoulder. Laura wrapped her arms around her. Bree seemed small and frail, not at all what Laura would expect of her. It was easy to assume that Bree's personality was strong; therefore, she must be strong.

Bree sighed.

"Is there anything I can do for you, Bree? Any way I can help you through this?" Laura asked.

Bree sighed again. Then, with a slight chuckle, she said, "Yeah, can you maybe find me a big, strong football player to watch over me? Maybe even two?"

"Oh, Bree." Laura laughed. "If I could find you one, I would have found me one."

She thought about Abigail and all she had gone through over these past few months.

Laura didn't know whether or not Abigail was with Nathan or Tank or who *the one* was. She thought of Abigail's accident at the Ridge, the woods the other night, and all the other things Abigail had endured in her first year of college. All Abigail's fights with Nathan and Tank made Laura think a lot about wishing for one thing yet finding the reality of it to be something totally different. For once, she was certain that Bree was wrong. Knowing about Abigail, Laura was pretty confident Bree wouldn't want that.

"Well, if you do, you know where to find me," Bree said.

There was silence as the two sat close to one another. It was an unusual instance at best, and Laura could feel their connection grow. It reassured her of what few people knew about Bree. She was kind, she was lovely, and she was, more than she knew, strong.

Laura listened as her breathing slowed, and so did her sniffles.

Laura didn't move as she spoke, "Bree, can I ask you something?"

"Sure."

"Do you believe there is someone out there for each of us? I guess what I'm asking is, do you believe in fate?" Laura's voice quivered.

Bree raised her head. Her eyes, swollen and beautiful, searched Laura's face to make sure she was not joking around. She was serious, and she wanted to know.

Bree sat back up. As if within moments of taking a deep breath, smoothing down her shirt, and tucking her hair behind her ears, she stated with utter and complete confidence, as though she had been waiting to be asked this question her entire life, "Call it fate or even destiny, but yes, I absolutely believe that, in one moment, our lives are meant to collide with another and change us forever. But I've always thought that chance meetings aren't necessarily unintentional. We can and should make our own luck in this world by opening ourselves to the possibility that possibilities happen."

And it was then that Laura knew Bree had spent a long time thinking about her fate and the "possibility that possibilities happen." A chance meeting had happened to her, and it'd changed her forever.

Thirty-Eight

FEBRUARY 25, 1996

Tank pulled into the parking lot of the Holiday Inn on Center Street just outside of Syracuse. Will pulled his car next to theirs and got out. He went to the back of the car, cracked the trunk, and took out his duffel bag. Tank nodded his head as Will went into the main lobby of the hotel to check in. His father had reserved the room for him because he did not want Will driving back late at night. About ten minutes later, he motioned through a side door for them to come in.

"Abby, ready?" Tank asked quietly.

She started to uncurl her legs. He got out and came around to her side, holding her crutches.

"Thanks," she mumbled.

"Sure. Over this way." He motioned toward Will.

She made her way toward the side door where Will stood. The wet snow soaked her hair and face. As she approached him, a pang of guilt washed over her, as it was the first time she had looked him in the face since Nathan arrived. She tried not to let her emotions crawl back up to the surface as she made her way past him. He gave her a sympathetic nod.

"Second room on the left," he said as she waited in the hallway.

The door was ajar, so she made her way in. Will and Tank were close behind. Tank was carrying her coat and bag along with a case of beer that he'd had in the back of his truck from the last football party.

She leaned her crutches on the wall next to the couch in the room. Then, she sat down and tucked her knees up to her chest, resting her chin on them. As she wrapped her arms around her body for warmth, she could feel her ribs through her shirt.

It had been weeks since she had eaten anything with real substance. She had mostly survived on plain turkey sandwiches and salads. Her anxiety over the situation with Nathan, Jonathan's book, and her diminishing friendships with everyone had all left her with little appetite, and it was starting to show.

Tank stocked the beer in the mini fridge while Will was in the bathroom. She barely had time to feel weird about being in this musty hotel room. She had so many other things on her mind that she couldn't possibly worry about this.

She could hear Tank twist the cap off three bottles of beer. She held her hand out slightly as he made his way toward her. He put the cold beer in her hand. She took a long sip. Will came out of the bathroom, and Tank handed him the other beer.

"Thanks." Will sat on the bed across from the couch and leaned back against the headboard.

Out of the corner of her eyes, she ogled Will. The striking resemblance to his brother was troublesome. If seeing this boy she'd just met for the first time caused such a stir of emotions within her, then she was truly starting to get an inkling into how it must make Tank feel. It could easily be him, Jonathan, sitting right there.

Finally, Tank stopped pacing in front of the window and peered out into the night. Then, he slowly turned around and faced the room.

She knew he was studying her, waiting. She took another sip of her beer and finally got up the courage to speak.

"Nathan knows about the book," she whispered. Before she would allow Tank to react, she added, "I don't know how or when, but it was Laura. I had no idea."

There was a loud bang as Tank slammed the empty beer bottle on the desk. He went over to the mini fridge and took another. He twisted the cap and threw it in the general direction of the garbage can.

Will raised his head and just stared at her.

"What are you going to do?" Tank asked her.

"What am I going to do, Tank? What am I going to do?" Her voice was hard.

"Guys, guys." He eyed Tank. "Please, let's not do this. This isn't going to help." His voice was calm and mature.

They both turned to him.

"Tank filled me in on…well, I guess what has been going on, but…" He played with his hands. "Abby, I'm just having a hard time with all of this. Not to say that you or Tank…"

Then, it hit her. This poor kid had lost his brother barely a year ago, and here she was, feeling sorry for herself for losing someone because of her own choices. It made her feel sick to her stomach with embarrassment.

"Not to say that you guys haven't been dealing with this, but..."

The silence was deafening.

Then, he said what he had wanted to say for the past hour, "Can I see the book?"

"Will, I don't think it's a good—" Tank was quickly cut off as Abigail raised her hand toward him in a gesture of silence.

"He needs to see it, Tank," she said.

"What? No, Abby, you don't know what that will do—"

"Tank, I can handle it. It'll be fine." He turned toward Abigail. "Please, can I?"

She slowly released her legs and put her beer on the floor. She took her bag and coat and made room for Will on the couch. He got up and came near her. He hesitated before sitting down.

She took the book out of her bag. "Please." She eyed the empty seat next to her.

He gradually sat down. She handed him the book. His hands shook as he took it from her.

"It's okay," she whispered.

Tank turned his back to the room and gazed out into the night. She could see his reflection from the windowpane, and much to her surprise, he appeared truly sad. It was as though the anger had finally washed away. He stayed like that for quite some time.

Will opened the book. Abigail could hear the air escape his lungs. She could almost catch the beat of his heart through his chest. She could not imagine in her wildest dreams what he was feeling in this very moment.

When he got to the first picture of her and Jonathan, he gasped.

"Are you sure," he said under his breath, "that you never knew him?" His voice was sick with concern.

"Never, I swear. I swear to you," she said in her sincerest and most honest tone.

"It's just unreal. I mean, it's you and him."

"Unbelievable, right?"

She sat next to him in silence as he flipped through each page. He read every note, every thought, line, scratch, and then he even went back to previous pages. She noticed one lone tear run down his cheek, and she knew he was starting to understand the severity—no, not so much the severity of the situation, but more the extremeness of this intertwined story, why the three of them were here now.

She didn't want to embarrass Will by getting a tissue or anything like that, so she left it alone.

Finally, he got to page thirty-two. He stopped at the pictures. Then, he said out loud, "Moon Pie? Is that why Tank called you..."

She quickly turned to him and gently put her hand on his leg. He stiffened at her touch. She hadn't meant to make him uncomfortable, but now that she had his full attention, this was her moment to show him exactly what they were dealing with.

She slightly turned her body, facing away from him, and she gently pulled down on her shirt, exposing her shoulder to him. There was silence. She let him take it in for a minute.

"My dad called me Moon Pie. It's his nickname for me. He's been calling me that since I was a baby. There is no way that..." She stopped to pull her shirt back up over her shoulder before she turned back to face Will. "There is no way that your brother could have known that, Will."

Will turned to her. "I don't understand what is happening here, Abby."

"Neither do I, Will. But I'm trying to figure that out."

Tank stood as still as a statue. He remained silent, which was unlike him.

"There is something I should tell you," she said. "I did not mean to offend you when I asked about when your brother passed, but, well, I haven't told anyone this, but what I realized tonight is that..." she said, hesitating.

"Tell me."

"I had a seizure last year on March first in the early evening. In fact, it was at seven forty-eight. I know because it was the last thing I remember, the last thing James said I mentioned was what time it was."

"Wait, a seizure? James? Do we know James?" He tried to get Tank's attention.

Tank still wouldn't turn around and acknowledge them.

"He was my high school boyfriend, and the doctors never knew what had caused the seizure. I was in a coma for a few days, and when I woke up, I didn't remember anything but the time..." Her voice choked.

Tank finally turned to face them. There was pain in his eyes, unlike anything she had witnessed so far.

So, she chose her words carefully. "I never felt right again, and I could never figure out why." There was extreme pain in her voice. She kept her eyes locked with Tank. She was no longer talking to Will. "I never felt the same. I couldn't explain it to anyone—not James, not my parents. No one understood. I always felt..." Her voice started to choke again, and her eyes welled up with tears. She fought them back. "I always felt like a part of me..." She wiped away a tear.

Tank finally spoke, "Died."

"*Yes*, a part of me had died." As the words escaped her lips, the most incredible sense of relief came over her. *Yes, finally, this all makes sense to me. Finally.*

She was able to understand what had happened to her a year ago and how it had been connected to the death of Jonathan Higgins. She truly believed now that there was a reason she never had any visions or dreams of Jonathan, like he had with her. He had known his life was nearing the end. He had known their paths were in some ways destined to meet, but he'd left before they had their chance. In doing so, her fate had quickly changed that evening last March. Her heart had broken a little because it knew someone she would have loved dearly had gone. Their chance had left this earth along with Jonathan, and it'd sent her on a new pathway, one directly toward Nathan Ryan.

She quickly came back to reality. "Yes." Tears slowly ran down both her cheeks. "But it never made sense…until now. Earlier, at the bar, it hit me. You can't imagine how much I worried my family and friends. It was awful, just awful."

She let Will take her hand. His face was wrinkled deep with concern. He was too young to be dealing with this. She tried to muster a smile in appreciation for his kind gesture.

"I am speechless, Abby. I'm so sorry. I wish I had known." He turned toward Tank. "How long have you known about all of this?" he asked.

Tank finally said, "A few months, buddy. Just a few months. As you can see, we are still trying to figure this all out." Tank finally walked away from the window and went toward the center of the room. He sat down on the other bed.

Tank's lack of acknowledgment of the impact this had been having on her life, both past and present, made her upset, so she quipped, "Figure what out exactly, Tank?"

Not in the mood to argue anymore, he said, "I don't know, Abby. I don't have all the answers here."

"You haven't had an answer all night, have you? Or in fact, the past few months. You just walked into my life and…."

"And what?" he barked.

"Tore it apart…"

Will quickly cut in, "Wait. Wait, guys. Come on, this is a lot for all of us."

She glanced at him, then back to Tank, and then back at Will again. "I'm sorry, Will. You don't need to hear all my crap. I'm sorry about your brother. I'm sorry about all of this."

"Ha!" Tank laughed. "You're sorry?" His anger was brewing as he, too, thought about the past few days for him. Getting kicked off the team, being humiliated in front of his teammates, watching Nathan take everything that should have been Jonathan's.

But for Abigail, she might never know if the laugh Tank had let escape from his mouth was meant to set her off or not, but it changed things between them. In that very second, Abigail became different.

"Excuse me?" she said, her voice as cold as ice.

His face transformed, too. He seemed bitter and angry, just like the old Tank.

"I said, ha!" he repeated.

"Tank!" Will barked. "Knock it off."

"No, Will, this has nothing to do with you. This is between her and me."

"Oh, really? Really? Now, this is between you and me, is it?" Abigail sneered.

"That's what I said."

"Well, that's news to me. But I guess I'm the idiot tonight then. This was only ever about you pulling me away from Nathan. Well, you won. I lost Nathan *and* my friends in the process by keeping your secrets. I've hurt everyone…all for you. You happy?"

"Abby," Will said, appalled.

Stunned by her own outburst, she immediately turned to Will. "That's not what I meant. I didn't mean…your brother… I'm so sorry."

Immediately, she sprang off the couch and ran into the bathroom. She locked the door, and she leaned over the sink as a wave of nausea hit her. She turned on the running water to drown out the noise she was making. She didn't want them to hear her throwing up.

They waited a few minutes. Tank let out a deep sigh. Will reached over and gave his arm a squeeze.

"Well, that sucked," Tank said.

"I know, but you have to put a stop to this, between the two of you, if you're ever going to make it right."

"I'm sorry you had to hear that, buddy." Tank moved closer to Will. "So, now what?"

Will leaned in and whispered, "Okay, here's the plan…"

Thirty-Nine

FEBRUARY 26, 1996

Abigail had done little to solve her own problems over this past year. Consider her relationship with James; she'd all but waited for it to end without doing a damn thing about it.

But what little she had done these past few months to solve her issues with Tank and Nathan was an all-time low for her, and she knew it. Broken heart or not, she knew she could have dealt with her issues a hell of a lot better than she had.

She heard the sound of their hotel door close, and as it did, she knew she was nothing but a coward.

She had stayed locked in the bathroom for the remainder of the night. She'd slept in the tub, wrapped in all the towels, as she prayed that something—not someone—would rescue her.

She slowly climbed out of the tub and turned on the light, but she was unable to check herself in the mirror. She was afraid she might actually see the real her, and right now, that was a horrific thought. She turned the handle, popping open the lock, and peered out into the room. It was empty. However much of it she deserved, it still made her feel terrible to truly be alone.

The room was littered with empty beer bottles, and the beds were unmade. The TV was on but with no sound. She went over to the sliding glass door and pulled open the curtains. There was a beautiful blanket of snow covering the ground. It was untouched, and as the sun shone down on the earth, it blinded Abigail's eyes, but she refused to close them despite the pain it caused her. She rested her head on the glass. The cold felt great against her forehead.

She was desperate for a glass of water. Her mouth was dry. She could not tell how long she'd stood there, resting her head, before her thirst overcame her, but it had to have been at least twenty minutes before she moved.

She walked back toward the bathroom, picked up the cup on the counter, and let the cold water run before she filled her glass. After two full glasses of water, she stripped off her clothes and turned on the shower.

She waited for the steam to fill the bathroom before she stepped in. The water was scalding hot, but she let it touch her skin regardless. Her lightly tanned skin turned red. She unwrapped the paper off the bar of soap and feverishly scrubbed her body until the bar shrank to half its size. Then, she just stood under the water, the suds falling down her legs and into the drain. She washed and conditioned her hair. Then, she turned off the water and grabbed a towel before tightly wrapping it around her body.

With so much steam in the bathroom, the heat became more than she could tolerate, so she opened the door a bit, letting some of the cooler air in. She wiped off the mirror, and for the first time, she saw her face. She looked exhausted, thin, and tired. She took the blow-dryer off the wall and began drying her long hair.

When she was done, she took her clothes and went back out into the room. She turned up the volume on the TV. It was then she noticed the light on the phone blinking. She went over and pressed the message button on the phone.

"Hello, Mr. Higgins. We received your message that you will be staying another night. We have charged your credit card accordingly. No need to come to the desk. Enjoy your extended stay, and if you need anything, please let us know. Also, don't forget that breakfast is included. Just give the waiter your room number in the restaurant."

She pulled on her clothes and went over to the couch to get her bag when she noticed the note.

Abby,

Sorry I had to leave without saying good-bye. I feel like we have some unfinished things. I'm sure you can agree with that. So, I'm asking that you meet me at this address tomorrow at noon. Please say you'll come. There is something you need to see.

45 Pleasant Street

Fairmont, NY

Please come.

Will

As she picked up the letter, she saw the room key resting on top of the book, which rested on top of her bag. Then, she recognized the Onondaga State football keychain. There had to be a reason they were making this so easy for her. Will had paid to have her stay another night, so she wouldn't have to go back to her dorm, and Tank had left his truck.

What are they up to?

She decided to go down to the restaurant for breakfast. She was starving and needed time to think.

She entered the main dining area and was greeted by a young hostess.

"One?" she asked.

"Yes," Abigail said quietly.

"Of course. Right this way." She sat Abigail next to the window.

Does anyone know where I am? Is anyone even looking for me?

She thought about calling her dorm, but the idea of getting Laura on the phone made her stomach churn with uneasiness. Abigail was still sort of angry with her.

She savored the below-average hotel food one bite at a time. It took Abigail almost an hour to eat all her breakfast. She signed the card for the breakfast and left a nice tip on the table before heading back to her room.

Once inside, her loneliness began to set back in. Feeling as sad as she was, she couldn't say why she picked up the book, but she did. She took the book, kicked off her shoes, and lay back on the bed. She let out a deep sigh before opening the book again. It would be the last time she would.

Abigail shut the book, closed her eyes, and laid her head back on the pillow. She was immediately brought back to April of her senior year when she was in her room with her best friend, Rebecca.

"Are you all right?" Rebecca asked.

"Yeah. Why?"

"I don't know. I was just asking you about the prom, and you seemed to fade away there for a minute. You feeling okay?"

"Oh, sorry. I feel great. I mean, I feel good." She forced a smile.

"Abigail, you know you can tell me anything, right?"

"Of course, Rebecca. I know that."

"So, about prom. What do you think?"

"Yeah, a limo with all of us sounds just great to me."

"Okay, but did you ask James?"

"He sort of was hoping we could go alone, but it's fine. I told him it would be way more fun as a group. I mean, don't take that the wrong way. It's not you guys. It…"

"I never do take it the wrong way with him. He can never get you alone enough," she said with raised eyebrows.

Abigail blushed. "Come on, give me a break."

"He's hoping you will," she said with an even larger smile.

"You. Are. Terrible," she squealed.

"Got you to smile! It's rare these days."

"Thanks," she said, thick with sarcasm.

"Sorry. It's just that you seem so different. It's hard to explain."

"Hard to explain."

The words circled around in her brain as her body began to stir on the bed. She opened her eyes. She knew what she needed to do.

She reached over to the phone and picked up the receiver. She dialed Rebecca's number. It rang and rang.

"Hello?" Rebecca said.

"It's me, Abigail."

"Abigail! Hi! How are you? Miss you. What's up?"

It was just the sort of response she needed, and it reaffirmed why she'd called her one and only truly unconditional friend. The tears began to flow down her cheeks, and she was unable and unwilling to stop them.

"Abigail, oh my God, are you okay? Where are you?" she barked.

Not wanting to alarm her any more, she immediately answered, "I'm fine, I swear. I'm…" She squeezed her eyes shut and wiped away the tears.

"Are you sure? You don't sound like it. What's wrong? Tell me." She waited through the silence. She was good like that.

Finally, Abigail spoke, "Rebecca, I have to tell you something."

"Okay."

She sniffled before speaking, "You have to promise me that you won't freak out or think I'm crazy or…well, that no matter what, you'll never tell a soul. You promise?"

"You don't even have to ask me that," she said sweetly.

Abigail knew it, too, but she'd had to say it regardless.

"I know," she said through her tears. "I'll just start from the beginning, I guess."

"Okay."

"You remember when I had the seizure last year?" she began.

"Yes, of course."

"Well, I think I've finally figured out why it happened."

Over an hour later, half of a box of tissues, and the two beers Tank had left behind, Abigail had finally told someone the whole story. The weight lifted off of her shoulders was immeasurable, and for once in their relationship, she'd left Rebecca utterly speechless.

"I don't even know what to say, Abigail."

"I know." It was the most Abigail had spoken in months to anyone. She was drained, exhausted, and emotionally beat up.

"But it does explain a lot about what happened," she said, thinking back to the days following Abigail's seizure.

"I know. That was why I had to tell someone. I just never felt the same again."

"Poor Jonathan. I bet, in some ways, you could have met him, right? Just once."

"I know. I feel terrible that we had this connection, and he passed away before I could feel it, but I guess I'm feeling it now, right? It's like our paths slipped by each other, only to come back around."

There was silence. She could tell Rebecca was letting this all sink in. It was a lot to take in.

"Wow. I'm just blown away by all this. So, you're going to meet Jonathan's brother tomorrow?"

"Yeah, I feel like I owe it to Will. The way he left and the way I behaved…plus, he said he wanted me to see something."

"I'd be more curious than anything. And what's the deal with this Tank guy? Is he a good guy or what? Because he sounds a little…I don't know…"

"I don't know either. He means well, I think. I'm not sure. I'm mad as hell at him right now, but that's nothing new."

"And Nathan?" Rebecca had to ask.

It stung.

"He wants nothing to do with me. Can you blame him? And besides, if I told him this story, he'd think I was crazy."

"But you said he saw the book."

"Yeah, but he thinks…I don't know. He thinks I used to know Jonathan."

"But you did, right?"

"I don't know, Rebecca. Did I?" That question traveled across the phone line in a thick, confused, and uncontested fashion.

Did she *know* him? She honestly could not answer that question. No matter how she tried to slice it, it was maddening.

Finally, Abigail said, "I have to go."

"Okay."

"I love you."

"Be safe tomorrow, will you? Call me when you get back?" Rebecca asked.

"I will."

"Abigail?"

"Yeah?"

"Love you, too. It will be okay. I know it."

"Thank you." With that, Abigail put the receiver down and closed her eyes, gently resting her head on the thick wood headboard.

Forty

Abigail could not believe how well she'd slept, but the silence in the room and the huge bed to herself had made it all but impossible for her not to pass out for almost thirteen hours straight. She had been exhausted, and her body had finally succumbed to months' worth of stress and anxiety. She'd slept like a baby.

She woke around eight. It was Monday morning, and she would normally be at her first class by now. So would Laura.

Abigail took another shower and dried her hair. When she came out, she found the checkout slip under her door. She'd have to explain the phone bill to Will, but she had every intention of paying for that call to Rebecca. She stuffed the bill in her pocket, slung her bag over her shoulder, and walked out the side door to Tank's truck. She drove to campus and parked on the side of her building.

She left her crutches in the bed of the truck and made her way up the side stairwell and right to her door without a single person seeing her. She gently put the key in the lock and opened the door to an empty room. She let out a deep sigh as she quickly turned and shut the door. She locked it.

She went over to her dresser and pulled out a clean pair of jeans, a navy tank top, and a dark green V-neck sweater. She dressed, closely watching the clock. She knew she had to be out of the room within half an hour if she didn't want to see Laura. She wasn't ready to talk about Jonathan's book. She took out her brown leather boots and put them on. She went over to her makeup bag and dumped the contents out onto the dresser. She quickly put on her makeup, then ran a brush through her hair and let it fall gently past her shoulders. She applied lip gloss and sprayed on her perfume.

She opened the drawer of her desk and took out her journal. She quickly glanced at it and wondered if Laura had read that as well. The mere thought of it sent a rush of emotions through her body. She couldn't help but feel betrayed again, but she knew what a lousy roommate she had been to Laura in return. She placed it on the desk. Then, as if she were leaving forever, she quickly shoved her keys, water bottle, two granola bars, her lip gloss, Discman, and a few CDs into her bag along with Jonathan's book.

She pulled out a sheet of paper from her notepad and sat on the edge of the seat. She wrote a note to Laura.

> *Laura,*
>
> *I know why you did what you did. But since we are both being honest here, I felt betrayed that you had gone through my things. I haven't been a good friend though, and I guess I can say that you've been a better one than I deserved. So, thank you. For what it is worth, thank you.*
>
> *Please don't worry about me anymore. I'll be fine. I've gone out of town for a day, but I will be back. Promise.*
>
> *Abigail*
>
> *P.S. You have my permission to deliver my journal to Nathan. It's the only way I can truly explain myself.*

She left the note on top of her journal. She stood for a moment in the room, staring at her journal, before she grabbed her navy wool coat and her green knit hat and gloves. She put them on and placed her bag over her shoulder, and as if she were never there, she disappeared into the side stairwell.

Tank stood next to Coach Stanfield's office door. Half of him was too afraid to sit with the overwhelming sense of doom that tore through his stomach, and the other half was just too afraid he'd wrinkle his suit if he did.

He waited patiently, trying not to pace or move at all. He wanted to seem composed even though he was dying inside.

Then, the voice came from behind the closed door. "McPherson, you out there? Come on in."

"Yes, Coach," he stammered as he struggled to open the door. It popped open, and he burst in.

Coach Stanfield was leaning on the credenza behind Coach Bromley's desk. His arms were folded. This was not a good sign.

Tank awkwardly sat down in the wood chair across from Coach Bromley.

"You going somewhere, son?" he asked.

"Yes, sir, I have to attend a memorial service in a few days, and...well, I thought I should wear my suit versus shoving it in a bag."

"Interesting approach." Coach Stanfield chuckled.

They both laughed, making Tank terribly uneasy.

"So, we received a call from the police station," Coach Bromley said.

Tank's heartbeat quickened at the mere mention of the police. He had no idea what was coming.

Coach Bromley continued, "They called to tell us that they arrested the guy who had been attacking female students on campus. As you might know, he was not a student or a football player here. Unfortunately, they have linked him to other attacks at SUNY Plattsburgh and Oswego."

Tank's eyes got wide, yet he had nothing to say, so he just listened.

"They wanted us to know they would not be pressing any charges against you for the assault on him. In fact, they have made it clear to us that had you not been there, they can only imagine what would have happened to Miss Price. His physical attacks on the other women were brutal, to say the least. The police owe you a debt of gratitude for your incredible ability to hit like a Mack truck." Coach showed little emotion when he spoke. It was clear he took this seriously. "With that said, you must be careful, Tank, as to who you hit off the football field. You have tremendous strength, and we need to make sure you are a bit more aware of that. That includes your captain, Marcus. That altercation was inexcusable."

He squinted his eyes at Tank. "Had that guy not been the one they were searching for, you realize you could have easily been charged with beating him, and that would have no doubt ended your time here." Coach let those words resonate.

"I'm terribly sorry, Coach. I tried to tell Marcus, like you said, but I just couldn't tell him about Jonathan. I know I haven't been handling my time here very well, and, Coach, it's cost me a lot—my scholarship, my place on the team—so believe me, I get it."

"I hope so, son. That's why we need to talk to you about next year."

"Yes, sir."

In the face of the uncomfortable conversation that took place between Tank and his coaches, the outcome was more than he ever could have asked for. Despite repeated attempts to fight back his emotions, ultimately, he was brought to tears. For the first time in months, he knew what he needed to do.

"Coach, can I ask you for a favor?"

"Seriously?" Coach said with sarcasm.

Tank took a deep breath, slowly let it out, and then spoke with complete confidence, "Coach, if I'm going to be back on the team, then I need you to trust me unconditionally, like you once did. If you do this, I promise that I will never let you down again. You have my word as a man, a player, a teammate, and eventually, a Hawk forever." He waited only briefly before he said, "Now, I need to borrow the practice van. I'll have it back no later than tomorrow."

Nathan sat alone in his room. Webber was at the extra-credit Biology lab, trying to make up for the fact that his lab partner had been missing from the last two classes. Nathan half-enjoyed the time alone, but the other half was tortured with his own thoughts, so a distraction would have been nice.

He'd sensed that Webber was feeling some of the pain he was when it came to Abigail. They did share a connection, and Webber had noted on a few occasions that he never saw her anymore. When he had, his voice had been strained. It had not been helpful at all since Nathan was missing her twice as bad.

As Nathan sat at his desk, trying to study, his thoughts, unfortunately, kept wandering elsewhere—that was, until there was a faint knock at his door. He got up and pulled it open.

"Laura, hey," he said with little emotion.

"Hey, how are you?"

"Fine. You?"

"I'm okay, I guess. I can't stay. I just wanted to give you this and tell you she was back, but she left again. That's all I know." She reached into her bag and pulled out Abigail's journal.

"Oh no, not this again. I don't want—"

She quickly cut him off, "It's not that. She asked me to bring this by, and it's the least I can do. So, just take it, will you?"

With hesitation, he said, "Fine. Thanks."

"Sorry."

"No, please don't be. I'm sorry."

"Well, me, too. Guess I'll see you soon, okay?"

"Okay, and thanks, Laura."

"Sure. Anytime."

Nathan slowly closed the door and went back over to his desk. He set the book down on his desk, realizing that it was different than the one Laura had shown him before. It was navy and bound with frayed edges. His heart skipped a beat, and his face flushed with anticipation. He sat down and turned on the desk lamp despite the sunlight. He opened the book and saw Abigail's name written on the inside cover, and he actually felt physically weak.

"Oh my God," he said quietly as he read the first page.

It was dated September 23, 1995.

> *I still can't believe James showed up at school this past weekend. I guess I would be lying if I said I wasn't happy to see him. I was. That's what I get for not calling him back. I always knew he was persistent. We have a lot of history. He has always been there for me, especially when I needed him after the seizure. He took a lot of flak from people, and he never wavered. He never left my side, no matter what. I guess there is something to say for that.*

> *Still, I couldn't get myself to do it. Yes, it. That's what I'm talking about. It just didn't seem right, and believe me, it wasn't easy to turn down a guy who looks like that, but I had to.*

> *In my heart, I just know he is not the one. The one is out there though, and when I find him, I'll know it.*

He blushed as he turned the pages, searching for the night they'd met. A part of him felt like he was invading her soul, reading her every thought, but another part of him appreciated her even more, if that were at all possible. He read the entry in which she'd recanted the night at the Ridge—meeting him, her first impression of him, the scene, and the people around her.

He turned the pages, and he read about when they'd encountered the photographer outside the dorm and how she'd felt when she saw the two of them, hand in hand, in the paper and how that had made James feel. She admitted that it was the best thing that could have happened for James—to see her with someone else, someone she had feelings for even though she was unwilling to admit it at the time. She went on to talk about how being in the spotlight with the freshman quarterback was more than she'd wanted—that was, until that week before the Christmas break.

> *He kissed me. He kissed me. He kissed me! It was the best kiss ever.*

That was all she had written.

Nathan fondly remembered that night in the hallway of the English building. He missed kissing her. His heart ached as he envisioned her. He started to question even more why they were so far apart today from where they had been back on that day in December.

He closed the book. He couldn't go any further. It was so painful, and he could not get himself to read any more about the good days or, unfortunately, the bad days that were undoubtedly in the book as well. All it did was reaffirm that getting over someone like Abigail Luna Price would be the hardest thing he would ever have to do.

He put his head down on his desk and closed his eyes. He let out a deep sigh. He needed to return the book to Laura. He shouldn't have it. He didn't deserve to have every thought Abigail had ever had since she started school here. No matter how badly he wanted to believe there were more good things in the book than bad, he couldn't bear to keep it in his possession a moment longer.

He stood, slipped on his hiking boots, grabbed his coat and the book, and reached for the door. He pulled it open.

"Jesus!" he barked as he almost ran into Tank's fist.

"Shit, sorry. I was about to knock."

"Yeah, well, I'm leaving, so good-bye," Nathan quipped.

He tried to walk past Tank, but he stood directly in Nathan's way.

"Tank, not now. It's not a good time."

"Yes, please just hear me out." His low voice was nonthreatening, almost pleading.

Nathan stopped moving and looked directly at Tank. Despite their obvious size difference—Tank being the size of a small house and Nathan lean and fit, like a swimmer—they stood almost the same height, so Nathan was able to stare Tank dead in the eyes. He scanned Tank up and down. He noticed the suit and tie, the serious demeanor, the desperation in Tank's eyes, and he couldn't help but back up into the room. Tank followed him in and closed the door.

"You have two minutes." Nathan leaned on his desk, putting down his coat and Abigail's book.

Tank laughed at first, and then his expression quickly grew serious as he said, "I'm going to need much longer than that."

"Really?" Nathan said with obvious sarcasm.

"Dude, please, give me a little break."

Nathan crossed his arms.

"Hey, I know I don't deserve a second more from you, but for once, can you please just let me say what I have to say? *Please.*"

Nathan took a chance. He closed his eyes for a moment and finally said, "Okay." He pulled out Webber's desk chair and offered it to Tank.

"No, thanks. I'm better standing."

"Suit yourself." He hopped up on his desk. He leaned forward, resting his forearms on his thighs. "Shoot."

Tank took a deep breath in and slowly let it out. He had prepared for this moment. He had known two nights ago, regardless of what happened with him being on or off the football team, that this moment, this day, would have to come. For once in the past several months, he had to do what was right.

I have to let it all go.

"My best friend, Jonathan Higgins, died last year of brain cancer." *Whew, the hardest part is over.* He had not spoken those exact words out loud since the day Jonathan died. In fact, he had never talked about it to anyone, except Abby and Will.

"He was a quarterback, a damn good one, and we had planned since we were in fifth grade to go to the same college, get football scholarships, play together, and have the best rookie years the school had ever seen."

Nathan's jaw dropped a bit as he began to realize the depths of what Tank was telling him.

"I almost didn't come to Onondaga State because I couldn't stand the thought of coming here without him, to play without him, to see someone else play in his spot…" He trailed off.

A realization came over the two of them. They were both frozen in disbelief.

"Oh my God, that explains—" Nathan began to speak, but he stopped.

"You have no idea," Tank interrupted. "I haven't even touched the surface."

"Okay," Nathan said, not knowing how much more he could take today.

"When Jonathan was in the hospital, he was really sick. I spent every waking moment that I wasn't in school by his side. Half the time, he was coherent. The other half, the doctors had him on so many pain meds that he would ramble on about stuff, all kinds of stuff.

"But the sicker he got and the more time went on, he would talk about *her*. I didn't know whom he was talking about, so I would just listen to him. Sometimes, I'd just try to be a good friend by asking him questions about her—what she looked like, her favorite music, what she wanted to be. I'd do anything I could to feel connected to my friend, who was so obviously slipping away from me.

"Then, he gave me *that* book. He told me to keep it. At the time, I thought nothing of it. Why would I have? He didn't have a girlfriend. I didn't know whom he was talking about. So, I tucked the book away. Not to say my life went on, but I guess it did in some ways. It had to. Until I came here." He tried to gauge Nathan's reaction.

Nathan appeared to be in the early stages of shock.

"I was going to try to move on, play football, just like we'd talked about. If nothing else, I was going to do it for Jonathan. But then she walked by me…coming out of the union."

Nathan spoke, "She?"

"Yeah. Abby."

"Okay, but what does that have to do with me then?"

"At the time, nothing. I mean…" He knew what Nathan was getting at, and he wasn't quite ready to go there. "Well, I'll get to that."

Nathan nodded.

"The day she walked by me, she was singing the song he'd told me she loved to sing, and I knew. I just knew it. It was her. But I tried to put it out of my thoughts. It was just my mind." He pointed to his head. "My emotions were playing a trick on me. I convinced myself of that. But still, it ate away at me. I was miserable.

"Then, I saw Abby in the paper, and I knew it was her, the girl from his book. But how could it have been?" He stopped and started to think about it again. "Right? How could it be real? But then, there she was again, with you at the banquet, where Jonathan and I should have been. Seeing her with you sent me off the edge. I felt like he was dying all over again. Not only were you here, playing in his spot, but—"

"Now, wait a minute—" Nathan started to protest.

"I know; I know," Tank interrupted, hanging his head low. "Just hear me out, please." He pulled off his wool coat. Beads of sweat had begun to form on his brow. He tossed his coat on Webber's chair. "You got any water or something?"

"Yeah, Gatorade in the fridge there." Nathan pointed to the mini fridge.

Tank grabbed a Gatorade and downed about half of it in one huge gulp. He took another deep breath in. "I know, Nathan. More than anything, I know now that I did not handle myself well."

"That's an understatement," Nathan mumbled.

Tank glanced at him with hurt in his eyes. "I deserve that, and I know it, but I'm trying now to make it right. I'm here to try to make all my wrong choices right again. I know what I did was not cool, and worse, I did it to two really nice people."

Nathan couldn't believe what Tank was saying. "Do you actually mean that, or are you just now feeling bad?"

"I do. I honestly do. But put yourself in my shoes for just one second, if I can ask you to. Nathan, it's her. It's real. As real as I guess it could be, and then the mark on her shoulder was the exact one in the book!"

Nathan couldn't help but let his mind wander.

How often has Tank seen the mark on her shoulder?

Has he seen her without her shirt on?

Have they been alone a lot, talking about all this?

Did it happen while I thought she was thinking of me?

Is all this the reason she became so distant?

Did they fall in love with the idea of all of this? The idea of her loving someone else? Is this why she always said, "It's not like that"?

He was quickly brought back from his thoughts as Tank continued, "Her nickname, the songs she likes, her being here at Onondaga State—I mean, it all started to come together as quickly as I felt myself unraveling. And then I did the exact opposite of what I'd told him I would do. He'd made me promise I would protect her...but I hurt her instead."

Feeling his anger rise, Nathan sat up. "What do you mean, hurt her?"

"I hurt her. I know I did. You can see it in her. I was being selfish."

"What about that guy...Dan, right? You protected her that night, right?"

"Yeah, of course. I had a feeling in my gut that she needed me. I can't explain it. I can't explain to *you* what it is like to be near her, to be around her, to see her that night. I was out of my mind with anger. What if I'd never met her? What if I hadn't been there to defend her?

"Her very existence consumed my state of mind and, unfortunately, my actions. I'd made Jonathan a promise, only I'd had no idea what I was getting into at the time. He never made me promise him anything. We were best friends, so he didn't have to. So, imagine for just a moment that what he thought he had with her or just knew of her, he believed to be real...so he made me promise him as though it were just that...real." His last words dropped off. The exhaustion was setting in with Tank. He was tired, physically and emotionally. He dropped his head as the color drained from his skin.

"Dude, you okay?" Nathan had to ask.

"Yeah, don't worry about me."

"For what it's worth, I felt helpless—pissed in fact—that I wasn't there to protect her. But then again, you seemed to always be there..." Nathan's voice almost sounded sad. He was disappointed that he couldn't connect with Abby like Tank had. He didn't know when she needed protecting, and it made him realize even more that maybe he just wasn't the one for her.

"Well, I'm just glad they arrested him; that's all. I went to the police station with her, and she identified him."

Nathan's heart sank. His eyes were despondent.

Tank slowly spoke, "Oh...you didn't know."

"No, I had no clue."

"That's probably my fault, too. It was the day I got kicked off the team."

"You mean, the day *I* kicked you off," Nathan said with anger. Then, unable to help himself, he added, "The day you and Abby got drunk, the day we were all looking for her—*my* girlfriend—and she was off with you, believing that I'd had something to do with you getting kicked off the team. She believed what you told her!" He let out an exasperated sigh.

"I know; I know. I deserve every word of this."

"You're damn right you do!" he barked.

"I know. You won't hear me say otherwise, and to add insult to injury, we might as well consider all the other things I've done. The Ridge? It was my fault she was there. I chased her there, desperate for an answer, anything that would tell me I was crazy. But all it did was reaffirm that it was her. She showed me her birthmark, and I knew it was her. I knew he'd called her Moon Pie. Then, I showed her the book, and that was it. I had her. She was hooked.

"We were connected forever, only we couldn't understand why. The more I realized we were joined, the more I hated the thought of you, the idea of you and her. You stole my best friend's spot on the team, and you stole his one true love, the only love he'd ever known. And I couldn't let you get away with it."

Nathan's eyes grew wide with disbelief. Even though Tank's words had sounded threatening, they had been as softly spoken as words like that could be.

Nathan stayed stationary in his seat on the desk. He could tell this was not easy for Tank to talk about. In fact, it wasn't easy to hear about either, but Nathan allowed him to continue.

"So, I pulled her away…and she'll tell you I didn't because she has a heart of gold, but I did. I made her keep my secret, and I had no right to ask her to do that. It's cost us both more than I ever would have imagined. I realize that now. I broke her, and I'm sorry for that."

"What are you saying, Tank? You didn't know her before you came here in September?"

"Yes, but in some strange twist-of-fate kind of way…I did. I mean, we both knew *of* her."

"I just assumed you were in love or even obsessed with her. And then Laura showed me the book. I thought it was someone else, and you were both in on some sort of sick joke. For the life of me, these past few days, I couldn't figure out why the hell you would both do that to me!" The tone of his voice increased with irritation as he finished his sentence.

Tank stared out into the distance, almost beyond Nathan, and he was quickly taken back to a day ago in Will's car.

"Before I leave, I have to ask you one thing. Do you love her?" Will said as they sat in his idling car outside of Tank's dormitory.

"Do I love her?" He looked over at Will, his eyes wide.

When Tank didn't answer, he asked again, "Do you love her?"

Tank slowly turned his head toward the windshield of Will's car. It was a bright, sunny day. So many thoughts passed through his mind. "Do I love her?" Then, he said louder, "No. I don't love her."

"Then, why are you doing this?"

"Why? Because I…" He hesitated.

Will interjected, "You promised my brother? Is that why you are doing this?"

"Yes, you know that is why."

"So then, tell me, what does she mean to you?"

"What do you mean?" Tank said, feeling his heart begin to quicken. Before Will could respond, he quickly said, "Because she is my friend."

"Your friend? So, you're friends. I can see that, Tank. So, let me ask you this."

"What?" he said, like a child being scolded.

"If she is your friend, then why would you do this to her?"

"Do this to her? What the hell does that mean?" It was the first time in Tank's life he had risen his voice to Will.

They were family, and where they came from, family treated one another with respect. But Will was out of line, and Tank had to let him know.

"Tank, have you taken a good look at the situation, at what is happening to you both? I mean, Jesus, man, look at her. Look at you, for God's sake!" he barked.

"Dude, lay off!" He began feverishly rubbing his temples. "Do you have any idea what I promised your brother? Do you? When we made promises, we kept them, no matter what."

There was silence.

Will waited for Tank to tell him more. He knew so little but could only speak to what he had observed on this particular weekend, and it wasn't good. He didn't like what he saw of his brother's best friend, not one bit.

"I made him a promise that I would protect her, and that is what I plan to do. I don't even want to think about what would have happened that night in the woods if I hadn't been there, watching, waiting to see that she got home safe. It makes me so mad. That scumbag preyed on her!" he shouted. His breath was heavy.

Will remained silent.

"Don't you see? I don't have a choice. I was not given a choice. I can't take back what I said I would do. And, yes, I truly care about her. My love for her is undefined. Christ, she is the only person who has ever given me another chance here. The only one."

Will killed the radio, as it had been playing quietly through the speakers. They watched for a time as the students began walking back and forth in front of his car, going to the cafeteria or the library or whatever, just as normal college students should be doing. It made Tank feel sad. He remained silent for what seemed like minutes.

"Was she happy when you met her?" Will asked.

"Yeah. Yes, I think she was."

"Does she seem happy now?" Will asked him.

Tank put his head down and shook it. "No, I guess she is not."

"Then, if she is your friend and you care about her, you need to let her go. Give her another chance at being happy again. Let this all go. I, more than anyone, know how you feel, Tank. But you have to do this."

"But I can't. If I do, then—"

"Then, what? You think you'll be letting him go? Do you really think that your relationship with my brother can simply be erased?"

With his head still hung, he said, "No."

"We can't change the past. It isn't an option, but you have some control over your future, Tank. I think you know my brother would not want you to go through this. This is not what he had in mind. She is suffering right now in that hotel room. That is a fact. Get your life back, man. You owe that much to yourself. So, stick to the plan, okay?"

He glanced at Will, his face serious, and in that brief moment, he could imagine Jonathan saying the same exact thing to him. He had always been Tank's voice of reason. He had, ironically, been everyone's rock. And that was why Jonathan was missed so much. And that was why, more often than not, Tank was lost without him.

"Jesus," he said with a slight snicker.

"What?"

"You're a smart kid, you know that?"

Will chuckled. "I know." He sported the same cocky grin his brother had had. "Now, get out of my car."

"You're just like your brother," Tank remarked as he opened the car door.

"Earth to Tank," Nathan said with a wave of his arm.

He was quickly brought back to reality. He knew how long it had taken him to grasp all this information, and he had Abigail and Will alongside him, helping him, as he tried to make sense of all this, regardless of the consequences.

But not Nathan. He had no one.

Tank noticed the pain in his eyes. "I know. It's a lot to handle. Believe me, we've been trying for months to figure this all out, and in the process, I made her push everyone away. I realize that now."

"Months?" He sounded hurt.

"Yeah, months. I mean, how could she tell you? *What* could she tell you? She was the ex-girlfriend or something of my best friend whom she'd never met before he died?"

"Yeah, well, maybe she could have tried to tell me." But even as he said the words, they sounded ridiculous.

"She couldn't, Nathan. I asked her to keep *my* secret."

"So, Tank, why now? Why tell me all of this today? It's done, over. I don't even know what I'm saying. This is all so bizarre."

"I know, but you saw the book, the evidence, all those clues, all those things that kept leading me back to her."

"Yeah, and?"

"Well, I'm trying to get my life back, her life back. I ruined my friendship with her. I hurt Jessica, you, my teammates. I got my scholarship taken away. And all for what? For what?" he repeated.

Although he knew for what—or better, for whom. It was Jonathan. It was always about Jonathan. He was the best friend he'd ever had, and although he wouldn't admit it now, he'd do it all again in a heartbeat.

"Yeah, you did. You let the team down. You made my life hell, and for what? For a spot I earned? I earned that spot, Tank! You saw the year I had. *I earned it!* I'd worked my ass off, just like you, my whole life. This," he said, motioning around his room, "believe it or not, was my dream, too, not just yours."

"I know." Tank, with overwhelming sadness, whispered, "It was fate."

Finally, Tank could see what he had done. He recognized that this was meant to be for someone else and not for Jonathan. Sadly, Tank was meant to be at OSU on his own, and although he hated the thought, it was *his* reality, and he had to accept it once and for all.

As Nathan lowered his head, Tank truly recognized the pain he'd caused Nathan, and he had to look away.

"And that is why you call me Two? Because, according to you, I was never going to be the number one quarterback?" Nathan was not able to hide the disgust in his voice. "In your eyes, it always belonged to Jonathan."

"Yes. Stupid, I know. So stupid. I was mad. Hell, I'm still mad that he's gone. Can you blame me?"

Nathan gazed at the picture on his desk of his father and mother holding him when he was three years old. "No, I can't. I still feel that way about my..." He trailed off. Then, picking up the picture on his desk, he said, "My mom."

It was then he realized the depths of what Tank was telling him, the torture and sadness of seeing a friend pass away and so young. It was just like his mother—so young in life, too young to go. No matter how many days passed, if you stopped for one moment and thought about them, you'd feel sad. It could come on at any second, tearing apart your day. You knew in your mind that it was not what they would have ever wanted to do to you, but it was a testament to how much a person, a mother, a best friend impacted your life forever.

The silence in the room was thick but necessary. There was so much history between the two of them, more than either of them had grasped until today.

"I'm sorry about your mom."

Nathan glanced up, feeling like he was meeting Tank for the first time. He saw a different person than the one he'd had countless arguments and scuffles with, the drunk who had badgered him at parties, the guy who had seemed obsessed with his life. No, today, for the first time, he saw a guy who had lost his best friend a year ago and had been suffering each and every day since.

Nathan sensed the tension release from his shoulders as he dropped his hands between his knees and lowered his head. He glanced at the picture of his mother, and he knew he was better than all this. His mother would have expected him to forgive and move on, and that was what he intended to do with Tank.

Nathan took a deep breath and placed the picture back on his desk. "I'm sorry about your friend. I had heard of him at Nationals. He was a great quarterback. Onondaga State would have been lucky to have him."

"You don't have to say that."

"I know," he said with conviction. "And the guy who was with you the other night?"

"Will. He is Jonathan's younger brother."

"Does he know?"

"He does now." Tank sighed, thinking of Will.

"Okay. So, thanks for coming by to tell me all this. I'm sure it wasn't easy."

"No, but I owed you at least a face-to-face explanation, and, well…"

"What, Tank?"

"Well, I need you to come with me. I have to show you something."

"Tank, really? Can't it wait? I'm not up for any more surprises today."

Tank stared at him for a moment and tried to carefully choose his words, but then he just blurted out, "You're coming with me even if I have to kidnap you, understand?"

Nathan noticed how serious Tank's expression was and couldn't help but laugh. It was the kind of laugh that grew the more you laughed, making it almost impossible to control. That was, until he saw that Tank's face never changed, not one bit.

"Okay, okay. Fine. Jesus, you are one pain in the ass."

"So I've been told." Tank grabbed his wool coat and gently put it on over his suit.

"I'm obviously underdressed," Nathan said.

"Nah, I've got to go home for Jonathan's memorial service."

"Sorry."

"Thanks."

Nathan pulled on his navy coat over his sweater and jeans. He took his keys, bag, and Abigail's journal. He shoved it in the bag before Tank noticed. Nathan would return it on his way home.

Tank pulled open the door and waited for him in the hallway. "This way." He headed toward the stairs.

They walked down the stairs in silence—if for no other reason than Nathan was in total disbelief as to what had been happening today, let alone the past few months.

Tank pushed open the side door and headed to the parking lot next to the dorm. He walked in front of Nathan, leading him to the van.

"Where—wait, what are we doing?"

Tank approached the van. "Get in." He unlocked the van door.

Baffled, Nathan went up to the passenger door and waited for him to unlock it. He got in as Tank started the van.

"Did you steal this? Jesus, Tank!"

"*Really*? After all I told you, you honestly think I would steal the practice van? Give me *some* credit, will you?" He backed out of his spot, the beeping noise alerting everyone around them of their presence.

"So, what's the deal then?" he asked curiously.

"Coach let me borrow it."

"Seriously? Coach let you borrow the van? What? Did you kidnap him, too? Is he tied up in the back of the van? Coach!" Nathan yelled toward the back.

For the first time, they laughed together. They were actually sharing a laugh.

"Ha, very funny. No, I asked him, and he said okay."

"*You* asked Coach? When? Today? So, does that mean..."

Tank hesitated a moment before he answered, "Yeah, and...I have you to thank for it."

Nathan wanted Tank to realize that, despite what he'd thought of Tank less than a week ago, Nathan had gone to bat for him. That was what a teammate did.

"Just remember that when you are driving me to God knows where and you plan to leave me stranded, alone, in the middle of nowhere." He smirked, and he could see out of the corner of his eye that Tank was doing the same.

Forty-One

FEBRUARY 27, 1996

Abigail pulled up in front of the white split-level home with the dark blue door and put Tank's truck into park. She checked the address on the note against the large black numbers screwed onto the mailbox in front.

This is it. She peered at the bay window that enveloped the front of the house.

She saw the curtain move, and her heart fluttered. Wherever she was, they knew she had arrived. The front door opened, and she realized almost instantly where she was—the Higgins' residence. She should have known.

It made her skin prickle and her heart pick up speed as she saw Will Higgins come down the front steps toward the driveway. His expression was determined but welcoming, much like the photos of Jonathan. It made her heart race even more. He showed no surprise whatsoever that she was here. He had known she would come. His confidence slightly bothered her since she had considered not coming.

He walked up to the passenger door and opened it. "Hey," he said with his killer grin.

"Hey," she responded softly, feeling slightly embarrassed about the events that had transpired in front of him the other night. "I owe you money for the hotel," she blurted out as she went to reach into her bag for money.

A bit surprised at her first full sentence, he responded, "Don't worry about it. Honestly."

"I insist," she said formally.

"Really, no, I insist."

"Okay. Thank you."

"Good. Can I get in?" he said with a shiver.

"Yes, please, of course."

"I'm glad you decided to come, Abby."

"Okay, but I'll be honest; I'm not sure why I'm here."

"If you'll drive, I can show you."

"Okay. Sure. Where to?"

"I'll show you," he repeated, waiting for her to put the truck in drive. So, she did.

He gave her turn-by-turn instructions but never said exactly where they were going. He'd point out a few things here and there along the way—the place all the high school kids hung out at, the best place to get pizza, the place they got together to play pond hockey, the high school, the movie theater. It was all the typical places you'd find in a town just like this, but each held their special attachment to the teenagers who lived here.

As they drove along what appeared to be the main street, she couldn't help but wonder what it would have been like, coming here and having Jonathan show her around, him taking her out for pizza and a movie. As Will sat next to her, she could see him out of the corner of her eye, and it was easy for her to envision what it would have been like to be with Jonathan. Their resemblance was uncanny, and she even imagined their voices sounded the same. She couldn't help but feel emotional. As the tears began to fill her eyes, she quickly grabbed Tank's Oakley sunglasses from the dashboard and put them on.

"This is hard for me, Will." Her words were filled, despite so few of them, with deep pain and sadness. Her whole life, she had been difficult to read, but now, she was an open book.

"I know," he said quietly. "Take a left here. I'm not trying to make things harder for you. Please know that."

"No, I do. The way Tank and I left it the other night, it's hard, and with you seeing all that and…" She trailed off. When he didn't speak, she said softly, "And meeting you. You look so much like him."

"I know. Believe me, I know." He turned his head as he let out a deep sigh. "Take another left here."

She turned down a gorgeous tree-lined road. It was like something you'd see in a calendar.

She could see a large wrought iron gate up ahead, and as she approached, she had a sinking feeling in her stomach. She slowed the truck down to almost a crawl as they came close to the gate.

She read the overhead sign silently to herself, *Pine View Cemetery.*

"It's okay," he said softly.

She didn't speak.

"Just go straight for a bit."

She hesitated and glanced at him. He kept his face forward, staring into the distance, and it was in that moment that she realized how much older

Will appeared. He was a boy who had been through a lot, had seen a lot, and this was only the tip of the iceberg for him.

Neither spoke until she made a conscious effort to press her foot down on the gas, slowly forcing the truck through the gate.

If a place like this could be welcoming, then this was just that. The weeping willow trees throughout the grounds, although sad in their own right, gave off a sense of peace. There was always something calming about a weeping willow tree.

The hard winter grass was covered ever so slightly with a recent dusting of snow. It appeared to be untouched throughout the plots, leading Abigail to believe there were not a lot of visitors here.

They drove down the small gravel road and up and around a small curve that led to a slight hill. As Tank's truck slowly made it up and over the hill, she realized the depths of the grounds within these iron fences, the amount of land still untouched. It was remarkable yet so devastatingly sad. Her longing to know Jonathan began to resurface. She wished more than ever that she had at least met him face-to-face.

But as each stone passed, so did each life, and it was then that she realized how fortunate she had been in her short nineteen years. She had had little time to reflect on death, and she knew how grateful she should be to have been afforded that—until now.

Tank's truck seemed to move forward even though she felt unattached to the steering wheel and gas pedal. The farther they drove, the more recent the headstones got. She sensed they were getting closer.

"You can park here."

"Okay."

She wished there were something she could say, but she had no use for words in the moment. She tossed Tank's sunglasses on the seat, opened the truck door, and climbed out. She had decided yet again to forgo the crutches—this time, for good. She pulled her coat tighter around her body and put on her green knit hat and gloves. It was colder out today than it had been in the past week.

Fitting almost, she thought to herself as she walked around the front of the truck to meet Will.

He stood, motionless, but for some reason, there was a tranquil countenance about him. It was hard to explain, but she got the sense he had done this many times before.

"Come." He took her hand.

Strangely, it did not feel weird to hold his hand. In fact, it felt natural and reassuring.

She followed him through the first row of headstones and then the second, making sure to be respectful of each one they passed. Finally, he stopped next to a large dark gray stone. He walked her around to the front, and she tried with all her might not to react. But reading Jonathan's name sent her into a place she'd never known was within her, and she began to cry. Will released her hand and draped his arm around her shoulder. He squeezed her tight, and for the first time, she truly cried over *all* of this. It was all coming to this moment. The tears that streamed down her face were for every second of her life she had spent since October—no, even since last March when she'd had her seizure. The tears were for that and every fight, every lie, every heartbreak, every injury and attack, the deception, the love she'd gained and lost. It was all for now, this moment, and it finally hit her like a ton of bricks.

She stared at his name chiseled in the stone that rested above the earth. Seeing his name sent a wave of incredible wretchedness over her entire body, and had it not been for Will holding her up, she feared she would have collapsed. He noticed her body give way, and he squeezed her tighter.

"It's okay, Abby. It's okay."

She could hear the quiver in his voice, and she dared not to look up at him.

"I don't know what this all means. I don't know what to do, Will," she barely whispered.

"I'm hoping you will find that answer today, that we will somehow figure this all out," he said with such care and sincerity.

They stood in the cold for what seemed like eternity.

But what is eternity in a place like this?

They barely spoke a word to one another as they stared at the stone in front of them. She thought of the life that had passed that she was so unknowingly a part of. This boy that now lay in rest had been in love with her, and she, in love with him. She felt, for the first time, to be a true part of his life. Standing here, next to his only brother, she did belong here. This was where she was supposed to be today. Right or wrong.

"Do your parents know you are here?"

"No, they don't come here much. So, I guess I'm the only one besides Tank..." He hesitated for a moment and then said, "I talk to him a lot when I'm here."

"You do?"

"Yeah, I guess, in some ways, I spill my guts to him. It's silly, I know."

"No, not at all. I'd do the same."

He laughed quietly.

"Do you think he knows I'm here?" she asked, not feeling silly in the least.

"I do, Abby. I certainly do."

"Did he ever mention me to you or just..." *Tank.* Instead of speaking his name, she just let her words drift off.

"Yes, that's why I asked you to come."

She had not known that. She'd thought the day at the bar was the first time he had heard of her. She was wrong.

The silence between them grew as he held her tight. She finally closed her eyes and rested her head on the side of his chest. She took a deep breath in and held it. She waited, not willing to breathe until she had some clarity. She needed some kind of a sign, an awakening of sort, a vision of what her life was supposed to be.

They stood, side by side, in total silence, still clutching one another. She could only hear the faint sound of a cardinal whistling in the trees as her eyes remained shut. Her breath held tight within her lungs. They burned as the wanting for new air remained, but she was determined not to let go. Then, as she neared the brink of passing out, it came to her.

She could feel him, and she could see him as she squeezed her eyes shut, tighter and tighter. He was coming near her. She began to make out his figure, this man coming toward her—tall, wavy and dark hair, beautiful gray eyes, slim, athletic build, and an incredible smile. She felt the warmth of his presence as he got closer and closer to her. Her lungs burned, and her heart quickened. Will slowly released her body, and she was weightless as she stood alone, her eyes still shut tight. Then, as if by some sort of intervention, a higher power of sorts, she knew it was time.

She slowly let out her breath as she began to open her eyes.

"Abby?" Will said softly.

"Yes?" She wiped away what was left of her tears.

She turned toward him, and much to her surprise, he grinned at her. It was warm, and she could not help but return the favor.

He reached over and took her by the hand. "I want you to know how much I appreciate what you did for my brother, that you gave him hope and love. Quite honestly, it's something we might never understand, but it meant something to him, so it will always mean something to me," he announced.

Normally, Abigail would protest. She would tell him she had done nothing. She would tell him she'd caused more harm than good, ruined relationships, produced heartache everywhere she had gone. But, for once, her self-deprecating chitchat held no place here today.

Instead, she glanced at Will and could see in his eyes just how much his words meant. Therefore, she decided to step outside of herself. She chose her words with more care than she normally would have.

"You're welcome, Will, truly," she said with sincerity, plain and simple.

Hand in hand, they began to walk back to the truck.

As Abigail passed Jonathan's stone, she gently kissed her fingertips and brushed them along the top of the stone as she whispered, "Good-bye at last."

The drive back to the Higgins' home was quiet. Only the faint sound of Sarah McLachlan filled the truck.

This is the good kind of silence.

They needed no words to be spoken to understand where they both were in this moment. The sense of peace was enough to carry them home.

Abigail pulled in front of Will's house, the same spot she had parked in before. She put the truck in park and killed the engine.

He then glanced forward and let out a deep sigh. "Before you go, you asked me if I knew about you before. I answered yes, but in theory, I knew nothing." He reached inside his jacket pocket. He took out a folded envelope. "My brother asked me to keep this. He said I would know what to do with it. So, I took it and never asked him any questions about it. The other night, when we were all in the bar, was when it hit me. It's *your* name on the envelope, Abby." He played with the letter-sized white envelope folded within his hands. "It was then, Abby, that I knew you had to come and see me. I was worried that, if I told you why, you might not come."

"I understand, Will. I do." She thought back on that night in the hotel, that horrible night. "But what about Tank. Did he know?"

"Yes, I told him at the bar after he told me about the book when you were outside."

"So, he knew then that you knew more."

"Yes, Abby, and that is why we did what we did."

"What? I don't understand."

"You see, we had—we didn't want to make you upset, Abby, but we had to break this."

"What? Will, what are you saying?"

"Tank acted the way he did because he had to. Whether or not he did the right thing, I can't say. But he knew he had to change the course. I'm sorry. What I'm trying to say is, we acted the way we did on purpose. Listen, please trust me. I only have your best interests in mind. We both do. I know it doesn't feel that way, but I hope after all this, you'll know you can trust me, Abby." His words pleaded with her.

She couldn't speak.

He reached over, took her hand, and gently put the envelope in her open palm. "Read this, Abby. It's for you."

She simply closed her fist.

"I don't…" she started to speak but noticed Will grab the door handle.

"Wait, please don't..." Only her words were pleading this time. She suddenly felt so alone again. She had no Nathan to talk to, no Laura or Tank, and now, Will was leaving her, too.

"Abby"—he turned back toward her—"please read the letter, okay?"

He could see the hurt in her eyes. He was leaving her at a time when she needed someone, but he couldn't stay. He got out of the truck.

"You trust me, don't you?" He held open the door.

Without hesitation, she nodded her head.

"Good, Abby. Please understand that I have to go, but I need you to do one more thing for me, for my brother."

Surprised by his request and too shocked to protest even if she wanted, she again nodded her head.

"Tank feels terrible about what he's done. He asked me to tell you to meet him at the house within the clearing, where it all began. He said you'd know exactly what he meant." Will glanced at his watch. "You have to go now, okay?" Before he shut the door, he reached in again and squeezed her hand.

"Talk soon?" she asked.

"I'd like that." He gently shut the door.

She turned the key and let the truck roar before she put it in drive. He stood on the snow-covered grass in the front yard and waved slightly as she pulled out. She did all she could to muster a smile. She peered at him in the rearview mirror as she drove down the street. Her heart ached. A surge of anxiety ran through her, urging her to turn the truck around. She had so many unanswered questions but ultimately, she knew Will wouldn't allow it.

And she couldn't blame him for that.

Forty-Two

MARCH 1, 1996

The letter sat next to her on the seat. As soon as she saw the first gas station, she pulled in. She filled Tank's truck with gas and then moved his truck to an open spot on the side of the mini-mart. She reached over with a shaking hand and picked up the letter. On the front, it simply said, *Abby*.

She gently slid her finger into the sealed end of the envelope and tore it open. She unfolded the one-page letter and took a deep breath.

February 19, 1995

Dear Abby,

If you are reading this, then you have found me. I am not sure what led you here today, but I'm glad you came. I'm sure you have more questions than I have answers, but I will do whatever I can to try to answer them with what little I know.

I truly believe that fate brought us together. If for nothing else, then it was to give me a glimmer of hope in what remains of my life. This letter is not meant to make you sad or to bring sadness to anyone who might read it, but I hope more than anything that it will be a reminder to us all that love, in whatever shape it takes, is powerful and real.

I felt all along that you were brought to me as a sign that, despite all that is happening to me right now with my cancer, there is someone looking out for me, so much so that it has led me into the future, allowing me the rare opportunity to see what my life would have been.

Although that sounds sad, it is not. I feel blessed to have been able to see all of that in the brief time I have left.

As each day passes, I try to focus more and more on all the good I have had and continue to have, largely in thanks to you.

I can still remember the first time I saw you. You were wearing a navy V-neck sweater at the football party, and you just took my breath away. I knew then that we would be together. You're so beautiful in a way you might never know, but I hope you will one day, Abby. You will see what I have seen. It is amazing, and it has kept me wanting each day to come again.

I still pray that every night when I go to sleep, I'll dream of you, so I can see you, this beautiful angel who has kept me clinging on to the idea of forever. You will be my forever, although I realize I will not be yours.

I asked Tank to watch over you. I asked him to protect you. He did not ask me any questions. I trust that he will. I trust him with all of this despite how crazy I might sound at times. He has believed me from the beginning, and that is why he will always be my best friend. I know you will need him in your life—that, I can promise you. He will look out for you always.

So, I would like to leave you with the words Jeff Buckley wrote for us. I know you know the song. Listen to it and think of me. It's our story.

This is our last good-bye, Moon Pie. So, thank you from the bottom of my heart.

Those words are not enough, but it is all I have to give.

Jonathan

She read the letter even though the tears in her eyes made it almost impossible to see the paper. He was saying good-bye. It was all making sense to her now.

She folded the letter and put it in her jacket pocket. She pulled out of the mini-mart and was back on the road toward campus.

The ride back went faster than Abigail remembered the ride to the Higgins' house. She barely had time to think about Tank before she was turning down Route 20 and heading toward the cabin near the clearing. It was almost three thirty, and it would be getting dark in a few hours.

She didn't know what she would say to Tank, and to be honest, she was still unclear about where they stood, but it did feel suitable that they would find themselves once again back at the cabin where it had all begun for her and Jonathan, where it had all begun when Tank showed her the book.

After what Will had said about what had happened in the hotel, that Tank treated her badly on purpose, she was even more confused as to their relationship. But she was, at a minimum, willing to hear Tank out, particularly after what Jonathan had written in the letter.

She pulled down the dirt path toward the clearing. Her heart raced with anticipation, and her breath quickened as her nerves started to get the best of her. *What am I so nervous about anyway?*

As she got closer to the clearing, she saw a large white van parked in front of the cabin. She pulled in next to it and quickly realized it belonged to the football team. *But how in the heck did Tank get ahold of it?* She could only pray he hadn't stolen it just to get here to see her.

She turned off the engine but left the keys in the ignition. She opened the door and saw Tank standing on the porch.

He was wearing a suit, and she was taken aback by how different he appeared. He looked handsome, regal almost, and most importantly, sober. It caught her a bit off guard.

"Hey."

"Hey," she said back.

He walked closer toward her. She took a few strides toward the cabin.

There was silence. He never took his eyes off of her. She gazed toward the field.

"Will you look at me?" he said softly. "Please."

She turned to him and swallowed hard. She scanned his face and tried not to react, fighting back her grief. "You look nice. Going somewhere?"

"Yeah, home."

He was surprised when she spoke first, "Oh, right, the memorial for Jonathan." His named flowed so easily off her tongue.

"Right, yeah. You remembered."

"Of course I did."

He walked to the top step and sat down. She hesitated for a moment before walking up the steps to meet him. She sat next to him. Whatever this was between them was different, much different than it had been in the past.

The memories of the last time they had been here came rushing back. It was the first time she had seen the book. It was the first time she'd begun to grasp the depth of their connection, and it seemed almost fitting that they found themselves here again.

"Finally gave up on the crutches, I see." This was his attempt to make small talk.

"Yes, just couldn't do it anymore." Although she was referring to her crutches, her words could have taken on many meanings.

Tank sensed this and turned a bit more toward her. He searched her face for a clue, a sign, something to indicate what she meant. Instead, he saw the same face he had seen over the past months, one that housed a look of confusion with an underlying hint of sadness.

"I take it, you saw Will?"

"Yes, I did. He told me you wanted to see me here."

"Yes, I'm glad you took a chance on me."

He hesitated, again searching her face for something to tell him this was all going to be okay, but instead, she appeared thin and drawn. She seemed like she had been crying.

"Abby, I'm so sorry for everything. Really, I—"

She quickly cut him off, "I know, Tank. Me, too." She met his eyes.

Surprised, he remarked, "You are? For what?"

"For everything. For just…I don't know…lots of things, I guess."

"Me, too, Abby. I'm sorry that I hurt you the other day, but I hope you know I had to try and separate us, so we could see clearly. I had to break this cycle. Only then could I see what pain we were causing ourselves and everyone around us. I…" His voice choked a bit. "I had to let go, and I just needed someone to tell me that it was time. Who better to do just that than Jonathan's brother?"

Abigail reflected upon her time with Will over the past few days and how, out of all of them, he seemed to be handling the situation the best. He'd been strong and supportive to the both of them despite the fact that he was the one who had lost his brother. She felt shame flood over her, shame mixed with gratitude.

"He is a wise seventeen-year-old, now isn't he?" She laughed slightly.

"He sure is. He's just like his brother."

Tank had always envied Jonathan and Will's bond notwithstanding all their efforts to make him feel like a brother as well.

"I hope you know I never meant to hurt you, Abby. I just wanted to be close to you, to protect you, like I'd promised I would. I just wanted to be a part of your life, like he'd so desperately wanted to. You were the reason he hung on. You gave him so much hope. I just want you to know that I'll never hurt you again."

"Oh, Tank," she said, taking his hand. "I know, and I have myself to blame for the choices I made. I ruined things with Laura, Webber, and…well"—she choked back tears— "Nathan. I take full responsibility for all of that."

"I appreciate you saying that, but you and I both know it's not true," he said firmly. "I caused your problems by asking you to keep my secret, and I asked you here to try to fix all that."

"And how do you propose to fix all my problems here…today?" From behind, she heard the creak of the floorboards inside the cabin. A chill ran up her spine.

Then, she heard, "For starters, he asked me to come."

It would take a million lifetimes for her not to recognize his voice, that reassuring and sexy deep voice she swooned over. Her heart beat faster as she could feel his presence behind her. Tank's face said it all.

He looked back at Nathan and then again toward her. "I'm trying to make all my wrongs right again, and I knew there was only one place to start."

Still holding her hand, he placed his other one on his knee as he pushed off and stood, gently taking her with him. It wasn't until she was finally standing that she was able to turn and see Nathan.

"Nathan," she breathed as she searched his eyes for a clue as to how he was feeling.

He appeared confused and tired but still as gorgeous as she'd envisioned he would. Her heart fluttered, and her stomach turned with unmistakable desire.

Tank, not wanting to let her go, slightly squeezed her hand. She noticed a corner of Tank's mouth drew upward in an attempt to smile. She realized then that Tank was truly struggling with letting this all go. Regardless of all her problems and heartaches that she had encountered, he had suffered far greater over the past year. She squeezed his hand back.

"I'm trying," he said quietly.

"I see that."

Nathan stood, motionless, and observed the two of them as they struggled to move, to move on from their connection. In many ways, it was good for him to see them together, to see that this bond was far deeper than anyone could have anticipated. It was real, and it would be everlasting.

"I hope you do, Abby. I'm so sorry." Tank's voice quivered.

She could see the moisture fill his eyes. She moved closer, and in one swift motion, she wrapped her arms around his massive body and gave him a hug. He reached around with one hand and enveloped her with the other. He pulled her head toward his chest, and she rested it on his suit coat. They stood there as if they were the only ones on earth, allowing this moment to sink in because they owed it to one another. They owed it to Jonathan.

Finally, Tank cleared his throat and pulled away. "I've got to go." He tried to wipe away the tears without success.

Abigail reached up with her hands, straightened out his suit coat. "You've got to go," she said matter-of-factly. She stepped back and smiled at him. "Thank you, my dear friend," she whispered.

"Always," he whispered back.

Then, he stepped over toward Nathan and reached out his hand. Without hesitation, Nathan took it.

"Thanks, Tank," Nathan said.

"No, thank you." He bound down the stairs. He got near his truck and then turned. "Hey, have the van back by tomorrow, no later, or Coach will have my ass. Keys are in the back."

Abigail glanced at Nathan and then at Tank. "You mean, you're back on—"

"Yep, all thanks to him." Tank motioned back toward Nathan. With that, he was in his truck, starting it and putting the gear in reverse.

The two watched as he drove away from the clearing and toward the road.

As Tank pulled out onto Route 20, he let out a sigh of relief as the sun began to fade across the gorgeous pink and copper sky. Then, a huge smile spread across his face. He was free from the anguish that had lived inside of him for the past year. He was *finally* free.

Abigail did not even know where to begin. She had no idea as to how much Nathan knew and what, if anything, Tank had filled him in on. But she didn't have to wait long before she knew her answer.

She felt his presence from behind her, and the fear of turning to face him was far greater than she had anticipated. She stood frozen and waited, and then his arm reached around the side of her waist. His torso pressed up behind her, and her blood rushed to all the organs in her body.

"Nathan," she whispered, "I am so…" She could feel him get closer to her.

He buried his face in her hair. He turned her body to face his, and one look into his eyes said more than she could have ever hoped.

"Abby, I'm the one who is sorry. I just wish you could have told me."

"I know, but I just could never find the words, and it was all so crazy. It's like I've been living in two worlds that were happening at the same time, side by side. I just couldn't get it together." Her eyes filled with tears.

"Please don't cry, Abby. Please," he begged.

"I've just ruined everything, Nathan. I don't know how to fix my life or what I think is supposed to be my life." She took a step back.

"Please don't pull away from me." His voice sounded gruff.

He seemed hurt when she wouldn't come close again.

"I'm afraid of getting close to anyone."

"I'm trying to understand. Really, I am." His face wrinkled with concern.

"But why?" she asked. "Why would you want to? Apparently, the world has decided that I was supposed to be with someone else. Look at this." She ripped the letter from her coat. "Read this and tell me you want to understand, that you want to even try because I know you won't. There is something wrong with me, and this is proof." She thrust the letter toward him.

He hesitated. "I don't know if I can read one more thing, not after you left me with your…"

Journal.

Oh no, she had forgotten all about her damn journal, the one that contained all the intimate details of her life. He knew more about what had happened to her this past year, more than he was letting on, and although her nerves should have gotten the best of her, instead, her frustrations started to surface even more.

"Take it, and we can be done."

He reached out and took the letter. He opened it and went over toward the steps to read it in what light was left of the fading winter sun.

He took careful measure to read each and every word. In some way, she regretted giving him the letter to read, imagining how painful it must be for him to read about her and this supposed love from some other person neither one of them knew. But the other half just hoped he'd read it and want nothing to do with her once and for all, so she could go about her broken life and someday find someone who knew nothing of these two worlds she was living in. Only then could it truly be erased from her mind. But she knew, deep down, she did not want that. She did not want to forget about the love she had given to Jonathan. She did not want to forget about the love she had for Nathan, the love she would always have for him.

She observed him as he scoured over the letter, taking great pains to absorb the words. He finally stood straight again and folded the letter back up. He reached out his hand with the letter gripped tight and handed it back to her. She reached forward, hardly noticing the shaking in her hand, and took the letter.

He took a deep breath and slowly let it out.

He is hurting. She'd hurt him again. Enough was enough.

After what seemed like an eternity of silence, she spoke, "We should go. It's getting dark."

He spun around in a hurry, so much so that she reacted by stepping back toward the railing.

"What?" He sounded utterly annoyed. "You want to leave? Just like that?"

"Yes." She tried to sound confident. But once she saw the glare in his eyes, she backed off. "I think it's best, Nathan."

"So, that's it then." Before she could say another word, he spoke, "You think you can just hand me a letter like this and then leave or that Laura can give me a book and expect me to then move on. Or, even better, you leave me all those details of your life that just made me want you even more, and then you just leave me…again. Is that so?" There was anger in his voice.

He waited, his breath quickening, as he longed for her to respond.

She was motionless, so he pressed on, "So, everyone else gets a second chance but me, is that it?"

"No," she stammered. "That's not it…I'm trying, Nathan." She just stood, immobile, her arms like weights hanging off her shoulders.

"Then, what?"

Getting defensive, she snapped back, "Well, you read the letter, and I guess that's that. What more can I say?"

He started to laugh a bit, only it wasn't a friendly, nice-joke-you-just-made kind of laugh. It was that sarcastic I-want-to-provoke-you type of laugh.

"Ha, so he gets a say," he said, pointing to the letter in her hand. "And Tank gets a say, and you get your say, but I don't?" He ran his hand through his hair.

She noticed it had gotten a bit longer. The waves of his hair fell gently around his ears. She had to snap out of her daydream.

"That's not fair," she said.

He laughed again. "Want me to tell you what is not fair?" His words oozed with disdain. "What's not fair is that, for one second, you thought that I had something to do with Tank getting kicked off the team. What's not fair is that, I, above anyone else, was *your* friend, and you never once came to me. Instead, you went to the one guy who hated me the most, and for what? Because his friend died a year ago, and for some reason, I had something to do with replacing him on the team?

"You knew me the best, Abby. I thought you would know that I didn't steal his place on the team, and just to top off, I didn't exactly go and steal his girl, too. Remember *we* met, and no one else had anything to do with that. Just *you and me*. Does that sound fair enough?"

When she didn't speak, he added, "Did it ever occur to any of you that this is my fate that I am standing here today? Something brought me here. I'm really sorry about his friend, I *truly* am, and I told Tank that, but I also told him that I'd worked my ass off to get here. Despite what anyone else thinks, I believe that this is my shot, and unfortunately, it wasn't his. But I refuse to make excuses for that to anyone.

"The first day I met you, Abby, I knew we were meant to be, and I know you felt it, too." He searched her eyes. "Don't you see, Abby? Everything happens for a reason. Jonathan happened for a reason, you happened for a reason, and we—you and me—happened for a reason.

"And I'm just so sick of fighting against something or someone that I have no control over. I never did, and I never will. But what I do have control over is this." He pointed back and forth between them. "And me, being here today. And I swear to you that I will never speak of this situation again, or I will talk about it every time you and Tank and whoever wants to, but those are my only two options right now, Abby, because being without you is not an option."

"Being without you is not an option." His words echoed in her mind over and over.

He took a step closer to her.

"Nathan"—her voice cracked—"you have to know, I never meant to do this to you, to hurt you so badly."

He took another step closer. "I know you didn't, Abby," he said, sounding slightly defeated.

"But I've just been so confused by all of this. I've been pulled in so many directions, and I let myself be pulled." Tears dripped from the tips of her eyelashes. "I never wanted any of this. You have to know that."

He tried to come closer, but she put up a hand in an attempt to keep him back. He stopped.

She waited for him to remain in his spot before she said, "I went to see his brother today. I had to, and I didn't know why until I got there. Then, I knew exactly what I was doing, and it all became so clear." She reflected back on her day with Will.

"When I was in the hotel…" She searched his face to see how much he knew exactly, and she could tell he did not know that. "We went to the hotel that Will was staying at after I saw you at the bar. We wanted to show him the book to try to figure out what he knew, to see if I was the one who was in the pictures even though we all knew it was me."

She took another breath. "And I—we just tried so hard to figure this all out, but we were more confused. Tank and I fought. He was so cold and angry with me, and I was with him, too. I was tired and irritated, and after seeing you, it was just too much for me. So, they left me alone with a note and Tank's truck. They wanted me to go and see Will today. So, I did. I went." She tried desperately to fight back the tears that flowed. "So, I went to their house, and I met him. He took me to the cemetery—"

Nathan cut in, "Oh, Abby, that must have been horrible." His understanding tone made her burst into more tears.

"It was. It was awful. Being there with Will, seeing Jonathan's name engraved in a stone, there in the cold. Forever gone…this boy I never knew, but somehow, he knew me. It was just so sad, so terribly sad. I wanted more than ever to have known him, to see what he saw in us, to understand how this all could have happened. I just…waited. I waited for a sign to tell me something…" She trailed off as she wiped the tears from her eyes with the edge of her coat sleeve.

His face was filled with concern and sadness. He was truly sympathetic to what she had been experiencing all along.

"And?" he said.

"And I got one." She took a step closer toward him. "I did, Nathan. I got a sign."

"What?"

"I was standing there, next to Will, and I just closed my eyes. I held my breath. I waited to see what I might see if I were on the brink of being gone. What would *I* see?" She recalled how her lungs had burned for air and how she'd felt her body become weightless.

She closed her eyes again and tried to re-create what she had seen.

As she kept her eyes shut, she said, "And then you…you came to me, Nathan, no one else." She let her words linger in the cold air as her breath crossed the porch.

She slowly opened her eyes, and he was standing there, right in front of her, just how he had been in her vision.

"It was you. It had always been you, and it just took me a bit longer to wade through all this to get to the place I already knew I had—no, the place I wanted to be all along."

"So, why then did you want to leave here and not tell me this?"

"Because I needed to know that you—after all this, after seeing the letter, knowing all the things I'd been doing, all the lies and secrets—would still want to be with me. If you didn't, then I would have tried to understand, but more importantly, I would have known that it was not in your best interest to be with someone like me. You have too much to lose."

He came closer to her. In fact, he was so close that she could smell his cologne and the mix of his soap on his skin. It was intoxicating. She closed her eyes for a moment, and that was when his arms wrapped around her waist.

"Yes, I do." He sighed and then said, "I have you to lose."

She gazed up at him. His eyes sparkled regardless of the setting sun. She felt weak in his arms. She was immediately brought back to the night that had started it all in the library—the way he'd commanded she leave with him, the first time he'd held her in the hallway and kissed her with such confidence and it took all her might not to let her knees buckle.

He held on tight to her, never taking his eyes off of hers. She was so drawn to him, like she had always been. She missed being in his arms more than anything in the world.

"Nathan, I am so sorry…for everything."

"Please, don't be sorry anymore. This was out of your control, Abby."

"I know, but I never told you…" Her voice faded. She realized that it was time to grab ahold of each and every moment of her life. She took a deep breath and said, "I love you, Nathan Ryan."

She sensed his muscles tighten as he grabbed on to her. He lifted her up off the ground. In one swift motion, he brought her toward him, so they were close, face-to-face, and he kissed her. It was even better than the first time they'd kissed, if that were possible. His lips were soft and full as he pressed them hard onto hers, and she, too, returned every bit of passion within her soul as she wrapped her arms around his neck, unwilling to let him go. Their kiss was deep and loving. Then, he gently lowered her to the ground but did not let her go.

He whispered, "I love you, too, Abigail Luna Price, with all my heart."

She smiled, and it was one of the biggest smiles she had ever had. For Abigail, that said a lot.

They stood there on the porch of the old cabin, holding one another, and it was timely that she was here, full circle, now with Nathan.

She closed her eyes and knew as she breathed in deep that she was meant to be here today with him. She knew that she was ready to let Jonathan go. Even though he never had her, she had in fact belonged to him. She accepted that now, but even more so, she accepted the fact that it was time to say good-bye. This was what he would have wanted for her. She was ready to take his offer. She was ready to move on. She knew now that Tank would understand, that Will would, too, and that they would always have these days and these memories, and no one could take them away.

She shivered as the cold air brushed across the porch.

"Abby?"

"Yes?"

"Can we start over?" he said.

She waited before answering, "No."

He pulled apart from her, and with concern, he said, "But I thought you meant—"

"Oh, I did, most certainly. But why start over when we have already come this far?"

He gazed at her with amazement. "You're going to keep me on my toes, aren't you?"

"I hope to, if you'll let me."

"I'll do more than that," he said with a suggestive smile.

Her heart pounded with force in her chest.

"Then, let's go."

He grabbed her hand and headed toward the stairs. He walked up to the van and went to go to the driver's side, leaving Abby standing at the front. He opened the driver's door and saw the keys were not in the ignition.

He peeked over at her and said, "Wait, in the back, right?"

He closed the door, and at the same time, Abby went along the passenger side toward the back.

He pulled open the double doors to the back of the van just as Abby said, "That's weird. Why would he have put the keys—" But she stopped talking as he got the two back doors completely open.

There in the back, next to the keys, were two sleeping bags with pillows, a radio, a cooler, a twelve-pack of Natty Light, and a grocery bag filled with food and all the necessities you'd need to camp out for the night.

Oh, Tank. You did good.

Without saying a word, he climbed into the back of the van, unfolded the sleeping bags, and propped the pillows behind his head. He reached out his hand toward her. She took it.

"You ready to spend the whole night with me?" He pulled her in toward him.

She slid in next to him and leaned her head on his chest. "I've been waiting a long time for this," she said with sincerity.

"And I've been waiting a long time for this." He rolled over, taking her with him.

As he lay on top of her, he gazed into her eyes and grinned. He leaned close and gently kissed her lips. Every muscle in her body contracted with delight, but before she could wrap her arms around him and squeeze, he got up on his knees and gently unbuttoned her coat. He pulled it open, and then with agile fingers, he took off his coat. As she admired his body, she pulled her arms out of her coat before he sank back down onto her. They could feel their bodies more closely now, and she was home. She heard his breath quicken as he kissed her over and over, each kiss growing with passion. She wrapped her arms around his neck and held him close to her, never wanting to let him go, never again.

As they lay in the back of the van in one sleeping bag, Nathan softly traced her birthmark with his fingertips. She moaned slightly as the feeling of being so close to him along with the trace of his fingertips were lulling her to sleep.

As she began to close her eyes, she whispered, "Beautiful moon tonight."

"It sure is, Abby," he breathed as he, too, closed his eyes.

Epilogue

OCTOBER 18, 1996

Abigail waited by the tunnel near the back of the field in the same spot she always did. Family, friends, and students gathered here after the home games to wait for the players to come out after they showered and changed. There were a lot more people than usual on this gorgeous Saturday afternoon, and she couldn't blame all these fans for sticking around. The Hawks were off to their best start in over twenty-six years. In fact, after every game, more and more people would be waiting for the players than the time before. It was exciting to watch and even more exciting to be a part of.

No matter how many times she waited for him after a game or practice, she would still get butterflies when he came out of the tunnel and walked straight toward her. Countless people stopped him for autographs or to shake his hand, and he would oblige, but he would never take his eyes off her. It was just one of the many reasons she was so in love with him.

"Here they come." Laura grinned.

"Finally, this waiting around gets longer and longer every week," Webber said with full sarcasm. "You'd think these guys had invented the wheel with the way all these people—"

Logan quickly cut him off, "Oh, you are so jealous that it's sickening." He laughed as he patted Webber on the back.

"Jealous? Please. Look at him." He pointed in Nathan's direction. "Who could be jealous of that?"

They all turned as Nathan maneuvered through the crowd of students and, more importantly, all the swooning girls. He headed straight toward them. His navy suit fit him like a glove, and he had loosened his tie just enough to expose a little bit of his chest.

"Yeah, who could be jealous of that?" Melissa laughed as she squeezed Logan's hand.

"Hey," he scoffed, "not fair."

She playfully reached up and kissed him on the cheek.

Abigail could hear all the talking, but she barely paid attention to their banter. She was practically drooling as Nathan made his way toward her.

"The guy behind him isn't so bad either," Jessica remarked as she moved closer to Abigail.

Abigail turned to her with a big grin and nodded in agreement. Then, she glanced right back toward Nathan as he approached.

He greeted everyone, "Hey, guys. Thanks so much for coming."

They all spoke at once with the typical, "Great game!" or, "Nice job!"

Then, he turned to her and wrapped one arm around her waist as he pulled her in close.

"Hey," he said with a sultry tone.

He leaned down and kissed her. She blushed, like she always did in front of a crowd of people, but she kissed him right back regardless. Then, they pulled apart.

"I see I won the coin toss," Tank said, smiling at Abigail. He draped his arm over Jessica's shoulders.

Abigail quickly spun around, showing off the jersey she wore. The name McPherson was on the back.

"Yep." She turned back around. "It's always going to be a toss-up—my boyfriend or my best friend. It's a game-time decision."

"Hey, aren't I your best friend?" Nathan said to Abigail, pretending to be hurt.

"Wait a second," Tank said, eyeing Nathan. "I thought I was *your* best friend," he said, acting as if he had been stabbed in the chest.

"You are, buddy. You are. Coach just won't let me wear your jersey; that's all." He laughed.

"Ha-ha, very funny," Tank scoffed.

"Can you guys *please* stop fighting over each other?" Bree said in the background, half-kidding but half-serious. She pushed off the fence she had been leaning on for the past twenty minutes.

They all turned toward her. Then, seeing her face break into a grin, they all started to laugh.

"Besides, you *all* know how I hate to wait, so let's go. I'm starving!" she announced as she started to walk toward the field house.

One by one, they followed her back toward campus. Tank, Abigail, and Nathan headed up the rear as Jessica, Webber, Logan, Melissa, and Laura caught up with Bree.

Once Tank knew the rest of the group was out of earshot, he said to Nathan, "Hey, I appreciated what you said back there, to the press and all."

Hearing the tone in Tank's voice, Abigail quickly peeked up at him and then to Nathan. "What did you say?" she asked.

Before Nathan could respond, Tank stopped and turned to Abigail. He cleared his throat, his face softened, and then he spoke, "He said that everyone should make sure to come to the game next week, rain or shine, because all the proceeds from the ticket sales would be going to the Jonathan Higgins Memorial Scholarship Fund…" He tried not to let his voice quiver, but it proved to be too difficult, even for him. "The best quarterback that Onondaga State never had."

Abigail turned slowly with a tear in her eye and glanced up at Nathan. His face was flushed, and he shifted uncomfortably on his feet. She wiped the tear that had fallen to her cheek and took a deep breath.

Just moments before, as she'd viewed him walking toward her, she would have sworn she loved Nathan Ryan with all that she had, but she was wrong. She loved him even more now.

He gazed down at his feet, too embarrassed to respond. Abigail took his hand and squeezed it once, and then she turned to Tank and smiled. He winked at her and then started to walk again.

Sensing the moment was coming to an end and not a moment too soon, Nathan spoke, "So, what are you guys thinking for dinner?" He draped his arm over Abigail's shoulders.

Tank and Abigail looked at one another.

In unison, they both said, "Steak and cheese." Then, they burst out laughing. "Pickles and mustard."

"You two!" Nathan shook his head.

Abigail beamed while she walked between them. Nathan gently squeezed her shoulder. She peered up at him, her eyes squinting in the afternoon sun.

"What?" She noticed the beautiful expression on his face.

"Nothing. Nothing at all."

She knew exactly what he meant. There *was* nothing, nothing at all. It seemed like it had taken them forever to get to the place they were today— a place filled with respect and acceptance—and it was all because they had decided to believe in the unbelievable. They'd had to. They'd opened themselves to the possibility that possibilities happened because, in the end, it was about their undying love for one another, the devastating loss that had connected them, and without question, one girl's fate.

About the Author

Laurel (Kupillas) Ostiguy was born in Queensbury, New York—a town sandwiched between Lake George and Saratoga Springs—where she still visits with friends and family. She currently lives outside of Boston, Massachusetts. She commutes into Boston for a job she loves at a financial firm.

She attended Plymouth State University and graduated in 1997. She is now married to her college sweetheart, Jeff, and they have two sons. She also received her master's degree from Northeastern University in 2003. When she is not working in Boston, she loves to spend time with her family and friends as well as skiing, skating, swimming, writing, or just enjoying the beautiful New England seasons.

What's Next from the Author?

A wealthy girl from the Hamptons, Bree has known nothing but good fortune.

But a horrific encounter on her first night in college has left her broken, confused, and scared.

Gradually, as Bree begins to heal, she finds solace in the arms of a forbidden man on campus. Knowing their infatuation with one another could cost him his job, Bree has a decision to make. Walk away before anyone gets hurt or risk it all?

What will Bree decide?

Made in the USA
Middletown, DE
07 November 2019